W9-DEU-040

Four Dogs and Their Tales

By

Marcella Bursey Brooks

authorHOUSE®

AuthorHouse™
1663 Liberty Drive
Bloomington, IN 47403
www.authorhouse.com
Phone: 1-800-839-8640

© 2013 Marcella Bursey Brooks. All rights reserved.

No part of this work my be reproduced or used in any form or by any means—graphic, electronic, or mechanical, including photocopying, recording, taping, or information and retrieval systems—without prior written permission from the publisher.

Published by AuthorHouse 4/24/2013

ISBN: 978-1-4634-2771-9 (sc)
ISBN: 978-1-4634-2770-2 (hc)

Library of Congress Control Number: 2011910612

Any people depicted in stock imagery provided by Thinkstock are models, and such images are being used for illustrative purposes only. Certain stock imagery © Thinkstock.

This book is printed on acid-free paper.

Because of the dynamic nature of the Internet, any web addresses or links contained in this book may have changed since publication and may no longer be valid.

The views expressed in this work are solely those of the author and do not necessarily reflect the views of the publisher, and the publisher hereby disclaims any responsibility for them.

Acknowledgements

I feel very blessed to have shared much of my life with my dogs all of whom were the inspiration for this book. I'm grateful for having had their love and companionship. Some have passed on but my love for each of them is as strong as ever. Dogs love unconditionally—I wish I was capable of loving so unreservedly.

My late husband never doubted my ability to write this book and his faith in me helped greatly. Thank you, Clint.

My resolve to write this book was strengthened after I attended Tom Bird's class at a local college on How to Write a Novel in 45 Days. I became one of his Intensive Writing Students. Tom always called me author which helped me to think of my dream as being an attainable reality. For other aspiring authors Tom's website is www.tombird@tombird.com

I had the good fortune to take computer classes from Shelia Lilleston who subsequently set up the manuscript template on my computer and typed the original draft of this novel. I can't thank Shelia enough for being so helpful and supportive.

Hope Smith, of the United States Dog Agility Association (USDAA) was my pleasant and co-operative resource about the sport of dog agility who graciously and patiently answered my many queries about dog agility during the writing of this book. I sincerely thank her.

Bob Taschetta is a computer expert who helped me when my computer had a glitch causing me to lose much of the manuscript. Thank you, Bob, for being such a kind neighbor and friend.

Jackie Parker Earnhart, a contact through Tom Bird, edited my book. I regard her as a friend. Thank you for your excellent input.

Many thanks to the team at AuthorHouse who turned my manuscript into this book.

Dedications

This book is dedicated to my late husband Dr. Clint Brooks
and to all my pets and everyone else's, too.

CHAPTER ONE

The scruffy mutt looked at his paws in despair. He couldn't remember when he had last eaten. He always felt exhausted and inside his chest he felt pain all the time.

He drank from puddles and streams of dirty water that flowed beside the raised stone sidewalks. There were several large piles of sand used by construction workers to make cement for the houses being built in the area. As the nights grew colder, he slept on them because they held the warmth of each day's sunlight.

He occasionally rested on the front stoop of someone's home because it had an overhang that sheltered him from rain; however, he never interacted with the people whose front stoop he used because he always ran away whenever he heard them coming to the front door. He even ran away whenever he saw that woman approaching him, though he knew she brought him food. He resolved to never love and trust anyone again because he could never be hurt if he didn't open his heart. He was free and he vowed that he would always remain free.

His throat no longer oozed blood and didn't hurt much anymore. Night had fallen and he brooded over the events that had brought him to this pile of sand where he lay alone.

He could barely recall leaving his mother and brother and two sisters. He now knew that he had been sold in a marketplace because he always remembered the confusion of sounds, colors and many people moving all around him and last week he had followed the scent of food and found himself in such a place. It was a Mercado and the sounds and sights and smells evoked that first memory.

The people who had taken him home from the marketplace had placed him beside Blanca. His first impression of her was that she was large and very light in color. She had also seemed old. They had always lived outside in a courtyard. He used to snuggle close to her for warmth and comfort at night. It had taken him awhile to realize and accept that Blanca did not love him like his mother had, but she tolerated him.

His owners had always been angry with him. He had never known what to do, or not do, to please them. At meal times he had gobbled the scant amount of food given him but had never felt full and satisfied. In spite of so little food, he had grown and he now recalled the surprise he had felt the day he stood beside Blanca and realized that he was bigger than she was.

He wasn't sure what his name was or if he even had one. He remembered, that when he was a puppy, his owners said the word "Mozo" whenever they spoke to him, but as he grew bigger, he became nameless.

Life had been so limiting and boring that sometimes, when the courtyard gate had been left open, he had run through it to investigate the world that lay beyond. He remembered how scared he had felt that first time he saw other dogs roaming around. He had only known Blanca, who never said or did anything except to get up every so often to change her position and lie down on her other side. The dogs in the outside world had ignored him as had the people, except for that one time he had approached a couple walking with a child. He remembered wagging his tail to let them know that he wanted to be friends, but they had stamped their feet and yelled at him. When the man raised his hand, threatening to strike him, he had run away.

When he returned from those excursions, his owners had been angry at him. Of course, they had always been angry with him even when he hadn't left the courtyard or done anything that he knew of to cause their anger. After that last adventure, his owner had whipped him with a rope and then tied that same rope around his neck and lashed it to a hook embedded in the stone wall of the courtyard. He had never again been free of the rope and his confinement had been so great that he hadn't even had the freedom of the full run of the courtyard.

The mistress of the house had been mean, or perhaps just thoughtless, because she had frequently placed a bucket of fresh water so far from him that the short length of his rope didn't allow him to lap water from it. Before being tied to the stone wall, he had enjoyed the luxury of laying in the shade of the courtyard tree when the hot sun was high in the sky. After he had been so completely confined by that rope, he had always had to lie on the stone floor of the courtyard and endure exposure to sun and rain.

He winced as he remembered how the rope had rubbed and chafed the flesh under his chin and had caused him great discomfort and misery. At first, he had been offended and hurt by Blanca's indifference to his plight, but after he had thought for awhile about her attitude, he had concluded that all curiosity and sense of adventure had been leached out of her by her acceptance of the disregard of their owners and the boredom of their everyday existence.

His thoughts turned back to that fateful day of celebration. Colored lights had been strung on the tree and courtyard walls and because that had been something new and different to look at, it had lifted the boredom of his humdrum existence. The mistress had been cooking food over an open fire in the courtyard while the children had run in and out of the house and shouted to one another in excitement as strangers arrived and were greeted with hugs and laughter. He had greeted the strangers, too, until his owner had tied him so close to the stone wall that there had been just enough length of rope left to allow him to lie down. He now realized that no one had wanted him to greet or touch the strangers who had come for the celebration.

Everyone had been drinking, laughing and eating food. The food had smelled so tempting that his drool soaked the fur on his chin as he had pleaded to be given some. The master had kicked him and spoken angrily. He trembled as he recollected what had happened next.

The smell of smoke and sounds of people running and shouting had awakened him and he had been shocked and mesmerized by the sight of the courtyard tree burning. People had run in and out of the house carrying buckets of water to douse the fire. Someone had tried to spray water on the blazing tree but the hose had been too short to be dragged close enough to wet the tree and only the courtyard floor got watered. His master and mistress, the children and all the strangers ran through the courtyard door and left it open. Even Blanca had roused herself and loped after them.

The noise and heat of the flames was still fresh in his memory. He had pulled so hard against the rope around his neck in his effort to escape that he had almost passed out from choking himself but the rope had held fast. He relived the terror he had felt when a fiery tree limb had hurtled through the air, hit the stone wall directly behind him and snagged on his rope. Luckily for him, it had been a charred branch with very little flame left and had burned through the rope.

He remembered running through the courtyard gate, vowing never to return to those people who abandoned him in the courtyard with the burning tree and had not cared if he lived or died. Somewhere inside his chest, he still ached as he remembered the horrors of his early life.

He had been on his own for a while now and that suited him just fine. He would never ever let anyone get close enough to hurt him again—not even that pesky woman who was trying to tempt him with food.

CHAPTER TWO

Topaz rested contentedly on the stone pathway that had been warmed by early spring sunshine. She loved lying on it almost as much as she loved lying on her soft comfortable bed on the floor in her mom and dad's bedroom. Her favorite resting place was on the couch with her head cradled in her mom's lap.

She thought of how she used to climb into her mom and dad's bed during the night whenever she heard strange noises outside, but that had been when she was a puppy and had been frightened by the unfamiliar sounds made by animals going about the business of living after nightfall. She would snuggle between the two of them and feel safe and secure. When they awakened in the morning, her mom and dad looked startled, but they laughed and her mom always hugged her.

Now that she knew what caused the night noises, they no longer seemed strange and threatening to her. Owls often hooted and deer sometimes noisily thrashed about in the thickets. Foxes lived nearby and sometimes she heard a male and female barking as they tried to find one another after dark.

Upon awakening each morning, she loved listening to the joyful and busy sounds of birds greeting a new day. Occasionally, the birds abruptly became silent and she knew that, at those times, a hawk was flying overhead looking for a meal.

She recalled an incident when she had been resting on the grass with her paws tucked under her, lazily looking around for squirrels, and had realized that all bird sounds had ceased. Suddenly, a low-flying hawk snatched a morning dove in flight. It had happened so close to her that some of the dove's feathers had been carried by the wind and fluttered onto her head and settled on the grass near her paws. She had been terribly shocked and had run faster than she ever had before, through her special dog door into her home. She hadn't stopped running until she found her mom sitting in one of the big, comfortable chairs in the family room watching television. She had jumped up onto the big chair and squeezed herself into it beside her mom, who laughed and scooted over to make room for her.

Topaz had become used to the wildlife events that took place on her property. She liked the deer and there were lots of them to like. Sometimes she rested on the lawn close to them.

As her thoughts focused on deer, she saw a pair of fawn. They looked so small and fragile. She wondered how they ever managed to run on their thin, little legs. She looked at their large eyes and innocent expressions. They were so sweet and appealing. Topaz decided to get a closer look, maybe sniff the baby deer and lick their muzzles and let them know that she liked them.

She pushed herself up from resting pose and ambled slowly toward them so as not to alarm them. They stood gazing at her in wonder. Just as she was getting close enough to greet them, their momma doe sprang out from behind an overgrown forsythia bush. The doe was gigantic and she whistled and snorted as she charged toward her. Topaz was so terrified that she couldn't move for several seconds. Just before the big doe monster got close enough to kill her, Topaz managed to move her legs and ran for her life through her dog door and into the kitchen looking for her mom. When she found her, she bumped the back of her mom's legs with her head. Her mom spread her legs apart and Topaz sat between them, feeling safe at last.

She was still trembling in fear when her dad stomped into the kitchen and began talking to her mom. Topaz knew he was angry because she had run from the giant monster doe. He often pointed to the deer, then looked at her and said, "Sic 'em." She always pretended not to know what he wanted her to do. She just didn't want to chase them. She liked deer. Besides, they were lots bigger than she was.

While Topaz sat trembling between her mom's legs, she was comforted as her mom stroked her head and neck. Her mom spoke sharply and with authority to her dad and she knew her mom was defending her flight from the monster momma doe.

She and her mom had a special connection with one another. Sometimes her mom knew what to do for her before she herself knew that she wanted or needed something. Last night, at bedtime, her mom had covered her with a soft blanket as she lay resting on her dog bed. Immediately afterward, Topaz realized that she had felt chilled but hadn't known it until her mom had put the blanket over her.

Yes, she and her mom had a magical bond and she loved her mom more than anyone or anything else. She loved her dad but not with the deep passion that she had for her mom.

Her dad had gone back outdoors. He wasn't angry with her anymore, but Topaz knew she was a continual disappointment to him because she didn't want to hunt or chase the critters on her property. Her dad had never praised her for having taught herself to swim in the pond on her property. Her mom had made a big deal of it and told her over and over that she was the smartest dog ever. Topaz loved getting wet all over and often prowled her property during heavy downpours. Once, when her mom was toweling her dry after one of those excursions, her dad had said, "Topaz is too stupid to come in out of the rain." She had intuited exactly what her dad had said to her mom.

Jeanette Bancroft looked down at the beautiful German Shorthaired Pointer sitting between her legs. Topaz was a treat to look at with her dark liver-colored head and neck, the solid color broken only by the liver and white-ticked coloration of her muzzle, which gave the impression of freckles. Her trim, well-muscled body was mostly white with liver ticking and three large liver patches that were evenly spaced and traveled from the withers, down the center of her back to the base of her tail. She had a great chest and well-developed, strong hindquarters. Her top line was straight. She was a show dog in appearance, but not in personality.

Jeanette caressed Topaz's silky ears and softly said to her, "You're supposed to love hunting. You come from a long line of Conformation and Field Champions, but the hunting gene didn't get passed along in your DNA. I love you anyway, and everything about you is perfect as far as I'm concerned!"

Like Topaz, Jeanette was slender yet well-muscled. Her hair was black and straight and her eyes were almost as black as her hair. Her skin was creamy white with a tendency to freckle. Cole often remarked that her freckles looked cute even though they detracted from her goddess appearance. She was five feet nine inches tall and favored the Irish half of her heritage except for the exotic slant of her eyes, bestowed upon her by her Japanese ancestry.

Topaz followed her mom into the family room and watched her light a fire in the hearth. Topaz stretched herself in the down dog yoga position, yawned and settled herself comfortably on the rug in front of the fireplace. Her last thought before she was lulled to sleep by the crackling noise and warmth of the fire was that her practically perfect life would be totally perfect if she had some dog friends.

CHAPTER THREE

Essie Kilmer ran her fingers through her short, straight blonde hair, squinted her vivid blue eyes, then rubbed the side of her small, straight nose with her forefinger. She gnawed her pretty, bow-like lips with even teeth that had recently been professionally whitened. She was five feet five inches tall—a slim, trim energetic woman who worked at maintaining the weight that she had been in her twenties. She was in a quandary as she watched the breeders lifting puppies out of their van. Her husband, Evan, was gifting her with a Tibetan Spaniel puppy for her forty-ninth birthday.

She looked at Evan, who had turned the half-century mark a year and a half ago. He smiled at her and laugh lines crinkled around his gray eyes. Evan would go unnoticed in a crowd, she thought, because everything about him was average in appearance. He had a medium build and was just under six feet tall with brown hair, liberally sprinkled with gray, and even features that gave him a pleasant face but not a memorable one. Once you got to know him, though, you realized what a remarkable man he was. He had a great sense of humor, was extraordinarily intelligent, efficient, honest, dependable, quick-witted under stress and so far, had not shown any tendency to an over-fifty, jelly belly.

She raised her shoulders and spread her palms upward in a helpless shrug to indicate her inability to pick a puppy. She had always risen to any occasion and accomplished whatever she attempted. She made decisions quickly—today was the exception.

The first thing that the Tibetan Spaniel puppy noticed after she had been lifted out of the vehicle was the awesomely gigantic tree. She quickly paced toward it and touched the trunk with her nose. It felt rough and hard. Her exploration disturbed a large spider that had been resting in a groove of bark, and the puppy was so startled as it scuttled away, that she jumped backward. The puppy sat at the base of the tree and took stock of her surroundings. She saw a man and woman standing in front of a stone house that had a tall, peaked roof and lots of windows and was so huge that she had to swivel her head from side to side and up and down to see all of it. They stood on a lawn dotted with tall trees and shrubs of various sizes and colors. It was so vast that she couldn't see the end of it. Besides the scent of grass and trees, there were other unfamiliar and enticing fragrances that beckoned her to explore their origins. She watched the other puppies tentatively exploring the lawn near the vehicle, except for one who remained aloof and sat in the grass looking around.

She made a momentous decision: she wanted to live here. What could she do to gain the attention of the man and woman? Why, she could run faster than any of the other puppies! She pranced daintily around the base of the tree, picking up speed until she looked like a little merry-go-round running out of control.

"Choose me," she cried out in her mind. "I can run faster than the others." She aimed the fervent little prayer at the hearts of the man and woman.

Essie's attention was captured by the puppy who had been sprinting around the half-century old White Ash tree and who now streaked toward her like a tempest in a swirling sea of grass. The puppy stopped so abruptly at her feet that it almost somersaulted, then flopped onto its back in a gesture that clearly said, "Pick me up. I'm yours."

Essie laughingly said to Evan, "I've been chosen," as she bent down and tenderly lifted the puppy into her arms.

The puppy had blonde fur with a white muzzle, white legs and a white, bushy tail. White fur surrounded and enhanced sparkling, big, brown eyes that gazed into her own blue ones with curiosity. Small ears flopped downward in Spaniel fashion, framing a face so pretty that Essie felt sure the puppy was female and further investigation proved this to be so. Essie's heart melted as she bonded with the puppy thinking, "We're both blondes with some white hair." She closely cuddled the puppy who responded by licking her lips and cheeks.

Essie declared, "I'll call her Kissy because she's such an expression of affection and a gift of love to the world!"

The warmth of the woman spread into Kissy and she felt loved and special and she knew that she wanted to live with this person and the man for always. Yesterday, one of her brothers had been taken out of the small room where they lived and hadn't returned. Her mother had explained that he had gone to live with other people and that someday she and her other brother and sister would also leave to live in another home. Kissy had been happy to hear that because she had been bored by the confinement and predictable routine. She had longed to have playtime and to live in a home where she would be the center of attention. She could hardly believe that she had just gotten what she wanted. She licked the woman's face over and over in gleeful celebration of being chosen to be part of their family. Kissy then barked in joyous exuberance to the world, "I've been chosen!" She licked the woman's soft, smooth cheek once again.

As Evan walked toward the breeders to pay for Kissy and collect her pedigree papers, he saw the pensive puppy sitting in the grass apart from the others. It had slightly wavy, amber-colored fur and a black muzzle. The fluffy tail was amber and black and the fur on the ears was finely crimped, as though it had been braided and then released. The strong jaw line and neck that was thicker than Kissy's suggested maleness. He approached the puppy, who looked at him with a questioning, bewildered expression and, as their eyes met, the puppy quickly looked away and shifted position so that its back was presented to Evan. Evan surmised that the puppy was telling him that he didn't want any interaction, didn't know what he was doing here and didn't want to stay around long enough to find out. Evan's evaluation was correct.

The puppy was thinking, "I don't know what I'm doing here. I could easily get lost in this great, big place and no one would ever find me."

His mom had explained to him that he would eventually leave her to live in another home. He hoped this place wasn't the new home that his mom had talked about. He wasn't ready to leave her just yet. He had watched another puppy sprint around a towering tree to draw attention to herself and then dash toward a man and woman asking them to pick her up. He knew she wanted to be chosen to stay here and it looked as though she had been so maybe, just maybe, he could go home to live with his mom for a while longer. He had been so absorbed in his thoughts that he hadn't noticed anyone approaching until the man was almost beside him.

Evan felt that the puppy was a lot like him when he had been a young boy. He recalled how, during the first month of kindergarten, he had stayed on the sidelines during recess and had tried to remain unnoticed in class. That had changed after he was familiar with everybody and the routine and had seen how his abilities measured against everyone else's. He was the kind of person who liked to evaluate a situation before he felt comfortable with taking action and he sensed that this puppy was like that, too.

He wanted this puppy to be a part of the family, too, and wondered if it would be too much to give Essie two puppies for her birthday—one of which she hadn't chosen. He decided that the best course would be to ask her to give him this puppy for his birthday. She always said that she didn't know what to get him for his birthday because he had everything that he wanted. Well, her dilemma was solved! He wanted this puppy and so what if the gift was six months early. He knelt down and gently picked up the puppy and held him at face level so that he could maintain eye contact.

"Don't choose me," the puppy pleaded wordlessly from the depths of its being.

"Hey, buddy, I see that you are, indeed, a male puppy. You size up situations before you make up your mind about anything and I'm kind of like that, too. I think we're suited to one another and I'd love to have you as a member of the family. You think over things, which means you cogitate. I'll call you 'Codgie' or something like that."

The puppy was calmed by the low voice, but he refused to relax in the man's arms. He rested his chin on the solid and comforting warmth of the man's shoulder and decided not to think or do anything. He would just watch what everyone else did and cogitate.

Evan walked back to Essie and, after asking her to give him "Codgie" as his "six-month-early birthday present", she laughingly agreed and said, "They will be companions—making the transition to a new home easier for them."

After Evan explained the name that he had chosen, Essie suggested that it be spelled 'Kawdje' because that made it seem like an exotic name suitable for a Tibetan Spaniel and Evan readily agreed.

Kissy snuggled against Essie's neck, but after she was carried into the big house, she alertly looked around and her exhilaration grew as the realization that this huge, exciting place was now her home. This was the real beginning of her life. Kissy suddenly remembered that she hadn't said goodbye to her mother and was momentarily downcast. Well, this lady who held her so securely was now her mother so she licked Essie's warm cheek to tell her, once again, that she loved her.

Evan placed Kawdje on the grass while he paid the breeders and they gave him helpful advice about raising puppies. Kawdje's mother licked him on his muzzle and told him to love and obey his new family. She reminded him of the many discussions they had had about him eventually leaving her to live in another home and that a dog's purpose was to bring unwavering love and loyalty to a human family. She gave him another good-bye lick before jumping into the vehicle for her return trip home. Kawdje felt bereft, as though some physical part of his body had left him and he trembled at the thought of living the rest of his life without his mother.

The sensation of having part of himself missing lessened after the man picked him up, cradling him in his big hand against his warm shoulder. Kawdje experienced the same sense of security that he had always felt with his mom. It helped him release the panic and sadness he had just experienced when his mom had left. His trembling lessened and he felt steady enough to take advantage of the view. He liked being up high because he could see more and farther into the distance. The grass and trees and house didn't seem so overwhelmingly huge from this height. He was glad that he would have the other puppy to play with. He sensed this man and woman were kind and caring but, for now, they were still strangers.

As Evan entered the house, Essie said, "Let's show them their kennels where they'll sleep and where their water will always be kept and the piddle pads that I've placed on the floor near the back door because they may not be house-trained. They'll get used to going to the back door when they need to relieve themselves and soon, hopefully, they'll just bark at the back door when they want to go out into the yard for a potty break."

"Good idea. Let's hope they get that good idea, too. I suggest putting them in the same kennel while they're so young and small. It will probably be comforting for them to sleep together."

Kissy and Kawdje were relieved when they were shown the huge bowl of water because they were thirsty. They lapped water until their tongues became cold and tired, after which, the tour of their new home continued. There were so many rooms that it was confusing, and neither of them could remember the path they had taken. Kawdje couldn't smell the return pathway because of the many new scents that confounded him and Kissy didn't even try. They felt intimidated by the immensity of their new home and the many pieces of furniture and interesting, large areas of material on the floors that reminded them of grass.

Both felt the need to relieve themselves of all the water they had drunk a while ago and decided that any of the large pieces of something like grass that lay on the floor was a good place to do so. Immediately after squatting, they heard their mom and dad saying, "No! No!" and they were picked up and carried outside where they finished the job.

Kawdje couldn't remember which pathway led to the door that opened onto the grassy yard and sat on the grass pondering how he could get outside whenever he wanted to. Kissy was action-oriented and immediately began running around trees and under bushes until she had to stop and catch her breath. She wanted to remind her mom and dad that she was a fast runner in hopes that they would forget the mistake she had made. At last, she ran up to her mom and dad and begged to be picked up. When she was settled in her mom's arm, she licked her face and sent her the thought that she loved her and was sorry for the mistake.

Essie laughed and said, "We've chosen their names well, because Kissy is kissing me and Kawdje is cogitating."

That evening, Kawdje moped in the kennel, longing for his mother, brother and sister and refused to come out and interact with his new family. He dolefully watched Kissy dividing her affection by sitting on their mom's lap for a while, then on their dad's lap and then back to their mom's. He recalled the confusing day and all the new rules and routines that went with this new home. His head hurt trying to remember them all and the effort made him sleepy.

After Essie tucked Kissy in the kennel beside a sleeping Kawdje, Evan suggested, "Let's have a bedtime snack, maybe something decadent like whole milk and chocolate chip cookies."

Essie said, as she spooned dough onto a cookie sheet, "It's great having you home with me. I was lonely after Joy married and moved out. Now we have these cute little puppies. It's kind of like having kids around, and fortunately, you're home to help me clean up the messes."

As Essie tended to baking cookies, Evan thought to himself that he had been clever with his and his brother, Gordon's, investments over the years and had managed to turn the inheritance his father had left them into a sizeable retirement fund. Being head of the accounting department of a large firm with international holdings and varied interests, had been a high-pressure job that had paid extremely well, but he had been happy to be able to take an early retirement. Now he had plenty of time to devote to his and Gordon's investments and enjoy leisure time with Essie.

They had traveled some during the first six months after his retirement, but he hadn't felt satisfied. Something had been missing and he had decided that youthful, noisy energy was what their home needed. Since he didn't expect to be enjoying grandchildren anytime soon, he thought a puppy would be perfect. Not a large breed that could yank Essie's arms out of her shoulder sockets or pull him along on a walk faster than he ever thought he could run but, rather, a small dog that would always fit on his lap. Kissy and Kawdje were perfect—one for Essie's lap and one for his.

Evan studied the puppies' pedigrees. "Essie, we have two very well-bred puppies whose pedigrees are far more illustrious than ours. Kissy is three days older than Kawdje and they are four months old. They have different parents and are not directly related to one another, although they have some of the same kennels in their backgrounds. They each have an impressive number of champions in their backgrounds. These papers go back eight generations."

The next few weeks were happy, interesting and exhausting for Kissy and Kawdje. They memorized the pathway to the door that opened into the big, wonderful outdoor kingdom and familiarized themselves, frequently, with the piddle pads that lay on the floor directly in front of that door. Each learned to respond to the sound that they knew was their own. Kissy loved her name because it seemed soft and happy and the s-s-s-e-e sound was soothing. At first, Kawdje wasn't sure that he liked his, but after he thought about it, he decided it was sharp, commanding and male—awesome!

When their mom and dad put a collar around each of their necks, Kissy loved hers immediately. It was an adornment and she enjoyed it. It took Kawdje several days to decide that a collar was okay. He sensed that it was some sort of family identity thing and he was now happy to be part of a family with his dad, mom and Kissy.

The day that Kissy and Kawdje were taken for their first family car ride, Kissy became so upset wondering if they were being driven back to the place they had come from or to another home where they would live, that she upchucked. Essie quickly pulled a towel onto her lap, preventing the car from becoming a disastrous mess and spoke soothingly and reassuringly to Kissy. Kawdje perched himself up high and looked out the back window and watched the ever-changing scenery as it whizzed by. People walked in and out of buildings, eating food, carrying packages, standing and talking to one another and occasionally walking dogs. He barked warningly to other dogs to let them know that he had a powerful family and was a force to be reckoned with! When Evan lowered a window, Kawdje jumped onto the back seat, stood on his hind legs and hung his head out. Although the car was moving slowly, there was enough wind to flap his ears and the rushing sound and force of it felt awesomely wonderful. He decided that a car ride was one of the best perks of life!

Kissy and Kawdje looked forward to mealtimes with anticipation. Sometimes they were hand-fed small, bite-size morsels from the table. Kawdje loved lima beans and asparagus tips, preferably drizzled with butter. The slightly mushy texture of the lima beans and the distinctive taste of asparagus appealed to him. Before she had ever tasted one, Kissy loved gingersnaps. The scent of them was tantalizing and she had begged to be given one until Evan had finally indulged her by breaking one into bite-size pieces. It was everything she had imagined and more! The crunchy texture and spicy flavor was indescribably delicious and, upon first bite, Kissy decided that a gingersnap was one of the best perks of life.

Essie and Evan wanted the puppies to develop into well-adjusted members of the household and achieve their highest potential so, over the next six months, the couple began training the puppies for Conformation Dog Shows. The Shows required interaction among the four of them and was a good bonding tool.

Kissy and Kawdje learned how to walk on a lead without pulling or having to be pulled, how to heel, sit on command, stand still on a table while their teeth were being examined and to assume a "stacked" position that showed their physical conformation to best advantage. Kissy also learned that she wasn't permitted to kiss her mom and dad during training sessions. She loved being with them, but thought that the whole training process was boring. Kawdje wondered why he had to stand still and look at a piece of dried liver that his dad held in his hand. He had chewed it once and thought it tasted terrible. Fortunately, Evan discovered that he could use oatmeal cookies as "reward bait," after an incident when Essie had accidentally dropped one of her homemade oatmeal cookies on the floor and it had broken into small pieces. Kawdje had immediately licked up the mess and then sat on his haunches and begged for more. Kawdje preferred to be hand-fed the treats. Both puppies enjoyed training time with their parents because they loved the attention and felt close to their mom and dad. Kissy and Kawdje were happy and content.

CHAPTER FOUR

When the alarm clock screamed shrilly, Essie snuggled deeper into the bed. She knew Evan wouldn't get up to silence the nasty little machine. She flung back the covers, stomped across the bedroom, punched the off button and silenced the scream in mid-wail.

"Rise and shine, Evan. We've got to get an early start to make it to that dog show."

Evan groaned, "Are you sure we want to make champions of our two little darlings?"

"No, I'm not but we're going to stick to the plan and see what happens."

Kissy and Kawdje were happy to have a car ride and wondered if this trip was a visit to the vet, a walk in a park or just a lot of stops while Mom and Dad went into big houses and came back with bags of food and other things. After the ride they were lifted out of the car and immediately picked up the scent of many dogs and heard a wide variety of barks. Kawdje decided to warn the dogs that he not only had a powerful mom and dad, but that he was well able to defend his family. Kissy thought that Kawdje was saying everything appropriately but decided they ought to put up a united front, so she echoed the sentiments in her shrill, commanding bark.

Essie picked up Kissy and remarked to Evan, "They're so small compared to all these large breeds. Maybe this is a frightening experience for them, especially since this is their first dog show. Perhaps you should carry Kawdje. You know how he likes to stand on anything that will make him taller. I think he wishes that he was a big, tall dog."

Kawdje was relieved when his dad picked him up in his arms. He felt much better when he could see over the crowd. He noted that both he and Kissy were wearing their short leads and wondered if all those times when they had to walk closely beside their mom and dad, or stand still, or have their teeth examined on a table, had something to do with being here today.

They were set down near other small dogs who looked the same as they did. This was okay so they waited quietly. Soon Kissy walked into an open area beside her mom. She saw other girl dogs whose moms kept them leashed closely.

She watched them take turns walking up and down the area that was called a ring. A man spoke to her mom and gestured with his arm. He seemed to be directing everyone. After they had paced around the ring together, her mom lifted her onto a table and the man felt her body. All the people who came to her home were friendly and always gently stroked her head and ears, spoke softly to her, and smiled. She knew they liked her. This man seemed so—Kissy searched for the correct description and chose "impersonal". Yes, that was it. He didn't like her, but he didn't dislike her. He just didn't seem to care about her at all.

She felt insulted when the stranger stuck his fingers in her mouth and examined her teeth, so she lightly bit him to let him know that she didn't like him invading her space without her permission.

The judge yelped and backed away. Essie was mortified as she was commanded to remove her bitch from the ring. Kissy sensed that her mom was upset and embarrassed as they hurriedly scuttled out of the ring.

When they joined Evan and Kawdje, Essie said, "Kissy bit the judge!"

Evan laughingly said, "Good for her! He's a pompous ass anyway."

"Evan, I don't think I can ever show Kissy again after an experience like that. I'll always be nervous about what she might do, and that will affect her performance and it will definitely affect mine."

"I'll handle Kissy in the ring from now on and you handle Kawdje, except for today. You're much too upset to take him in the ring. Besides, you've done your duty."

It was time for the male Tibetan Spaniels to parade around the ring. Kawdje stood quietly beside his dad and waited to see what would happen. He knew he had to remain alert and try to understand what the purpose of all this was.

Time dragged by and he began to feel uncomfortable because he had to relieve himself. His gaze roved around the ring looking for piddle pads or a tree trunk, but he couldn't see anything suitable. He couldn't wait any longer and decided the best place was against his dad's leg. He reasoned that it was the most similar thing to a tree trunk and, most important of all, it was available.

Evan heard the laughter of some folks standing outside the ring. The handler standing behind him laughed, too, and told him about Kawdje's hilarious breach of ring etiquette. Evan looked down at his very wet trouser leg. He found the situation more amusing than embarrassing. He just hoped the judge hadn't seen the deed.

The rest of the time in the ring went smoothly. Kawdje was unsure about what was expected of him and just followed his dad's directions. At last, his dad was given a ribbon and they exited the ring and joined Mom and Kissy. His mom hugged and kissed him.

"Oh, Evan, you were both great in the ring and he's won second place."

As they made their way through the crowds toward the building exit, they decided that in the future, they would always take the pets for a potty break before entering the show ring. Both agreed that Kawdje had been nervous and Kissy had been defensive because of the confusion and noise of the crowds and the presence of so many large dogs.

During the next few months the four of them attended more dog shows. Kawdje won four blue ribbons, plus a Best of Breed. Kissy, however; usually placed second because the white coloration of her legs drew attention to the fact that they were slightly too long for the breed standard. Kawdje's legs, which he always wished were as long as Kissy's so he could run as fast as she could, were the correct length in relation to his body and he conformed perfectly to the standard set for a Tibetan Spaniel.

Although Kawdje had won four blue ribbons and a Best of Breed, the classes had been small because the breed was not well known so he had not earned a lot of points for those wins. A dog had to acquire fifteen points in order to attain the title of Champion and must collect some of those points by being awarded first place over enough other competitors to be given at least two three-point majors or one five-point major.

As Kawdje became familiar with the routine of dog shows, he relaxed to the degree that he felt confident. He always looked up into the judge's eyes trying to sense what kind of person he, or she, was and watched for some indication of what he ought to do next. Essie and Evan loved his habit of giving the judge a searching and inquiring look because it seemed as though he was asking the judge to give him the win. It worked to his advantage, in this instance, that he was a contemplative dog.

Kissy liked it best before she went into the ring and after she exited the ring. It was at those times that people gathered around her, telling her how sweet and beautiful she was.

At one of the shows, Kissy and Kawdje watched some dogs performing in a way they had never seen before. They ran through tunnels and climbed something that looked like stairs, walked on a plank and ran in and out between poles. It looked challenging and lots of fun to Kissy.

They noticed that the dogs weren't on leashes and their moms and dads ran alongside them. It appeared to be some sort of race that the fastest dog won. Kawdje thought that if it were a race, he would never win. He couldn't even outrun Kissy.

Kissy wanted to play this obstacle course game. That very day she began her campaign of sending her desire to her parents by imagining herself doing this activity and placing the picture into the hearts of her parents.

The next week the four of them attended another Conformation Dog Show where the sport of Dog Agility was, once again, being demonstrated. Essie and Evan stopped to take a brief look but lingered when they noticed Kissy's obvious interest and enthusiasm. They watched her eyes darting back and forth taking in the performances of the dogs. Every so often she would bark her approval and encouragement.

Kissy longed to participate in the active, challenging sport of Dog Agility especially after she heard the applause for each dog's performance. She understood that Kawdje was being chosen over her and many other dogs in Conformation Dog Shows because the judges liked him for being the best. The best at what, she didn't know. All she and Kawdje did was pace around a ring and then stand waiting until a judge picked you out of the line-up, or not. For some unfathomable reason, Kawdje was chosen over her. People noticed him and neglected her. She was sure that she would be a winner and a star if she could run that obstacle course. She was more agile than Kawdje and never afraid to try something new, and he never caught her when they played tag. She mentally placed herself on the obstacle course and became so animated that she almost jumped out of Evan's arms.

He said, "I wonder if I could train myself to handle her in the ring. She's so quick and agile, has a fantastic memory and is very intelligent. I'm thinking she'd do well in this sport; however I'm not so sure that I would."

They introduced themselves to the attractive woman who was standing beside them and holding onto an unidentifiable breed of dog who was large, shaggy and fifty shades of gray ranging from dirty white to charcoal. The dog had the coarse, wiry fur typical of most Terrier breeds, but he obviously was not a purebred Terrier. He somewhat resembled a smaller-than-average Irish Wolfhound except for having longer fur growth over the withers and on the back of the hindquarters. Essie thought he looked like a very homely crossbreeding between an Airedale and an Irish Wolfhound; however, the intelligence that shone from his brown eyes combined with his regal bearing gave him presence.

"Do you know anything about Dog Agility and does your pet compete in the sport?" Essie asked.

Sarah Pullman introduced herself. She was short, measuring only five feet and one and one half inches tall. Her skin was tanned to a light golden shade and she had shoulder-length, light golden brown wavy hair that matched the color of her eyes. She had a delicately sculpted nose and the dimples that appeared whenever she smiled drew attention to it. The dog's large size and homeliness contrasted with the petite, pretty woman and they made an arresting pair. She replied that she had some dog agility obstacles at her home and that she and her pet, Michael Archangelo, had very recently begun practicing the sport.

"What a wonderful and unusual name for a dog!" exclaimed Essie. "There must be a story connected to a name like that," she added.

Sarah said, "I spent this past winter in San Miguel de Allende and saw Michael sheltering himself under a car parked on the side of the street. He was the homeliest dog I had ever seen. He looked scruffy and starved and there was an aura of fear and desolation around him. I sensed that he had been deeply wounded by someone or something and I felt such compassion for him. I felt compelled to help him but he ran away whenever I approached him. I knew something terrible must have happened to cause him to be so fearful of people. Street dogs never run away if you don't threaten them because they're hoping to be fed. Michael was wearing a collar and I wondered why he was frightened of people and so pathetically thin if he had a family.

During the next couple of months, I carried food and water with me whenever I walked around my neighborhood in the hope that I would see him. For the first few weeks, he ran away whenever I tried to get close to him, so I placed his food and water on the ground and left. When I returned and collected an empty bowl, I was never sure if Michael had eaten the food or if another dog had made a meal of it. Eventually, he trusted me enough to eat his food while I stood close by. He never wagged his tail in response to me.

After about six weeks of eating a daily ration of food, Michael's coat took on sheen and luster, and he had more energy. I was surprised to realize that he was a young dog. I had thought he was old because he moved like an old dog, but that was because he was starved and lacked energy."

"How did you manage to make friends with him so that he would allow you to touch him?" asked Essie.

Sarah related that she and some friends left San Miguel to take a trip to Guadalajara and were away for several days.

"Upon my return, I took my usual morning walk carrying food and water for Michael. I felt a wet muzzle nudging my hand. It was Michael. He was so happy to see me that he jumped around me in a clumsy doggy dance. In spite of whatever had happened to cause his distrust of people, he had decided to take a chance on me. I resolved then and there that I wouldn't betray his trust and I would bring him home with me when I left San Miguel in the spring.

By this time, I had fallen into the habit of calling him 'Michael,' which I'm sure you know, is the English version of Miguel. It seemed appropriate to call him after the name of the town where I found him and because Michael is the name of an Archangel, I added Archangelo. I wanted to give this superb, sensitive being an illustrious name to make up for his lack of pedigree.

He has a large, granulated scar on the underside of his neck. I have no idea how that occurred. Something, or someone, obviously hurt him deeply. I can't imagine whatever awful and painful circumstances led to his mistrust of humans. However, he now completely trusts me and I am honored that he does. He is a wonderful companion and a blessing in my life."

Essie and Evan asked if they could touch Michael, and Sarah replied that he was now very tolerant of people. Michael allowed them to caress his ears and smooth the top of his head.

Kissy and Kawdje could tell that Michael liked the attention because he half closed his eyes and raised his head slightly toward their parents' hands. Although Michael was very large, they were not afraid of him. They could tell that Michael was kind and disciplined. They sensed the bond of love and trust between him and his mom. They decided they liked Michael and, simultaneously, both of them moved close and sat looking up at him. He lowered his head and all three touched noses and wagged tails.

Essie remarked, "I've never seen my two spoiled little darlings ever be friendly with another dog at these dog shows, especially not a big dog. This is amazing!"

"Did you have to travel far to attend this show?" asked Evan.

"No," replied Sarah. "I drove here from Chadds Ford."

Essie exclaimed, "We're practically neighbors! We live in Media, Pennsylvania. Perhaps we could get together and discuss the sport of Dog Agility."

They exchanged contact information and Essie and Evan invited Sarah and Michael for dinner on Saturday evening. Sarah asked if they were sure that they wanted Michael Archangelo to accompany her. They assured her that Michael was equally welcome.

Because Sarah was wearing gloves, Essie couldn't see if she was wearing a wedding band or engagement ring so she asked, "Do you have a husband or friend that you would like to bring along too?"

"I'm a widow. My husband died several years ago. My daughter, and only child, married last year and that's why I over-wintered in Mexico. There didn't seem to be any reason to spend a cold winter in Pennsylvania, alone in my home and I thought the change would do me good. A couple that Charles and I had known for years were planning to spend the winter in San Miguel de Allende and I decided that enjoying winter in a warm, sunny place with friends nearby would be good medicine for me. And it was. I came home with a special gift from the universe—Michael Archangelo."

"I'm sorry for your loss," Essie said and then added, "You look too young to have a married daughter."

Sarah smiled. "Thank you. What time shall we come for dinner and what shall I bring?"

"Come about five o'clock and you don't have to contribute anything except some interesting conversation. What would Michael like to eat? I usually feed our pets cooked chicken livers or table tidbits and fresh veggies plus high-quality dried dog food."

Sarah smiled, "Michael will enjoy any and all of the aforementioned. It's nice to know that I'm not the only one whose pet dines on the same food I eat. Would you mind if I brought gingersnaps? Michael loves them and I occasionally give him some for dessert."

Essie and Evan laughed and said in unison, "So does Kissy!"

CHAPTER FIVE

When Sarah and Michael arrived for dinner, Michael held a basket, the handle of which was clamped between his teeth. Evan ushered them into the kitchen and announced, "Michael has come bearing gifts."

As Sarah motioned for Michael to place the basket on the floor, she said," He's got a present for Kissy and one for Kawdje." She held out a small stuffed dog toward Kissy, who loved toys. Kissy snatched it, ran into the family room and proceeded to untie the ribbon around its neck. Then Sarah showed a small, soft, colorful ball to Kawdje. He sniffed it suspiciously before gingerly accepting it from Sarah's hand. As he closed his mouth around it, it squeaked. He was so startled that he dropped it. Michael smacked the ball with a paw and it squeaked again. Kissy darted back into the kitchen to see the cause of the commotion. She went straight for the small ball and pressed her nose against it. It squeaked again. By now Kawdje had regained his composure. He clamped the ball in his jaws and ran into the family room with Michael and Kissy in hot pursuit. Then, while Sarah, Essie and Evan sat in the living room sipping wine, the dogs nudged the ball around, stepping on it or biting it to make it squeak.

Finally, the pets settled down on a plush Oriental rug facing one another.

"You have a comfortable home," said Michael.

"What is your home like?" asked Kissy.

"I have a big, wonderful home with mistress Sarah and I have my own soft, comfortable bed to sleep on, but that was not always so," replied Michael. "I didn't always live with Sarah."

"Where did you live before your life with Sarah? Why did you leave your first home?" Kissy asked.

Michael told them of being sold in a marketplace, the meanness of his owners, the indifference of Blanca, the boredom of life in the courtyard, the misery and pain of being tied to the courtyard wall by a rope that chafed his neck, the blazing tree and his flight to freedom through the courtyard door.

Kissy and Kawdje listened in wonderment and compassion. Kissy laid her head on Michael's neck and Kawdje placed a small paw on Michael's large one.

"What happened after you ran out of the courtyard? How did you come to live with Sarah? Who fed you? How did you manage to live on your own?" inquired a concerned and curious Kissy. Michael continued with his story.

"I ran and ran until I was so tired and thirsty that I had to walk. I kept looking for a source of water and, at long last, I came upon a stream and took a long, satisfying drink. I decided to stay near the stream so that I could have another drink later. I slept on hard packed earth with my back against a rock. It was very much like sleeping in the courtyard except the earth was warmer and softer. I awakened at daylight. My throat felt painful and I smelled my own blood. I had torn my flesh while pulling on the rope as I tried to escape from the fire. I hadn't felt pain at the time because I was so frightened. The rope was no longer around my neck. It had dropped off while I was running.

I felt incredibly happy to be free of the rope and far away from those mean people. I vowed to never allow anyone to get close enough to hurt me or confine me again. I thought that people were cruel and thoughtless creatures who cared only for themselves and gave no thought nor love to anything else."

"But that's not true," exclaimed Kissy.

"I know that now, but at that time in my life, I had never known love."

"Tell us more," urged Kawdje.

Michael told them of days and nights searching for water to drink, raiding garbage cans for food, finding safe places to settle in for a night's sleep and trying to remain unnoticed.

"I didn't know where I was traveling to because I didn't have a destination other than finding a safe place where food and water were always available and a sheltered area to bed down at night. I kept walking and searching until my paws were so sore that I limped. Eventually, I came to a big town with lots of people and houses, cats and dogs. Vendors had carts filled with food that they cooked on the side of the streets. The people who bought the food sat at tables near the vendor's carts and, occasionally, they shared their meal with me and other dogs who begged for tidbits. I never had enough food to eat to feel full and satisfied, but I got by and was thankful that I was free."

"Did you make any friends?" asked Kissy.

"I knew some dogs that I trusted but I didn't have any companions that I roamed with. I was still wearing a collar, so other street dogs thought that I had a family.

I settled in the area that I told you about—the front stoop that I sometimes laid on to get out of the sun or rain and those large piles of sand that I often slept on at night. There was a stream nearby and a large grassy area. Other dogs and some cats hung out there, too.

People frequently walked in that area and some walked with dogs on leashes. A lot of homes had dogs who lived inside with their people. They would hang their heads out the windows and bark at me."

"What did they say to you?" Kawdje asked.

"Mostly they warned me to stay away from their property. I told them they could be kings of their castles, but that I was king of the streets."

"What a great answer!" Kawdje said admiringly.

"How did Sarah earn your trust?" asked Kissy.

"I could tell that the dogs who walked beside their people loved them, and were loved in return. I realized that walking beside their people was a happy adventure for them. I even saw some dogs riding in cars."

"How could you see them if they were inside cars?" asked Kissy.

"Because every dog rides in a car with his head hanging out a window so that the wind can blow through his fur, flap his ears and vibrate his muzzle. I do that myself now, and it's one of the best perks that life has to offer a dog."

"Amen to that!" said Kawdje.

"It must be a guy thing because it doesn't give me a thrill," said Kissy.

Michael continued, "I had a routine where I patrolled certain streets raiding trash cans for food, drinking from the nearby stream, sleeping on the front stoop or on a sand pile and begging to be fed by people as I sat near a vendor's cart. I always felt exhausted because I didn't get enough to eat but I was free and that was what mattered most. One day, as I was resting on a sand pile, a woman approached me and offered food. It was Mistress Sarah. Although I never felt threatened by her, I ran away because I was wary of everyone and everything, but she continued to leave food every day wherever she found me, and gradually I felt secure enough to eat her food while she stood nearby. The food was delicious—the best I had ever tasted."

"Good food and car rides are the perks of life," declared Kawdje.

"Males are so corporeal," said Kissy.

Michael and Kawdje looked at her in astonishment and said in unison, "Say what?"

"I mean that males judge everything by how their body feels rather than using their mind to evaluate experiences."

Michael was too confounded to respond to Kissy's remark so he continued with his story.

"Other street dogs avoided me because I was wearing a collar. One day that changed when I was pacing through bushes and my collar snagged on a branch. While I thrashed around trying to free myself, the collar broke and fell off me. I was happy because that meant I was really free. I just belonged to myself."

"I like being part of a family," Kissy said. "Just before I fall asleep at bedtime, I feel happy knowing that I'll see my mom and dad and Kawdje when I wake up."

"At that time, I had never had a close relationship. I didn't miss what I had never known. I sensed that Mistress Sarah was kind and genuinely interested in me but I wasn't willing to take a chance on loving and trusting anyone. If I never let anyone be a friend, then I couldn't get hurt."

"How did you come to love her?" asked Kissy.

"I didn't know I was opening my heart to her until something happened that made me realize I had begun to rely on her for food and companionship. Mistress Sarah always brought me food every morning and evening. After a while, I noticed that I felt stronger and could run faster and for longer periods without panting and that I slept soundly at night. There was a nice rhythm to my life. One day, that routine was interrupted. Mistress Sarah did not come at all!

I waited all day and looked for her to show up that evening, but she didn't. It was too late to stop by the vendor's cart because he always closed his place at nightfall so I lay down to sleep on my sand pile that night feeling hungry. I awakened at dawn and took a long drink of water from the nearby stream, mostly to fill me up—not because I was thirsty.

I waited for Mistress Sarah until the sun was high in the sky and when she didn't show, I sniffed the scent of her trail all the way to her house. I waited by her courtyard door and when she hadn't shown by sunset, I ran to the vendor's place and begged for food. Someone threw a piece of meat and half a roll onto the street in front of me. It didn't begin to satisfy my hunger. Also, now that I had become used to eating Sarah's food, the vendor's food didn't taste very good any more, but beggars can't be choosy and I was a beggar."

"Did Sarah come by the next morning?" asked Kissy.

"No. I sat outside her courtyard that day, too, but I could tell there wasn't any fresh scent and knew she had not touched the courtyard door for several days. I began to think that she had gone forever. My chest began to ache. I felt empty and it wasn't because I hadn't eaten much. I realized then that there is a difference between feeling empty and feeling hungry."

"What is the difference?" inquired Kawdje.

"Feeling hungry is located in just one part of your body, but feeling empty is all over. It's even in your head. It's an awful and frightening feeling. I had come to rely on Mistress Sarah for food. The scariest part was that I had come to rely on her for companionship. I wished with all my being that she would return home to me. I decided that, if she did, I would let her touch me and I would touch her to let her know that I appreciated and loved her. That night I slept outside her courtyard. I remember thinking how strange life is. I had spent most of my life trying to get outside a courtyard and now I was longing to get inside one.

When I awakened in the morning, I walked to my stream, lapped some water, lay down and wondered what to do now that Sarah was gone. There didn't seem to be any reason to live. I was terribly upset when I realized that life wasn't worth living if I didn't have someone to love and care about, and if no one loved and cared about me. I returned to my favorite sand pile and saw Sarah. I ran up behind her and placed my muzzle into her hand and licked her palm. I wagged my tail so fast it made my spine vibrate. I pressed my head against her and told her that I had missed her something awful and that I loved her and always would.

I even lay on my back and exposed my belly to her to demonstrate my complete trust.

She wrapped her arms around my neck. She stroked my back and muzzle. She murmured words in my ear that I didn't recognize, but I knew their meaning. She was telling me that she loved me! I felt such happiness, as I had never known! I sent a fervent wish up to the sky that I would live with Sarah all the days and all the nights of my life.

I walked beside her all the way back to her courtyard and up to her front door. I couldn't remember ever being inside a house, so I sat and waited for her invitation. She gestured for me to go inside so I stepped over the threshold. I felt so happy and excited that I thought I would float. That night I slept on a bed that was much softer, warmer and more comfortable than anything I had ever known.

Everyday with Sarah was filled with new and wonderful experiences. That first day, I walked through the streets with her to a shop where she bought a collar and placed it around my neck. I was happy to wear it because it meant that I was part of her family. She snapped a leash onto my collar. I quickly learned that when she tugged the leash, I was to follow the direction of the pull. I would have followed her anywhere with or without a lead. I was bursting with pride as we walked together through town.

My next experience was really strange to me. Sarah led me into a place where a woman washed me with warm water mixed with something that made it foam and smell pleasant. I had never felt warm water on my body before. She rinsed me off with clear, warm water and then blew very warm air all over my fur. My nails were trimmed and she cut off some of my fur, especially around my head, ears and neck. I had no idea what would happen next but the woman wasn't hurting me and I didn't want to offend anyone, so I stayed very still. When the woman finished grooming me, she walked me to the room where Sarah was waiting. I could tell she thought I looked good. I felt good! It was the first time in many, many days that I didn't feel gritty from sleeping on sand piles. I've been to grooming salons many times since, but that first experience was the most fantastic."

Kissy said, "Michael, tell us how you came to live here."

"Yes, I'd better get on with the tale of my life with Sarah during those first few months. We were living far away in a place that Sarah calls San

Miguel de Allende, Mexico. I now know that Sarah was just visiting the place where I was born.

I loved walking through the streets of San Miguel with Sarah. After I became part of Sarah's family, whenever I saw street dogs, I pitied them.

She is a kind and thoughtful leader and a fun companion. She's taught me the meaning of some words and to follow commands like sit, stay, heel, turn around, fetch the ball—stuff like that. Now I'm learning to climb on an A-Frame and use other agility obstacles."

Kissy asked Michael if he could teach her to do some agility tasks.

"I don't know, but you're welcome to come to my home and use the agility obstacles in my yard."

"Let Michael continue with his story," said Kawdje.

"The day after I had been to the grooming salon, Sarah took me to the veterinarian. Back then I didn't know what a vet was. He looked into my ears and my mouth and then he picked up something called a thermometer and lifted my tail. You won't believe what happened next!"

"Yes, we would!" Kissy and Kawdje exclaimed in unison.

"Say no more," said Kawdje. "We know the routine. Least said, best forgotten."

"Good advice," said Michael. "Let me tell you about the trip home. A man came to our house and helped Sarah put suitcases into the back of a car somewhere behind a seat upon which Sarah and I sat together. Sarah placed a towel on the seat where I sat—I think the man who drove us to the airport made her do that.

It was my first car ride and I was so excited. I wanted to hang my head out a window, but they were closed. I looked at the scenery, but it was difficult to focus on anything because everything whizzed by so fast. I knew we had been driven to a different town because the streets were wider and there were many more cars and people than in San Miguel.

Our destination was a huge building that Sarah called an airport. It was very confusing to me, but Sarah knew what to do. Some people put me into a kennel. I was afraid because I had never before been enclosed in something like a box. I could see out of the kennel and was glad of that but, to add to my fear, I was wheeled away from Sarah and I wondered if I would ever see her again.

I was rolled outside and saw a gigantic metal building that looked like a huge bird. I was lifted inside and after awhile a big door was shut and it was dark. Then I heard a loud, roaring sound and the huge bird, that I now know is called an airplane, began to move. The noise got louder, the airplane vibrated, it moved faster and faster and suddenly, I knew it had lifted off the ground and was flying like a bird. I had an unsettled feeling in my gut. I think that was partly due to the fact that I didn't know where Sarah was. I tried to sleep because there was nothing else to do, but I was too worried to relax, so I just lay there for a long, long time listening to the noise that seemed to become a part of me. I wished with all my being that I was cuddled up beside Sarah. I wouldn't have been afraid if I had been with her and knew that whatever we were doing or wherever we were going, we were experiencing it together.

At last, I sensed that the flying bird, I mean the airplane, was tilting downward. Then, there was a jarring bump and a roaring sound that hurt my ears and I knew it was rolling on the ground like a car.

I felt shaky and was very relieved when a huge door opened and I saw daylight. Two men lifted me outside and rolled my kennel across the ground and into a huge building. I knew I was in a different airport because everything smelled different and the sunlight had a quality unlike that of San Miguel. I saw Sarah walking toward me and when she opened the kennel door, I licked her hands and jumped all around her because I was so happy and relieved to see her. I wagged my tail and laid my head against her. She hugged me and stroked my neck and back. I knew that Sarah had taken me from Mexico to live with her for always. I didn't know where we were and I didn't care. It just mattered to me that wherever I was, I was with Sarah. She loved me and I loved her and we were together."

"Where do you live with Sarah?" asked Kissy.

"A man drove us to the biggest house I had ever seen. I jumped out of the car and breathed air that was quite cold. The wind carried unfamiliar scents that I couldn't identify because the trees and shrubs were not the same kind as I had been used to.

I took a tour around the place to familiarize myself with my property. I couldn't defend a property if I didn't know all about it. I decided to investigate an area that had a great many trees growing close together but I didn't have time to follow the scent of some critters because Sarah whistled for me to return to her.

We walked inside our home. Sarah took me into the kitchen and filled a bowl with water and placed it on the floor. I was grateful because I hadn't had water or food for many hours."

Kawdje said, "Speaking of food, are both of you hungry? I am. Let's go into the kitchen and let Mom know that we want to be fed."

CHAPTER SIX

While Michael told his life story to Kissy and Kawdje, Sarah related her experience in San Miguel de Allende with Michael Archangelo and their flight home to Essie and Evan.

"I was very unhappy with air travel accommodations for Michael. I'm sure that Michael was petrified to be separated from me and I don't really know how safe it was for him to have been stowed in the cargo area. I was told that he would be kept in a separate, temperature-controlled compartment but I don't know if the temperature was comfortable for him. I think that a separate area in the passenger cabin should be dedicated for traveling pets."

Evan said, "If Essie and I were flying with Kissy and Kawdje, we would have the same concerns. Our pets are small but too big to fit into a kennel that could be stowed under a seat and because of that, they would have to be housed in cargo. I'm going to ask my brother about this. He used to be a pilot who flew large commercial aircraft before he gave that up to become an archeologist. He still has a pilot's license and flies small aircraft and owns a helicopter."

"What prompted him to make that career change?" Sarah asked.

"My brother was always fascinated by archeology and took courses in the subject when he attended university, but he also loved flying and got a license to fly small aircraft. Gordon married immediately after he graduated from university. He needed to make enough money to support a wife and family, so he concentrated on becoming a commercial airline pilot and put aside his dream of become a full-time, in-the-field archeologist.

Financially, it was good for him, but not in any other way. He was away from his wife and their son much of the time because the job requires traveling. I think the frequent physical separation was the reason his marriage disintegrated. He divorced about ten years ago and hasn't remarried. His son, Kevin, is twenty. He's studying aeronautical engineering at Purdue University and is also taking some courses in archaeology. Guess the fascination with flying and with old bones got passed from father to son."

Essie added, "We haven't seen Elsa since the divorce. Gordon told us she remarried within a couple of years. Kevin lived with Elsa but spent most of his summers with Gordon on digs."

Evan continued, "Gordon persuaded Elsa to let Kevin attend an excellent preparatory school in this area during his high school years. He planned for Kevin to eventually attend a top-notch university, so he wanted to be certain that he had good schooling. We were happy with that decision because we got to see him often. It helped to soften the blow when our daughter left home to attend university and eventually became solvent enough to own her own pad after she graduated."

Sarah exclaimed, "I didn't know you have a daughter! As you already know, I have a daughter. You tell me about yours and I'll tell you about mine."

Essie replied, "Our daughter's name is Joyce but we call her Joy. We couldn't resist naming her, Joyce Kilmer, after the poet who wrote the famous poem 'Trees'. She inherited my straight blonde hair, blue eyes and slender build and looks a lot like me except she favors Evan's side of the family for height. She's five feet nine inches tall—almost as tall as her dad. She graduated from Swarthmore College with a degree in Liberal Arts, then took up photography and now works for *The Inquirer*. She was married last year to Sam Albright."

Sarah asked, half in jest, "That wouldn't be The Sam Albright, the famous basketball player, would it?"

Evan replied with a broad grin, "Yep."

"You lucky in-laws. Bet you all get fantastic seats at the basketball games when he's playing. Does Joy travel with Sam when the team's touring, or has she kept her job at the newspaper?"

Essie said, "She accompanies Sam occasionally but she's kept her job with the newspaper so we see her frequently. She and Sam bought a townhouse in the city and, for now, they're comfortable there. Now tell us about your daughter."

"Strangers would never guess that my daughter and I are related. Her appearance favors her father's side of the family. Pat is of medium height at five feet seven inches. She has her father's thick, dark brown hair and wears it long and straight. She has Charles' features—his straight nose instead of my turned-up one and his rectangular face rather than my heart-shaped face. She does have my eyes, though. Pat will soon graduate from the University of Pennsylvania's School of Veterinary Medicine. Her husband is a lawyer who specializes in corporate and international law. His name is Edward Palliser, so now her name is Patricia Pullman Palliser. Doesn't that have a great sound to it? I'm surprised that Pat doesn't have a pet, but I guess her life has been too busy for the past few years to make room for one. She used to show our dog, Chopsticks, when she was a junior handler."

"What breed was Chopsticks?" asked Essie.

"Pekingese. We all adored him. He lived to be 12 years of age and, of course, Pat, Charles and I were heartbroken when he died. We didn't get another dog immediately because Pat was about to leave home to attend university and I needed time to grieve over Chopsticks. When I felt I was ready to open my heart to another dog, Charles was diagnosed with stomach cancer. He had surgery and recuperated to the degree where he had good quality of life for several years. He returned to work and our lives carried on in normal mode, but we always had the underlying fear that disaster could strike at any time, and it did. Three years ago, my husband died."

"We're very sorry for your loss and grief," said Essie. "How did Pat cope? How did you find the strength to keep going?"

"Pat concentrated on her studies. She wanted to finish vet school, so that goal kept her going. I had to be strong for my daughter's sake. Charles had provided well for us financially so, thankfully, we didn't have the wolf at the doorstep.

I missed him terribly at first, but after the first year, that gradually lessened. I remember driving to the store one sunny day about two years after Charles' death and the trees were in leaf, tulips were blooming and the world looked exceptionally lovely. I suddenly realized that I was deep-down happy once again. My mourning was over.

Well, I'm not a very vivacious dinner guest. Let's get on to some happy topics. I wonder how Michael, Kissy and Kawdje are getting along. They've been very quiet!"

"Here they are now," Essie exclaimed. "I bet they want food. We should let them outdoors for a few minutes before they're fed."

It was still light enough outside to enjoy the trees and shrubs. Tulips were blooming, as well as some late-blooming varieties of daffodils. Pets and people strolled through the big garden in happy companionship.

The reverie exploded into an action scene when Kawdje saw a squirrel and took chase, followed by a yipping Kissy and a sprinting Michael who quickly overtook Kawdje in the chase. They all circled the base of the tree that was home for the squirrel.

"They're so companionable together," said Essie.

"I want to have all of you over to my home for dinner. You've mentioned that you think Kissy would prefer the sport of Dog Agility to being shown in Conformation Dog Shows. You can try Kissy and Kawdje on the Agility setup that I have for Michael. The jumps can be lowered to accommodate them."

"Thank you, Sarah. Evan and I would love to come for dinner and give our pets an Agility tryout. Let's go inside and discuss it over dinner. Will Michael eat pot roast and vegetables?" asked Essie.

"Michael loves almost all table food."

"I have crème brûlée for dessert. I know it's an odd combination with pot roast, but it's Evan's favorite dessert so I make it often. Kissy and Kawdje adore crème brûlée. If Michael doesn't like it, I can always give him gingersnaps."

Dessert was the pièce de résistance. Three pets and three people did justice to the crème brûlée. There wasn't a lick left over!

CHAPTER SEVEN

The following week Essie and Evan took Kissy and Kawdje to another Conformation Dog Show. It was a mild, sunny day with a cloudless sky and Kawdje's mood lifted to match the perfect weather conditions because the show was being held outdoors. He knew what was expected of him. He had learned that most judges pointed in the direction he was to walk toward, so he led Essie in the routine. When he stopped in front of the judge, he looked up at him inquiringly and mentally asked, "Well, did I do everything just right, or what?"

When they exited the ring, Essie excitedly joined Evan and Kissy and said, "Kawdje has won another Best of Breed. Now he has two majors. I know that means we have to hang around this show for the Non-Sporting Group competition, but if Kawdje wins that, he'll have his championship!"

"Fat chance," said Evan. "He's up against a Poodle and a Bichon Frisé and they are both cute, puff balls. He doesn't stand a chance! Oh well, let's stick around to give him a shot at the title."

They wandered around and stopped by the ring showing German Shorthaired Pointers.

They overheard a handler telling a tall, slender, beautiful Eurasian woman, "Topaz has beautiful conformation but she plods through being shown as though it's an ordeal for her. She doesn't look vivacious and happy, or even focused and because of her attitude, she will never show well. You're wasting your time and your money."

The woman glumly thanked her for the honest assessment. Her posture was regal as she watched the handler walk away, but her expression was forlorn. She turned and faced Essie and Evan and her expression changed into a beautiful smile as she saw Kawdje's Best of Breed ribbon.

She congratulated Essie and Kawdje on the win and said, "I guess this is the closest I'll ever get to that prestigious ribbon."

Essie thanked her and introduced herself and Evan. She explained that, although they were showing both of their pets, Kissy wasn't interested in being shown either and they entered her in Conformation Dog Shows primarily to keep Kawdje company and continue the activity as a family foursome.

Jeanette Bancroft introduced herself and informed them that her husband, Cole, rarely attended these shows because, as a cardiologist, he always had a heavy work schedule, plus emergencies.

"He wants Topaz to become a Champion in Conformation Dog Shows because he knows it's a hopeless cause to train her to become a Field Champion. Topaz regards deer as friends and never chases them off our property."

Jeanette related an incident when Topaz was chased by a doe who became concerned for the safety of her twin fawns when Topaz ambled too close to her offspring.

Evan and Essie laughed heartily and Evan asked, "Do you think that Topaz would be interested in the sport of Dog Agility?"

Jeanette said she would love to train Topaz in Dog Agility if the dog showed an interest in the sport and asked how she could find out more about it.

"Essie and I have a friend who has some agility obstacles set up on her property and she's training her dog. She has invited us to try out Kissy and Kawdje and see if either has an aptitude and, more importantly, an interest in the sport."

"Do you think your friend would allow me to bring Topaz over sometime to try out the setup? If Topaz shows an interest in Dog Agility, I'd be willing to have a workout as her handler. I believe that dogs need to have a learning program to help them evolve. They have decent reasoning ability, a need for companionship and a desire to please. I have a couple of neighbors and each has a dog that is always alone in the backyard with no stimulation or friendship. What a boring and empty life!"

"We are of like mind," Essie chimed in. "Let's exchange telephone numbers. I'll contact my friend and put your request to her and get back to you. Where do you live? I live in Media and my friend's home is in Chadds Ford."

Jeanette wrote her contact information on a slip of paper as she informed her that she lived near New Hope in Bucks County. Essie hurriedly tucked the paper in her waist-pack and said that she had to get to the Non-Sporting Group ring to show Kawdje. She and Evan waved goodbye and promised to get in touch soon.

Kawdje knew as he was led into another ring with many dogs of other breeds that something special was up. He stood directly behind a large dog, but since he had become familiar with Michael, large dogs no longer terrified him. He knew they were all kept on leashes so he was safe from attack. Maybe the big dog in front of him liked riding in fast cars and hanging his head out the window just like he and Michael enjoyed doing. His thoughts turned to Topaz. He had instantly liked her. She was big and beautiful and not at all threatening or aggressive. "Yes!" he thought. "Some big dogs are worth knowing."

He was in a good frame of mind as he paced the ring with his mom. When he stopped in front of the judge, he looked up directly into her eyes. When his mom lifted him onto the table, he stood very still in the stacked position and didn't shuffle his paws as the judge checked his teeth and felt his back and legs.

After his mom placed him back onto the floor of the ring, he carefully watched where the judge pointed and knew just what direction he and his mom should walk toward.

He paced a little ahead of his mom and when she tugged slightly on his lead, he quickly turned around without losing stride and walked toward the judge. Kawdje wagged his tail to tell her that he liked her as he gazed up at her face.

His mom walked him toward the side of the ring and he stood still while other dogs performed for the judge. The waiting was boring and tiresome, but he tolerated it because it was part of a routine that he knew well and he felt secure knowing the routine. He looked up at the judge whenever she walked by him, trying to pick up any signals that would tell him what to do next. She pointed at him and made a motion that meant he should step out of the lineup and walk to the spot she indicated. His mom was suddenly very happy and excited. He watched the judge point to several other dogs and they were positioned behind him. Then the judge gestured that he should pace around the ring. His mom tugged on his lead and almost ran as she led him around the ring, so he paced faster than he ever had before to keep up with her. He heard loud applause and then his mom picked him up in her arms and the judge gave her a huge ribbon. Kawdje knew he had won something. He posed in the stacked position while his picture was taken.

His dad managed to hug him and his mom, while still holding Kissy in his arms.

"Essie, you were great in the ring and Kawdje was 'on' today. What an accomplishment to have a group win! He's won a five-point major, so he's a Champion now."

Kawdje thought the show was over and was surprised to be led back into the ring again. He was puzzled to see only six other dogs. He decided to do exactly what he had done just a little while ago—stand still in a stacked position and carefully watch the judge indicate what he should do next.

Evan watched ringside and his hopes of Kawdje winning Best in Show dimmed as he looked over the incredible Bloodhound who represented the Hound Group. An equally wonderful Newfoundland from the Working Dogs Group and a shaky little Shih Tzu from the Toy Group looked like winners, too.

"They all look like winners and they are," he thought.

He had to admit that Kawdje was still "on." He looked steady and self-assured and stacked himself whenever he wasn't pacing in the ring. Evan's jaw dropped and his eyes widened in disbelief as he watched the judge walk toward Essie and give her a huge rosette. Even if he hadn't been holding Kissy in his arms, he knew he would not have found the strength to applaud. He was too overcome with emotions. He watched Essie accept congratulations and slowly make her way through the throng of well wishers toward him.

"Evan, I'm flabbergasted! I never imagined that Kawdje would be a Best in Show winner when he and Kissy came to live with us. He was the reserved one who always held back in new situations and assessed people and circumstances. He really put himself out there today, and I could tell that he felt good about himself. He liked the judge, too, so that helped."

"Obviously, the judge liked him and that sure helped, too. Well, Essie, is the Westminster Dog Show in Kawdje's future?"

"I'm not getting my hopes up that he would be accepted to compete in Westminster and I don't know if I'm up to handling him in that prestigious show, although sometimes I think he handles me in the ring. He's always contemplating everything and today his mind and heart connected and he enjoyed himself. He showed like a true champion."

Kissy knew that Kawdje had just had a big win. He was receiving attention from people crowded around him. She loved people and loved having everyone notice her. She was sure that if she was performing on agility obstacles, she would be a winner and everyone would pay attention to her.

Essie noticed that Kissy was subdued and said, "I wonder if Kissy is feeling left out or jealous because Kawdje has gotten so much attention today."

"Maybe so. We'll have to begin agility training soon. We'll include Kawdje but I suspect Kissy will do better at Dog Agility than him because she's more daring. Remember how long it took him to learn how to climb the open tread staircase at home?"

"Evan, I think that's because he was fearful of falling through the spaces between the stair treads. He's definitely not afraid of heights. Even though he contemplates and thinks a lot, his reasoning isn't always logical by human standards.

Let's go home and celebrate, Evan. I'll have to phone Joy and Sarah and tell them all about Kawdje's big win and that he is now a Champion. Also, I must ask Sarah if we may bring along Jeanette Bancroft and Topaz for a tryout on her Dog Agility setup to find out if they enjoy the sport. You also need to know if you would like Dog Agility teamwork because you'll be partnering Kissy. I'll handle Kawdje in Agility if he wants to participate in that kind of dog event."

As Essie and Evan, Kawdje and Kissy made their way through the dog crates and grooming paraphernalia that were being packed up, they were stopped frequently by handlers who wanted to have a good, close-up look at Kawdje and inquire about the personality traits of the Tibetan Spaniel.

Kawdje basked contentedly in all the attention and thought that this day had been almost as good as a car ride with his head hanging out an open window.

During several encounters with other handlers, Kissy barked to draw attention to herself and the handlers complied by stroking her head and remarking what a pretty face she had. She wondered what Kawdje had won a ribbon for. "I can run faster than he can. Why would he win something for walking around a ring? Oh well, I'll find something to do that's more exciting and challenging."

CHAPTER EIGHT

Sarah stroked Michael's head as she looked over the setup consisting of three Jumps, an A-Frame, a Rigid Pipe Tunnel and Weave Poles and was satisfied that there was enough equipment for the pets to have a good agility workout. Michael's body suddenly went on full alert and several seconds later, Essie and Evan's van drove up her driveway followed by the Bancroft's SUV. Car doors opened and people and pets poured out. Michael ran to greet everyone and stopped momentarily when he saw Topaz, then resumed wagging his tail even more enthusiastically. Her scent was more delectable than the juiciest bone he had ever gnawed on. She was of a size to look him in the eye and her warm, brown eyes were the kindest, friendliest and most beautiful that he had ever gazed into—other than Sarah's, he hastily amended. He very badly wanted to touch her nose in greeting but wasn't sure how she would react so he restrained himself.

Sarah caught up to Michael and Essie and Evan introduced her to Jeanette and Cole. She thought that the tall, elegant, Eurasian woman with the air of serenity and friendliness and the tall, lean, dark-haired man with the intense expression and piercing, hazel eyes that were framed by rimless eyeglasses, suited one another. An exquisitely beautiful German Shorthaired Pointer was pressed closely against Jeanette's leg and Sarah sensed the close bond between the two and knew that Topaz was "momma's girl" and not "daddy's girl."

Sarah shook hands with Jeanette and Cole, then slid a hand down one of Topaz's incredibly silky ears, "She's exquisitely beautiful. Her body is a perfect balance of elegance and sturdiness."

Jeanette said, "Being shown for conformation bored Topaz so she didn't do well. My husband and I are hoping she'll enjoy agility training. Thank you for extending your hospitality to us."

Cole studied the agility setup and asked, "How will all the pets be able to use the same setup? Kissy and Kawdje are miniscule compared to Topaz and Michael."

"All jumps are adjustable so pets of any size can use the same setup. Before we start the training session, would anyone care for something to drink? I have iced tea, soft drinks, juice, and water. Also, there is water for the pets near the area of the lawn that I've dedicated to the agility ring. Let's show them their water bucket now."

They all walked over to the bucket. Kissy and Kawdje were barely tall enough to lap from it without having to stand on their hind legs to reach their heads over the rim. They loved it! It felt great to be able to drink from the same water pail as large dogs. Michael wedged his head into the bucket and slurped up water with them. Topaz waited politely until the other three had finished before taking a drink.

Kissy noticed the Dog Agility set-up and excitedly hoped that she was going to have a chance to demonstrate her swiftness and learn how to perform on the obstacles. She shared her thoughts with the others. Kawdje immediately felt wary and concerned as he always did when faced with a new situation. Topaz said that she thought it looked like more fun than standing around waiting for her turn to pace in front of a judge and that it would really be great if it was going to be an activity that she and her mom did together. Michael told the other three that he and Sarah had been practicing for awhile and that he enjoyed the activity especially because they did it together.

The Kilmers and Brancrofts declined anything to drink and everyone agreed they should get started on the agility training tryout.

Sarah suggested that she and Michael give a demonstration after which everyone could choose an obstacle to begin training their pet to use and then progress to another, and so on.

Sarah signaled Michael to ascend and descend the A-Frame. She pointed to the two contact points on the obstacle. Each was located on the lower portion of the frame where it touched the ground and went up for about 20 inches. She explained that a dog must touch the safety contact zone when ascending and descending the obstacle.

"Failure to touch contact zones and an early jump-off are faults. Every fault is given points, usually five, and faults are added onto the time that a team takes to get through the course. A team is comprised of a handler and a dog. The team that wins is the team with the fewest faults and the fastest time. There are different types of agility classes. Some classes require that a team collect as many points as they can within the Standard Course Time and the team with the most points wins. In those classes, scoring ceases after a fault. It wouldn't be fair to have a team win by accruing the most points because they had the most faults."

While Michael zigzagged through the Weave Poles, Sarah said that the dog must always enter the poles on the right side.

Evan asked, "Does the right side change depending on the approach? Could the left side be the correct side sometimes?"

Everyone looked confused.

Sarah apologetically said, "I've read that Weave Poles must always be entered from the right side. I think Michael will always have to enter from his left. I have terrible difficulty remembering my right from my left. I'm trying to teach him to differentiate between his right and left. I call out 'left' to him as he enters the poles, but I've made many mistakes because it takes me so long to translate the right side of the poles and his left side in my mind that I confuse him."

Evan asked how he could get more information about Dog Agility.

Sarah said, "There is a website that you can log onto and I'll give you that information after practice. If anyone decides that Dog Agility is something you want to pursue, I suggest we meet frequently among ourselves to practice. My home and setup is open to all of you. Also, you may want to consider joining the Keystone Capers Dog Agility Club. I'm going to. I've been to one session as an observer and it was helpful."

Evan said, "Let's go to work," as he jogged Kissy over to the first jump obstacle.

Kissy thought that the top bar looked at least three times higher than the top of her head and considered squirming under the jump. Evan jumped but Kissy didn't. Everyone clapped and cheered and complimented Evan on his jumping prowess. He laughed and took a bow, then picked up Kissy and lifted her over.

Sarah walked over to the jump and removed two poles. "Let's start her at a very low height, appropriate for her size. Later on we can add to the difficulty of the jump."

Evan and Kissy jogged up to the jump again and this time Kissy wasn't intimidated and she jumped up and over the top pole. She was elated by her success but decided that high jumping wasn't one of the best perks in life.

Essie had Kawdje try the jump while it was set at a low height and he cleared it with plenty of room to spare. He felt strong and daring and altogether wonderful and decided that Dog Agility just might be a fun thing to do. He reasoned that because the obstacles prevented this activity from being a race, he might be able to do as well as Kissy.

Sarah replaced the top bars on the jump. Jeanette and Topaz jogged toward it and Topaz easily jumped over without breaking stride. Jumping was a commonplace activity for Topaz who easily cleared old fences and other obstacles on her property.

Sarah suggested that they snap short leads on the pets and lead them up, over and down the A-frame to teach them to touch the contact zones and prevent an early jump-off.

Jeanette led Topaz to the A-Frame who just looked at it. Jeanette placed Topaz's front paws on the base of the frame and said, "Contact." Then she stood alongside the obstacle and tugged on her lead to let her know that she should ascend. Topaz was flummoxed by the odd thing that wasn't a staircase and wasn't like anything she had ever climbed up and over on her property. She looked inquiringly at her mom, who kept saying, "Up. Up."

She began to climb and was encouraged by her mom's praise for her effort. After she had reached the peak, Topaz easily and quickly descended, touching the contact zone that her mom pointed to, saying, "Contact." Topaz understood that she was supposed to walk on the lower area of the plank.

Her mom then led her over to another jump that was higher than the first. She cleared it with ease. She wasn't sure what to do when they reached the Weave Poles, so Michael gave another demonstration after which her mom and dad physically helped her weave her way between each pole. Topaz felt awkward, which was a new experience for her.

Meanwhile, Essie and Evan were coaching Kissy and Kawdje to use the A-Frame. Kissy loved it. It was like climbing stairs at home. Kawdje balked. To him, it looked something like a staircase but it wasn't. Then the thought came to him that he would be able to view everything from a better vantage point at the top of this thing, so he quickly ascended and refused to descend. He took a good look around and enjoyed the view. Essie was just about to lift him off the A-Frame when she suddenly understood that he liked being up so high.

She turned to Evan and said, "I hate to spoil his fun, but we need to teach him not to stop at the top. What shall I do?"

"That's a tough one, Essie. If he's ever going to be a serious agility competitor he has to be trained now not to hesitate at the top of the A-Frame."

Essie agreed and she tugged on Kawdje's lead to make him descend. As soon as he touched ground, he turned and faced the ramp he had just descended from and rapidly ascended to the top. A giggling Essie tugged him down the other side. He abruptly turned and faced the A-Frame, prepared to ascend it again. She picked him up. "You're a stubborn little fellow," she said as she cradled him in her arms.

Essie and Evan carried their pets over to the Weave Poles. Once again, Michael demonstrated weaving in and out. Kissy and Kawdje were guided between the poles and seemed to enjoy the activity. Evan removed their leads and coaxed Kissy to repeat the maneuver. She slid between the poles quickly, loving the sinuous weaving motion that reminded her of the way she had once seen a snake move. Kawdje plodded along after her, feeling that, once again, he was trailing in Kissy's path, which is what always happened in any activity that called for speed.

After an hour, everyone took a break.

The pets gathered around the water bucket. Each had been given a big dog biscuit and, although Kissy and Kawdje did not care for dog biscuits, each nibbled at their biscuit because they were pleased to have been given the same size as Michael and Topaz.

Topaz said, "You perform well on all the obstacles, Michael. How do you manage to slide between the poles so effortlessly?"

"It takes practice. Sarah and I have been doing this almost every day for weeks. We began soon after I came here to live."

Kissy said, "Michael, tell Topaz your story of how you came to live with your mom, Sarah."

Michael summarized a version of his life in Mexico and meeting Sarah.

Topaz said sympathetically, "I've never known what it's like to not be loved or to be on my own. I'm glad that you have a home and family now. You have a big property to look after. It's large like mine is. I'm expected to keep deer off my property and that's a problem because I like deer. Also, they're much bigger than I am. When I try to chase them away, they refuse to run. I'm a disappointment to my dad because he says I'm a hunting dog and he expects and wants me to hunt and, frankly, I just don't like to. I especially don't like to hunt and chase anything bigger than I am. I chase off groundhogs, rabbits and chipmunks, and I race the squirrels to their home base trees. I can run fast enough to almost catch them. I'm not sure what I'd do if I actually caught a critter. I like them and I don't want to hurt them or have anything or anyone else hurt them."

Michael said, "We have deer around here, too, but they run from me. I've warned them not to damage our trees and to stay away. They come onto my property at night but there's nothing I can do to prevent that because I sleep in the same room as Sarah and my priority is to protect her and our home. The deer won't harm Sarah or our home so I just keep my senses on alert for any intruder who might pose a threat to her safety."

The other three were impressed.

"What would you do if someone tried to get into your house without your mom's permission?" Kawdje asked.

"I would snarl in warning and do whatever had to be done to protect Sarah, including sinking my fangs into the intruder."

"I guess Kissy and I would do that, too," Kawdje said uncertainly.

"We're small," said Kissy, "but we have sharp, shrill barks and we could wake up our mom and dad, who would know what to do and would look after us."

Kawdje agreed. "Our dad and mom can handle anything but I guess I would actually bite someone if I knew that person meant to harm them."

"I guess I would, too," said Kissy, "but I've never met a person that I didn't like except for that judge at my first dog show, and I only bit him lightly because he stuck his fingers in my mouth."

Michael snickered.

Topaz said, "I guess I could bite someone who meant to harm my mom. I can sense what my mom is feeling and I often know what she's thinking. If I ever sensed that she was afraid of someone or something, I'd do my very best to protect her but, most of the time, she protects me."

The dogs saw their family members walking toward them.

"I guess we're in for more training now," said Michael.

The next hour sped by quickly for everyone, and, when Sarah suggested that they go inside and have dinner, people clapped hands and pets wagged tails. The kitchen was a busy place as Sarah delegated tasks. Cole opened a bottle of wine and poured a glass for everyone. Sarah removed oven-roasted potatoes and a roasted leg of lamb from the oven. The scent of garlic and rosemary made everyone's mouth water and the pets drool. Evan carved roasted lamb and Sarah placed the slices on a platter. Jeanette tossed a salad and apportioned it in bowls that Essie carried to the dining room table. Then Sarah, Jeanette and Essie heaped scraps into four dog bowls while Cole and Evan spread newspaper on the kitchen floor for the dog dishes to be placed on.

The afternoon workout had made everyone hungry and those who ate in the dining room cleaned their plates almost as quickly as those who ate in the kitchen.

Dessert was a hit!

Cole remarked, "My grandmother used to make rice pudding and it was always one of my favorite desserts. My mother made it, too, but it was never quite as good as Grandmom's. Your pudding ranks up there with Grandmom's."

Sarah beamed with pleasure as Jeanette and Essie asked her to share her recipe. She said she would and related that it was an old family recipe of her great, great grandmother's and passed down through the generations to her.

The pets were just as enthusiastic about dessert. Each devoured their portion with speed, greed and pleasure, then checked everyone else's bowl for leftovers.

As the friends sipped coffee and tea, they decided to continue agility practice at Sarah's because the obstacles were set up on her lawn, and to gather for practice on weekends. Weather conditions would dictate if it should be Saturday or Sunday. Essie and Jeanette insisted they would take turns bringing dinner and lift the burden of cooking from Sarah.

Everybody shared cleanup chores. It had been an exhausting but satisfying day so, as soon as the last dish had been rinsed, dried and put away, the Bancrofts and Kilmers said their goodbyes. Michael and Sarah escorted them to their cars.

Before the cars were out of sight, Michael ran into the house, up to the bedroom and stretched out on his bed. He felt exhausted from demonstrating over and over how to weave between the poles. In spite of his exhaustion, he had thoroughly enjoyed the practice. He liked everyone, especially gorgeous Topaz, whose scent was even more delicious than rice pudding. He could hardly wait to see everyone again.

During the drive home, Essie said to Evan, "Let's come up with a plan to introduce your brother to Sarah. I think they would suit one another. Any idea when Gordon will pay us another visit?"

Evan said he didn't know, but promised to phone his brother and find out.

CHAPTER NINE

The following week, Essie and Evan, Sarah and Jeanette joined the Keystone Capers Dog Agility Club that met every Tuesday evening at the estate of Mavis Lowden.

Mavis was a tall woman. Everything about her was gray. She had gray hair, wore dark gray trousers and a lighter gray blouse and looked to be between over fifty and under seventy. She had a firm, no-nonsense-but-kindly-manner and demonstrated everything with her Pembroke Welsh Corgi and Flat-coated Retriever.

New situations usually stressed Kawdje more than the other three pets, but even he took this unfamiliar circumstance in stride after quickly noting that there were only eight dogs, other than himself and his group, and they were all on leashes except for a small dog and a big dog that the owner of this large practice place used to demonstrate the obstacles.

Mavis had various techniques for teaching dogs to follow commands and the meaning of left and right. A whistle or clicking gizmo could be used instead of voice commands if the handler preferred that. She showed how the same course setup was changed to accommodate dog breeds of all sizes.

"Only the hurdles and jump heights are changed. Some of our first-time attendees may be wondering why large and small dogs use the same setup and questioning the fairness of such a practice. Height differences are factored in, and Standard Course Times are different for each height category."

Mavis explained that a Standard Course Time was different for each class and each course setup and was determined by the judge who factored in the path that the dog must take, the distance of that path, the number of obstacles and the degree of difficulty.

"A Standard Course Time for the same class and setup will be slower for small dogs and faster for large dogs, so even though a small dog must run the same path through a course setup, the small dog is given a longer Standard Course Time in which to run that distance."

She informed them of the procedure for determining a dog's jump height and the four jump height categories. "A dog must be able to jump at least its own height at the withers and even higher. I'm going to take the opportunity to measure our four new canine clients."

Michael, Topaz, Kissy and Kawdje were measured from the shoulder to the ground. Michael and Topaz fell into the 26-inch jump height category, and Kissy and Kawdje into the 12-inch jump height category. Mavis said she would send the information to the USDAA officials.

Mavis then discussed course-handling etiquette.

"A handler must guide the dog off the leash while in the ring and have control of the dog while performing. It is cause for elimination if a dog is running out of control on the course, or runs the course setup the wrong way or, heaven forbid, runs out of the ring. Make sure that the four-legged members of your team have a potty break before performing because fouling the ring is another cause for elimination.

Also, always be on time for your scheduled entry into the ring. If you are entered in several classes in an event and you think there is the possibility of a time conflict, talk to the event officials and they will adjust your performance placements so as to avoid having you scheduled to be in two rings at the same time."

Mavis finished her talk by asking if there were any questions.

Sarah said, "Weave Poles must always be entered on the right side and the right will depend on the approach to them. I'm training Michael by using verbal commands so, should I call out 'left' to him because he will always enter between the first and second poles by turning toward his left side?"

Mavis said, "Yes. His entry into the right side of the poles will always be on his left."

After class, Mavis informed them that dogs must be at least eighteen months old to compete in Dog Agility events and that a veterinarian's certificate was required to confirm this.

Sarah was in a quandary because she didn't know Michael's age.

Jeanette said, "Your vet can make an estimate from examining Michael's teeth. Humans have molars that come in at 2 years, 6 years and

12 years of age and dogs have comparable and predictable dental growth. I'm guessing he's about Topaz's age and she's 18 months old."

As they walked to their separate vehicles for the drive home, Evan said, "I logged onto USDAA's website since we last met at Sarah's and made printouts that describe the obstacles and the various classes. I also ordered their Official Rules and Regulations book and should receive that soon. We can go over everything at our practice session this coming weekend."

During the drive home, Evan suggested dropping Conformation Dog Shows for Kissy. "I know she loves Dog Agility. She weaves in out of those poles like a comet."

"Comets don't weave," laughed Essie. "They blast their way through space leaving a trail."

Evan said, "Kissy blasts her way through those poles so fast that she almost leaves her tail at the Weave Poles entrance."

"We should nickname her 'Kissy the Comet'," declared Essie. She added that Kawdje was more relaxed at tonight's practice than he had been at Sarah's.

Evan said he had noticed that, too. "Let's keep him in Agility. He might become a great competitor and I'd like to keep it a family activity. Serious Dog Agility competition is time-consuming and requires travel to competitions. Let's plan on doing it together unless he lets us know that he hates it. Also, let's buy a Dog Walk to contribute to Sarah's agility course.

They met on Saturday at Sarah's for their agility practice. Essie and Evan arrived early so that they could place the Dog Walk in the setup. Evan also brought two hula hoops and everybody helped affix them to poles that Evan pushed deeply into the ground. One hoop was set at a jump height for Kissy and Kawdje, and the other one at Michael and Topaz's jump height. Jeanette surprised everyone by bringing a Collapsible Tunnel.

Practice was fun for everyone; however, Sarah struggled with her right/left discrimination. The problem was compounded as she tried to remember Michael's left and right.

During lunch break, Evan passed around printouts describing all the obstacles.

He announced, "Contact obstacles are those that the dog touches when performing and that would be all the obstacles other than Jumps and Hurdles. We ought to get a See-Saw because none of our pets had a chance to use it during the Keystone Capers Dog Agility Club meeting.

The various Jumps and Hurdles are: Tire Jump, Wishing Well, Long Jump, Brush Jump, Spread Hurdles, Winged Hurdles and Non-winged hurdles.

A Spread Hurdle is like a low bridge that must be jumped over rather than walked over. It's always lower and shorter in length for small dogs than for larger breeds. All Jumps can be raised or lowered to accommodate the four different jump height categories that are 12 inches, 16 inches, 22 inches and 26 inches in the Championship Program that our pets are entered in. There is a Performance Program that is less strenuous and has lower jump heights. It would be suitable for veteran dogs or breeds that aren't quick and agile due to their bone structure or for any number of reasons. We just need to concentrate on the Championship Program."

Everyone thought they ought to get a See-Saw and Spread Hurdle. Evan offered to make a Spread Hurdle for Kissy and Kawdje and a larger one for Michael and Topaz and order a See-Saw to be delivered to Sarah's home. The group agreed to share expenses.

Sarah said, "We'll soon have enough obstacles for a complete course setup. By the way, my daughter checked out Michael's teeth and estimated that he is at least eighteen months old."

Several weeks later, Essie and Kawdje returned home from a Conformation Dog Show that had been held in the area and Essie announced as they walked through the front door, "Kawdje won another Best in Show today."

Evan gave an exuberant whoop and picked up Essie in a bear hug. "You gorgeous little handler. I bet I'll see you on TV at the Westminster Dog Show. I have good news, too. I just hung up the phone from talking with Gordon. He's coming to come visit us tomorrow."

Kissy and Kawdje recognized the excitement in their parents' voices and responded by chasing one another around the kitchen. Kissy had missed Kawdje, who had left early that morning with their mom.

Essie said, "We'll bring Gordon with us to our weekend agility practice at Sarah's. We're going to introduce them to one another sooner than we thought and it's going to happen without any elaborate plans that we hatched. The simplest plans always work best anyway. I'd better let Sarah know so that she sets an extra place at her table."

CHAPTER TEN

Jeanette hung up the phone and her expression showed obvious distress as she turned to Cole. "That was Brant Prescott, my sister's brother-in-law. He said Iris and Don have been seriously injured in an auto accident. Both have broken bones and have been taken to surgery. He doesn't know the full extent of their injuries yet. We'll need to look after our niece while Iris and Don are recuperating. Jenny is with Brant, but he can't look after her for more than a few days. His job requires a lot of traveling plus, he's going through a divorce. I'll drive to Chicago tomorrow. I expect I'll have to remain there until Jenny completes her school year in a couple of weeks and then I'll bring her home with me. She'll probably be living with us during the summer, maybe even longer. I'll take Topaz along. Then you won't have to come home a couple of times during the day to let her out, or worry if you've left her outside for the whole day, that she'll bolt across the electric fence and come to harm."

"Maybe that is the best solution," Cole said and then asked, "How will you get into their home?"

"I'll call Brant back and tell him I'm planning to drive there tomorrow. We'll arrange to meet at the hospital and he can give me the key to Iris's home or tell me where to get one."

Cole said, "It will be tough for Jenny to be so far away from her parents."

"I know, but it isn't as though we're strangers to Jenny. Maybe Iris and Don will be discharged soon and have home care. Whatever the case, I'll drive there tomorrow with Topaz, assess the situation and decide the best course to take when I have more information. I'll call Sarah now and let her know that I can't attend agility training this weekend."

Sarah listened with concern as Jeanette related the turn of events. She immediately offered to keep Topaz while Jeanette was away.

"Thanks for your offer, Sarah, but I know that she'll be extra work and she might mope because she misses me."

"Here's another suggestion, Jeanette. Leave her with me during the day while Cole is working. He can pick her up every evening. Topaz is welcome to stay here all night whenever Cole is on emergency call. That way it won't be such a big adjustment for her. She's a sweetheart and I think Michael is in love with her."

Jeanette laughed, "I know she likes you and Michael and would feel comfortable in your home. I'll talk it over with Cole and call you back real soon."

Topaz sensed that her mom was sad, excited, worried and uptight all at the same time. She watched her mom pack a suitcase and knew that meant she would get in the car and drive away. Sometimes, she took her along, too. She jumped up delightedly when her mom called for her to get in the car. When they arrived at Michael's home, Topaz felt confused. Why would her mom pack a suitcase just to take a trip to Michael's home?

She leaped gracefully out of the car and looked around. Michael ran up to her and touched her nose. Kissy and Kawdje weren't around, so Topaz decided that this was not an agility practice. She watched her mom give her food bowl to Sarah and then pull her favorite soft blanket out of the car and carry it into Michael's home. What was happening, she wondered?

When her mom came back out, she hugged Topaz and whispered in her ear. Topaz then understood that she would be staying here with Michael and Sarah. She didn't know for how long, but she knew that it wouldn't be for always.

Michael licked her muzzle and told her how happy he was to have her companionship. Sarah caressed her ears and Topaz relaxed. She knew that Sarah genuinely liked her, and Topaz's mood lifted as she remembered that Sarah always served tasty food. Good food was one of the great perks of life.

Her mom had been talking to Sarah and now she turned and gave Topaz a last goodbye hug. As Topaz saw her mom climb into the car, heard the hum of the engine and watched the car disappear, she felt queasy. She missed her mom already. Sarah offered her a piece of cooked, chopped liver, but Topaz refused it. She had a lump in her throat so big that she was sure she would never be able to swallow anything ever again.

Michael suggested that they take a run around the property and Topaz agreed. He showed her the stately pine tree that he loved to lie under.

They picked up the scent of deer and Michael said, "Watch and I'll show you how I make them run from me."

Michael ran around sniffing until he picked up the trail and he followed it with Topaz close behind him.

"Turn this way," said Topaz as she cut to the left. Sure enough, behind a cluster of tall bushes stood a small herd of deer. Michael gave a series of short, sharp barks warning them that they must leave his land pronto! About four doe and two young deer, just past the spotted fawn phase, ran and leaped deeper into the woods. One young buck stood his ground uncertainly. Michael assumed an aggressive hunting posture. He slowly stalked the young buck while emitting a low, rumbling growl. Michael did not waver in his progress and the young buck turned tail and ran after the herd.

"That's how it's done. You slowly stalk forward, giving them plenty of time to run, and letting them know that you're the boss and you won't retreat. They always give in."

"But, Michael, I feel sorry for deer. They would never harm anyone except to protect their young."

"Topaz, you're supposed to hunt and chase critters. You have a great nose for picking up scents. I guess that's because you come from a long line of hunting masters."

"I know, Michael, but my problem is that I like most critters and I'm afraid of chasing those that are larger than I am. Thanks for showing me around your land. Let's go inside now. I think I'd like something to eat and drink."

Cole developed a daily routine of dropping off Topaz at Sarah's home in the early morning and picking her up just before dinner. He was glad to have Topaz's company during the evenings. She was gentle, intelligent and well-mannered. Topaz and Jeanette were alike in some ways. They were both quiet and capable; then he quickly amended the thought. Jeanette wasn't exactly quiet. It was just that she seemed to do everything with an economy of movement and effort. He loved his wife so much that he sometimes felt excluded by the uncanny psychic bond that she and

Topaz shared. Maybe while Jeanette was away, he and Topaz would grow closer.

Cole attended Saturday's agility training in Jeanette's absence and arrived at Sarah's just ahead of the others. Michael bounded out of the house to greet them just as Essie and Evan drove up. When Gordon got out of his vehicle, he introduced himself to Cole.

Michael and Topaz crowded around Gordon, sniffing his shoes and licking his hands. They both instantly liked and trusted him. Kissy and Kawdje loved him almost as much as they loved their parents. Gordon shuffled slowly and awkwardly toward Sarah's front door. He was afraid to lift his feet and walk in a normal fashion for fear of stepping on a paw of one of the pets who milled around him exuberantly.

Sarah walked through the front door and smiled in greeting. Gordon was speechless as his brother introduced her. She seemed so familiar. Everything about her was exactly right, from the color of her golden brown wavy hair that matched her eyes to the golden hue of her lightly tanned skin. "She's a golden girl," he thought. "Her smile would light up a dungeon."

He shook her outstretched hand and said something that he couldn't remember immediately after having said it. He hoped it had been something polite that made sense.

It seemed to Sarah that the sun suddenly shone brighter as she shook hands with Gordon. She felt as though she had met him before and thought, "He doesn't look much like Evan but they're related, so there's got to be a genetic similarity in many ways such as the way they move, the cadence of their speech—something. He's taller than his brother and has blue eyes instead of gray like Evan's, plus his hair is thick and blonde. He has the same build as Evan except his shoulders are broader. He's a hunk of gorgeous man!"

Sarah knew she was a sucker for tall men and Gordon was at least 6 feet 2 inches. She was acutely aware of not being quite 5 feet 2 inches, and she felt it balanced her to be with a tall man. She knew that Topaz minded having a very short tail and that Kawdje didn't like being so small. She could relate because she had always wanted to be tall, so she made up for her lack of height by preferring tall men. If she couldn't be tall, the next best option was to be with someone who was. She got a grip on herself and offered everyone some liquid refreshments before they started practice.

Gordon suggested a mock agility trial and offered to time them. Everyone helped mark a path through the course setup by attaching a number on each obstacle. The course would begin with the number one, progress to number two obstacle, and so on.

"I don't have a stopwatch, so for this practice my wristwatch will do. You have several minutes to walk the course and plan where you will run between obstacles, or stand so that you can best show the dog member of your team what to do and where to go next."

Gordon walked the course with Sarah and said, "You're a wonderful hostess and generous to open your home to everyone on weekends."

"It's not much effort for me. We usually have a potluck dinner so I don't have to do much cooking. Everyone helps with cleanup chores. I feel blessed to have my weekends filled with congenial companions and a common purpose. The friends I had when I was married drifted away after my husband died."

"I'm sorry for your loss. Evan and Essie did mention that you were widowed. They also told me that you have a grown daughter. Do you get to see her often?"

"Not as much as I would like to. Pat has a busy life but I content myself knowing that she is well and happy and fulfilling her dream of becoming a veterinarian."

Gordon said, "I guess she inherited your love for animals."

"I guess she did. I've observed that they are so much like us. They have the same range of feelings we do; they have reasoning ability; they enjoy many of the same activities we do, plus, they have an appreciation for the comforts of life just like humans have. For example, Michael loves sleeping in his comfortable bed just as I do in mine. He adores riding in a car and enjoys the scenery as much as I do except that he loves to hang his head out the window while appreciating it. He behaved in a very humanlike way when he became distrustful of people and afraid to take a chance on loving again because he had been abused."

"Essie and Evan told me that you brought him back with you from your trip to Mexico and that his full name is Michael Archangelo. I bet that exalted name has a story behind it and I'd like to hear it."

"I can't tell it now because our break is almost over. Maybe I can tell you during dinner if the others don't mind listening to the story one more time."

Gordon seized an opportunity to ask Sarah out. "Why not tell me over dinner tomorrow evening? I'd like to take you out if you're free."

"Thanks for the invitation and I accept. What time will you pick me up?"

Gordon quickly decided to ask her to spend the afternoon with him, too. "If you're free during the afternoon, I'd like to come by about 2 p.m. We could visit the Philadelphia Art Museum. They usually feature some special collection on loan. Would you be interested in that?"

"That's a wonderful idea, Gordon. If you can come here about 1 p.m., I'll have lunch ready for us. We may need food to fortify us for all the walking we'll be doing."

Gordon said, "Great! One o'clock it is."

"I'd better walk the course setup again to plan my strategy. I wasn't paying much attention while we were talking."

Sarah jogged back to the hurdle that had been designated as number one while Gordon positioned himself slightly off to one side of the course setup.

He gave her a couple of minutes, then took out his whistle and announced, "Okay teams! Everyone get set. Sarah and Michael are Team One; Cole and Topaz are Team Two. We'll lower the jumps before Essie and Kawdje who are Team Three perform, followed by Evan and Kissy, who are Team Four."

As Gordon watched Sarah and Michael perform, he observed her looking at her left hand and noticed a mark on it. She hesitated when commanding Michael to turn left or right. It slowed their performance, which was fast in spite of her obvious right from left orientation problem. Michael used every obstacle without hesitation or difficulty. Gordon thought they had the makings of a champion team and an idea came to mind of how to help Sarah with her right from left dilemma.

Meanwhile, it was obvious to Gordon that Cole and Topaz weren't used to working together. Topaz was graceful and a natural jumper who needed more time to become familiar with Weave Poles. Her performance was impeded by Cole's lack of experience, but in spite of that, their time was not much slower than Sarah and Michael's. In fact, Topaz was deliriously happy that her dad was practicing with her and she wanted to please him so badly that it had a negative effect on her performance because she wasn't as relaxed as when she practiced with her mom. She couldn't tune into her dad's thoughts and feelings as she could with her mom's, and the result was that she felt alone on the practice course.

Gordon saw that Essie and Kawdje worked like a team. Their experience in Conformation Dog Shows supported their dog agility teamwork. Kawdje had a natural spring to all his jumps. He wanted to hesitate on the Dog Walk long enough to look around, but Essie urged him on. Kawdje complied out of habit but also because he was beginning to understand that this type of activity called for speed and action. No one ever stood still or waited patiently for a judge to look you over in Dog Agility practices. The Weave Poles were his least favorite obstacles and he plodded through them. Gordon had no idea if Kawdje's time was excellent or dismal. He couldn't compare his performance to either Michael or Topaz's. He would have to wait until Kissy had run the course to determine an acceptable Standard Course Time for dogs in the 12-inch jump height category.

Gordon smiled at Kissy's aggressive and enthusiastic attitude. She was undecided about waiting for Evan's guidance or charging ahead and doing her own thing. She was not a natural jumper and lacked the spring that Kawdje had, but she more than made up for that by being so agile and hustling from one obstacle to another. He calculated that her course time compared to Kawdje's was faster by almost two seconds.

Everyone enjoyed the mock agility trial, so much so, that they switched the numbered pieces of paper to different obstacles to delineate a new path through the set up. Gordon announced that every team's time had improved.

Gordon's contribution to the practice session had been invaluable and everyone told him so. It had been a long and satisfying afternoon, and when Sarah asked if they were ready to eat dinner, Essie and Evan, Cole and Topaz, Kissy and Kawdje jogged to the front door and tried to hustle through it together.

Gordon walked over to Sarah and Michael and said, "I hope you won't be offended by my saying that I noticed you have difficulty differentiating right from left. I have a suggestion that might help your dilemma."

Sarah groaned and held up her left hand showing Gordon the 'L' mark she had inked on her palm. "This doesn't help me to quickly distinguish

Michael's left and right. I know my problem slows down our performance. I welcome any suggestion that could provide a solution."

Gordon said, "I often spray paint lines to mark off areas when I'm on a dig. It's easier than pounding stakes into hard-packed earth and it prevents the possibility of damaging any shallowly-buried artifacts. It gave me the idea that if you sprayed your left hand and Michael's left ear in a bright color that could easily be seen, you would always have a visible reference and reminder of his left and your left. Or, you could spray his right ear and your right hand, whatever suited you."

Gordon's breath caught in his throat and he felt his heart flip-flop as Sarah smiled radiantly while looking directly into his eyes.

"That's a fabulous solution! I'll buy a non-toxic, water-based spray paint tomorrow morning and try out your suggestion before you arrive for lunch."

Michael saw a brightness that surrounded Sarah and Gordon and he moved closer to be included in its radiance. He reveled in the sensation of floating and the feeling of joy that made him tingle all over. It felt as though he were basking in sunshine as he sat quietly while they talked.

When the three of them walked into the house, Essie was warming lasagna in the oven and Evan was tossing the salad they had brought. Cole had purchased a decadently rich chocolate cake from a bakery. Knowing that dogs should never be fed chocolate, he had also brought rice pudding for the pets. Everyone clapped and laughed as the desserts were apportioned out. When the evening drew to a close, pets and people were reluctant to leave, in spite of feeling tired.

As they were taking their leave, Cole asked Sarah if he could leave Topaz overnight during the coming week.

"I'm going to have a long, busy day next Tuesday and won't arrive home until 11 p.m. or later. The following morning, I'll have to leave home about 6 a.m. Will it be okay if I bring Topaz over Tuesday afternoon and leave her until Wednesday afternoon?"

"No problem, Cole. Will you bring her bed with you or shall I provide blankets for her to sleep on?"

"I'll bring her bed. I think it's best to keep her sleeping routine as normal as possible. I can't thank you enough for generously opening your home to Topaz and to all of us every weekend."

Meanwhile, Gordon reluctantly departed with his brother and

sister-in-law, inwardly fuming that he had not been able to have more time alone with Sarah because Cole had engaged her in conversation.

When Cole and Topaz arrived home, the message light was blinking on the answering machine. Cole punched a button and listened to Jeanette's voice say, "I'm glad I didn't bring Topaz with me because I'm usually at the hospital, picking Jenny up from school or shopping for food. Iris has a crushed pelvis and her right leg and arm are broken, plus she has muscle contusions and torn ligaments and tendons. Both of Don's legs are broken and he has cracked ribs. Thankfully, neither of them has internal injuries. I expect that we'll have Jenny all summer. She's bright and well-mannered. You'll love having her around. How are you coping? Call me, please."

He phoned her and related the day's events.

Jeanette said, "Sounds as though Gordon was a real plus factor during the practice. How did you and Topaz perform together?"

"She didn't give a peak performance because she's used to being teamed with you, but we managed. Want to speak with her?"

Topaz recognized her mom's voice. She wished with all her heart that her mom was with her. She barked into the phone a couple of times to tell her mom that she missed her but that she was okay.

CHAPTER ELEVEN

Michael alerted Sarah of Gordon's arrival by barking at the closed front door. She had just finished tossing the salad that would accompany hot pastrami sandwiches. Hot tea and coffee were ready because it was a cool, rainy day. She welcomed him and they dined at the kitchen table while Michael devoured his pastrami in his bowl that Sarah had placed on the floor near her.

Michael watched Sarah shrug into a jacket and when she walked over to him and touched his back six times, he knew she was telling him how long she would be away from home. He also knew his special dog door would be locked because Sarah always locked it at night and whenever she would be gone for a long time or when it was raining or snowing. He stretched out on the back hallway rug. It was a good place to rest while he was on guard duty. He decided to dream of Topaz and himself chasing deer through the woods.

Sarah and Gordon trekked through the museum and discovered that they both loved Impressionism and did not enjoy Modern Art. Later, over dinner at an Italian restaurant located in South Philly, Sarah related the story of how she and Michael found one another. She described how upset Michael was when he was rolled away in a crate to the cargo area of the airport for the flight home to Pennsylvania.

"I was worried about his accommodation, but I didn't have any choice. I hadn't taken my car to Mexico so driving home wasn't an option. I can't think of any valid reason why every airline doesn't have certain flights and specific planes that have passenger cabins modified to accommodate pets traveling with their families. There must be folks like me who would be willing to pay the airfare to have their pet travel in the cabin area. It would be comforting to be able to periodically visit the cabin section that housed the kennels and talk to the pet member of the family. I think that on very long flights, a potty break should be allotted for each pet. Letting one pet out at a time and keeping the pet leashed while leading them to an area set up for potty duty should be available."

"How would you regulate breaks? Would flight attendants be involved or would in-flight care of pets be the sole responsibility of family members? What kind of setup do you envision for the pet bathroom area?"

Sarah said, "I haven't thought this through in detail; however, I would not expect flight attendants to be involved in any interaction with the pets. That wouldn't be comforting to pets or people passengers. There should be a vacant/occupied sign at the pet area just as there is at the toilet area for people. No more than one pet should be out of a crate at any time. That would prevent any possibility of fights between upset and stressed-out pets. I also think there should be a partition between dog and cat crates.

Also, piddle pads that are used during training time for puppies could be used for each pet's potty break. They should be in plentiful supply on each flight. They could be easily disposed of after pet usage and removed with other garbage after the flight."

She smiled, then added, "Sorry. Sometimes I get on my soapbox about this."

Gordon gazed at her admiringly and said he thought her idea was very viable. "Sarah, it's worth looking into and I'd be happy to help you do research if you like. Maybe we could interest an airline company in the idea. Many of them are having financial troubles and your idea might help to increase their revenue."

Sarah was startled when she heard a man say, while passing by their table, that it was 7:45 p.m.

"Gordon, it's almost 8 p.m. Michael's dog door is locked. I need to get home pronto."

Gordon motioned for a waiter and paid the bill. They grabbed their jackets and hurried out of the restaurant.

When Sarah opened the front door, Michael greeted them both with equal enthusiasm before dashing outdoors. Sarah brewed some coffee and unlocked the doggy door. Just as they settled into chairs at the kitchen table, Michael entered through his dog door. To Sarah's amazement, Michael padded over to Gordon, sat beside him and rested his head on Gordon's knee.

Michael was sensing the incredible energy that enveloped Sarah and

Gordon, and billowed outward to include him. It made him feel as though he were expanding to match that warm, happy energy. It was like basking in warm sunshine but much, much better. He knew they both felt happy, and he did, too.

When Cole dropped off Topaz the next day, Michael described to her, the beautiful energy that he sensed generating from Sarah and Gordon. "Do you feel that same kind of energy flowing between and around your mom and dad?"

"I've never thought about it, Michael. There is always an underlying calm, steady happiness in my home. I've never known anything different. Was Sarah sad before she met Gordon?"

"No. We have always been happy together. It's just that I've never experienced such a special and uplifting energy before. It makes me feel as though I could float."

Topaz touched her nose to Michael's and said, "It's a drizzly day. Let's lounge together on the window seat while I tell you about my experience of trying to chase away deer."

After they had settled themselves comfortably, Topaz continued, "My dad called me outdoors yesterday evening and told me to 'sic' a herd of deer off our property. I copied your method of dealing with them. I slowly stalked forward while growling as menacingly as I could. The does and their young immediately clustered together and ran into the woods. I never wavered in my progress and kept growling and pacing toward the bucks who were whistling and snorting. I sensed their uncertainty about how to deal with the situation. I recognized some of them, having slept in the grass close to them not long ago and they probably recognized me, too, and wondered why the sudden change in my behavior. All the bucks turned and followed the doe except for one. My dad kept urging me to 'sic 'em'. I barked and jumped around but the remaining buck pawed the ground and lowered his antlers. I was afraid he was going to charge me! I was caught between the determined buck and my bossy dad. I was so scared and I wished that my mom was with me or that you were beside me to drive the buck away. My dad ran toward the buck shouting and waving his arms and the buck loped off into the woods. Once again, I disappointed my dad."

While Topaz and Michael communicated with one another, Cole told Sarah that Jeanette would be bringing their niece home with her and asked if it would be okay if they brought Jenny to the weekly agility practices.

"Sure thing! Isn't Jenny about eleven years old? Does she like dogs?"

"Yes, she's eleven and I don't know if she likes dogs. There aren't any pets in her household."

"Cole, I bet having Topaz around will be a real treat for Jenny. I see that you've brought Topaz's bed. I'll have her sleep in my bedroom and place her bed close to Michael's. Don't worry about her. Topaz is used to being here and feels comfortable."

Later that day, Gordon arrived at Sarah's home carrying a huge bouquet of lilies, larkspur and asparagus fern. She put the flowers in a vase that displayed them to perfection and placed the arrangement on the large coffee table in the living room. Topaz climbed down from the window seat and ambled over to sniff the flowers.

"She's so sweet and gentle, Gordon. I don't believe she has a hunting bone in her body."

The both laughed and each gave her a hug before hugging one another. Topaz felt a wave of bright, happy energy wash through her. It was like the energy that pervaded her own home, except this was much more intense. She padded back to the window seat, climbed up and snuggled beside Michael, then told him about her perceptions of the energy.

Sarah and Gordon sipped hot chocolate in the kitchen and discussed air travel for pet family members.

"Gordon, supposing a pet got lost like luggage sometimes is, or wasn't transferred to the correct connecting flight or left on the original flight and ended up at the wrong destination or in another country, does the airline take responsibility for caring for the unfortunate pet, or what?"

They agreed it would definitely be safer for a pet to travel inside the passenger cabin and have the family member be sure that the travel crate was removed off the airplane and through the terminal to catch a connecting flight.

"At small airports that don't have ports to connect an aircraft directly to the terminal, would passengers have to embark and disembark directly outdoors via stairs? If so, it would be difficult to get a crate up or down the stairs," said Sarah.

"If an aircraft is that small, I think pets could be leashed and negotiate the stairs themselves. I know that in some very small airplanes dogs are allowed to lie on the cabin floor during the flight," Gordon replied, then asked, "Are you up for doing some field research in an airport? We can eat an early dinner downtown if you like."

"Let's come back here for dinner. That way Michael and Topaz won't be confined inside as long. I have a meatloaf chilling in the refrigerator, just ready to be popped in the oven when we get home and a gingerbread cake for dessert."

The afternoon sped by as they visited airlines. They were denied access to view the cargo area where a pet would be housed. They inquired about space allotment and temperature conditions and were informed that the animal would be taken to the ticket area and, from there, placed in a kennel and taken to the hold area. The animal would travel separately from luggage in an unlit, pressurized room at a temperature of about 67°-70° Fahrenheit. Also, animals were not permitted to travel if the outside temperature was less than 10°F or greater than 85°F because the cargo door was open during the loading and unloading of luggage and all parts of the hold area could become cold or hot, depending on outside temperatures. They were told that the cargo area had comfortable traveling conditions for any animal with no greater noise level than cabin passengers would experience.

As they walked through the short-term parking lot at the airport, they agreed that airline companies regarded domestic pets as animals and not beings who were bona fide family members.

"Michael had real separation anxiety when he was taken to the cargo area. If I could have visited him during the flight, he would have been reassured and known than everything was okay, even though it was a new and strange experience for him."

"He's so intelligent and companionable, Sarah. I'm honored that he's become my buddy so quickly."

"He loves you, Gordon. I think I'm a wee bit jealous about that."

By now they had reached their car and Gordon turned to Sarah and said, "Speaking of love, I just have to blurt this out in a straightforward and unromantic way, 'I love you' and I have from the first moment that I saw you. This sounds like a cliché, but I feel as though I've always known you. When I was introduced to you I felt like saying, 'Haven't we met before?' But I was afraid that you'd think it was a hackneyed, pick-up phrase and drop me off your radar screen."

Sarah looked up at Gordon with a look in her eyes and a smile that could change ice to hot water. "I instantly had that same feeling of familiarity, but told myself it was because you're Evan's brother. I can't find words to describe how unbelievably happy I am that you love me, because I love you, too."

Gordon wrapped his arms around her, looked at her as though he had just found the most precious treasure of a lifetime, and kissed her with passionate abandon. Sarah wound her arms around his neck and released all thoughts of everything except Gordon and the delicious perfection of the kiss. Just last week she had felt old—well not exactly old, but middle-aged for sure and now she felt young and vigorous. Love was a better energizer than a mountain of vitamins.

Cars in the short-term parking lot drove by and some of the occupants honked horns, rolled down their windows and cheered and yelled encouragements but Gordon and Sarah had blotted out the rest of the world. When they finally left their alternate reality, they found themselves standing beside Sarah's car with a slowly moving, ever-changing audience of drivers clapping and cheering. They grinned and waved to everyone.

During the drive home, Gordon proposed marriage and Sarah accepted. He wanted to get married right away but Sarah demurred, saying that they needed to tell their children and be prepared for the possibility of their disapproval and objection to their marriage.

Gordon suggested that they elope, thus making it useless for their families to raise any objections.

"That would hurt our children and I want my daughter to be my Maid of Honor. Wouldn't you like Kevin to be your Best Man? If we include them in our wedding, it will truly be a family affair. Let's break the news to our children first, then to other family members and hope they'll be glad that we have another chance to live a happy, married life."

Gordon said, "If Kevin and/or Pat object, I still plan to marry you no matter what. I hope you feel the same way."

"Yes I do, but I'd like us to be as diplomatic as possible and try to include our families and close friends in our wedding."

They discussed where they would live after their marriage. Gordon said that he was often away on archeological field trips and didn't have to live in the Phoenix area to pursue his career, so he could make his home base in Pennsylvania. They decided to sell their respective homes and buy a house that didn't have any ghosts of past memories for them or for their children.

Sarah said she would contact a real estate agent tomorrow to begin looking for a home for them and that she wanted enough property to accommodate the agility setup. Gordon wanted enough land for a helicopter pad.

"I'll leave my helicopter in Arizona for now because that's where I do most of my field work. Eventually, I'll look into getting on staff in the Department of Archeology at one of the universities in this area."

After more discussion about where to live, the topic returned to air travel accommodations for pets, and Gordon said, "Let's look into starting our own pet-friendly airline. My son is studying aeronautical and mechanical engineering. I'll ask him to design changes to aircraft that accommodate pet quarters inside the main passenger cabin plus install a lift to raise kenneled pets into aircraft during occasions when travelers have to walk onto the tarmac and climb stairs when boarding and disembarking. Most times when boarding is done from a port, the lift wouldn't be necessary because a kenneled pet could be rolled into the plane. Your son-in-law is a lawyer, isn't he? We could ask him to draw up a charter."

"I don't know if that is Ed's area of expertise. I'll discuss it with Pat and she can have Ed get back to us. It will give me an opportunity to tell her about us. Also, I'll invite her and Ed to this weekend's agility practice. It will make introductions less intense with others present and the agility activity taking some of the focus away from our upcoming marriage."

"Good thinking, Sarah. I'll clear it with Essie and Evan about having Kevin come for the weekend but I'll tell him about us before I invite him. That will give him a chance to think of a plausible excuse to refuse if he's upset by the news and feels that he can't accept the situation just yet."

"Gordon, if my daughter told me she wanted to marry someone she had only known for several days, my advice to her would be to wait."

"Do you have doubts about me or our relationship, Sarah?"

She squeezed Gordon's hand. "Definitely not!"

She was surprised to see her home and said, "That drive went quickly."

When they walked through the front door, Michael and Topaz greeted them with boisterous enthusiasm.

"It's a treat to come home to such a happy welcome. Everyone should be so lucky," said Sarah.

CHAPTER TWELVE

The weather was predicted to be perfect for the weekend agility practice. Sarah looked over the agility setup, which now included a See-Saw and Brush Jump that Gordon and Evan had assembled yesterday. At that time, Evan told her that he had checked USDAA's website and discovered that the Northeastern Dog Agility Regional Championship event was being held locally and in the very near future. She was glad that the pets would have some intensive practice on the newly installed obstacles before competing in the Regionals. Jeanette would also get in some needed practice with Topaz before the event because she and Jenny had arrived home a couple of days ago.

Gordon and Kevin were the first arrivals. Sarah noted that Kevin was as tall as his dad and bore a close resemblance to him. He had his dad's grin, easy bearing and air of competence. His blonde hair was darker than Gordon's and his eyes were hazel and not blue like his dad's. She gave him a brief hug when Gordon introduced them.

"You're very much like your father in appearance, Kevin, and perhaps because of that you seem familiar to me. Welcome! I'm delighted to meet you."

Michael walked around Kevin sniffing him thoroughly, then sat beside him and pressed his head against Kevin's leg. Kevin responded by hunkering down to look directly into his eyes.

"So you're the wonder dog that my dad has told me about. Thanks for the warm welcome."

Michael placed a paw on Kevin's thigh and touched Kevin's face with his nose. Michael could tell from Kevin's scent that he was related to Gordon. He knew that Kevin was younger than Gordon and concluded that this was Gordon's offspring. He instantly loved him just as he had

Gordon. He looked into Kevin's eyes and knew that he was good and strong and kind, like his father.

Kevin stroked Michael's ears and neck and scratched him under his chin. "I'm glad we're part of the same family."

Sarah's heart warmed to Kevin. She recognized his innate kindness and sensitivity. She and Gordon grinned at one another. The initial meeting had gone very well, thanks in part to Michael.

They heard car doors opening and closing, followed by yipping sounds from Kissy and Kawdje, who bounded into the kitchen through Michael's dog door. Kevin was still hunkered down facing Michael. Kissy scooted between them and stood as tall as she could on her hind legs to kiss Kevin's face and then lick Michael's muzzle. She was happy to be with some of her favorite beings and meet someone new. "What a great day," she thought.

Kawdje hung back until Kevin reached out and pulled him into the circle. Kawdje wished he could be as outgoing and sure of himself as Kissy.

Essie and Evan brought food and Sarah busied herself putting everything in the refrigerator. In the midst of the flurry of activity in the kitchen, Pat and Ed arrived carrying chickens and cornbread stuffing that had to be prepared and baked.

Gordon was surprised that Pat bore so little resemblance to her mother and he thought that she and her husband looked enough alike to be related. Ed looked to be several inches taller than Pat and his hair was thick and dark brown like Pat's but his eyes matched his hair color whereas Pat's eyes had her mother's golden hue. Pat had her mother's active efficiency but in a more assertive, take-charge manner. Gordon surmised that she must have inherited her mother's compassion for animals because she was a vet—well, almost. Ed was quiet by comparison although his affable and unassuming affect probably won him friends and helped his career as a lawyer.

Sarah felt jittery as she made introductions because she wasn't sure how Pat would react to Gordon. Pat had been appalled by the news of her mother's impending marriage to a man she had known for only a week. Sarah hadn't corrected Pat's assumption regarding the brevity of her courtship and hoped that she would never find out that she only known Gordon for a mere three days before accepting his marriage proposal.

Pat immediately liked Kevin. How could she not like someone who so obviously loved dogs and, more importantly, was so obviously loved by dogs? She thought that dogs had good instincts about people and an innate sense of who could be trusted with the gift of their love and loyalty. She grudgingly admitted to herself that Gordon seemed to be the great guy that her mother had said he was. Plus, he was easy on the eyes. She amended the thought and told herself that he was downright, drop-dead handsome, as was Kevin. Somehow, her mom and Gordon looked like a couple and it wasn't just because they looked good together. There was an invisible bond between them that made them seem like two halves of a whole. She felt a twinge of sadness as she thought of her dad, then sternly told herself that he would want her mom to be happy and not live the rest of her life lonely and in mourning for him. "I want that for Mom, too," Pat thought.

She suddenly realized that Michael was nudging her leg with his head and felt Kissy's forepaws pressed on her shins to help her balance herself on her hind legs. Pat laughed, knelt down and put her arms around them.

Michael had sensed an unease flowing from Pat. He had never known her to be anything but happy whenever she had visited. Kissy had also sensed tension in some of the people present and decided that the best remedy for promoting happiness and joy was to kiss everyone, and so she did.

Kawdje noticed Ed standing slightly apart from the others and immediately understood that Ed was a lot like him. He padded over to him, sat up and begged. Ed picked him up. Kawdje's high perch delighted him! He felt a bond with this quiet man, so he laid his head against Ed's cheek.

Essie said, "Everyone—look at Kawdje. He has chosen Ed as a friend. Ed, feel flattered because Kawdje is reserved and aloof and it usually takes him awhile to bestow trust and friendship."

Everybody crowded around them. Ed and Kawdje were pleased to not only be included, but to actually be the center of attention.

Just then, Jeanette, Cole, Jenny and Topaz arrived with more food. Introductions were made and Sarah and Essie each gave Jeanette a welcome home hug and then hugged Jenny. They had expected Jenny to somewhat resemble Jeanette and were surprised to see that she was small for her age. Jenny's mother, Iris, lacked her sister's height and the Asian part of Jenny's genetic make-up was further diluted by her father's Caucasian addition to her gene pool. Jenny's hair was light brown and very straight. Her eyes were her outstanding feature, not only because of their unusual green color and exotic upward tilt but also because of the strong, focused energy that emanated from them like a laser beam. Essie and Sarah noticed that she had her Aunt Jeanette's economy of movement, when Jenny quickly jumped out of the way to avoid being whipped by Michael's vigorously wagging tail as he enthusiastically greeted Topaz.

Kissy sensed that although Jenny wasn't unhappy, she wasn't exactly happy, either. She decided her kiss remedy was needed and, as she walked toward Jenny, Kissy wagged her tail so enthusiastically that she wiggled all over. Once again, she stood on her hind paws and braced herself by putting her front paws on Jenny's legs. Jenny was enchanted by Kissy. She plopped down on the floor and pulled Kissy onto her lap. She giggled as Kissy licked her face.

"There," thought Kissy. "I've made her happy."

Evan announced that he had printouts describing each of the various types of agility classes and suggested they go over the requirements before starting their weekend practice.

After everyone, including each pet, was settled comfortably in the living room, Evan said, "The obstacles that are used in Dog Agility are: A-Frame, See-Saw, Collapsed Tunnel, Rigid Pipe Tunnel, Weave Poles, Dog Walk, Table, Tire Jump, Wishing Well Jump, Long Jump, Hurdles and Spread Hurdles.

There is one Standard Agility Class and four Nonstandard Classes. The four Nonstandard Classes are Gamblers, Snooker, Relay and Jumpers."

As Evan passed out diagrams that he had drawn, showing a proposed obstacle arrangement for each type of Dog Agility class, he suggested that they study the information just prior to practicing that particular class.

"Because we're going to practice the Pairs Relay soon, everyone might want to look over that diagram while I read information about the rules for that class.

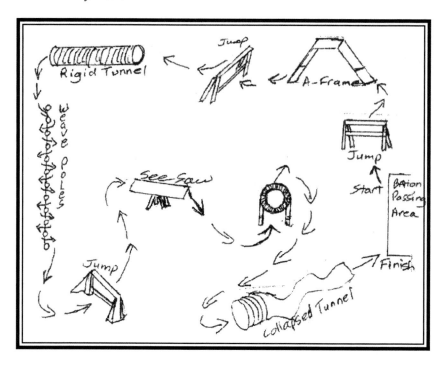

The Relay course is much like a Standard Agility setup except that all the contact obstacles don't have to be included and the Table is never included as an obstacle to be used. The Relay winners are the teams that have the fastest time and the fewest, or no, faults. Faults are added to the time.

It's called a Pairs Relay when two teams perform a course and a Three-dog Relay when three teams perform a course. In my opinion, this class calls for real sportsmanship because if a mediocre team is paired with a team that performs superlatively and the mediocre team is slow and accrues faults, the overall team score will reflect that and the terrific team will have a placement much lower than their performance deserved. Also, if one team is eliminated, the other team goes down, too. USDAA requires that each team must not perform the Relay class with the same partner team more than once at each titling level. That rule prevents two topnotch teams from always partnering together.

Sarah said, "As I understand it, Michael and Topaz can be partnered for the Pairs Relay once at the Starters Level, once at the Advanced Level and once more at the Masters Level, if we ever get that far."

"That's correct," replied Evan. "I also want to mention that a handler is allowed to hold his or her dog while the other team is running the course."

"What a relief!" exclaimed Sarah. "I could just see Michael dashing off to join Topaz and jump the hurdles with her.

Essie said, "We had better make contacts on the agility circuit and arrange to pair up with other teams in our respective jump height categories before we register for each Relay event or take the luck of the draw by having event officials pair us up with other entrants."

Pat asked, "Does USDAA stand for United States Dog Agility Association?"

That's correct," said Evan.

"What constitutes a fault?" she asked.

Evan replied, "Some ways to accrue a fault would be failing to touch the contact zones on contact obstacles, missing a Weave Pole, failing to cleanly clear a jump, or refusing to use an obstacle. Some infractions are cause for elimination; such as fouling the ring, three refusals on the course, signs of aggression, leaving the ring before the performance has been completed, and running the wrong course which includes taking a jump in the wrong direction."

Pat asked, "Who sets the time limits for performances?"

Evan replied, "Another good question and I'm proud to know the answer. Every class, in every event, has a Standard Course Time that is set by the judge of that class. Standard Course Times will be faster for large dogs performing the same course than it will be for smaller dogs. Let's say that at the Starters Level in the Standard Agility Class, a dog performing in the 26-inch height category has an SCT of 50 seconds, a dog in the 22-inch height category performing on that same course will be given more time to complete the course, and a dog in the 16-inch category would have even more time. The dog in the 12-inch height category will be allowed the greatest amount of time to complete the course.

The more advanced the level, the trickier the course setup will be, with additional obstacles added to all of the classes and less time to complete the course."

Pat asked, "Is the Masters Level the highest level at which a dog can compete?"

"No," replied Evan. "The Championship Level is higher than the Masters Level; however, all classes at the Masters Level and higher are competed under Masters rules. Many teams continue competing after achieving the Champion Level and earn the title of Tournament Master and Bronze, Silver, Gold and Platinum Metallic Designations."

"I guess you could keep competing for a lifetime," Pat commented.

Evan said, "I looked up last year's World Cynosport Agenda and there are non-titling events such as Disc Dogs and Dock Dogs. I also looked up the meaning of cyno. It's Greek for dog."

Jeanette chimed in, "I'd be interested in Dock Dogs. Topaz loves the water. It would be fun to enter her in that competition. Cole and I have a dock on our pond and everyone is welcome to bring the pets over anytime and use the pond. I'll find out more about the Dock Dogs competition."

Evan said, "It's always held every November in Arizona. All the classes are run under Masters rules and none can be used for titling purpose even though all the USDAA rules and regulations must be adhered to. I think that teams from other countries compete in the event. It would be a good learning experience for us."

Sarah said, "Maybe none of us will have enough experience or expertise to be able to compete in such an event. November will be here before we know it."

Essie exclaimed, "We'd better stop talking and start practicing."

Everyone picked up cups and glasses and carried them into the kitchen, then headed outside for the agility setup.

Sarah asked Gordon to be timekeeper.

"Only, if you'll give me a kiss and a big hug."

Sarah turned and intended to give him a brief kiss but Gordon, unconcerned by the onlookers, gathered her to him and gave her what a grinning Jenny called "a mile long kiss." Everyone applauded!

"Okay, okay," Evan, reminded them. "Time to arrange the obstacles for a Relay class."

"We don't have a baton to pass," said Essie.

"No problem," Sarah said. "I'll break a branch off a bush."

"I'll help you," offered Gordon.

"Forget it," said Pat. "I'll help her. You two might get lost in the woods and who knows when we'd see you again."

Jenny giggled. While Sarah and Pat searched for a suitable stick, the men moved some obstacles and Jeanette and Essie decided where the baton-passing zone would be.

The jumps were set for the 26-inch height category, so Michael and Sarah performed first while Topaz and Jeanette stood in the designated baton-passing zone.

Michael was puzzled because Sarah was holding a stick in her hand as she directed him from one obstacle to another. He decided that Sarah wanted to play so he made several attempts to wrestle the stick from her. She kept saying "no" in a firm, no-nonsense tone so he finally concentrated on running the course.

When Sarah passed the stick to Jeanette, Michael lunged for it. So did Topaz, and the dogs beat Jeanette to the prize. Michael and Topaz thought that this was a game of Tug of War and they loved it. This was the most fun that agility practice had ever been. Topaz sank her teeth into the wood. Michael clenched one end with his teeth and shook his head back and forth.

Kissy saw the mock battle and got into the fray. The stick was long enough for her to get a jaw hold on it. She was almost lifted off the ground. She didn't care. She loved and trusted Michael and Topaz and knew they would never hurt her. Suddenly, Kawdje was beside her trying to get a good bite-hold on the stick.

They all heard Sarah saying, "No. No. Stop!" They ignored her. Everyone else was laughing too much to say anything.

Finally, Kissy felt her dad lifting her up and she let go of the stick. Topaz became aware of her mom stroking her back. Kawdje was pulled away by Essie and held in her arms, and Michael gave his attention to Sarah who held out her hand and commanded him to pass the stick to her.

After the laughter subsided and the jump heights had been lowered, Essie and Kawdje began the Relay. Essie held the stick with her left hand and tried to keep it out of Kawdje's range of vision. Because Kawdje was not very familiar with the See-Saw, Essie wanted to be sure that he touched the contact zone during his descent so she touched the area with her right hand saying 'contact' while holding her left hand, which was curled around the stick, away from her body. Kawdje smoothly descended the See-Saw, touched the contact zone at the bottom part of the plank and clenched the stick firmly between his teeth without breaking stride. Essie reacted automatically by pulling the stick up and away from him but Kawdje hung on with all his might. He tucked his paws in toward his body and let her carry him out of the setup.

Evan was holding Kissy in his arms, which prevented her from joining Kawdje in his quest to conquer the stick. Fortunately, Jeanette and Sarah had collared Topaz and Michael, thwarting their attempts to join the game.

Everyone hooted and laughed and Pat, who had been inside setting the dining room table, came out just in time to see Kawdje's breach of dog agility etiquette. She laughed so hard, her eyes watered.

When the laughter subsided, Pat announced, "I've set the dining room table. The chickens are roasted. The salad has been tossed. Someone needs to carve the chickens and then pet guardians can fill the dog bowls. You each know how much food your pet will eat."

Kevin asked as he walked toward her, "Pet guardians? What does that mean?"

Pat said, "I don't believe people should consider pets as their property. People can own jewelry, houses, cars and such, but pets are sentient beings who think and feel, act and react. They even dream. One being shouldn't own another just because of greater reasoning ability or higher intelligence—that is, as we humans measure intelligence."

"My dad told me that you're a veterinarian. You're in the right profession. Your attitude toward pets is commendable and very forward-thinking. Whenever I get a dog, I'll remember to think of myself as a guardian rather than an owner."

Pat confided, "I've promised myself a dog when I graduate from vet school but I'll wait awhile and see how events develop before making such a big decision. After all, a pet is with you for many years and has a profound effect on your life."

By now, they were in the kitchen and Pat put Kevin to work carrying salad and bowls to the dining room table. Ed carved the chickens while Jenny spooned stuffing into a bowl.

Ed said, "Pets surely can change your life. Think about the big changes in your mom's life, Pat. She brought Michael Archangelo home with her and because of that, she met Essie and Evan when they attended the same dog show. Through Essie and Evan, she met Gordon, Jeanette and Cole. All our lives have changed because your mom rescued Michael. We've met those same people, plus Kevin and Jenny. We all met because of the four dogs. They are the hub of our wheel of friendship."

Jenny, Kevin and Pat stopped their tasks and looked at him. Pat walked up behind him, wrapped her arms around his waist and laid her cheek against his warm back. "Ed, you don't talk much but when you do, you express yourself poetically. The dogs are definitely the hub of our wheel of friendship. We'll have to toast to that during lunch."

The others came through the kitchen door like a gaggle of geese chattering and laughing noisily—or barking, depending on the species.

After pet bowls were filled and people were seated at the table, Ed stood, raised his glass of iced tea and said, "Here's to Michael, Topaz, Kissy and Kawdje. They give us love, loyalty, joy and companionship, all of which are the components of friendship, and we reciprocate. Most of us would not have met one another had it not been for these four dogs. They are the hub of our wheel of friendship and I'm including the pets when I say that all of our lives have been enriched by our friendships."

Everyone clinked glasses and sipped their water, tea or soda pop. They clapped, and complimented Ed on his eloquent toast. The four dogs ran into the dining room to see what was going on. They didn't want to be left out of any fun and games and were disappointed to see that everyone was seated.

"Let's get back to our food," said Michael.

After they had gobbled their food and checked out one another's bowls to make sure that one of them hadn't left a morsel that another could finish, they assumed resting pose and discussed the morning's practice. None of them could understand why they weren't allowed to play the "grab-the-stick" game.

"Why should my dad get to carry the stick and not me?" asked Kissy.

"Sarah often throws a stick and has me fetch it and carry it to her," commented Michael.

Kawdje said, "They want to carry the stick and give it to each other and not let any of us have it. I don't know why, but I'll think about it and maybe I'll come up with a reason."

Topaz said, "Our moms and dads keep changing the setup. I wonder why they do that."

Kissy declared, "I like the changes. It's fun not to know what's going to happen next."

Michael said, "Maybe they want us to be able to work through different setups. It sure makes me pay more attention to Sarah because I never know which obstacle I'll have to use next."

Kawdje chimed in, "I find it unsettling not to know what obstacle to use next; however, even though the setup changes, the obstacles and how we are are supposed to use them doesn't change."

Kawdje looked at Topaz and said, "You always seem to know what your mom wants you to do. Why is that?"

"My mom and I have always had a special connection that helps me to know what she wants me to do," replied Topaz.

"Does it work the other way? Does she know what you want her to do?" asked Kissy.

"I think so. Lots of times, she knows what I want or need before I know myself. For example, one night when I was lying on my bed, and my mom was just about to climb into her bed, suddenly she got a blanket from the closet and covered me with it. After she had done that, I realized that I had felt chilly. We have a special bond and I can't explain how or why."

Michael told the others that he could see and sense feelings and described to Kissy and Kawdje the brightness and the feeling of great happiness that flowed between and around Sarah and Gordon and that it made him feel as though he could float in the air when it surrounded him. Topaz told them she had seen and felt it, too, when staying at Michael's home during the time her mom had been away.

Kissy and Kawdje described their method of putting a picture of whatever they wanted into their mom or dad's heart.

"We just keep doing that until one of them gets the picture," said Kawdje.

Meanwhile Evan was telling the group in the dining room about the history of the sport of Dog Agility. "The United States Dog Agility Association was established in 1986 and its rules were patterned after those already in effect in Great Britain. Many countries around the world now participate in the sport of Dog Agility and the number keeps growing. Every other year an international competition is held in one of the countries that is a member of the International Federation of Cynological Sports. Our country is a member of the IFCS. An international competition has already taken place this year so we have plenty of time to climb the titling ladder, gain experience, and spend next year collecting as many points as we can in hopes of being chosen to represent Team USA in the spring of the following year."

Sarah spoke in a quavering voice, "It scares me to think about international competition. None of us has even entered a local event."

Jeanette announced, "I'm going to take care of bringing a baton for tomorrow's Relay practice. I have an idea of how to stop our pets from using a baton as a 'fetch-the-stick—free-for-all' game."

Essie suggested, "Let's practice Gamblers this afternoon. It will be a challenge to exercise control while standing so far away from our pets."

Everyone agreed and there was a clatter of dishes being gathered up and taken from the dining room to the kitchen.

Evan, who hated doing dishes or any kind of cleanup chores after a meal, suggested that the men go outside and rearrange the course for a Gamblers setup while the women washed dishes and put away leftovers. He hurried through the kitchen door before anyone had time to comment. Gordon, Kevin, Cole and Ed followed him as fast as they could.

Essie put her hands on her hips and said, "Evan hates cleaning up after a meal. I guess most men do. Somehow, they always weasel out of kitchen duties."

The three women made quick work of the cleanup, after which

they studied the diagram that Evan had made of a Gamblers course and carefully read the rules for that class before joining the others outdoors.

Evan passed the diagram and rules for Gamblers to Gordon and Cole and then, for everyone's sake including Jenny's, he announced a summarization of the rules with some timely tips thrown in for good measure.

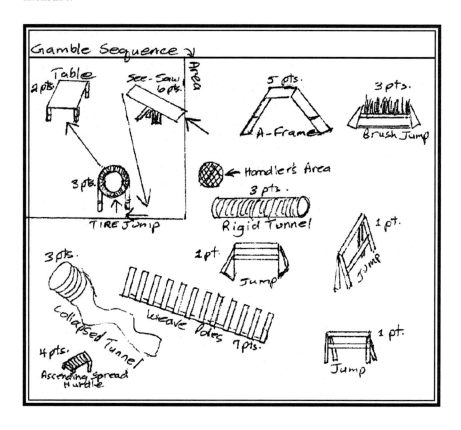

"During the opening period, dog and handler try to accumulate as many points as they can. All obstacles may be used an unlimited number of times, but points may only be earned twice on each obstacle. It makes sense to not waste time by using an obstacle more than twice. When the judge's whistle signals the end of the opening period and the start of the "Gamble" sequence, the handler must be in, and remain in, the designated handler's area while directing the dog to perform the "Gamble" obstacles.

Although the opening period doesn't have any pre-determined route, the Gamble sequence does. At least three obstacles are always used and the direction in which they must be taken is clearly marked. During the Gamble sequence, the handler is at least 9 feet from the dog at all times: that distance increases to 15 feet at the Masters level. This class requires strategy and distance control on the part of the handler. If a dog faults an obstacle, points are not earned for the fault, as would be the case in the Standard Agility, Jumpers and Relay Classes where the team with the fastest time and fewest faults wins. In this class and in Snooker, the team with the most points wins and time is the tiebreaker."

In twenty minutes, everyone was ready to begin Gamblers. Sarah had sprayed her hand and Michael's ear neon orange. Jenny pronounced them to be the coolest team ever. Michael couldn't see his ear and once the spray paint had dried, it didn't feel different from the other, so he forgot about it. Topaz, Kissy and Kawdje's eyesight didn't interpret his ear as being a shockingly bright orange so they ignored it.

The course had been set up for the 26-inch height. Topaz and Jeanette went first. They were superb. When Jeanette stood in the defined handlers' area during the Gamble, Topaz followed directions as though she had done the course a hundred times.

Cole's heart swelled with pride as he watched Jeanette and Topaz. He thought that even though Topaz was too dumb to come in out of the rain and not brave enough to chase off deer, she sure pulled it together when it came to Dog Agility thanks, in no small part, to his incredible wife who seemed to have a talent for anything she decided to do.

Sarah's innards quivered while waiting to begin. She looked at Michael's bright orange ear and hoped that would help her to quickly discern his left and right. She fervently prayed that her performance wouldn't be a big letdown after Jeanette and Topaz's classy display of teamwork. Most of all, she didn't want to hold back Michael, who had the potential to be a fabulous agility dog.

She took a deep breath and said to Michael, "Let's go."

She remained close to him during the opening sequence, so remembering right from left wasn't a problem because she was able to point to and say the name of each obstacle that she wanted him to use. Her major concern during the point-collecting opening period was to stay ahead of Michael and position herself so that he could clearly see her signal which obstacle she wanted him to use next and the direction he was take it. When Michael approached the A-Frame, Sarah saw that he was poised for a leap and quickly called out "Contact" so that he wouldn't jump halfway up the ascending plank and miss the contact point at the beginning of the ascent. "I'll have to work with him on contact points," she thought.

When they finished the opening period, she had worked their path through the setup so that she was inside the handlers' area and Michael was in good position to use the See-Saw, which was the first obstacle of the "Gamble." She held her neon orange left hand in front of her at chest level so that she could easily see it and kept turning her direction to correspond with Michael's direction as she called out her commands. It helped ease her right/left dilemma.

Because it would be good discipline for the pets to assume and remain in resting pose for a 5-second count, while at a distance of almost 10 feet from the handlers' area, they had decided to use the Table as the last obstacle in the "Gamble" even though it would never be used that way in official competition. Michael finished the course by staying in resting pose on the table for the 5-second count. Sarah was very proud of him and sent a thankful prayer heavenward that, at least, Michael knew left from right.

"He's smarter than I am," she thought. She had found it somewhat distracting to keep checking her left hand and then looking up to orient herself to the position of Michael's left ear but the spray paint sure helped diminish her right/left dilemma.

It was a good performance, but not quite as smooth and coordinated as Jeanette's and Topaz's had been. Gordon checked the stopwatch and, although Michael's performance wasn't as fast as Topaz's, he knew it was due to Sarah's slower calculation of which direction to command Michael to take. He had watched her glancing back and forth from her orange hand to Michael's orange ear during their performance, but she had not made a right-from-left error. The cue was a helpful physical reference and Gordon was certain that as Sarah continued to use it, she would become more relaxed and confident and the team's performance would improve.

Everyone pitched in and quickly lowered the jumps to accommodate Kissy and Kawdje's 12-inch jump height. Essie and Kawdje's performance preceded Evan's and Kissy's. Kawdje dutifully followed his mom's directions throughout his performance and focused on her while maintaining a 5-second, resting pose on the Table and waiting for her signal to jump off. Essie hugged and kissed him and told him he was the best little fellow anyone could ever have the pleasure of working with. She had worried that Kawdje might stand and arrange his posture in the stacked position that was required when on the table in a Conformation Dog show but, he didn't seem to recognize any similarity between the large surface, low square table used in Dog Agility, and the higher, smaller table used in Conformation Dog Shows for the purpose of aiding the judge in examining small dogs.

Evan waited impatiently to show off Kissy's prowess. She was a fast and fearless competitor. He had her use the Weave Poles twice during the opening period because she could slither through them so quickly and they had the highest point value. As he stood in the handlers' area during the Gamblers sequence, he called out directions as fast as he could form the words and she responded with amazing agility and speed. She jumped onto the Table and, at his command, assumed the resting pose but ignored him when he directed her to stay. She kept half rising, then assuming resting pose as he called out for her to stay, then after a second had passed, she once again half rose in anticipation of jumping off the Table. It looked as though she was doing a doggy version of push-ups. It was obvious that Kissy wanted to keep moving and didn't think that assuming a resting pose for 5 seconds counted as performing.

Everyone tried to hide smiles except for Jenny, who giggled delightedly.

Essie smugly said, "I think that each time Kissy refused to remain in resting pose was a fault. I'm sure she accrued at least 20 points. I don't know if that's cause for elimination but, if not, it sure gives you and Kissy the slowest time."

Evan called for Kissy to come to him. He held her in his arms as he said, "Little one, you're over eager. Sometimes holding still is part of the performance. We have work to do. You have to learn to wait for my direction."

Everyone decided to call it a day, agility wise, and eat a dinner of warmed-up leftovers. Sarah announced that she had made a yummy dessert of mascarpone and ricotta cheeses that could be shared with the pets. It was a convivial evening for pets and people. While strategies for accumulating the most points in Gamblers were discussed at the dining room table, the pets, who dined in the kitchen, reminisced over and decided upon favorite desserts.

Michael thought that the new dessert was almost as delectable as crème brûlée. Topaz wavered awhile before deciding that she, too, thought crème brûlée was still her reigning favorite. Kissy and Kawdje said the tasty new dessert was as good as rice pudding but ranked second to crème brûlée. They all agreed that desserts were one of the best perks in life; not as blessèd as being part of a happy family nor as gratifying as having loyal friends, nor as comfortable as a soft, clean bed to sleep upon, nor as challenging and exciting as agility, but very, very soul satisfying.

CHAPTER THIRTEEN

The next morning about 11 a.m. everyone gathered again on Sarah's lawn for agility practice, with the exception of Kevin who was on a flight back to his university. The friends had decided the previous evening that the Pairs Relay and Snooker classes would be the only events that day.

Jeanette had an enigmatic smile on her face as she pulled on a pair of garden gloves. She asked Sarah if she had a sturdy pair of garden gloves and suggested that she wear them. Sarah jogged into the garage to collect a pair.

Topaz and Jeanette began their performance without mishap. Jeanette could see that Topaz looked at the baton longingly, but she obeyed all commands and took each obstacle as directed and made no effort to grab the new stick. When they reached the baton-passing area and Jeanette passed the baton to Sarah, Michael wagged his tail because he was so happy that Topaz was close to him. He wanted to play so he lunged for the stick. Topaz had seen Michael shift his weight to his haunches in preparation for a stick-grabbing leap and decided to beat him to it. They both reached the prize together and easily snatched it from Sarah, who hadn't had time to properly grasp it before their intercession.

Kissy and Kawdje had been sitting on the sidelines between their mom and dad. With happy yips, they ran pell-mell across the setup and joined the fray. Suddenly tails stopped wagging and several unhappy yelps were heard. The baton was dropped and the pets quickly paced away from it.

Gordon gaped at the spectacle of Michael and Topaz, Kissy and Kawdje pacing toward their parents with heads down, ears down and tails down and asked, "What happened?"

Jeanette raised her voice. "I bundled together rose canes and left some thorns on them. It's a mean-and-nasty, but quick-and-effective way to teach them that the baton is not a toy."

Cole thought, "She looks like a goddess, but she's wily."

Pat asked, "Were you a teacher in your former life?"

Jenny said, "Aunt Jeanette, you're a grinch!"

The Pairs Relay class continued without further mishap and the pets behaved as sedately as little old ladies at a tea party.

The friends decided to practice the Snooker class while the pets were still in an obedient frame of mind. Everyone moved around the obstacles, to comply with Evan's diagram of a Snooker Set-up.

Evan then quoted the rules. "In Snooker, all obstacles are assigned a color. Each color always has the same point value as follows; red will always be worth 1 point, yellow—2, green—3, brown—4, blue—5, pink—6, and black—7 points.

Red obstacles are always hurdles that can be modified to accommodate the different jump height categories. Colors assigned to other obstacles can change from event-to-event; however, point values of 6 or 7 are usually assigned to more difficult obstacles such as the See-Saw or Weave Poles rather than, for example, the Pipe Tunnel. During the opening period you want to collect as many points as possible up to a maximum of 24, when 3 red obstacles are used. There is a protocol that must be followed. A red obstacle must be used first, followed by any color obstacle, then one of the two remaining unused red obstacles, followed by any color, then the last red obstacle that hasn't been used, then another color. There is a catch—scoring ceases if a red obstacle is not successfully taken or if the "red—color—red" protocol isn't used.

During the closing, which is the Snooker sequence, the obstacles must be taken in the correct color order, beginning with yellow which is 2 points and working up in ascending point value. Scoring stops in the Snooker sequence if the dog accrues a fault, or if the course time expires. As with the Gamblers class, the team with the most points wins and time is the tiebreaker."

They decided to give the See-Saw the highest point value of seven because it was the newest obstacle and its unfamiliarity probably made it the most difficult obstacle for the pets to use, although Topaz and Kawdje still plodded through the Weave Poles.

Evan, Essie, Sarah and Jeanette walked the course and decided on their strategy for the opening sequence. The See-Saw was placed at the opposite end of the course from the three red Jumps, which meant that valuable time would be used trying to collect the maximum number of points in the opening sequence. Time would be accumulating as the pets dashed back and forth the full length of the setup.

Everyone knew that the team with the most points won and that time was the tiebreaker. They also knew that they couldn't collect any more points during the opening sequence if a red obstacle was not taken successfully so they knew they had to be careful. The opening period definitely called for strategy.

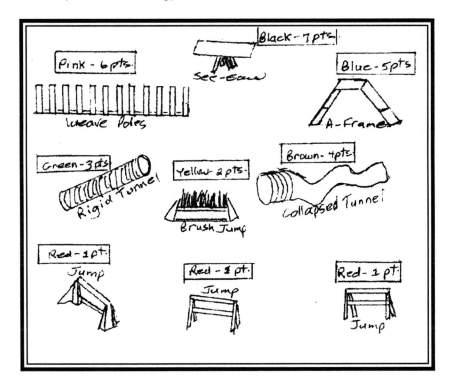

Jeanette knew that Topaz was a natural jumper and physically strong. She decided to have her use the See-Saw three times—once after each red Hurdle—in the opening sequence. She would then be collecting the maximum number of points. Although the Weave Poles were closer, Topaz hadn't developed a natural rhythm for sliding between the poles and they were worth one point less than the See-Saw.

Sarah also chose to have Michael collect the maximum number of points by using the See-Saw three times in the opening sequence. He was a strong, well-rounded competitor who was comfortable using any obstacle.

Essie decided it was a no-brainer to have Kawdje use the See-Saw three times in the opening sequence. He was small but a strong and well-conditioned competitor who could run the length of the course back and forth three times and still be able to jump the red obstacles with ease because he had a natural jumping ability. He was a plodder through the Weave Poles, so the fact that they were closer to the red obstacles wouldn't help him time wise.

Evan reasoned that Kissy loved to run and was fast. He didn't think that having her run back and forth the length of the course between each red obstacle jump would exhaust her and prevent her from performing each jump cleanly. Kissy didn't mind jumping as long as she didn't have to repeat one jump after another.

Taking size disparity into consideration, the handlers calculated that Kissy had the fastest time. None of the pets accrued faults.

Lunch was a feast of leftovers except for a fresh, warm gingerbread cake with warm lemon dessert sauce for the topping. Sarah said she made it using an old family recipe of her great, great grandmother's. Before Essie and Jeanette could request the recipe, Sarah said that she would e-mail it to them. They beamed with gratitude.

As they lingered over tea and coffee, Evan announced that the Northeastern Dog Agility Regional Tournament was going to be held in Kennett Square in two weeks. "We've got to get started on our quest to become Champion Dog Agility Teams. The event begins Friday morning at 10 a.m. and ends 2 p.m. on Sunday. I've downloaded schedules from the USDAA website and have ticked off the classes we should enter. They will all be Starters Level classes that count toward titling. We can manage to compete in two Standard Agility classes, two Gamblers, two Snooker classes and two Pairs Relay. If our pets make a qualifying score in each of those classes, they will have completed two-thirds of the Championship Program at the Starters level. We can consider entering our fearless foursome in the Steeplechase, which is a Jumpers course, and the Grand Prix, which is similar to a Standard Agility Class, both of which are performed under Masters rules. That means that Standard Course Times will be much faster than at the Starters and Advanced levels."

He distributed the printouts. Everyone, other than Pat and Ed who had left after lunch, perused the schedules, discussed the classes and whether or not to bring a tent and a hot lunch each day. They decided to use the agility setup every day on an informal and individual basis in preparation for the upcoming Dog Agility Event.

Early Monday morning, Pat phoned Sarah and confided that she really liked Gordon but was very concerned about their commitment to marry after having known each other for such a brief time. She asked when they planned to marry and Sarah said that they would probably not marry before the end of summer.

"That's three whole months away, Pat."

"Mom, you would have been beside yourself if Ed and I had married after having known each other for just three months. Where are you going to get married?"

"Here. Not in this home, I mean, in this area. You know that Gordon and I have a realtor looking for a home for us."

Pat said in a husky voice, as though she was holding back tears, "I'll miss the home I grew up in with you and Daddy, but I'm glad you're happy and busy again, Mom. I really like Kevin and that's good because he's going to be my stepbrother. He's a lot like Gordon. They are nice folks and I think we'll get along together. We all have something in common—we adore dogs. Anyone who loves dogs has his heart in the right place and is okay in my book. So, it will be a fall wedding, Mom. Can I help you plan it?"

Sarah felt giddy with relief that her daughter had accepted the new turn of events. "This summer is going to be like a roller coaster ride. By the way, this past weekend was so busy that Gordon didn't get a chance to talk to Ed about having him draw up a charter, or whatever is required, for the purpose of creating an airline company that transports both people and pets inside the cabin area. Evan and Essie want in on it. I expect that Jeanette and Cole will, too. Gordon discussed the matter with Kevin and asked him to think about the alterations required in order to install a lift for kenneled pets and redesigning cabin space to create an area for pet crates."

"Mom, I love that idea! I'm sure Ed will do whatever legal work is required. How can this great project be accomplished money wise? Is Gordon rich?"

"I don't know, Pat. Neither he nor Evan needs to do the daily grind routine in order to live comfortably. Evan is an astute investor and he handles most of Gordon's investments for him. I expect we'll find out when we get together with you and Ed and everyone for a dinner meeting soon. Essie and Evan's daughter, Joy, and her husband, Sam Albright, will be at the meeting, too. Joy wants to meet the lucky woman who is going to marry her Uncle Gordon. She's a journalist and photographer with *The Philadelphia Inquirer* newspaper. Her husband plays basketball."

Pat squealed, "Is he THE Sam Albright?"

"The one and only!" Sarah replied.

About an hour later, Michael heard a vehicle coming up the driveway. He exited the house through his dog door and was surprised and happy to see Topaz. He rubbed her muzzle, then gave a quick greeting to Jeanette and Jenny before running toward the Kilmer's big van that was rolling to a stop. After Kissy and Kawdje joined him and Topaz, they sat together and watched with interest as Evan and Gordon unloaded a Dog Walk obstacle from the van.

While they assembled it, Sarah told the others that she had spoken to Pat about having Ed handle the legalities of setting up a pet friendly airline company.

"Gordon, she'll have Ed phone you this evening after he gets home from work."

Jeanette asked, "Is this something Cole and I could be part of, too?"

Sarah gave her a brief explanation of their plans for a pet friendly airline company and said they were welcome to be included.

Essie said, "Let's begin discussions over dinner at my home. That will take the burden of providing the meeting place from you, Sarah. After all, we're all going to descend upon your dining room yet again this coming weekend."

Jeanette said that Cole was usually available Thursday evenings. Everyone then agreed that would be the evening of choice for the meeting, if it suited Ed.

Sarah snapped on Michael's lead and together they jogged over to the Dog Walk. He performed flawlessly! Topaz and Jeanette also had a very creditable performance although Topaz was more hesitant and less sure of herself as she walked across the horizontal plank. There was no need for Jeanette to remind Topaz to touch the contact portion during her ascent and descent because Topaz was obviously being cautious. Kissy ran fearlessly up, across and down the Dog Walk. Evan had to step lively to keep up with her. She was too tiny to leap past the contact zones, which was probably a good thing. Otherwise, in her haste to perform at top speed, she might have missed them. Kawdje paced sedately up the ascending plank and decided to stop and enjoy the view while walking on the horizontal plank. Jenny giggled as she watched Essie coaxing a dawdling Kawdje across the horizontal plank of the Dog Walk. After he reluctantly descended, Evan suggested they have the pets repeat the performance minus the short leads because they would have to perform without leads during official Dog Agility events.

"Let's have a Standard Agility Class practice incorporating the Dog Walk," suggested Jeanette.

Sarah leaped on the suggestion. "Good idea. In case none of you has the diagram for that class, I can fetch mine from the house and we can do that setup."

Essie and Evan agreed.

Evan reminded them that the rules for the Standard Agility Class were the same as for the Relay Class, in that the team with the fastest time and fewest or no faults won. "All the obstacles are used in this class, including the Table, which isn't used in the Relay.

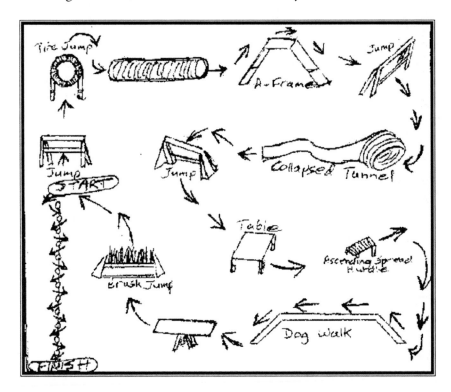

Everyone taped numbers on obstacles to mark the path to be taken through the setup.

Because the jumps were set at the 26-inch jump height category, it was decided that Michael would perform first, followed by Topaz and, after adjusting the jumps for the 12-inch height category, Kissy would perform and Kawdje would be last.

Kawdje watched the others in a dour mood. He wondered why he was always last to perform. He was disgruntled because there was now another obstacle in the setup. He noticed, as he watched the progress of the others that the tippy, tricky See-Saw had to be performed upon immediately after using the Dog Walk.

He plodded onto the course and made it obvious that he was not enthusiastic. During his performance, he was nervous because he had to use that tricky See-Saw and finish up bumbling through those tiresome Weave Poles.

When his mom signaled for him to take the Dog Walk, he dutifully walked up the ascending plank and across the horizontal plank. His enjoyed the extra height it gave him and his mood lifted. He felt secure enough to look around while walking forward. He saw a deer near the edge of the woods. He barked to alert the others and ran down the Dog Walk toward the deer so fast that Essie couldn't grab him.

Michael and Kissy took up the hue and cry and raced in hot pursuit. Topaz reluctantly ran after them in a leisurely, loping gait. She didn't want any confrontation with deer and didn't want her friends to hurt them.

The shortest path to the deer required Kawdje to jump over hurdles. He cleared them like a high jumper. Michael was still behind him but gaining. Kissy was yipping enthusiastically and Topaz was loping alongside her.

The startled herd was stupefied to see a very small creature running swiftly toward them. They were used to Michael and weren't sure what this small, speedy thing was. As it drew closer, the deer recognized the scent of dog. The herd shifted focus and saw Michael and Topaz, whose scent they were familiar with, plus another very small, yappy dog. The deer turned and vanished into the woods.

The pets heard their families calling for them to return and, as Michael, Topaz and Kissy abandoned the chase, Kawdje, who wanted to pursue the deer into the woods, decided that discretion, at least for now, was the better part of valor. He wasn't sure how many deer comprised the herd and, he reasoned, with no one to back him up, who knew what might happen to him? Briefly, he entertained the thought of chasing the whole herd of deer rather than face the See-Saw, but decided that he would be really brave and tackle that tippy obstacle. He reluctantly turned back toward the agility setup.

Jenny was delighted by the break in routine and laughed until she gasped for breath. Gordon and Evan also laughed until they had to wipe tears from their eyes.

"It was like a fox hunt, except that it was a deer hunt, with a wee Tibetan Spaniel in the lead," said Gordon.

"Who knew that inside Kawdje beats the heart of a hunting warrior?" exclaimed Evan.

Kawdje swaggered up to his dad who lifted him up and nuzzled the neck.

"What a guy you are! You're so full of contradictions. You were afraid to climb the stairs for such a long time when you were a puppy, and you're suspicious and wary of anything new, but you're ready to round up a herd of deer. I wonder how you would react to buffalo, or lions and tigers."

Gordon was stroking Kawdje's head so Evan passed him over into his arms. As Gordon was cuddling and praising Kawdje, Michael experienced an unfamiliar feeling sweep through him as he watched the loving attention that Gordon was bestowing upon Kawdje. He suddenly felt unhappy and depressed and wanted Gordon to love him so he walked over to him and pressed his head against Gordon's leg. Gordon hunkered down and placed Kawdje on the ground and divided his loving between the two of them.

Essie grumpily observed that Kawdje deliberately created a distraction because he wasn't in the mood to practice agility. "I know he doesn't much like the See-Saw."

"Oh well," said Sarah. "He gave us all a good laugh. Agility should be fun."

Kawdje decided he had better make amends with his mom so he pranced over to her, stood up on his hind legs and braced his front paws against her legs while looking up at her as appealingly as he could. He knew his special look won over judges at Conformation Dog Shows and he hoped it would melt his mom's heart. Essie sighed in resignation and picked him up.

"Okay, pal, let's get back to work." She carried him over to the Dog Walk and placed him on the horizontal plank where he had stood before taking off to chase deer. He quickly performed on that obstacle and ran toward the dreaded See-Saw. Kawdje felt more relaxed now and he paced surefooted up the plank. As he reached the pivot point and felt the plank beginning to shift into a horizontal position under his paws, he slowly placed his one paw forward, then another and the plank moved to the level position.

"This is cool," he thought. "If I stand still, the plank will remain level and I can look around and see far into the distance. Maybe I'll see more deer."

He heard his mom urging him forward so he reluctantly continued walking forward and the plank tilted down all the way until it touched the grass. He ran down and onto the lawn.

"Well, that wasn't too bad," he thought. "Actually, it was kind of fun."

Much to Essie's surprise, Kawdje indicated that he wanted to repeat the exercise by turning around and facing the See-Saw and placing his front paws on it. She let him perform on it again and this time he did it with speed and perfection. Kawdje and Essie were elated!

The rest of practice went well and the morning sped by. Everyone settled upon arriving at the Kilmer's home about 5:00 p.m. on Thursday.

CHAPTER FOURTEEN

Late Thursday afternoon, Essie had just finished setting the dining room table and Evan was putting glasses on the bar countertop when Kissy and Kawdje barked, announcing the arrival of Jeanette, Cole, Jenny and Topaz. The three 2-legged guests carried in delectable trifle and rice pudding desserts and remarked on the lovely country setting. Essie offered to show them the property. They tramped around the grounds as Essie pointed out her prize specimen curly needle pine and some old varieties of azaleas and rhododendrons that clustered among small groves of dogwood.

Kissy and Kawdje were occupied showing Topaz their property. "See those low-growing juniper shrubs?" asked Kawdje. "A mole lives under them. It's made a hole under the roots that it escapes into whenever we come close to catching it."

"I see you've tried to dig it out," said Topaz as she observed a small hole that had been dug. "Would you like me to help you?"

Kissy and Kawdje simultaneously said a resounding, "Yes."

Essie heard Sarah, Gordon, and Michael arrive. Because Gordon was staying longer than he had planned, he had driven over to Sarah's earlier that afternoon to fetch her and Michael in a car he had rented. Pat and Ed had followed Gordon in their own car.

Michael leaped out of the car, bounded over to his pals and looked with interest at the hole they were digging. Kissy brought him up to speed about the mole that lived under the roots of the juniper bush and Michael literally dug in to help. Soon, the four dogs had uprooted the small bush but, to their disappointment, there was no mole to be found. They could see a maze of small tunnels so they all continued to dig with tenacity and diligence. They uprooted another bush.

After chatting and sipping wine for awhile with her friends, Essie wondered where the pets were and excused herself to check on them.

Evan was refilling Jenny's glass of 7 Up and he almost dropped it, when they all heard Essie's scream. Everyone leaped to their feet and ran in the direction of the commotion. Essie's low-growing juniper bushes, which had been planted in a scalloped arrangement to mimic the scalloped cedar shakes that encircled the house in a four-foot-wide trim, had been uprooted and tossed aside in a jumble of exposed roots. She stood beside them with a horrified expression on her face.

"I knew that Kissy and Kawdje were interested in this area and had dug small holes. I assumed that there was probably a mole, or a vole, under one of the junipers but I never dreamed that Michael and Topaz would help them dig up my bushes. My garden is ruined," Essie wailed.

Joy and Sam, who had just arrived, quickly ran from their car toward the group.

"Mom, what's wrong?" asked Joy.

Essie pointed to the destruction and said, "Just look at my Blue Star Junipers. The planting arrangement is ruined."

Sam's shoulders shook and he turned away as he put a hand over his mouth to muffle his laughter. Jeanette felt terrible and also felt responsible, as did Sarah, since it was obvious that Topaz and Michael had contributed to most of the damage.

"Oh, lovely," thought Jeanette. "It's my first time here and the evening has not started off well." She apologized for Topaz's behavior and said, "Give me a shovel and a bucket of water. If the junipers are replanted immediately, I think they can be saved."

Evan and Gordon brought shovels to the area while Cole attached two hoses together and screwed one end onto an outdoor spigot. Essie retrieved some stakes from the garage and everyone helped replant and stake the junipers upright.

Michael, Topaz, Kissy and Kawdje watched with rapt interest at the efforts to replant the shrubs.

Kissy said, "They're rebuilding the home of that critter."

Kawdje replied, "That will give us another chance to dig him out again."

Topaz said, "I sense that my mom is definitely upset that we dug up those bushes."

Michael summed up the situation, "All of us had fun digging together to catch that critter, but none of our families understand us."

"Let's discuss this over dinner," Kawdje suggested. "It smells to me that we'll be dining on ham."

Kissy added, "It's rice pudding for dessert. Yummy!"

They paced briskly toward the house and waited by the door for their families to catch up.

During dinner, the logistics of starting up an airline company that catered to the complete family was discussed. Everyone wanted to give their airline a catchy name that promoted the idea of pets being full-fledged family members who are provided full-service, too.

Jenny cut through the chatter and simply said, "Pal."

Everyone stared at her. Then Joy exclaimed, "Yes, that's perfect and it should be spelled with a double P, as in PPAL, which would stand for People Pets Air Line."

There was a series of resounding yeses.

"Why did you think of PAL?" asked Jeanette.

"Topaz senses when I'm feeling blue because I'm missing my parents and worrying about them and she comes to me and lays her head on my lap or cuddles up beside me. I was thinking that she is my pal. Then I thought those letters could stand for Pet Air Lines."

"Good thinking," said Cole. "You've named our airline company."

The conversation covered the charter that Ed would draw up, how much airfare to charge for traveling pets, how many aircraft to start with and which airports and flight paths to offer.

Gordon suggested, "We should just offer service in this country and, if it takes off, no pun intended, we could add flights to Canada and some of the Caribbean Islands. We want to offer flights to places where some hotels/motels are pet friendly."

Pat said, "I can draw up guidelines for pet air travel. For example, all shots must be up-to-date, plus documentation showing a recent veterinary health clearance, and I think that all pets should have a photo ID just like people have. It could prevent an unscrupulous person from using the certificate of someone else's healthy pet and passing it off as belonging to their unhealthy or unvaccinated pet. It would also help to prevent pet theft."

"Those are good points," Gordon said.

Sam interjected, "How much money will we need to come up with to get this airline company off the ground?"

Joy said, "There you go again, speaking in puns."

Everyone discussed how much they could invest in PPAL and came to the conclusion that it would be a miniscule amount compared to what would be needed.

Jeanette said that they shouldn't give up too soon and suggested having questionnaires available for distribution at some of the upcoming dog agility events. "People who participate in Dog Agility are our potential clients. Let's find out if they would utilize a pet-friendly airline, which flight paths would be most convenient for them, and how much they would be willing to pay for the service. Also, we should accompany the questionnaire with a brochure describing the service we hope to offer for pets traveling by air with their family."

Everyone thought that was a great idea and promised to call Jeanette with their ideas and suggestions regarding the content of the questionnaires.

After the meeting was over, Jeanette invited everybody to her home on Sunday to try out Michael, Kissy and Kawdje as "Dock Dogs." Joy and Sam, Pat and Ed declined the invitation saying that their weekend schedules were full, but the others promised to come about 11 a.m. and leave before lunch.

"Oh no," said Jeanette. "Stay for lunch. It will give us another opportunity to discuss PPAL."

As Gordon drove Sarah and Michael home, Sarah said that their real estate agent had found a house in Bucks County that she thought might be just what they were looking for but that it wouldn't be on the market for another few days.

Gordon said, "If the property is large enough and local law doesn't prohibit it, I could keep my Bell Jet Ranger on the property. If not, there is a small airport in Bucks County and maybe I could keep it there."

"Let's not get our hopes up yet," cautioned Sarah.

Inwardly, she had a feeling that this house might be the very one that spoke to them as soon as they walked through the door, saying, "I'm yours."

Michael drowsed sleepily in the back seat. He heard the word home spoken several times as Sarah and Gordon talked to one another. He was aware that his and Sarah's home was not Gordon's and wondered if they were talking about a place that would be home for all three of them. He loved his home with Sarah but he would happily leave it for another if it meant that Gordon would live with them.

CHAPTER FIFTEEN

Sunday morning, the aspiring Champion Dog Agility Teams arrived within a few minutes of one another for Dock Dog tryouts. Sarah gasped in awe at the beauty of Jeanette and Cole's place. The driveway was long and winding and because of all the mature trees and the luscious growth of fern beneath them, she didn't see the beautiful fieldstone and stucco home until the driveway ended and opened into a parking area that could accommodate six vehicles.

Large expanses of lawn on both sides and behind the house gave it an air of stateliness. Some Tree Peonies were blooming and the flowers were so large and exquisitely formed and perfect that they looked artificial. Beautiful flowers bordered a side lawn, with a forest of mature trees as a backdrop. The lawn on the opposite side of the house surrounded a large stone patio and, as Sarah and Gordon walked toward it, they stopped to enjoy the magnificent view. The lawn off the patio was level for about fifty feet before sloping downward. It was so steep that trees growing at the edge of that portion of lawn did not obscure the grand vista that stretched out for miles.

"I wouldn't mind living in a home like this," Gordon said. "In fact, I would love it."

They walked to the front door with Michael ambling between them. Jenny opened the door at their knock and invited them in. Jeanette appeared in the hallway wiping her hands on her apron. Topaz was close beside her and she and Michael licked each other's muzzles as their families greeted one another. Cole came in the back door carrying a load of firewood that he placed in the hearth before hugging Sarah and shaking Gordon's hand.

Sarah said she and Gordon were so impressed with their home and surrounding grounds. Jeanette and Cole offered to give them a tour if they would like one.

The back lawn was outstanding. A rose arbor arched over the entrance of a stone pathway that beckoned to be walked upon. The end of the pathway opened into a round courtyard laid in stone that was surrounded by metal arches with climbing rose bushes trained over them. Weathered clay urns filled with colorful flowers were placed around the perimeter of the courtyard, as were several stone benches that appeared to be centuries old although Jeanette and Cole had just purchased them the previous year. A fountain at the other end of the courtyard completed an exquisitely beautiful and tranquil outdoor room.

Gordon and Sarah gazed in silent admiration.

At last, Sarah said, "What an incredibly lovely setting! This is beautiful beyond words. You could rent it out for weddings and make a fortune."

Jeanette asked, "Would you like to be married here? It would be our pleasure and honor to host your wedding."

"What a wonderful offer! You are such kind and special friends, but Gordon and I wouldn't want you to go to that much effort for our wedding."

Gordon interrupted, "Who says we wouldn't? I think this is a perfect place for our wedding ceremony and I'm accepting the offer, on our behalf."

Sarah sputtered, "Jeanette and Cole, I love your home and gardens. It's idyllic. It's just that I don't want to place the burden of hosting our wedding on you."

Jeanette smiled, "Cole and I want you to be married here."

Cole added, "The matter is settled."

Sarah thanked them and said, "I would love to have Jenny as my Flower Girl, if she's still here when the wedding takes place. I also want to have Michael take part in the wedding. Perhaps I'll walk down the aisle with him. Now that I think about it, all the pets should be present at the wedding and maybe even be a part of the ceremony. What do you think about that, Gordon?"

He pulled her close for a hug and said, "Suits me. They're part of our families so why shouldn't they be included?"

Jeanette laughed and said, "Topaz loves to sing. Maybe she could sing at the wedding. She sings to the moon, especially when it's full. Cole calls it baying but I know she's singing."

In the meantime, Michael said to Topaz as they paced around her house. "You have as much woods as I do, Topaz. You have even more lawn."

Just then, Essie, Evan, Kissy and Kawdje arrived. The pets ran toward one another and touched noses. Topaz said, "I've been showing Michael my property. Want to join the tour?"

They followed Topaz to the stone patio. Kawdje could see for miles and thought that sitting on this patio was even better than standing on his own stonewall, or at the top of the A-Frame obstacle. "Wow," he thought. "Not too shabby!"

Topaz then led them to the pond. They paced onto the dock and peered into water that was too murky to see bottom. None of the others had ever swum before, so Topaz led them off the dock toward the shore where they could wade in. She demonstrated her swimming prowess. Michael waded into the water until the bottom dropped away. He instinctively paddled furiously and, to his surprise, he was swimming. He swam in a half-circle and headed to shore.

Kissy saw Michael's success and was encouraged to try. After taking a few steps into the water, she couldn't touch bottom. She tried to swim along the shoreline but couldn't get the hang of it. She had to make a tremendous effort to keep from sinking. Her wet fur weighed her down. She felt panicky and heavy and clumsy, which was a new sensation for her. She quickly decided that she didn't enjoy swimming so she got out of the water and shook herself vigorously.

Kawdje looked with concern at Kissy's attempt to swim. He gingerly put a paw into the water. It wasn't warm like the water his mom or dad used when he was bathed in the big sink at home; however, the others hadn't come to harm so he walked into the pond a little ways. The water was cool but not unpleasantly cold. Suddenly, there was no bottom to walk on, so, like Michael, he instinctively paddled and, to his surprise and pleasure, he managed to keep his head above water. He was swimming like Topaz and Michael and his elation gave him confidence. He swam forward a little ways before swimming in a half-circle and dog paddling to the shore's edge. When he could touch bottom, he swam along the shoreline. He thought that swimming was easier to learn than climbing the open-step staircase at home.

When their families arrived at the pond, they were surprised to see Topaz, Michael and Kawdje swimming and even more surprised to see that Kissy was not. They could see from her wet fur that she had already tried swimming.

When she refused to re-enter the water at Evan's coaxing, they concluded that she had decided that it wasn't her kind of sport.

Jeanette said, "I'm not sure that Kawdje will become a star in Dock Dog competition. It isn't weighted for smaller dogs."

Evan said, "If he decides he enjoys diving into the water after a ball, we'll support his efforts. Who knows? Eventually Dock Dogs may open a class for smaller breeds."

Jeanette stood at the end of the dock and called for Topaz to come to her. When Topaz was about 10 feet away, Jeanette threw the ball into the water as far as she could and commanded, "Fetch."

Topaz ran to the end of the dock, jumped into the water and swam toward the ball. She retrieved it and swam to shore holding the ball in her mouth. She waded out of the water, not stopping to shake water off her fur and bounded joyfully toward her mom. Jeanette took the ball, praised her, then positioned Topaz about 20 feet from the end of the dock. She walked back to the end of the dock, made a high sweeping arc with her left arm, snapping her fingers as she finished the arm motion while saying, "Jump," and then, "Fetch." She threw the ball a good distance into the pond.

Topaz ran toward the end of the dock. She now understood that her mom wanted her to make a big leap so she launched herself into the air and stretched out her front legs as she landed in the water.

It was a prodigious leap! Jeanette reckoned it to be about 20 to 22 feet before splashdown. Everyone whistled and clapped. Topaz felt very proud.

Michael walked onto the dock and made it obvious that he wanted to try his paw at Dock Dog so Sarah followed him and threw the ball a short distance because, to the best of her knowledge, Michael had just learned how to swim.

Michael was relieved that he didn't need to leap very far from the dock to fetch the ball because this was the first time he had ever jumped into water. He belly flopped but managed to keep his head above water. "So far, so good," he thought. He retrieved the ball and swam as fast as he could to shore. He climbed out of the water, dropped the ball, shook himself off, then picked up the ball again and brought it to Sarah, who was standing on the dock.

Everyone applauded enthusiastically. Twice more, Michael performed the Dock Dog routine and with each attempt, he jumped further in distance.

Essie and Evan decided Kawdje should fetch the ball from the shoreline, at least for his first tryout, and see how he managed the routine. Kawdje watched his mom throw the ball into the water and say, "Fetch," to him. He knew what to do because he remembered what Topaz and Michael had done, so he waded into the water and swam toward the ball.

He tried to retrieve it but he couldn't open his jaws wide enough to grasp the ball. It bobbed away with every attempt he made. He kept swimming toward the ball until he heard his mom calling him. He was in a quandary. He was supposed to bring the ball back to her but he couldn't clench his jaws around it. He decided to give it another try. No luck. He just couldn't hold the ball in his mouth. He heard water splashing close to him and then saw Topaz. She grasped the ball in her jaws and swam toward shore, staying just a little ahead of him. He was shocked to see how far from shore he had swum. Topaz released the ball into the water a little ways ahead of him. He swam toward it but before he could reach it, she clamped it in her jaws and swam toward shore and, once again, dropped the ball a little ahead of him. She did this until he reached shore. He was greatly relieved for Topaz's assistance and told her so as he waded out of the water and watched her drop the ball onto the grass. Kawdje nudged the ball with his nose toward his mom until it touched her shoes. Then he shook water out of his fur and everyone squealed.

Essie picked Kawdje up and everyone took turns praising him for his courage, tenacity and resolve. Essie passed Kawdje into Evan's arms, then she lavished praise on Topaz for rescuing Kawdje.

Evan said, "I should have realized that the ball was too large for his mouth. I'll get him a smaller one."

"Evan, he can't compete in Dock Dogs against large breeds."

"The rules could change and levels in Dock Dogs could open up for smaller breeds, Essie. Besides, he enjoys being in the water. Tibetan Spaniels aren't supposed to like the water but Kawdje doesn't know that."

Kissy had barked non-stop while Kawdje was in the water to encourage him, as well as sound the alarm that he was in trouble. She had been very upset and worried that Kawdje would come to harm. Now that he was safely back on shore and the center of attention, she was annoyed and jealous.

"Somehow, he always manages to grab the spotlight," she thought.

Jeanette fetched towels from the house and everyone set to work toweling the pets dry.

The pets were still damp as they devoured a lunch of chopped liverwurst and cooked lima beans mixed with dry dog food and drizzled with homemade chicken broth.

After they had eaten, they discussed the morning's event.

Kawdje said, "I really enjoyed myself. I knew I was supposed to retrieve the ball but it kept slipping away because it was too big to fit into my jaws. Topaz, thanks again for guiding me back to shore. You're a good swimmer and I felt confident because you were close beside me."

Michael said admiringly, "Topaz, you can really take long leaps off the docks. You were great."

"Thanks, Michael and Kawdje. I thought both of you were amazing. You did a great job of swimming for a first time practice."

Kissy felt left out. "I hate swimming. My wet fur weighed me down. I don't like cold water and I will never do something as useless as jumping off a dock into cold water to fetch a ball. Give me a warm, comfortable window seat with a soft pillow to rest my head upon and a nice view to look at."

Topaz, Michael and Kawdje understood that Kissy was upset because she had finally found something that she couldn't immediately conquer. Being unwilling, disliking or afraid to do something was a new experience for her. Michael gingerly changed the subject to agility practice.

Meanwhile, in the dining room, the topic was real estate.

Gordon said, "Sarah and I are going to look at a home in this area in a couple of days. It's not far from a small airport where I could rent space for my helicopter. Also, there's enough land with the house that I could have a pad cleared for it if local ordinance permits."

"Would you be up for taking Jeanette, Jenny and me for a ride sometime?" asked Cole. "I've always wanted to fly in a helicopter."

"Absolutely," said Gordon. "My chopper is a Bell Jet Ranger that will hold up to eight people if it's not loaded with cargo."

Jeanette suggested to Sarah, Essie and Jenny that they sit in the living room and discuss the wedding, and leave the men to talk about flying.

Jenny asked to be excused because she wanted to play a handheld video game.

When they had comfortably settled themselves, Sarah said, "I was listening to an old recording of Mario Lanza singing that wonderful song, 'Because,' a few days ago. You know, the one that begins, 'Because you come to me with naught save love,' well, I want to have that sung at my wedding. It's an oldie but goody. I think a small, intimate gathering in this lovely setting would be ideal. I want to wear a long wedding dress and carry roses because there is a line from that song that says something like, 'I see the roses blooming at your feet.'

I'll mail handwritten notes to my deceased husband's family telling them of my impending marriage, but not invitations. None of his siblings is well enough to travel and I don't think any of them will want to come, although I'm sure they'll be happy for me. I'll just have you and our children, some of my church friends and a childhood friend that I've always kept in touch with plus my pastor, who I would like to perform the nuptials, and his wife. My brother and his family will want to come. I haven't asked Gordon yet who he wants to attend the wedding. I want Jenny to be my Flower Girl, if that's possible, and I want all our pets to attend. What do you think?"

Meanwhile, Michael, Topaz, Kissy and Kawdje sat on the stone patio that overlooked the beautiful vista. Jenny sat on a chair nearby and played a hand-held video game. They discussed Dock Dogs practice. Topaz told the others that the sweeping gesture her mom had made with her arm just before she had thrown the ball into the water meant that she wanted her to make a huge leap.

"I think we're supposed to leap way out into the water as far as we can instead of jumping in the water close to the dock."

"Want to do it again?" asked Michael.

"I know I'd do better if I didn't have to retrieve that ball," said Kawdje.

Kissy, who was sitting on Jenny's lap chimed in, "Not me. I do not like swimming and I don't think our moms and dads want us to get wet again." Jenny lifted Kissy off her lap onto the patio, stood up and walked inside the house. She found her Aunt Jeanette discussing the upcoming wedding with the other women.

She announced, "Topaz, Michael, Kissy and Kawdje talk to each other. They make sounds that aren't barks. I don't know what they're saying but they definitely talk to one another."

Her aunt smiled at her and said, "Yes, of course they do, dear."

Essie and Sarah nodded in agreement and Essie said, "That's right. They do, indeed, communicate with one another."

CHAPTER SIXTEEN

Two days later, Sarah's real estate agent informed her that the house they had been waiting to go on the market was now officially for sale. Sarah immediately called Gordon and they arranged with their agent to meet at her office in the early afternoon and follow her to the property. Sarah phoned her friends and let them know that, although the morning agility practice was still "on," she and Michael would not be attending Dock Dogs practice that afternoon because she and Gordon were going to look at a house in Bucks County that they had been waiting to see. Jeanette offered to take Michael home with her after agility practice.

"Thanks, Jeanette. We'll pick him up late afternoon or early evening. I'll call you after we've seen the house and let you know a specific time."

After agility practice ended, Michael was puzzled but not unhappy when Sarah made it clear that he was to go home with Topaz. She touched him on the back once so he intuited that she meant just for today.

After they arrived at the real estate agent's office, the agent pulled up the statistics of the house on her computer. There was a large, eat-in kitchen with its own entrance, plus a laundry room and bathroom off of it. A dining room was situated between the kitchen and a large living room. There was a large master bedroom with its private bathroom plus two other large bedrooms and a small one that could be used as a den/office. There was another full bathroom plus a powder room. It was situated on 12 acres that were mostly wooded.

They followed the agent in their own vehicle and drove up a long, paved driveway that was in good condition. Both of them had a good feeling as they glimpsed the roofline. The home was a two-story structure with the upper story consisting of two large unfinished rooms. Sarah and Gordon were pleased to see dormer windows plus side windows and visualized them being turned into bedrooms or an office.

The kitchen had a slate tile floor and the rest of the home had lovely yellow pine flooring. The windows in the dining and living rooms were almost floor to ceiling and framed a view that was spectacular and similar to Jeanette and Cole's, with its long sweeping vista on the south side of the house. The only drawback was that the garage was small and unattached to the house, the lawn area was not large, and the plantings were unremarkable.

Gordon asked, "Is this home for you?"

Sarah laid her cheek against Gordon's chest. "This is home. The house said, 'I'm yours,' as soon as I walked into it. How about you?"

"Me, too."

The smiling realtor wrote up their offer. Sarah phoned Jeanette while Gordon called Evan with the news.

They dined at the only restaurant in the area that served paella, which was Gordon's favorite dish. They discussed their wedding and decided to set a date.

Sarah suggested that they marry in early October.

Gordon asked, "Why wait until October?"

Sarah said, "Because we don't know if the offer we made on the house will be accepted and if it is, we signed for a settlement date of August 25th, which is barely more than 60 days away and the present owners may not want to vacate that soon even if they accept our bid. Also, I'd like to have at least a couple of weeks after the Dog Agility events wind down to pull together all the details of our wedding. Another thing, since it's taking place at Jeanette and Cole's place, I know she would like a little extra time, too. I'd go for the 24th of September, which I happen to know is a Saturday because I looked it up earlier."

Gordon groaned, "Couldn't we just elope?"

Sarah smiled. "You won't have to concern yourself with details. Basically, you have to show up and say, 'I do,' when the pastor tells you to. I expect you'll be busy with PPAL and arranging for garage renovations and pad clearing if our offer is accepted. Plus, you have to sell your townhouse and move to Pennsylvania whatever items you intend to keep."

The waitress brought their flan dessert. A very small package, wrapped in gold foil, nestled beside Sarah's dessert. She looked questioningly at Gordon.

"What's this?"

"Open it and find out."

Sarah tore away the wrapping which revealed a small jeweler's box that she quickly sprung open. A stunning diamond and sapphire engagement ring glittered like moonlight on water. She felt tears well up in her eyes as she looked at Gordon.

"You're not going to cry, are you? Don't you like it? Don't you want an engagement ring?"

"I'm crying because I'm happy. It's beautiful. It's a perfect expression of our love."

"May I put it on your finger?"

Sarah passed him the ring box and held out her hand. He slipped the ring on her fourth finger, left hand. It fit perfectly!

"Now we are officially engaged to be married," Gordon said as he pressed her hand to his lips and kissed it.

Later, when they stopped by Jeanette and Cole's house to pick up Michael, everyone admired the ring and warmly congratulated them on their official engagement. Jenny begged to be allowed to try on the ring and Sarah indulged her. Michael knew something special had happened because that wonderful, light, happy energy that always enveloped Sarah and Gordon was stronger and steadier and it flowed out and wrapped around him and everyone else. He saw everybody looking at something that appeared to be a tiny, brilliant collar encircling one of her fingers the way his collar encircled his neck. He remembered how important it was for a dog to wear a collar in Mexico. The street dogs of San Miguel who didn't wear a collar were not part of a family. He recalled how happy and loved he had felt when Sarah had encircled his neck with the collar that he still wore. He shared his thoughts with Topaz and they decided that Gordon had put this small, glittering collar on Sarah's finger.

Topaz said, "My mom has two collars on one of her fingers and she wears them all the time. Occasionally she puts other small collars on other fingers. She even wears collars around her neck sometimes!"

They concluded that the collar that their moms and dads wore all the time on the same finger must be important, and signified that they were members of the same family, just as their own neck collars did.

Gordon and Sarah described the house they had just put a buyer's bid on.

"It's located about five miles from here. It's very private and you can't see your neighbors, but I guess this is a safe area," said Gordon.

"It is, although we have had several car thefts in the past six months," Cole replied.

"One of the first things I plan to do, if our bid is accepted, is to have a security system installed and a garage built that adjoins the house," Gordon said.

After a few more minutes of conversation, Sarah, Gordon and Michael said their goodbyes amidst congratulations and drove to Essie and Evan's home to show them the engagement ring.

Once again, they received hugs and congratulations. Although Essie and Evan had known that Gordon planned to give Sarah an engagement ring, this was their first look because he hadn't wanted anyone else to see the ring before Sarah. They thought it was magnificent. Kissy and Kawdje were picked up and shown the ring.

The dogs immediately understood that something special had happened because Sarah had never worn anything so shiny on her finger before and their mom and dad were making such a fuss over it. They asked Michael about it. He explained that he thought it had the same significance as the collars they each wore.

"Oh, so it shows what family you're part of," said Kawdje.

"Then Sarah and Gordon are a family and you're part of their family, Michael," Kissy reasoned.

"Yes," Michael said proudly. "I used to live by myself on the streets in Mexico and now I have a mom and dad and a home. I loved and trusted Gordon as soon as I sniffed him."

"Maybe now you'll all live together in the same home," Kissy said.

Gordon drove Michael and Sarah home and departed soon afterward. Michael was so disappointed that he barely had the strength to climb the stairs and flop onto his bed. He thought the finger collar meant that Gordon would live with them always. He lay awake wondering why Gordon had not stayed, and then a thought occurred to him. "Maybe Gordon smells that faint scent of another man in this house and he doesn't want to live here because of that." He fell asleep puzzling over it and wondering how Gordon would solve the scent problem.

CHAPTER SEVENTEEN

Early Friday morning, the group, with the exception of Cole who was working, met on the grounds where the Northeastern Dog Agility Championship was being held. Gordon accompanied them and took the responsibility of looking after Jenny. Many out-of-town participants had driven to the event in RV's. They had unfurled the awnings on their mobile homes, set up dog pens and looked comfortably settled in for the next few days. It was obvious that many competitors had a cheering section with them.

It was a cloudy day and, although no rain was predicted, tents had been erected over the rings where the dog agility performances would take place. The sides were rolled up making it easy to walk under and out of them. The friends had brought a small tent to shelter themselves from sun or rain plus a portable fence barrier to contain the pets. They had also brought Pak-n-Fold kennels, mostly for the purpose of having a designated, safe, comfortable place for the pets to nap between classes and keep them off the grass that sometimes felt damp and chilly to lie on. Everyone had a portable chair. They stacked a huge hamper of food and several thermoses of hot coffee and tea under their tent.

All first-time competitors in a USDAA event were measured to verify that the stated height was accurate. Kissy and Kawdje qualified for the 12-inch jump height category and Michael and Topaz for the 26-inch jump height category.

They were amazed to see so many other dogs. Kawdje relaxed when he realized that all the other dogs were on leashes just like in the Conformation Dog Shows.

"This must be a very special agility practice," he said.

"I wonder if we'll do the same things that we always do during practice on Michael's lawn?" wondered Kissy.

"I'll do what I always do—follow Sarah's directions and just do it as fast as I can," announced Michael.

"That's a good plan," pronounced Topaz.

The pets had been entered in every Starters class available that day. They competed in Snooker and Gamblers in the morning.

Sarah and Jeanette experienced pre-performance jitters while doing the "walk-through" for their first class, which was Gamblers. Fortunately, their nervousness abated with the physical activity of competing and didn't adversely affect Michael and Topaz's performances in spite of Topaz having sensed her mom's anxiety. Jeanette and Topaz's uncanny connection served them well during the closing sequence when they were always at least nine feet apart from one another.

Topaz and her mom won the Starters Gamblers Class. Michael and Sarah placed second.

Essie and Evan's first class was Snooker. Both remained calm, due in no small part to having had the experience of competing in Conformation Dog Shows. Kawdje also remained composed from having contended with the hustle and bustle of those shows while blotting out the commotion around him and focusing on his performance. Kissy felt an unfamiliar quivering sensation in her gut prior to her first performance. She was reassured when her Dad stroked her back and remembered that he would be with her all the time.

Kawdje competed just before Kissy, and when she heard loud clapping for his performance she thought, "Anything he can do, I can do faster." It spurred her on to her fastest performance ever. She exulted in the applause she received and thought, "Hooray for me! I love this!"

Kissy placed first in the Starters Snooker Class and Kawdje placed third. A little Rat Terrier named Zippy came second.

When Kissy competed in her next class, which was Gamblers, she was overconfident and wanted to make independent decisions. She ignored her dad's signal and used a nearby hurdle for the third time so she didn't accrue any points for that jump and her action placed her further away from the high-point-value Dog Walk that Evan had wanted her to use. Getting her back into position to use the Dog Walk added extra seconds to their performance time.

Kawdje won Starters Gamblers and Zippy came second. In spite of her undisciplined behavior, Kissy placed third which was no small feat because it was a large class.

After each class, a brief ceremony took place in which winning teams were presented with a ribbon and trophy, the color of which designated their placement. Kissy, Kawdje and Topaz immediately understood the significance of receiving awards for their performances, from having had the experience of competing in Conformation Dog Shows. They took turns explaining the meaning of the awards to Michael.

Kissy loved the recognition and applause. It was like the elixir of life to her! Kawdje enjoyed winning but he just didn't have Kissy's passion for winning and inherent need for recognition. He mostly set his mind to figuring out the purpose of things. Topaz loved winning mainly because she sensed that it pleased her mom and because she shared the ceremony with her mom and she loved doing any activity that meant she would be with her mom. Michael was very gratified by the recognition of his agility prowess. Before Sarah came into his life, no one had recognized anything about him worth applauding for. Nonetheless, the gratification that he felt from the crowds' approval was insignificant compared to the pleasure that filled him when he sensed Sarah and Gordon's pride in his accomplishment.

The rest of the morning went smoothly. All the pets had fault-free performances that were well within the Standard Course Times. In the 26-inch category, Michael and Sarah won Snooker and Topaz and Jeanette placed third.

Everyone was more than ready to take time out for lunch. The couples collected their portable chairs, hastened to their tent, re-opened the chairs and collapsed onto them. Gordon and Jenny poured tea and coffee and opened the cooler.

Pet bowls were filled with food that disappeared like a magic vanishing act. Kissy and Michael crunched gingersnaps for dessert and Kawdje and Topaz ate rice pudding after which they were happy to lie in their Pak-n-Fold kennels for a well-earned nap.

"They'll need some sleep. It will be a long afternoon," said Essie. "We have the Jumpers, Pairs Relay and Standard Agility classes."

Jenny told the adults that she had made friends with a couple of kids who were entered in the Junior Handler Trials that would be held on Sunday and that she wanted to be a Junior Handler.

Jeanette asked if she wanted to perform with Topaz at a future event.

"No. I want to team up with Kissy. She's the right size for me and she likes to sit on my lap."

"We'll have to ask Uncle Evan and Aunt Essie's permission," Jeanette said.

Evan put his arm around Jenny's shoulder. "Next time we're all practicing at Aunt Sarah's, I'll show you how to handle Kissy. She can be tricky because she has such a competitive spirit. She attacks a course and doesn't want to be held back. Because of that she is more prone to make a mistake by choosing her own path if you let her get ahead of you. It will probably be good for her to work with more than one handler."

Jenny wrapped her arms around Evan's waist and hugged him. "Thanks, Uncle Evan."

As they relaxed sipping iced tea and munching cookies, Jeanette brought up the topic of PPAL.

"I ordered five hundred brochures and five hundred questionnaires. Cole will pick them up at the printer's this afternoon. We can set up a small booth beside our tent tomorrow. The questionnaires will have to be handed back to us after they've been filled out. Cole and I thought it best not to have them mailed back and make any of our home addresses available to strangers."

"What info did you put on the brochures and what questions did you ask on the questionnaires?" asked Evan.

"More or less what we had discussed during the dinner meeting. The questionnaires ask, 'how much would you be willing to spend for safe, comfortable air travel accommodations for your pet; would you be satisfied to have your pet housed in a separate compartment of the aircraft cabin; how often would you anticipate using a pet-friendly airline; would you travel internationally with your pet if safe and comfortable accommodations were available for your pet;' and so on.

The brochures describe the accommodations that we envision for pets, plus information about pet health documentation requirements including vaccines, pet photo ID, plus the type of check-in and embarking for pets that we want PPAL to provide."

Sarah interjected, "Pat and Ed have volunteered to stay with the pamphlets during the weekend. Pat is hoping that someway, somehow, PPAL will take off, no pun intended. She has her heart set on being the airline's full-time veterinarian."

Jeanette continued, "Pat contributed a great deal to the information brochure content. A lot of space is devoted to the vaccines required for this type of air travel for pets, as well as info about airline-approved kennels that pets must be crated in

We've described PPAL's proposed in-flight protocol, such as, passengers not being permitted to visit pets while the seat belt sign is on, nor entering the pet area whenever the 'Occupied' sign is displayed, indicating that another passenger is in there and may have removed their pet family member from the kennel. Pat even thought of informing potential clients that piddle pads, for pet usage, would be available to purchase before or during the flight. Also included is information about a designated potty break area and the protocol to be followed."

Gordon asked with interest, "How do you plan to keep the pet toilet area from being soiled by male dogs who lift a leg to urinate?"

Sarah said, "I posed that same question to Pat. She said the potty break area should have rows of clips on the wall, placed at varying heights, so that piddle pads could be secured against the wall, thus protecting it from being soiled, plus another pad placed on the floor to cover it."

Jenny piped up with the comment that it would be more expensive to travel with a male dog than a female because males would need two pads every time they used the potty break area and females would only need one.

They all laughed and Evan reflected that it would probably be the only occasion when a male of any species incurred more expense than a female. Gordon grinned but wisely kept his mouth shut while the ladies glared at his brother.

The afternoon was a blur of activity for all of them.

In the Starters Pairs Relay, Kissy and Kawdje had been entered as a pair and Topaz and Michael as a pair in their respective jump height categories.

The Pairs Relay began with the 12-inch jump height category. Kissy and Kawdje were held in their parent's arms, while they waited their turn near the entrance gate. They saw the baton being carried by the handlers, and because they were familiar with that type of practice session, they knew what to expect and became completely relaxed.

Kissy loved the Relay course setup because it had a variety of obstacles and she attacked the course with confidence. She saw her dad use the signal that meant a long jump was to be taken next, so she prepared for her least favorite hurdle—the ascending spread hurdle. She unconsciously adjusted her rhythm so that she placed her front paws just in front of the hurdle and then swung her hind legs under her, placing them where her front paws had been as she pushed up and forward in a mighty effort. She cleared the ascending spread jump with room to spare and was so elated and proud of herself that she momentarily forgot to keep watching her dad and slowed her pace without realizing it.

She heard her dad call, "Right," and that brought back her concentration. She veered right, ran through the pipe tunnel and finished the rest of the course with ease. She knew in her heart that she had done very well. Her dad picked her up and murmured into her ear, "You cleared the spread hurdle in high style. Daddy's little girl is the best!"

Kissy licked his face and thought, "Now I know how to make a long jump. I know where to place my paws so that I get a good push off. I'll remember to do that every time I jump. I'm getting better and better, and soon, I'll always be the best!"

Later, when Evan and Essie checked the point sheet for Pairs Relay results, Kissy and Kawdje had placed first in their height category.

"I'm as proud as I ever was when Joy did something exceptionally well," said Essie.

"Me, too," agreed Evan.

In spite of their hectic schedule, Essie and Evan were able to watch their friends compete in the 26-inch category of Pairs Relay. They sat beside Gordon and Jenny in the chairs that Sarah and Jeanette had recently vacated. Essie held Kawdje in her lap while Jenny held Kissy and cooed into her ear telling her that she was the very best, most beautiful doggy in the whole world. Kissy wiggled until she had positioned herself so that she lay on her back with her head cradled in the crook of Jenny's arm and presented her tummy to be rubbed. Jenny giggled and slowly ran her hand in a circular motion on Kissy's tummy. Soon Kissy was fast asleep. That spread jump had been hard work.

Meanwhile, Essie hand fed pieces of an oatmeal cookie to Kawdje as a special treat for a performance well done.

During their Pairs Relay performance, Sarah noticed that Michael seemed distracted and quickly realized that whenever he was parallel or facing Topaz, he was torn between watching her for direction and looking over toward Topaz. She fumed inwardly because she couldn't run fast enough to always place herself between Michael and his view of Topaz.

When Michael was running through the collapsible tunnel, Sarah realized that he would emerge facing the baton-passing area where Topaz stood. Her heart pounded and she gulped air as she ran as fast as she could move her legs, with the aim of being a few feet in front of him when he emerged, thus blocking his view of Topaz. She made it! Thankfully, the next obstacle required Michael to make a 90° turn to his right, which meant he would be moving away from the area where Topaz and Jeanette stood. The whole experience was nerve-wracking and Sarah prayed that Michael would stand and stay during the baton-passing interlude.

About halfway through Sarah and Michael's performance, Jeanette noticed that Michael was not devoting all his attention to Sarah and his performance, and realized the reason was Topaz. She kept moving to block Michael's view of Topaz. As they neared the finish, Jeanette commanded Topaz to "stay," then placed herself in front and a little away from her and held her arm straight out to receive the baton from Sarah.

As soon as Sarah released the baton, she grasped Michael's collar because she knew that he had been poised to leap enthusiastically toward Topaz. Jeanette and Topaz sped away from the handler's baton-passing area.

Topaz performed flawlessly and was not distracted by anything. She had sensed that her mom hadn't wanted her to greet Michael after he had finished the course and had wanted to get away quickly and start their own performance as fast as they could. Topaz responded by performing faster than she ever had.

As they ran to the finish, she could hear applause and felt momentarily downcast because the practice was over. Her favorite time was whenever she and her mom were just concentrating on one another.

The group gathered under their tent cover for a snack and beverage break before packing up their gear and departing. Sarah and Jeanette expressed relief that Topaz and Michael wouldn't be paired together for the next two Starters Level Pairs Relay classes. The two women hoped that by the time they could be partnered together for a Relay at the Advanced Level, Michael and Topaz would be more seasoned competitors and familiar with the behavior protocol during the baton-passing sequence. The dogs and people congratulated each other on their good performances. Michael and Topaz placed first in Starters Pairs Relay for their height category as had Kissy and Kawdje. Kissy won the Standard Agility

Class and Kawdje came second. The Rat Terrier, Zippy, had probably performed that class faster than Kawdje but had accrued five faults and that put him in third place. Michael won the Standard Agility Class in his 26-inch height category. Topaz placed a very close second. Kawdje won the Starters Jumpers Class for the 12-inch jump height category and Kissy placed third. Topaz placed second in Jumpers for the 26-inch category and Michael came third. These were excellent performances for beginners!

As they discussed tomorrow's Steeplechase Round 1, the pets lapped water thirstily and then, without being coaxed to, lay down in their kennels for a short rest.

The friends decided that if schedules permitted, they would watch some of the Grand Prix Semifinals being held tomorrow. Like the Steeplechase, it was a non-titling event. It, too, was run under Masters rules and open to all competitors regardless of titling. The course setup would be equivalent to the Standard Agility class. Winners would not receive any money as they would in the Steeplechase. They had decided when registering the pets in the Northeastern Regional Championships that nothing would be gained by also entering them in the Grand Prix.

Performing the Steeplechase would give them some idea of the Dog Agility caliber of their pets and their astuteness as handlers with the incentive of possibly winning money, plus exposure to seasoned agility teams. The Grand Prix would offer the same experience and exposure without the possibility of winning money. They had decided to wait for another Dog Agility Tournament before entering the Grand Prix.

As they pushed themselves to a standing position and folded up their portable chairs, Evan said, "I feel creaky. Kissy will have to pull me through tomorrow's classes."

CHAPTER EIGHTEEN

It was sunny but slightly cool when Pat and Ed, Sarah and Michael arrived early Saturday morning and set up a table beside their tent to display the PPAL brochures and questionnaires. Jeanette, Cole, Jenny and Topaz arrived about five minutes later with brochures and a cooler filled with food. After a discreetly sized sign about pet-friendly air travel had been set up with brochures and questionnaires placed in front of it, Essie and Evan arrived carrying Kissy and Kawdje. Joy accompanied them carrying a cooler filled with food and beverages. Gordon followed the group with folding chairs hanging from his shoulders, elbows and hands. Joy's husband, Sam, had weekend games that prevented him from attending.

Joy watched her parents perform with Kissy and Kawdje. She was amazed by Kissy's performance in the Jumpers class. Her dad had said that Kissy didn't like jumping but, as best as she could tell, Kissy seemed to fly over the hurdles effortlessly. She noted that Kissy jumped forward and barely cleared the hurdles whereas Kawdje jumped upward and left airspace between his body and the top pole.

Joy strolled back to their tent and suggested to Pat and Ed that they take a break if they wanted. They acted on the offer and hustled toward the ring where the 26-inch category of the Starters Jumpers class would soon take place. Essie and Evan followed Joy to their tent. They wanted Kissy and Kawdje to have some water and a treat.

Several groups of people stopped to read the brochures and fill out questionnaires, which kept Essie, Evan and Joy busy for the next few minutes.

Pat, Ed, Sarah, Gordon, Jeanette, Cole, Jenny, Michael and Topaz ambled toward the tent. They all had broad grins on their faces, including Michael and Topaz.

"We done good!" announced Gordon.

"We don't know how we placed in the Jumpers Class but Michael and Topaz didn't accrue any faults and they were well within the Standard Course Time," added Sarah.

"We were, too," said Essie.

After Michael and Topaz had been given their treats, Jeanette asked, "Pat, Joy and Ed, would you mind staying with our pets for a few minutes while we check the Point Sheet for the Jumpers Class?"

"Sure thing," replied Ed.

To everyone's surprise, Kissy had posted the fastest time in the 12-inch category Jumpers Class. Kawdje placed second. Topaz placed first in the 26-inch height category and Michael came second.

Essie said, "Kawdje isn't revved up today. Kissy is always ready to compete with all her heart."

Sarah added, "I think Michael has the same attitude. He was coasting but I'm not sure he could have been faster than Topaz. She has wonderful jumping ability."

Evan announced, "It's almost time for Round 1 of the Steeplechase. If we do well, we may be eligible to compete in Round 2 on Sunday. A Steeplechase consists mostly of jumps plus an A-Frame and Weave Poles. We'll have a choice of using the A-Frame and Weave Poles once each or using one of those obstacles twice and not using the other. It will have a fast course time because it will be run under Master's rules. Remember, it's a pre-determined course, so we'll have to take the jumps in the order they're laid out. This is not a class where strategy counts. The team with the fastest course time and the fewest faults wins. Competitors who place in the top four or five spots win money."

Sarah said, "Too bad our pets don't know that. Maybe they'd run faster if they knew."

"Maybe not," said Jeanette. "They already lead happy lives. More money wouldn't buy them anything they don't already have. We'll be competing against more experienced teams since it's open to all dogs regardless of titling. Let's be sure not to impart any nervousness we may feel to the pets."

"Are you nervous?" asked Cole as he gave his wife an encouraging hug.

"Just a little," responded Jeanette. "A Steeplechase feels like big time compared to the Starters Classes. I don't mean to disparage the Starters

Classes. It's just that I felt that all of us at the Starters Level were on the same playing field."

"I feel a bit uptight myself," admitted Sarah.

"Me, too," added Essie.

The all looked at Evan. "I'm feeling secure. I'm teamed with Kissy the Comet."

"I'm going to vomit," retorted Essie.

"I don't blame you," said Evan with a grin. "You're teamed with Kawdje the Stodgy."

"Well, I'm with Topaz who's a real live gem," bragged Jeanette.

"I have you all topped because my partner is the namesake of Archangel Michael," said Sarah as she caressed Michael's bright orange left ear.

"I don't believe what I'm hearing," murmured Joy to Pat and Ed.

"Children," admonished Pat. "It's time you take a pre-performance walk-through of the course. Joy, Ed and I will stay with pets while you do that. Gordon, Cole and Jenny, are you going with the children or staying here with the adults?"

Cole replied, "I'll set up our folding chairs at ringside. Jenny can help me."

Gordon's cell phone rang and he excused himself to take the call as Sarah, followed by Jeanette, Essie and Evan, walked toward the Steeplechase ring.

Later, as they gathered to watch the start of the Steeplechase, Gordon hugged Sarah and whispered in her ear. "Our real estate agent called. Our offer has been accepted and the sellers requested to move up the settlement date to August 15th."

Sarah wrapped her arms around Gordon's waist and they kissed. Michael stood up on his hind legs to be included in the lovings. As they whispered to him, he understood the word home and sensed they were not referring to the house where he and Sarah lived. He knew something wonderful and important had happened. The happy, uplifting energy that flowed between Sarah and Gordon enveloped him, too.

Later, when Michael watched Kawdje run the Steeplechase course, he thought he was fast and climbed the A-Frame like a big, strong dog. Michael knew Kawdje was very focused on his performance and running as fast as he could. He wanted to bark encouragement, but Sarah's hand was resting alongside his muzzle and he knew she wanted him to remain quiet. When Kawdje and his mom left the ring, Michael saw a small, short-haired dog swagger into the ring with great self-assurance. The dog had an amazing performance and Michael judged it might have been faster than Kawdje's.

Next, Kissy daintily pranced into the ring. Michael could tell she was excited and that it took all her control to remain still while waiting for the sound of the start whistle. Even though she was petite, she ran through the course setup with incredible swiftness. He watched with satisfaction as she cleared the Spread Hurdle and then sped toward the A-Frame. When she was descending that obstacle, she jumped off early before touching the last contact point. In her haste to finish, she had not watched her dad pointing to the last portion of the descending plank just before it touched the ground. Michael didn't know why this part had to be walked upon. He just knew that Sarah always made him go to the very bottom of the A-Frame before he left that obstacle and that whenever he began to climb the A-Frame, she always made him touch that first step instead of allowing him to leap halfway up the ascending plank. He watched Kissy clear several more hurdles and then zip through the Weave Poles and exit the ring.

Later, when he and Sarah, Topaz and Jeanette waited near the entrance gate for their turn to perform, Michael spied a dog who looked like a huge wad of white, curly hair with legs. He asked the "hair-on-legs" his name and heard him say, "Mop." Michael and Topaz heard Sarah and Jeanette chatting with Mop's mom, who informed them that his name was Champion Mama's Swish N' Mop of Keystone's Corner, but his nickname was Mop and he was a Komondor. Michael asked Mop how he managed to run and jump with all that hair flopping around and weighing him down.

"It isn't easy, but I enjoy this type of event more than the shows where I stand around a lot and walk in front of a judge. My mom and I just began to attend Dog Agility shows. Sometimes my dad comes, too, but he doesn't perform in the ring with me. I can't have my hair clipped because they plan to enter me in the Westminster Dog Show. I was in that dog show last year and placed second in my breed."

Mop then asked Michael, "Have you ever been in that other kind of dog event where you have to look the perfect example of your breed?"

"Um, no. My mom isn't interested in any kind of dog show other than Dog Agility."

"What is your breed and name?" Mop asked Michael.

"My name is Michael Archangelo."

Topaz quickly said, "Hello, Mop. My name is Topaz and I'm a German Shorthaired Pointer."

"Oh, you like to hunt," said Mop.

"No, Mop. I don't like to hunt. I'm a great disappointment to my dad because I won't chase or hunt other creatures. On the plus side, my mom doesn't care and loves me anyway. We have a special bond with one another. I can usually sense what she's thinking or feeling."

Mop observed, "You probably channeled that hunting instinct into an intuitive bond with your mom."

Topaz was surprised at his perception.

"I never thought of that, Mop. Thank you for your very insightful observation."

Mop turned to Michael and said, "I don't believe you told me your breed."

Michael thought quickly and said, "I'm a Callé Dog from San Miguel de Allende in Mexico."

Topaz hid a smile because she knew that "Callé" meant "street" in Michael's native language. Michael had just told Mop he was a street dog.

Mop said, "That sounds like a rare breed."

Michael replied, "Not in San Miguel, it isn't."

It was Topaz's turn to enter the ring and as she paced toward the entrance gate, she wished Michael and Mop good luck.

"Swift course, Topaz," said Mop.

"Hear! Hear!" added Michael.

Topaz thought Mop was a really nice fellow. "It's a pity he has all that heavy hair to contend with while running a course setup," she mused.

Topaz then put everything out of her mind and attuned to her mom. She heard her mom say "Fast," and knew she was being asked to perform as swiftly as she could manage. She watched her mom signal her toward the first hurdle and Topaz concentrated on the course before her.

While Mop and Michael waited their turns, Mop inquired why Michael's ears were two different colors. "I don't mean to be rude, and if you'd rather not tell me, Michael, just say so and I won't be offended."

Michael explained, "My mom sprays paint on my left ear and her left hand before every practice. Somehow that helps her know which direction to tell me to turn or run toward."

Mop's mom walked up to him and removed his leash and collar.

As they paced toward the entrance gate, Michael barked, "Jump high and touch the sky!" to Mop.

Michael watched Mop perform. His abundant fur was flopping, swinging and swishing with every movement he made. Michael hoped it wouldn't snag on any obstacles.

Sarah also watched Mop's performance. She thought he looked like a huge, unruly wig having an emphatic conversation with itself.

Michael was still in an elated and lighthearted frame of mind when he began his performance. Sarah and Gordon's whisperings about home was still on his mind. He hoped the three of them would be living together soon. He heard Sarah quietly say his name, and he set his mind on the course.

He kept alternating his sight from Sarah to the obstacle he was to run to next. It seemed so effortless. Even the Weave Poles seemed slippery and he had never zigged and zagged so quickly between them. After he and Sarah exited the ring, they ran toward Gordon and all three embraced.

After all performance times had been posted for their class height, Michael had won Round 1 of the Steeplechase. Topaz had come third and Mop had placed within the top 30% so he, too, was eligible to perform in Round 2 of the Steeplechase on Sunday. A Miniature Pinscher called Olé had won in the 12-inch category. He was the little dog that Michael had seen swagger into the ring. Kawdje had placed second and Kissy made it into the top 30%, in spite of her 5-point penalty for having missed a contact point.

Over lunch, the friends exulted over their good showing in the Steeplechase. Evan discussed, with Jenny, Kissy's tendency to make independent decisions while performing because Jenny was going to be a Junior Handler with Kissy as her partner. Jenny summed up Kissy's problem by telling her Uncle Evan that he wasn't urging Kissy to perform even faster than she already was.

"She thinks that you're satisfied with her performance because you don't think she's capable of being better than she already is. She's decided you don't care how she performs. You always hug and praise her. When we're practicing again on Aunt Sarah's lawn, you ought to make her touch those contact points over and over again. Whenever she tries to anticipate you, let her know that she's wrong. She's aggressive and if she thinks you aren't strong and fast enough to be the leader, then she'll be the leader."

The others stopped their conversations to listen to Jenny and they marveled at her insight.

Evan said, "You may be right! I think you'll be a topnotch Junior Handler, Jenny. I can hardly wait to watch you work with Kissy."

Their afternoon activities began with the Standard Agility Class. This time Topaz and Michael's height class was slated to be first to perform. Michael was still in a lighthearted, euphoric state when he and Sarah entered the ring. The thought that Gordon might soon be living with Sarah and him kept circling round and round in his mind. He felt especially close to Sarah. It was as though they were both inside a big balloon of love. He concentrated more on the bond between them than the obstacles and it made their performance easier for Sarah.

Because he was so attentive to her, Sarah found it easier to remember her left from her right, and Michael's left from his right but she was still glad to have her orange hand and Michael's orange ear for reference. They finished well within the SCT and didn't accrue faults.

Gordon was waiting near the exit. He hugged Sarah, then hunkered down and laid his cheek next to Michael's muzzle.

"Did you notice how well Michael behaved in the ring? He was very attentive to me. I believe we're developing that special bond that Jeanette and Topaz have."

Gordon said, "I think he's different since we discussed having our offer accepted on the house we're buying. Do you think he understands that we'll all be living together soon?"

Sarah said thoughtfully, "He understands the word 'home.' I also know that he doesn't want you to leave us when you drive back to Essie and Evan's. I suspect he knows something is up."

When they checked the Point Sheet, Sarah did a little jig after she saw that Michael placed first. Topaz was third.

Evan followed Jenny's advice and was more emphatic when directing Kissy to touch contact zones and to follow his direction. She seemed more subdued than usual. In spite of her diminished ebullience, she placed first in the Standard Agility Class. Kawdje was second.

The Starters Pairs Relay was the last event of the afternoon. Michael,

Topaz, Kissy and Kawdje had all been entered into the registration pool with others who needed a relay partner. Kawdje was paired with Zippy, the Rat Terrier, and Kissy was partnered with a Boston Bull Terrier called Sam. Topaz and a large Border Collie, whose name was Brew, were teamed together. Michael, and a mixed breed bitch who looked like a combination of Doberman and Shepherd and whose name was Hattie, were paired together.

Essie and Evan conferred briefly with the other handler each would be paired with in order to decide upon a method for passing the baton.

Zippy performed first and Kawdje was impressed with the energy, speed and enthusiasm he displayed. It spurred him on to his best performance ever because he wanted to outperform Zippy.

Kissy ran the course before her partner did. She gave it all she had while being careful to watch and wait for her dad's direction. She had a fast and fault-free performance, but Sam was another story. He was nervous and very unsure of himself.

Watching Kissy's fast and flawless performance intimidated him. He gave a faltering performance. He ran past a hurdle and had to be directed back to it. He displaced the top pole on one of the hurdles. Evan's positive mood vanished as he watched Sam's performance. He hoped Kissy's performance had been good enough to pull the pair up to a qualifying score.

Michael was extraordinary and Hattie's handler, a woman from Connecticut, praised his performance effusively. She generously said that if they won the Pairs Relay, it would be due to Sarah and Michael's performance. Sarah responded by saying that Hattie and her handler were a great team and that it had been a pleasure to be paired with them.

Topaz and Jeanette were outstanding, but Brew and his handler were a stodgy pair. Jeanette pressed her lips together and reminded herself that they were at the Starters Level and she shouldn't be critical. Brew appeared to pause in front of each obstacle as though he were trying to remember how he was supposed to use it. This behavior was a mirror image of his handler, a young man, who approached the setup with a puzzled expression as if he was wondering where he was, how he got there and what he should do next. Jeanette prayed that Brew and Horace would manage to finish within the SCT. She tried to remember what the fault limits were for the Starters Level. She knew more faults were allowed than at the Advanced and Masters Levels before being eliminated. Brew and Horace were 30 seconds over the SCT. They hadn't accrued any other faults. Jeanette hoped that, in spite of the time limit fault, she and Topaz, Horace and Brew would have a qualifying performance.

Afterward, Jeanette asked Sarah to check Topaz and Brew's performance rating on the Point Sheet. "I don't have the courage to look and see for myself."

Sarah walked toward her a couple of minutes later and hugged her. "You and Topaz, Horace and Brew had a qualifying score. I won't tell you how far down on the placement list you are because all that matters is that your Pairs Relay was a qualifying performance."

"How did you and Michael and your partners do?" she asked Sarah.

"We placed first. Hattie had a wonderful performance."

Jeanette congratulated Sarah and said, "I watched Hattie and she did have a really good performance, but Michael was phenomenal. He ran the course as though he had been shot out of a cannon. He floated over the hurdles. I think he gave his best performance ever. He keeps getting better and better, and you seem to have conquered your left/right dilemma. I thought you and Michael demonstrated a special connection in the Pairs Relay. You're both improving at a phenomenal rate. I'm predicting that you'll be a part of Team USA at the next International Federation of Cynological Sports."

Sarah blushed at the praise, but shuddered at the thought of competing internationally.

As they packed to leave, Cole announced that a lot of their pamphlets had been taken but that they still had brochures available for tomorrow.

"Everybody I spoke to said they would pay as much for the safe, comfortable air travel conditions that we espouse for pets as they would for themselves. Some even said they would be willing to pay twice as much to have their pet inside the cabin as they would for their own seat."

Evan suggested that, because tomorrow's schedule was light, it would benefit them to watch some Masters Classes and see what they would have to contend with at more advanced levels because those courses would be trickier to negotiate than the Starters Level setups.

After the chitchat died down, Gordon and Sarah announced that their bid on the home they had looked at had been accepted. They were hugged and congratulated.

Pat said, "Let's all eat out and celebrate!"

Jenny replied, "Then, we couldn't include the dogs. Aunt Jeanette and Uncle Cole, couldn't we have everyone over to our place so the pets could be with us? We could order pizza to be delivered."

Jeanette hugged her and Cole announced, "Great idea! Pizza's on us. Let's all caravan to our place."

It was a boisterous, happy group who left the event grounds.

CHAPTER NINETEEN

Sunday morning, while everyone unpacked coolers and prepared for another competitive day on the event grounds, Gordon told Sarah that he had received a bid on his town home with an August 29th settlement date requested. They kissed and hugged and Michael nudged them, demanding to be included in the lovings.

"Gordon, I'll phone our realtor right now and tell her to list my home for sale immediately. I hope prospective buyers won't be turned off by the dog agility equipment that's spread all over the lawn."

Pat had accompanied her mother and Michael on the drive to the tournament grounds because Ed had to work on legal briefs. "You two are like a pair of teenagers," she complained.

Her mom replied. "Come and join us for a four-way hug."

"Humpf!" was all Pat said, but she walked toward them and wedged between Michael and her mom.

Joy and Pat stayed with the brochures while the others watched some Advanced and Masters Levels performances. The pets rested in their kennels.

As Sarah watched a Masters Level performance by a Border Collie in the 22-inch jump height category, she turned to Gordon. "The Masters course setup looks complicated compared to the Starters Level. I'm not sure I'll ever be able to handle Michael on a tricky course that has a fast Standard Course Time while trying to keep up with Michael's pace, plus remember my left from right and his left from right. Some people have asked me why Michael's left ear is colored orange. Most thought it had been injured. You should see the odd looks they give me when they see my orange hand."

"You will both be great," Gordon said encouragingly.

Starters Gamblers began with the 26-inch height category.

Michael remained euphoric because he kept hearing Sarah and

Gordon speak the word "home." He felt sure that the three of them would live together soon. He loved and trusted Gordon as much as he loved and trusted Sarah. He thought, "If the three of us lived together, it would be even would be even more fantastic than hanging my head out an open car window during a fast ride."

Michael performed superbly in Gamblers, in part because he felt happy and lighthearted. So did Topaz, who was ecstatic that her dad was present and showed affection and approval toward her. Topaz and Jeanette won Gamblers. Michael and Sarah were a close second.

Cole hugged his wife and then knelt down and put his arms around Topaz's neck. "You may be worthless as a hunting dog, but you're worth gold as an Agility Dog."

Meanwhile, Kissy's performance was outstanding but so were Kawdje's and Zippy's. The three tied for point accumulation. Kissy won. Her course time was a half second faster than Kawdje's. Kawdje placed second and Zippy ranked third.

After drinks and snacks, the pets snoozed in their kennels. Soon it was time for Round 2 of the Steeplechase. The 26-inch jump height category was slated first on the schedule, followed by the 22-inch, 16-inch and 12-inch categories.

Essie and Evan urged Pat to watch her mom perform in the Steeplechase and encouraged Joy to accompany her while they stayed with the PPAL brochures. When everyone returned, Sarah had to drink almost a full bottle of water before she could speak. Essie busied herself pouring water in bowls for Topaz and Michael to lap.

"Okay. Don't keep Essie and me in suspense. Who won and how did Michael and Topaz place?"

Jenny blurted out, "Michael won. He was so fast; it was awesome. He beat a sharp-looking um, oh, what was that dog, Uncle Cole?"

"A Rhodesian Ridgeback," he replied.

"Yeah. He was as big as Michael and came second. Topaz placed third," Jenny said as she stroked Topaz, who was standing close beside her.

Evan inquired about the number of dogs who competed in Michael and Topaz's height category and Gordon said he thought that there had been about thirty.

Soon it was time for Essie and Kawdje, and Evan and Kissy to perform in the Steeplechase. Pat offered to remain with the brochures and dog-sit Michael and Topaz, who were taking well-earned naps in their kennels, and let everyone else watch ringside. Sarah promised to return as soon as Kissy and Kawdje finished performing.

While Kissy and Kawdje waited to perform, Olé, a Miniature Pinscher, swaggered up to them with head held high.

"I'm Olé and I always win this Steeplechase," he announced.

"Why are you called Olé?" inquired Kissy.

"Because my mom and dad say that I'm worth cheering about."

"Maybe you didn't hear them correctly. Maybe they said you were something worth sneering about," retorted Kissy.

Other dogs within earshot snickered.

Olé looked down his nose at Kissy, which hard to do because they were both about the same size. He yipped at her telling her she was a little bitch.

Kissy calmly stated that officially, she definitely was. Once again, all dogs close enough to hear the exchange snickered.

Kawdje warned Olé that he and Kissy were partners and he wouldn't allow him to speak disparagingly to her.

"Eat my dust," Olé said as he turned his back on them.

"What a creep he is," a little Japanese Chin declared. "I've been paired with him in a Relay and he is fast, but because we didn't have the fastest time, he blamed it on me."

"What is your name?" inquired Kissy

"I'm Chrysee."

"It rhymes with mine, which is Kissy."

"Kissy, wouldn't it be fun if we ran in a Pairs Relay together? Kissy and Chrysee—sounds good together, doesn't it?

Essie and Evan noticed Kissy and Kawdje being friendly with the little black and white Japanese Chin and they introduced themselves to her handler. They found out that Chrysee wasn't qualified to be a show dog because her nose leather was a deep flesh color, which was considered to be a fault.

"Why is that a fault?" asked Evan.

The woman, who had introduced herself as Nancy Feldman, replied that black and white Japanese Chin must have black nose leather, whereas a lemon or red-marked Chin must have red or deep flesh-colored nose leather.

"In spite of her improper nose color, I think she's beautiful," Essie said. "Perhaps we could team our pets together for a Pairs Relay. We're still at the Starters Level but we hope to begin working toward Advanced Agility Dog titling very soon."

"Chrysee will achieve her Advanced Agility title this weekend; however, your pets may catch up to her level before the summer is over because my husband, Chrysee and I are going to spend the summer at our daughter's cottage in Ontario, Canada, and we won't be competing. Let's exchange contact information."

Olé and his dad entered the ring. Kissy begged her dad to lift her up, so Evan perched her on his shoulder and Essie held Kawdje in her arms. Nancy Feldman felt Chrysee patting her leg so she obliged by lifting up Chrysee so that she, too, could see the action in the ring.

All three pets were dismayed to see that Olé was swift and assured and was performing the course with ease. When his performance was almost over and he was about to use the Weave Poles, he started with the second pole instead of the first and had to begin over, thus accumulating faults plus adding unwanted time.

Kissy barked in delight.

Chrysee murmured, "It couldn't have happened to a more deserving dog."

Kawdje kept his counsel but his eyes sparkled with happiness.

Chrysee and her mom entered the ring next. Kissy and Kawdje were still held in their parents' arms so they watched her perform. It was obvious that she was quick and jumped well, clearing all hurdles. She didn't have any problems as best as they could tell.

Evan carried Kissy to the entrance gate and set her down before they entered the ring. She was excited but not nervous and felt more confident since she had learned how to jump the Spread Hurdle. She still didn't enjoy having to jump so many hurdles during a class, and much preferred the obstacle variety of the Standard Agility Class, but she was feeling strong. She cleared all hurdles. The Weave Poles were her favorite and, as always, she moved through them with a fast snake-like rhythm. Her dad picked her up and carried her in his arms after they exited the ring.

He walked until they had a good vantage point for viewing Essie and

Kawdje perform. Kawdje had a great performance and, although he could never weave as fast as Kissy through the Poles, he didn't miss any. He had natural jumping ability and the Steeplechase course favored that. Evan put Kissy down and, as they walked toward the exit gate to greet Essie and Kawdje, they met Olé and his dad.

Kissy sweetly said as they were passing one another, "Olé, Olé, you missed a polé (which she pronounced as pōlāy).

Evan was astonished when the Miniature Pinscher, who he recognized as having performed a little while ago, turned and snarled at Kissy for no reason. He picked her up and held her in his arms protectively. She snuggled against her dad's shoulder. She could hardly wait to tell Kawdje how she got even with Olé.

When Essie and Evan arrived at their tent Jeanette said, "Congratulations on two fine performances. We watched the 12-inch category of the Steeplechase until Kawdje was finished and then we all came back here to prepare lunch. What are the final results in your category?"

Essie's pride was obvious as she squealed, "Kawdje is Numero Uno! He won!"

Kawdje was startled when everyone crowded around him. He was stroked and passed from one person to another. He decided he must have won the event that had all those wonderful jumps.

Joy asked tentatively "How did Kissy place? I thought she gave a great performance."

Evan lifted Kissy up over his head and announced, "Kissy was Numero Dos. The comet cutie placed second in spite of not being a natural jumper. She's smart and she's developed a method for jumping all kinds of hurdles."

Kissy basked in the attention showered upon her. She knew she, too, had done well. All the hard work and effort it had taken to clear all those jumps was worth the attention she was now receiving.

Hot meatloaf and lima beams were served to pets and people. Kawdje licked his chops and dug in because lima beans were one of his favorite foods. The pets refused fruit salad but ate gingersnaps or oatmeal cookies for dessert.

The Starters Level Snooker Class began about 1 p.m. Essie, Evan, Sarah and Jeanette did a pre-performance walkthrough. The Weave Poles had been given the highest point value of seven. Essie and Jeanette were well aware that Kawdje and Topaz were not spectacularly fast on the Weave Poles, but the See-Saw had been given a point value of six and was placed further away so using it after each "Red" obstacle would be more time-consuming as well as racking up less than the maximum points in the opening period. They knew that the team with the most points accumulated won. Time was the tiebreaker.

Kissy was superb in the opening sequence. Weave poles were her specialty and using them after each of the three red jumps in the opening period lifted her spirits and got her off to an incredibly swift start. She loved the closing Snooker sequence because of the variety of obstacles and, to her supreme joy, not one of them was a hurdle. In spite of her euphoria, she disciplined herself to keep her dad in her sight at all times and let him lead.

Kawdje's performance was fault-free and reliable but not stellar as Kissy's had been. Weave poles were his least favorite obstacle and having to plod through them four times during one class was almost more than he could stand.

When he and his mom exited the ring, he saw that his dad and Kissy were waiting to greet them.

Evan said to Essie, "Well, Kissy the Comet lived up to her nickname in Snooker and so did Kawdje the Stodgy."

Essie glowered at him. "His nickname is Kawdje the Careful and I'd like to remind you that slow, but steady, wins the race."

Michael and Topaz each had fault-free and well-executed performances. Michael used all the obstacles with ease and because he was still on an emotional high, his performance seemed effortless. Weave poles were still Topaz's least favorite obstacle but she had developed a rhythmic method for using them and now felt confident. Michael won Starters Snooker in his height category. Topaz placed second. Kissy the Comet won Snookers in the 12-inch jump height category. Kawdje the Stodgy was third.

Everybody took a break before packing up. Pet bowls were filled with water. Sarah flipped gingersnaps into the air, which Michael deftly caught and hardly bothered to crunch before swallowing. Jenny hand fed Kissy pieces of gingersnaps. Essie had brought a large enough supply of her homemade oatmeal cookies to share with Topaz who was as fond of them as Kawdje was. Jeanette crumbled some into Topaz's food bowl and they disappeared in two licks. Essie painstakingly fed Kawdje one small piece at a time. He crunched up each one thoroughly before swallowing.

Everyone agreed that the Northeastern Regional Championships had been a great event. The pets had made a qualifying score in every class they had entered and each had won money for their placements in the Steeplechase.

Joy declared, "None of you should ever feel intimidated by competing against more experienced teams. Handler and dog competence was admirably demonstrated in the sport of Dog Agility by all of you."

Pat poured iced tea and soft drinks into disposable cups and passed them around.

"Let's toast the agility heroes," she suggested.

"To our fantastic Agility Teams," said Gordon.

"Chug-a-lug," Jenny said.

Everyone grinned at her.

"Where did you hear that expression?" asked her Uncle Cole.

Jenny shrugged, "From some of the kids at school."

Evan said, "The money we won for placing well in the Steeplechase will offset what we've spent on the dog agility equipment that's flattening the grass on Sarah's property."

"Speaking of my property," Sarah said, "my home goes up for sale tomorrow. I would prefer to attend local events because I'll be busy packing and trying to keep my home in show condition. Fortunately, the place that Gordon and I will be calling home has plenty of grounds to accommodate our communal agility setup."

Essie said that the next Regional Championship would be held in July in the state of Washington.

"Evan and I don't intend to drive that distance to attend the event. If there was pet-friendly airline service, we would consider flying there, but like the rest of you, we wouldn't house Kissy and Kawdje in cargo except for a dire emergency."

Pat said, "Most PPAL brochures were taken and many people filled out the questionnaires. We'll have to read the responses. Maybe there are ideas we haven't thought of."

Joy said, "Maybe some of them will contain information about possible financial backers."

"We can hope," Jeanette said.

Gordon said, "Back to real estate! My townhouse sold. The settlement date is August 29th. I'm going to fly back to Arizona, arrange to sell or donate my furniture because it isn't worth the cost of transporting here, pack my books, clothes and other personal belongings into my SUV and drive back. For now, I'll leave my helicopter in Arizona. It's safe in the rental hangar where I keep it."

"It'll be great to have you living near me, little brother," Evan said.

"Hey, old man. I've got a few inches on you," said Gordon, who was taller than his older brother.

As the others chatted, Gordon quietly said to Sarah, "I'm going to suggest something that I want you to think about before saying 'no' immediately. Let's get married before the August 15th settlement date on our Bucks County home and be together during the drive out west for the settlement on my townhouse. Afterward, we could drive to the Southwestern Regional Championships in California and then attend the South Central Regionals in Texas on the way back to PA. It would be good for you and Michael to experience competing in those two really huge Dog Agility events. We could postpone our honeymoon until just before or after the World Cynosport Games that are held in Arizona in November and then go to a warm, sunny island or wherever you want."

Sarah immediately said, "Gordon, I . . ."

He interrupted, "Don't say no without giving my suggestion some thought."

She remained silent for a few moments, then smiled and said, "Yes."

He stared at her with an expression of disbelief for a few seconds, then whooped and stood up. He pulled her to her feet, wrapped his arms around her waist, lifted her up off her feet and swung her round and round.

Pat stopped packing and looked at them. "You're like a pair of teenagers. I feel like the mommy, and it's a very unsettling feeling."

Cole inquired, "What's up? Anything you want to share?"

"We're going to get married before the August 15th settlement on the home that we're buying. We'll drive to Arizona for the settlement on my townhouse and attend the Regional Agility Championships in California and Texas. We'll have a real honeymoon somewhere romantic just before or after the World Cynosport Games," Gordon said.

Sarah said to Jeanette, "Don't feel obligated to have our wedding at your home. Events are fast-forwarding at warp speed and there isn't enough time to prepare for the lovely ceremony that you're planning."

"Of course there's plenty of time, Sarah. We have almost six weeks. No problem."

After hugs and congratulations, they finished packing equipment and dismantling the tent and decided, by common consent, to forego the morning practice sessions at Sarah's during the coming week.

CHAPTER TWENTY

Topaz abruptly awakened before sunrise. She heard something that wasn't any of the familiar sounds made by deer and varmints, as Michael referred to outdoor animals. She growled, but her parents didn't awaken. She groggily climbed out of her bed and padded into the hallway and down the stairs. She heard the unfamiliar sound again and growled as she paced toward the back hallway door. She heard Jenny quietly descending the stairs.

"Do you want to go out, Topaz?" she whispered.

Topaz lifted a front paw and placed it on the door. Jenny raised her hand to turn off the house alarm and discovered that her aunt and uncle had neglected to activate it before retiring to bed the previous evening. She opened the door to let Topaz outside and was surprised to see that Uncle Cole had not closed and locked the garage door after he had come home late yesterday evening. She decided to manually pull down the garage door rather than walk through the house all the way to the door that connected the garage to the house via the laundry room, in order to press the button that automatically opened and closed the garage door. She walked outside toward the open garage door, stretched up as high as she could to reach the door handle and froze in shock when she saw a strange man in Uncle Cole's fabulous Jaguar. He swiftly got out of the car while commanding her, in a low voice, not to scream or even speak. Jenny turned and ran as fast as she could toward the back hallway door.

The man tackled her from behind and she was thrown to the ground, landing face down. The breath was knocked out of her. She could only gasp and whimper. She felt the man's knee on the back of her waist pressing her into the hard asphalt driveway. He grabbed a handful of her hair and her head was pulled backward until she thought her neck would snap. Her face slammed onto the driveway. The unbelievably hard, cracking pain that jolted through her head was like nothing she had ever experienced before. She felt nauseated. She couldn't even feel the weight of the man's knee any more.

Topaz looked at the stranger and confusion paralyzed her. She watched as he threw Jenny to the ground. Topaz had never bitten, nor even so much as snarled at, a person before. She had never seen any person hurt another and she didn't know what she should do. Maybe she should "sic" the strange man. When she saw him slam Jenny's face onto the driveway and heard Jenny give a feeble cry of pain, she became enraged.

Jenny was her pal and she recognized that Jenny was still, well, sort of like a puppy, and needed to be protected and looked after. Topaz ran snarling toward them and jumped on the man. She bit the back of his neck and began pulling him off Jenny. He yelled and tried to twist so that he could get his hands on her. Topaz's grip on his neck loosened but she chomped onto the back of his collar and held on with the tenacity of a bulldog. Suddenly, she was only holding onto a jacket. The stranger had pulled open his jacket, ripping off buttons in his haste to shed himself of it.

He turned to face Topaz and, as he was pulling a gun out of his waistband, she lunged at him and knocked him flat on his back. The back of his head smacked the pavement and he lost his grip on the gun. As he rolled onto his side and attempted to get up, Topaz positioned herself behind him and held his neck between her jaws. She didn't know where this instinct came from. She just knew that she had to get a grip on his throat to defeat him. She heard him yelling and whenever he tried to twist and turn, or pound his fists on her head and pull on her collar or ears, she responded by clamping her jaws harder on his neck.

Suddenly, the outside lights were shining in her eyes and her mom and dad were beside her. Her dad coaxed her to release her grip on the man however; she remained within biting distance of his neck. Her mom was holding Jenny, who was now sitting up. Whenever the stranger attempted to sit up, Topaz growled as menacingly and authoritatively as she could. He remained lying down.

A car with flashing lights appeared. Two policemen got out and ran toward the group. Her mom pulled her away from the stranger and Topaz watched him being shackled, pulled upright and put into the police car. The police spoke to her mom and dad and Jenny. Then, they spoke to her as they stroked her head and ran their hands over her long ears. She knew they were praising her for rescuing Jenny.

Topaz walked over to Jenny and licked her face where she smelled blood. Jenny wrapped her arms around her neck and said, "You saved my life, Topaz. You are the best friend anyone could ever have. I will always love you."

Topaz felt her dad stroking her back and talking to her. "Topaz, my girl, you have your priorities straight. You go after harmful creatures like that sleazy, dangerous car thief and leave deer and groundhogs alone because they don't threaten us with bodily harm. It was a fortunate day for all of us when you came into our lives. I'm proud of you. I can't wait to tell everyone about the brave, smart pet that I share my home with."

Topaz lifted her head and leaned back against her dad, who put his arms around her and stroked her throat and chest.

"You're my special girl and I love you," he whispered into her long, silky ear.

Something inside her chest seemed to expand and move outward to meet the first rays of sunlight that beamed through the branches of the tall trees and warmed them all.

Later that morning, Jeanette phoned Sarah, then Essie and Evan and described the incident to them. Jenny had been taken to the hospital for a cat scan of her head to make certain she hadn't sustained a skull fracture or suffered subdural bleeding. Thankfully, everything was normal. They later learned that the car thief had been responsible for the rash of stolen cars in their area.

That afternoon, the police phoned and inquired if Topaz had an up-to-date rabies vaccine because she had punctured the thief's skin on his neck. Cole had taken that call and reassured the police that all of Topaz's vaccines were current, which was good because he and his wife were concerned for her health since she may have been contaminated by the car thief's blood.

Michael missed the frequent morning practices and the company of his friends, especially Topaz. He was happy that Gordon was at his home every day but he and Sarah were too busy packing things in boxes and carrying them to the garage to take walks with him. Several times, strangers came into his home and walked through every room. Sarah made him stay in the kitchen with her, but he could hear them and knew they had gone through the whole house.

One morning his friends drove up to his home and they were back in the Agility practice routine. He had a pow-wow beside the water bucket with Topaz, Kissy and Kawdje. Topaz described her episode with the nasty stranger who had hurt Jenny. Michael was very impressed when Topaz described the throat–hold she had subdued him with. He could tell that Kissy and Kawdje were also.

"My dad is proud of me now," Topaz said. "He doesn't seem to care anymore that I don't chase deer."

Michael told the others about the change of routine in his home and that Gordon and Sarah were happy about something and they said the word "home" a lot.

"I sensed that they were talking about living together in a home other than this one."

They other three looked stricken.

Topaz asked in a quavering voice, "Does that mean we might not see you again?"

"I don't think so. I had a fabuloso car ride to the place they looked at and the one that I think they're referring to when they say 'home'. It isn't very far away from here."

The others looked relieved.

Jeanette told her friends that Cole was planning to take the long July 4th weekend off and the following one, too, so that they could drive to New York State and enter Topaz in a couple of Dog Agility events. Evan and Essie said that they also would like to compete in those events.

"I wish I could go," Sarah said with obvious regret. "But I feel as though I'm tied to this place while my home needs to be kept in show condition."

Evan said, "Your home will sell with or without you being here. Why not clean it to your satisfaction and leave whenever you want to attend a Dog Agility event? Your real estate agent can take care of things."

Gordon put an arm around Sarah. "I second that suggestion. I even volunteer to stay here and keep watch over the place if you want to take Michael to that Agility event in New York; otherwise, I'd be happy to tag along."

Sarah gave him a sunny smile and said, "Let's go for it!"

The pets achieved Agility Dog titling during the competition that was held on the July 4th weekend in the Binghamton area of New York.

Topaz was elated that her dad was present for the event. Every time she and her mom exited the ring, her dad and Jenny greeted her with outstretched arms and hugged her. She felt so supported and appreciated that she aced all her classes, placing first in everything she entered. "My life is absolutely perfect," she thought.

It was a terrific weekend for everyone. Michael placed second in all his classes except for the Pairs Relay. Kawdje placed first in Jumpers and second in all other classes with the exception of Pairs Relay where he placed third. Kissy placed second in Jumpers, first in Snooker, Standard Agility and Pairs Relay and third in Gamblers.

As the handlers packed their gear, they decided to celebrate the Fourth of July, which was the next day, at Essie and Evan's. Everyone would bring a potluck dish and they would finish the celebration by watching a local fireworks display.

The week after July 4th was busy for all of them. Sarah couldn't find a wedding dress, at any of the local shops, that was suitable for a mid-forties widow to wear. Joy suggested that she and her mom, Sarah and Pat, Jeanette and Jenny drive to an exclusive dress shop, located in downtown Philly, where she thought that Sarah might find her perfect dress. The owner could make coordinating outfits for Pat and Jenny and the pièce de résistance, after they shopped, could be a roast beef sandwich at Nick's. The idea of a trip to Philly was met with enthusiasm.

When they arrived at the dress shop, Joy's instincts proved to be perfect. Raphaella, the proprietress, pulled a couple of selections off a rack for Sarah. After modeling them, the general consensus of opinion was that the sleeveless peach gown, so pale a shade that it was almost white, was the winner. The material was soft and fluid. The skirt fell close to the body but belled out below the knees and the hemline rippled when Sarah walked.

Raphaella suggested that she could make a modified train of gossamer chiffon that attached, by snaps, to the back of the waist so that it could be removed after the ceremony if desired, as well as a very short, close-fitting slip-on jacket made of the same material.

"It can be worn if your wedding day is unexpectedly cool. When you remove the jacket and train, the gown will be an ankle-length dress suitable for many occasions."

"What about the Maid of Honor and Flower Girl outfits?" Sarah asked.

Raphaella immediately pulled a deep peach colored, ballerina-length dress with a cowl neckline off the same rack. The skirt was similar in style to Sarah's wedding gown and the dress was sleeveless. Pat looked wonderful in it, and only a few alterations were necessary.

Raphaella said that although she did not carry children's clothing, her seamstress could easily make up a suitable dress for Jenny. "I'll take her measurements and perhaps you could bring her back in a couple of weeks for a fitting. I will have finished the alterations and accessories for the other two gowns by then."

While Raphaella rang up the sales, Sarah inquired if she knew of a store where a man's wedding outfit could be bought or rented. Raphaella recommended Carlo's Men's Wear for Special Occasions located several blocks away and wrote down instructions for getting there.

Later, as they sat in Nick's Restaurant tearing ravenously into roast beef sandwiches and with beef juice dripping down their chins and into their plates, Sarah mumbled between bites that this was her favorite sandwich.

"It sure is mine," Jenny managed to say between gulps. "Let's come here again after my fitting in two weeks."

Jeanette asked, "How about if we all come for Jenny's fitting and a trip to Nick's afterward?"

"You bet," said Essie. "I'm going to order several beef sandwiches to go. I'll serve two to Evan for his dinner and one for myself. Kissy and Kawdje might like the roast beef, so perhaps I'll order four to go. I can always scarf down two of these delectable sandwiches, if the pets don't want one."

CHAPTER TWENTY-ONE

The wedding rehearsal was a blast! For starters, the pets were dressed in their wedding outfits. Michael looked patrician in black bowtie and tails. He wore a white dickey in lieu of a shirt and it snapped to the inside of the jacket to hold it in place. When she selected the outfit, Sarah had decided not to torture him with a top hat. He looked bewildered as she dressed him in it with Gordon's assistance but, because he loved them, he tolerated the clothes.

Topaz wore a deep peach colored spandex tube with row upon row of ruffles. It covered her torso between her front and hind legs. A stretch band of peach material, with a silk, peach-colored rose attached, encircled her neck. Everyone thought she looked svelte. Topaz couldn't see herself, but she felt like a dork. She was thankful that, at least, her clothes didn't feel itchy!

Kawdje wore a black cummerbund and matching bowtie. He kept scratching his neck and twisting the bowtie so that it became placed at the back of his neck instead of under his chin.

Kissy looked dainty and precious in a pale peach ruffled chiffon skirt. She also wore a pale, peach-colored, silk rose, attached by sticky tape to the top of her head.

Everyone attending the wedding was invited to the rehearsal party. Sarah's brother, John Sandell, and his wife, Merrill, had arrived from California several days in advance of the wedding and had kept out of the way by touring historic Philadelphia and the Pennsylvania Dutch area of Lancaster County. Their son and his wife had remained in California because they were expecting the birth of their first child in a few weeks.

Sarah's childhood friend, Judy, and her husband, Clyde Hoskins, drove from Virginia with their nineteen-year-old daughter, Katie, and seventeen year old son, Clyde Jr. They toured the Pennsylvania Dutch area with Sarah's brother and sister-in-law because Clyde had never seen it, but he had wanted to ever since he had watched the movie, "Witness."

Sarah's pastor, Reverend Paul Tyler, and his wife, Belle, arrived. Sarah told her pastor that she planned to walk the wedding aisle with her dog and wanted the part of the ceremony, "Who giveth this woman in marriage to this man," deleted from her wedding vows. He readily agreed with her wish.

Gordon and Evan's sister, Melanie, and her husband, Joe Tate, had driven from Oklahoma with their sixteen-year-old daughter, Jillian, and eighteen-year-old son, Marlon, and had arrived that morning.

There were forty-two persons attending the rehearsal and wedding and that head count included the pets.

Everybody clapped and cheered as the pets walked down the stone path that would be the aisle at tomorrow's wedding. Chairs had been placed on either side of the stone pathway. Stone urns were filled with floral arrangements that transformed the area into a wedding bower. Two of the urns defined the area where a church altar would have been.

Michael walked sedately beside Sarah toward Gordon, Kevin, and a man he had never met before. He knew this whole gathering meant something special but he couldn't figure out what it was all about. Whatever was happening included him and that was reassuring.

The Master of Ceremonies that Evan hired had burned a CD of the old recording, "*Because*," sung by Mario Lanza and another of "*True Love*," sung by Bing Crosby and Grace Kelly, both of which were to be played as part of the wedding ceremony. It was a balmy evening—not too hot, not too cool, and not too humid. The wedding day weather promised to be just as perfect.

Sarah thought, "The universe approves of my wedding and is gifting me with wonderful weather."

Nick's roast beef sandwiches were served buffet style and accompanied by corn on the cob, tossed salad, various wines, beer and non-alcoholic drinks. Chocolate cake, ice cream and rice pudding were the desserts. The rice pudding was offered as an option mostly for the benefit of the pets, but it was almost everyone else's choice, too.

Sarah and Gordon were a tangle of intertwined arms and legs as they said a lingering goodnight to each other. Gordon had never slept overnight at Sarah's because he felt ill at ease staying in the home that her deceased husband had owned and lived in. Although Sarah's personality and style filled her home, Gordon always sensed an echo of Charles' presence. He decided early on in their relationship that when he lived with Sarah day and night, it would be in their own home. Michael wedged himself between them to share in the lovings.

The next morning, Michael was exercising on the agility setup and he was descending the A-Frame when Pat and Ed's car rolled to a stop. He wasn't surprised because they had visited frequently during the past week. Every time they came, they carried away a piece of furniture or another rug. He ran over to greet them and accompanied them into the house.

Michael watched with interest as Pat helped Sarah put on a long dress. He was lulled into a light sleep by their chatting and giggling sounds. He awakened with a start when he felt something being tugged up his front legs. He realized that Sarah and Pat were putting the same clothes on him that he had worn yesterday evening. He decided it meant he was being dressed for another party, so he stood up to accommodate their efforts. Excitement flooded him at the thought of another party with great food. He hoped there would be more roast beef and rice pudding and salivated thinking about it.

The car ride was okay but not great, in Michael's opinion, because the windows were kept closed so he couldn't hang his head out and feel the wind ruffle his fur and flap his ears.

Pat said to Ed, "If Michael whines, please do not open the windows because Mom and I don't want windswept hairdos."

After the car rolled to a stop and Ed opened his door, Michael jumped out and was overjoyed to see that they had returned to Topaz's home where last night's party had taken place. His enthusiasm dimmed a little after he sniffed the air and determined that roast beef was not on today's menu.

Topaz loped toward him and touched his nose in greeting.

"Are we going to get fed at this party, too?" he asked her.

"Yes, we are. I can't get into the kitchen because it's filled with strangers preparing food. Mom and dad seem to know them, so I guess everything is okay. The same people who were here last night are sitting down outside."

Kissy and Kawdje bounded toward them, followed by Jenny, who was wearing a long dress that, to Michael's appraisal, looked similar to

Sarah's. Michael sniffed the flower perched on top of Kissy's head and was just about to tell her that her flower didn't have any scent when he noticed Sarah standing beside him.

She slipped a hand under the neck of this jacket and lightly held onto him. He watched Jenny snap a lead onto Kissy's collar. He saw Pat standing in front of Sarah. Everybody else was seated and it had become quiet. Suddenly, he heard music and, to Michael, the traditional wedding march sounded happy and gentle.

Jenny and Kissy walked between the rows of seated people and Jenny heard them murmuring how sweet they both looked together. Kissy loved her outfit. Her mom had lifted her up in front of a mirror so that she could see her reflection. She thought the flower on top of her head made her look taller. She reveled in the attention she was receiving.

Michael quietly waited beside Sarah until Pat stopped walking and stood near Kevin and the pastor that Michael remembered from yesterday evening. Then he saw Gordon standing near the pastor and he tried to run toward him, but Sarah held him back and softly said, "Stay." She then commanded, "Heel," and they walked with slow, measured steps toward Gordon. His heart didn't feel big enough to hold all the happiness that he felt.

Sarah heard snatches of the wedding guests' whispered comments.

"Her escort is unusual but dignified."

"You can count on a dog to walk beside you no matter what the circumstances."

When they stood directly in front of the pastor, Michael felt Sarah release her hold on his jacket and then Pat tugged him toward her until he stood at her side.

Sarah stood quietly as the exceptional voice of Mario Lanza sang the recording of "Because you come to me with naught save love . . . I see the roses blooming at your feet." There were roses arranged in low containers placed to form a semicircle around the wedding party. Sarah saw Gordon gazing at her with such love in his eyes that she blinked to hold back tears.

Suddenly, another very strong voice was heard. It held a steady note for such a long time that everyone marveled at the lung capacity and breath control.

Michael instantly recognized Topaz's voice. He decided to contribute to the verbal celebration, too.

When Kawdje heard Topaz and Michael singing in accompaniment to a man's voice, he decided to join the chorus because he fancied himself as a bit of a balladeer.

Kissy did not possess a musical voice, but that didn't deter her from joining the canine chorus.

Topaz's voice soared strongly above all others, including Mario Lanza's. Jeanette and Cole were mortified and tried to muzzle her with their hands, but Topaz shook them off and pranced toward the altar. Kawdje jumped off his seat between Essie and Evan and ran toward Kissy.

Gordon pressed his lips together hard in an effort to suppress a grin. His face quickly clouded in consternation when he saw Sarah's bowed head and shaking shoulders. He thought she was crying and was just about to hold her in his arms to comfort her, when she raised her face and he saw, with relief, that she was laughing.

The pastor raised his prayer book in front of his face to hide his laughter, but it was a ruse that fooled no one.

Soon, all the wedding party and guests were howling along with the dogs.

The young man videotaping the wedding managed to keep the camera steady in spite of his laughter. "I've got a winner here," he thought, "but I'll have to get permission from Gordon and Sarah before I can send this to the *World's Funniest Home Videos TV Show*." When the laughter died down, the ceremony proceeded.

The pastor spoke words that Michael didn't understand, but when he watched Gordon slip another shiny collar onto one of Sarah's fingers and Sarah put one on Gordon's finger, he almost barked with joy. He recollected his discussion with Topaz, Kissy and Kawdje about the special finger collar that their parents always wore and he knew that Sarah and Gordon were going to live together as his mom and dad.

After the ceremony, the beautiful Bing Crosby/Grace Kelly recorded rendition of "*True Love*" played while Sarah and Gordon signed the wedding book. Everyone expected Topaz to once again lead the canine chorus, so, by unspoken common consent, everybody began to sing along with Bing and Grace. As before, Topaz's voice was strongly audible above all others.

The rest of the day was unusually relaxed and convivial for a wedding party. The pets were much admired by all. Several guests asked Jeanette and Cole if they had ever considered entering Topaz in the Singing Dog Contest held annually in New York City.

"She's a shoo-in to win it," declared Sarah's brother.

Meanwhile, the pets were busily dining on shrimp cocktail, which Kawdje the Particular refused to try, and Chicken Cordon Bleu, which they all ate with gusto. Kawdje ate some steamed, buttered green beans, but Kissy passed on those. They all ate the chilled, poached, wild sockeye salmon, although Kawdje nibbled at his portion, unenthusiastically.

"I like to swim but I'm not fond of eating anything else that swims," he grumbled.

Topaz and Michael gulped down everything offered them, including wedding cake and crème brûlée. Kissy ate sparingly of the cake and Kawdje sniffed and rejected it, but they both guzzled the crème brûlée.

"Now that is the king of desserts," pronounced Kawdje, and the other three agreed.

The deejay/master of ceremonies played a medley of moldy oldies and recent hits. Everyone danced. Essie danced while holding Kawdje in her arms, and Evan two-stepped beside them holding Kissy. Sarah, Gordon and Michael did a threesome boogie. Sam, Joy, Pat, Ed, Jeanette, Cole and Topaz formed a conga line and other guests joined, broke away and rejoined at will.

Topaz spent a great deal of time standing near the deejay and his recorder while belting out a doggy version of whatever tune happened to be playing. Kevin, ever the well-brought-up young gentleman, did a foxtrot with Belle Tyler, the pastor's wife and then many dances with Katie Hoskins. Paul Tyler loved the cha-cha and gave all the ladies a turn as his partner. Pat and Ed did several old-fashioned rock 'n roll dances. They were so good that everyone else stopped to watch, forming a ring around them and clapping to the beat.

Sarah and Gordon had gifted each attendee with a disposable camera, among other things, and everyone had a snapshot taken of themselves with Sam and another with the bridal couple.

During a dance break, Sarah threw her wedding bouquet. Katie Hoskins was very annoyed when Jillian Tate leaped in front of her and caught it.

Shortly afterward, Sarah and Gordon slipped upstairs in Jeanette and Cole's home and changed out of their wedding outfits. They were wearing less noticeable garb as they walked toward Gordon's SUV. They were shocked to see the condition of the vehicle. It was festooned with ribbons and empty cans tied to the rear bumper, and had "Just Married" written on every window. They spent the next fifteen minutes removing the writing and paraphernalia. Just before they climbed into the SUV, Gordon pulled Sarah close and gave her, what a grinning Jenny called, the mother of all kisses.

When they came up for air he murmured, "Mrs. Gordon Kilmer, we're off to spend a night in the honeymoon suite at the DuPont Hotel in Wilmington."

The wedding party was still revved up at full throttle when the newlyweds departed.

The wedding guests clapped, cheered and shouted their good wishes to Sarah and Gordon while Michael, in a state of disbelief and anguish, watched Sarah and Gordon drive away without him. He was held fast by Pat and Ed, and no matter how hard he struggled, he could not break free.

"Why did they leave me?" he asked himself over and over. He planned on the three of them living together for always. When he realized they had gone forever, he collapsed. Every part of him hurt and he groaned with every breath.

CHAPTER TWENTY-TWO

Pat and Ed were in a quandary. Michael refused to get up and they were unable to lift him themselves. Kevin was standing nearby and became aware of the situation. He knelt by Michael and attempted to coax him to stand, but to no avail.

"He's got a terrible case of separation anxiety," he said. "I know Dad and Sarah arranged for him to stay at your home overnight, but I wonder if he would feel more secure if he slept at Sarah's and on his own dog bed."

"We've got his dog bed in our car," Ed said.

"Ed, maybe we should sleep over at Mom's tonight. Michael looks so desolate that I'm ready to try just about anything that might cheer him up."

"Good Lord!" Ed exclaimed. "How will we cope when they leave him to take a two-week honeymoon on some enchanted island?"

"I don't know. Right now we have to solve this problem. Let's do as Kevin suggests and sleep at Mom's place tonight."

By now, Topaz, Kissy and Kawdje had gathered around Michael. They tried to comfort him but he was inconsolable. He kept moaning over and over, "They left me."

Michael felt Topaz's long, silky ears brush across his head and her warm tongue lick his muzzle. He felt Kissy and Kawdje's paws on his neck. In spite of their comforting gestures, a powerful wave of depression washed through him like a dirty river that deposited mud and debris into every part of his body in its wake. Sarah and Gordon had left him! He didn't want to live.

Gradually, the wedding guests became aware that something was wrong and they gathered around Michael. Pat, Ed and Kevin explained to everyone that Michael was in a state of emotional collapse because Sarah and Gordon had left without him.

Pat told the out-of-town guests, who were not familiar with Michael's background, that he had been a street dog that her mom had rescued in Mexico.

"Who knows what trials and tribulations he experienced before my mom brought him home with her? He's very emotionally attached to my mom and Gordon. Maybe he thinks they've left him forever."

Michael heard many kind voices murmur words of encouragement to him. Their concern and compassion did nothing to lift his desolation and loneliness. Topaz, Kissy, Kawdje, Jenny, Kevin, Pat, Ed and everyone surrounded him, but he felt as alone as he had when he used to lie on the sand piles in San Miguel and he felt far more abandoned now than he had felt then.

Jeanette offered to have Michael sleep at her home in the company of Topaz. Essie and Evan offered to take him home with them and have him sleep near Kissy and Kawdje. The majority decision was that Pat and Ed, Kevin, Essie and Evan, Jenny and Topaz, Kissy and Kawdje would all sleep at Sarah's to keep Michael company.

Jeanette explained that she and Cole couldn't leave their home until the caterers had cleaned up and left. Also, Cole had to get up very early in the morning to make patient rounds. They knew that Jenny would be safe with their friends and happy to have Topaz's company and Topaz would be comforted by having Jenny with her in the absence of her mom and dad.

Kevin, Sam and Ed hefted Michael into the back seat of Pat and Ed's car.

Jeanette hurriedly packed an overnight bag for Jenny and helped her change out of her Flower Girl dress and into shorts and a tee shirt.

Kevin, Essie and Evan drove home with Kissy and Kawdje to change into comfortable, casual clothes and pick up the pets' sleeping pads.

Sam and Joy drove Jenny and Topaz over to Sarah's. The other wedding guests said goodnight to Jeanette and Cole and each other, then sped away in their cars.

Cole observed as everyone drove off, "Well, Michael's emotional breakdown brought the wedding party to an abrupt halt."

The next morning Sarah and Gordon were surprised to see so many vehicles parked in front of her home.

"The wedding party must have moved from Jeanette's home to mine," Sarah said.

She opened the kitchen door, smelled coffee and saw Jeanette pouring juice into glasses and Jenny filling dog bowls. Kevin was sipping a cup of coffee and Ed was frying eggs while Pat set the dining room table because the kitchen table wasn't large enough to accommodate everyone present. Essie and Evan were making toast and buttering the slices. Kissy and Kawdje ran up to Sarah and Gordon wagging their tails in greeting.

"This is a wonderful welcome committee," Gordon said, trying to hide his puzzlement and surprise.

Everyone laughed and hugged them. Jeanette poured coffee for each of them and suggested they sit down while everyone took turns explaining why they were here.

From the deep pit of his misery, Michael thought he heard Gordon's voice, but dismissed it as a dream. He didn't have the energy to face another crushing disappointment in a standing position, so he decided to lie in his bed forever. Topaz was stretched out close to him and he was glad of that. He hoped she could be with him at the end. He cocked an ear because he was sure he had just heard Sarah's voice. "Yes!"

He leaped off his bed and jumped over Topaz in his haste to exit the bedroom. He charged down the stairs and exploded into the kitchen. He jumped onto Sarah and Gordon's laps. They were seated side-by-side at the kitchen table and he was large enough to cover both laps as he sprawled across them.

There wasn't a dry eye in the kitchen as everybody watched the three of them exchange loving greetings. Michael gave the most enthusiastic greeting to Sarah and Gordon that any pet had ever given. Sarah and Gordon hugged, stroked, kissed, patted and nuzzled Michael as they murmured loving reassurances to him.

Gordon said, "Okay, buddy, we're taking you to a motel with us tonight."

Sarah spoke with obvious determination in her voice, "Gordon, we can't go on a honeymoon in December to a warm, sunny place and leave Michael. He just might pine for us to the point of death. Wherever we go, we must take him with us."

"No argument from me, golden girl."

They had just finished eating breakfast when the phone rang. Sarah answered and recognized the voice of her real estate agent who asked if a late afternoon walk-through inspection of her home on August 19th would be possible because the August 20th settlement was scheduled for 9 a.m. Sarah assured her that this arrangement would be fine.

After hanging up, Sarah announced, "We're making settlement on our Bucks County home tomorrow morning and by noontime, it will be ours. You're all welcome to come over for a look-see. Gordon and I shopped for bedroom and kitchen furniture, which is scheduled for delivery tomorrow afternoon. This is the last time that we'll sit together in this house because the folks who purchased the furniture that Pat and Ed didn't want will be arriving this afternoon to take it away."

Essie said, "Evan, Kevin, and I will bring dinner to your new home tomorrow. We can hardly wait to see it!"

Gordon placed an arm around his son's shoulders and said, "Sarah and I bought a bedroom suite for one of the spare bedrooms so you can stay with us until you have to fly back to Purdue."

Kevin grinned at his dad. "You just want me around to help you move furniture, plus paint and whatever." Privately, however, he was elated that his dad and Sarah wanted him to be a part of their married life.

Sarah sensed how relieved Kevin was to receive the invitation to stay with them, so she suggested that they have lunch together at a state park that was close by. Then, she extended the invitation to everyone. "The park permits leashed pets. I know this is an impromptu invitation, but it will give me an opportunity to use up leftovers in my refrigerator to make sandwiches. I can buy whatever else we need."

Jeanette announced that nothing needed to be bought because her refrigerator was crammed with wedding feast leftovers.

"I'll drive home right now and start packing food into coolers. Maybe Cole will be home by the time I arrive and he can join us. Okay if I leave Jenny and Topaz here?"

Evan said, "Jenny and Kissy can practice Junior Handling Agility and I'll supervise."

Jenny danced across the kitchen and hugged Evan around the waist. "Thanks, Uncle Evan."

The next day, during Sarah and Gordon's house settlement at the local courthouse, Kevin drove Michael to a small park located nearby because it was too hot to leave him in the car. They snoozed under the shade of a huge oak tree until the ring of Kevin's cell phone startled him. It was his dad telling him to pick them up because the settlement was finished.

The four of them toured the entire house. Michael walked closely pressed to Sarah's side. He had remained within petting distance ever since his post-wedding reunion with her and Gordon. He recalled being here briefly once before, even though he had remained in the car. He never forgot a scent. He was certain that this was the place Sarah and Gordon referred to when they said "home".

There wasn't any furniture in the house and Michael didn't know what to make of that. He wondered if he would sleep on his soft, comfortable bed like he did last night at the motel. He wanted to go outside and explore, but not as much as he wanted to stay close to Sarah and Gordon. Finally, Sarah and Gordon walked outside and he and Kevin followed.

"Wow!" exclaimed Kevin when he saw the panoramic southern vista. Michael echoed the sentiment with an appreciative bark.

Gordon said, "There's a stream running through the lower part of the property. Maybe we should have a portion of it enlarged to make a pond. Let's all explore."

While walking through a wooded area, they found evidence of an old springhouse.

"We can have a pond put in. There's a spring to feed it," Gordon said.

Michael swelled with pride at the thought of all the property that he had to patrol and keep safe for Sarah and Gordon.

As they walked back toward the house, a furniture delivery truck rounded the curve of the driveway. The next couple of hours were spent arranging furniture.

"We need to have the whole house painted, the floors redone and the kitchen remodeled, but this will have to do for now," she said.

"Do you really think we need a new kitchen?" asked Gordon.

"Definitely! I need an updated kitchen just as much as you need a new garage."

Kevin hid a smile as he heard his dad say, "Okay, golden girl. A new kitchen is on the 'To Do List,'" and Sarah reply, "It's at the top of the list."

They had just finished arranging the living room furniture, when Jeanette, Cole, Jenny and Topaz arrived, bringing more wedding-food leftovers. While Jeanette, Cole and Jenny were being shown the house, Michael gave Topaz a tour of the grounds.

They heard Kissy's sharp, commanding bark and raced back to the house.

Essie and Evan, Joy and Sam carried food and wine into the kitchen. Kissy and Kawdje ran toward Topaz and Michael.

"This is a huge place!" Kawdje observed.

"Wait till you see the stream and springhouse," Michael said.

While they were pacing toward the woods, Pat and Ed arrived. Pat asked her mom if she wasn't worried about losing the pets.

Sarah replied, "This is the first time since the morning after the wedding that Michael has left my side. He has stuck to Gordon and me like a piece of flypaper. I know he won't stray far and because the four of them always stay close together, that means they'll all stay close by. Anyway, as soon as food is put on the table, they'll appear like magic."

Everyone had brought a housewarming gift. Essie and Evan gave them a huge firewood holder and fireplace set. Kevin's gift was a cord of seasoned firewood to be delivered in late September. Jeanette and Cole had divided some of their prize-winning roses and had a dozen potted specimens ready for replanting, plus, clippers, garden gloves and rose fertilizer. Pat and Ed gave a set of bed linens and matching bed skirt for Sarah and Gordon's bedroom suite. Pat remembered her mother admiring them when they had shopped together several weeks ago. Jenny's gift was a small dish in the shape of a dog's head and bore some resemblance to Michael.

"It's supposed to be placed near the kitchen sink and it's for putting your watch and rings, or bracelet, into it while you're washing dishes or rinsing vegetables. That's what my mom and Aunt Jeanette always do."

Sarah hugged her and said that it was one of the most special and useful gifts she had ever received.

They heard the pets barking. Gordon looked out the kitchen door and saw the moving truck rolling to a stop. It didn't take long to unload the agility equipment and the few possessions that Sarah was moving into their new home.

Gordon opened some wine bottles and after everyone had raised their wine glasses for all the various toasts that they could invent, they were feeling very happy.

The discussion turned to upcoming dog agility events.

Evan said, "The pets just need one qualifying score in each of the

Advanced Level classes to achieve Advanced Agility Dog titling, then it's on to achieving Master Agility Dog. It would be great if all our pampered, precious, peerless pet family members achieved Master Agility Dog titling before we attend the World Cynosport event in Arizona this November."

Everyone laughed as Evan stumbled over the tongue-twisting alliteration of so many words beginning with the letter "p."

Jeanette announced that she, Jenny and Topaz were driving to Chicago the day after tomorrow to see Jenny's parents and pack everything Jenny would need to spend a winter in Pennsylvania. Topaz would compete in Advanced classes in an event on the way and, after their return, in Masters classes at another event in Ohio if she had achieved her Advanced Agility Dog titling.

Evan said, "We've entered Kissy and Kawdje in two agility events in Massachusetts. If they make qualifying scores in the Advanced Level classes at the August 28th event, we'll change their registration in the September 3rd through 6th event from Advanced to Masters Level classes."

"What's your agenda?" Cole asked Gordon and Sarah.

"We'll drive to Arizona for the August 29th settlement on my townhouse, then travel to the Southwestern Regional Championships that take place near San Francisco from September 2nd through September 5th. After that, Sarah and Michael will compete in the South Central Regional Championships in Texas."

Essie exclaimed, "Wow! Our 'mile-a-minute' schedules should keep us busy for awhile!"

CHAPTER TWENTY-THREE

Michael watched Gordon pack suitcases into the SUV along with his Pak-'n-Fold kennel and his bed and bowl and wasn't sure if he was happy or disappointed. He loved traveling but he also loved this home they had just moved into.

"On the plus side," he thought, "they aren't going away without me."

It was a happy journey for all three of them. Sarah packed a cooler with food and replenished it along the way with purchases from supermarkets. Sarah and Gordon dined in restaurants for their evening meal and ordered extra for Michael so that they always had a doggy bag of delicious food to take back to the motel each night. Occasionally, they ordered take-out meals that they all ate together in a park or in their motel room while watching a video movie.

Several times the threesome hiked trails. Once, they stayed in a riverfront B and B in Missouri and rented one of the boats. Michael had his first-ever boat ride. After they put back to shore and secured the boat to the dock, Michael took a swim.

"That settles it. Michael loves swimming so we have to put a pond in on our property," Gordon said.

Upon arrival at Gordon's townhouse, Michael walked inside and immediately understood that Gordon lived here. His scent was everywhere. Michael didn't like this place nearly as much as the home they had left and hoped they weren't going to be living here for always.

The next morning, after breakfast, Michael watched Gordon place the cooler into the SUV. He knew it wouldn't be a long trip because suitcases hadn't been packed. After a not-so-very-long drive, Gordon parked and they all got out and walked toward an odd-looking vehicle. Michael had to high-jump to get into it. He knew it wasn't a car, but it did have seats. He jumped into one and Gordon strapped him in.

Michael detected the tantalizing scent of burritos in the cooler that

Gordon strapped into the seat opposite him. "Wherever the three of us are going there will be yummy food to eat, so it's going to be a great day," he thought.

Michael recognized the familiar floating sensation he had experienced during the trip from San Miguel de Allende to Sarah's home. The terrifying thought that they might fly him back to Mexico and leave him in the street grabbed hold and refused to let go. He howled in dismay.

Gordon said, "He always takes everything in his stride, except when you and I spent our wedding night away from him. We're both with him now, so what do you think is upsetting him?"

It occurred to Sarah that this was Michael's first flight since his trip from San Miguel and she shared this with Gordon. "I think Michael is afraid he is being flown back to Mexico. He began howling within seconds of take-off. He probably recognizes the sensation of being airborne and associates it with flying from Mexico to Pennsylvania. Maybe he thinks all flights are to or from Mexico."

"That's a keen insight, golden girl. Who knows how a dog reasons? What can we do to reassure him?"

"Would it unbalance the helicopter if I got up and sat in the seat opposite Michael so that I could reach over and touch him? Maybe that would comfort him."

"Just move slowly and place the cooler up front."

Michael felt better as Sarah stroked his neck. He wasn't sure what she was saying, but he sensed the loving concern that she and Gordon had for him and he relaxed enough to think clearly.

"They wouldn't fly me back to Mexico and leave me on the street, because they love me. I love them and I would never leave them, so they wouldn't ever leave me because they love me." He held onto that comforting thought but the nasty, queasy feeling in his gut, brought on by the thought that maybe, just maybe, he might be flown back to San Miguel and abandoned, wouldn't leave him.

After an hour's flight time, Gordon landed the helicopter near the kiva site that he had been exploring for the past year. Michael jumped out of the Bell Jet Ranger and looked around at desert wilderness. He walked so close to Sarah that he bumped into her several times.

She said, "I think Michael's fear of being abandoned will fade the longer he lives with us and the more he flies with us. "Good food always mellows him out. Let's eat lunch before you show us your kiva site."

During the return flight, Michael felt relaxed and composed. He thought, "I don't know why we couldn't have taken the trip in our car, but this is okay. Sarah and Gordon aren't going to fly me somewhere and leave me."

A couple of days later, Michael was relieved as he watched men come inside Gordon's home and carry away all the furniture. That same routine had taken place when he and Sarah left their home and moved into the place that they and Gordon now lived in. He reasoned that Gordon was leaving this home for always because now his home was the place with lots of land and trees and a stream that they had moved into just before they took this long trip.

Michael was happy to be on the road again. Much of the time he was able to hang his head out an open window and enjoy the wind whistling through his teeth and vibrating his muzzle. He felt such happiness, that his body could hardly contain the pleasure of it.

The following day, Michael was unprepared to attend an agility practice. It was not the usual routine. He always attended agility practices with Topaz, Kissy and Kawdje and their families. He wondered if they were somewhere among the crowds. He searched for them as he walked with Sarah and Gordon through the show grounds and finally decided his friends weren't at this event.

When Sarah sprayed his ear, Michael then understood he would be performing. As they waited to compete, he noticed a brown, curly-coated dog about his size. He decided this was a Pairs Relay because that would be the only time another dog with a parent would stand so close to Sarah and him at the entrance gate. They struck up a conversation and Michael learned that the dog was called Patrick and he was of the Irish Water Spaniel breed.

"My dad says I'm named after a saint—Saint Patrick."

Michael responded in kind, telling Patrick that he was called Michael Archangelo after his namesake Archangel Michael.

"Patrick, I guess this is a Pairs Relay and we're teamed together. Are you a good competitor?"

"Am I good? Michael, my boyo, you're paired with the best of the best. How about you? Can you run with four good legs under you or do you trip over your paws?"

Michael grinned. He liked this brash fellow in spite of his braggadocio attitude. At least Patrick hadn't looked him over and asked what breed he was.

He replied, "You and I are named after a saint and an archangel. We're winners!"

Patrick said, "I like your attitude, Michael boyo."

They paced into the ring oozing self-assurance. Michael and Patrick won the Advanced Pairs Relay in their jump height category at the Southwestern Regional Championships.

Sarah and Gordon noticed that Michael had adjusted to performing without the presence of his three pals. He wasn't as convivial as usual but he appeared to be confident and calm.

"If he qualifies in each of his classes in this event, he'll be an Advanced Agility Dog." Gordon said, then added, "I'll find a cyber café and e-mail the South Central Regional Championship officials to change his registration to Masters Level classes. Let's eat out after his last class tomorrow and hit the road again."

The afternoon of the next day, as they traveled to the South Central Regionals in Texas, Gordon kept congratulating Sarah on her and Michael's great performances. In spite of there being many competitors in every class, Michael won Snooker, placed second in Jumpers and Standard Agility, third in Gamblers and had won the Pairs Relay with Patrick.

"In spite of your right/left difficulty, you were remarkable, golden girl. I overheard comments about Michael's orange ear and some people noticed that your left hand was orange. Of those who noticed and commented, the general opinion was that it added to Michael's mystique."

Sarah leaned over and kissed Gordon's cheek.

"It was your idea. We owe our fame and success to you, my darling."

CHAPTER TWENTY-FOUR

Kissy and Kawdje rode in separate booster seats to the agility tournaments in Massachusetts. Kawdje appreciated being able to easily look out a window while sitting comfortably, but the windows were closed so he couldn't hang his head out and enjoy the rush of wind filling his mouth and nostrils and flapping his ears. It was one of his favorite perks of life.

Kissy was thankful that all windows were in the "up" position and that the air conditioning kept her cool. She disliked having her fur ruffled and tousled.

When Kissy and Kawdje heard the wide variety of barks, they knew they were at another agility practice. They were pleasantly surprised to discover that it wasn't hot here. They had no idea where "here" was, but both knew it was far from home. They were anxious to locate Michael and Topaz and immediately began tugging on their leads and darting from one side to another.

Essie and Evan realized that the pets were looking Michael and Topaz.

While they waited at the entrance gate for their turn to perform in the Advanced Pairs Relay, Kawdje announced that he wasn't going to perform.

An astounded Kissy asked him, "Why not?"

"I miss Michael and Topaz and their parents. I miss Jenny, too, even though she likes you more than me. This isn't nearly as much fun without them. I don't feel like performing."

Kissy knew she couldn't perform a Pairs Relay without a partner, so she set about coaxing Kawdje into a better frame of mind.

"I can't run a Pairs Relay by myself. Please do it for my sake."

"No!"

"You will disappoint Mom and Dad if you refuse to perform."

"I don't care. I'm just going to sit here on my tail. I'm used to having

Michael and Topaz around. I always liked returning to the tent, after performing, and having a snack and talking with them. I don't like this change in routine."

Ambitious Kissy always wanted to compete and win as many awards as she could. She felt frustrated and mulled over ways to budge Kawdje from his obstinate refusal to perform. Then she had an idea.

"Kawdje, if you won't compete with me, I'll eat grass and throw up on you today and tomorrow and every day until you compete again. I'll even throw up in your kennel."

Kawdje shuddered. He knew Kissy had the ability to throw up at will if she ate grass.

"Okay! Okay! I'll go in the ring with you."

"You had better perform fast enough to suit me or I'll still throw up on you and you know I can do it."

"Okay! Okay!" he said.

Essie was pleased with Kawdje's great performance. He ran as though he was being chased by a bogeyman. Little did she know that, in a way, he was!

Cole, Jeanette, Jenny and Topaz were enjoying themselves in a pet-friendly B and B in Ohio located near the Dog Agility Tournament. John and Marie Colbert, the proprietors, were enchanted with Topaz. They asked Cole and Jeanette if they were planning on puppies in her future.

Cole replied they weren't sure because she hadn't shown well in Conformation Dog Shows.

Marie was puzzled as to why Topaz hadn't placed well in Dog Shows. "She's so elegant and beautiful."

Jeanette explained that Conformation Dog Shows had bored Topaz and her indifference had been obvious to the judges.

"That's why we're pursuing Dog Agility. Topaz loves the activity and she's a great athlete."

"We think she's delightful," John Colbert said. "Keep us in mind if you ever have puppies available. Our kids are grown and our clientele usually come from April through October. We have time to devote to raising a puppy and enjoying the companionship of a pet. I wish we could spare the time to attend today's Dog Agility Show."

Jenny related the story of how Topaz had rescued her from a car thief and John said, "That clinches it! I want one of her puppies."

Cole explained that Topaz was worthless as a hunting dog. "She practically kisses the deer. Once she turned tail and ran from a doe who was protecting her twin fawns."

John and Marie laughed heartily.

"She has her priorities straight," Marie declared. "If a momma deer charged me, I'd run, too. I'm so impressed that Topaz would protect her family. Please be sure to keep us in mind if she ever has puppies."

Topaz had been entered in the Masters Standard Agility, Gamblers and Pairs Relay the previous day and had made a qualifying score in each class, placing second in Gamblers and the Relay. The competition had been tough because many dogs entered in those classes had already achieved Masters titling several years prior and had been competing to earn Agility Dog Champion and Tournament Master titling plus Bronze, Silver, Gold and Platinum Metallic Designations.

Today, as Jeanette did a pre-performance walk-through in the Masters Snooker class, she noted that the layout for the opening sequence had four red hurdles instead of three. For this class, after successfully using the second red hurdle, the judge required that a combination of three "color" obstacles had to be performed upon as though it were a single obstacle. Each obstacle would be scored individually; however, if a fault occurred, no points would be awarded for the combination, not even for any obstacle in that combination that had been used correctly.

Because of the direction in which the combination had to be taken, when Topaz descended the A-Frame, it would place her near the first red obstacle that had already been used. While Topaz was being directed toward the third red hurdle, she would have to turn right and pass two obstacles that were not to be used. Jeanette knew she would have to stay ahead of Topaz to make the pathway to the third red obstacle explicitly clear and to signal the direction in which it had to be taken.

After the third red hurdle had been used, Topaz would face a two-obstacle color combination—the Dog Walk and Collapsed Tunnel—before the fourth and last red hurdle could be taken; however, the second combination was not as tricky as the three-obstacle combination. Because the fourth red hurdle was situated near the Weave Poles, Jeanette decided she would have Topaz use them because they had the highest point value. After that, the closing Snooker sequence would begin by using the lowest point value obstacle (other than a hurdle) and working up in ascending point value.

As Jeanette thought about the SCT, she remembered that, in order to earn the title of Snooker Master, Topaz would have to place in the top 15% in three of the five Master Snooker classes. Topaz was up against tough competitors and part of that tough competition was a superb Border Collie mixed breed dog called Harry Houdini. He was slightly larger than Topaz. Jeanette knew that Harry had earned Bronze, Silver and Gold Metallic Designations from having chatted with his handler, Mark Lederman. She had noticed pins displayed on Mark's shirt and had inquired about their significance. Mark had explained that he had bought them to have something visible to wear at tournaments in recognition of Harry's dedication and ability because USDAA just gives a paper certificate for each Metallic Designation.

Jeanette recalled that a Bronze Metallic Designation signified fifteen qualifying performances had been acquired beyond the Champion/Tournament Master level; the Silver meant that twenty-five had; the Gold required thirty-five; and the Platinum signified a whopping fifty performances beyond the Champion/Tournament Master level.

Harry Houdini and Mark had earned three Golds and two Silvers, plus quite a few Bronzes. Wow! Another team with Metallic Designations was Zelda, a beautiful Weimaraner, and her handler, Jessie Northrup.

A total of twenty-six dogs were entered in this Masters Snooker Class. Jeanette calculated that four dogs would comprise 15%. She thought, "I'm betting that Harry Houdini and Zelda will be two of those four dogs, which leaves two slots for Topaz."

She groaned inwardly and then decided not to worry about placing in the top 15% in this competition.

Butterflies fluttered wildly in Jeanette's stomach as she walked onto the course. She hoped that Topaz, with her uncanny ability to sense her mom's thoughts and feelings, would not tune in until after she had composed herself.

"This is supposed to be fun. It's not a life-and-death situation," she thought.

She immediately felt calm as she put the competition into proper perspective.

Topaz walked closely beside her mom into the ring. She had been puzzled by her mom's attitude a few minutes ago and had wondered if her mom had felt sick but now she seemed fine. Topaz heard a whistle and then her mom pointed to a jump obstacle and they were off.

They had a fast and fault-free performance and made a qualifying score but Jeanette wasn't sure how their performance compared to the experienced Bronze, Silver and Gold winners. Jeanette's mouth felt dry as she checked the Point Sheet. Relief flooded her. Topaz's performance was a mere half second slower than Harry Houdini's. She came second. Zelda placed fourth.

Topaz's performance in the Masters Jumper Class that afternoon was brilliant; however, once again, Harry Houdini won and Topaz placed second.

Afterward, Jenny and Topaz competed in the Junior Handler Elementary Class. Topaz was so relaxed by the simplicity of the course layout that she was almost bored into a trance. She had a whole minute to perform on ten obstacles arranged in such a way as to make the course pathway obvious. She tried to remain interested for Jenny's sake but Topaz felt as though she was helping to train a puppy. Thankfully, it went well and Jenny earned her Junior Handler Elementary Agility Certificate.

That evening, John and Marie enjoyed Topaz's company while Cole, Jeanette and Jenny dined at a nearby restaurant. They ordered a rib roast take-out dinner for Topaz and bought a cheesecake at a bakery on the way back to the B & B. Everyone enjoyed the dessert, including Topaz who delicately licked her chops after devouring her portion. Marie and John looked longingly at her and Marie said, "I wish she was mine. Please remember to call John and me if she's ever expecting puppies."

Kissy and Kawdje enjoyed traveling. They loved the excitement of sleeping in a different motel every night and stopping for walks and picnics in parks. They were prepared for another full day's journey but today proved to be a short ride. Their mom and dad walked them onto the grounds of another Agility Show.

The event was being held outdoors. Kissy and Kawdje had been entered in their first Masters classes and their day began with Jumpers.

Kissy felt exuberant and could hardly wait to compete. Kawdje missed

Michael and Topaz but he loved traveling and if he had to compete in Dog Agility events between travel days, he decided it was a fair trade-off.

Their parents held them as they all waited their turn to perform. Kissy and Kawdje could see that the course had a lot of jumps and that was because the number of jumps and hurdles used in a Masters Jumpers class was greater than in the Starter and Advanced classes. They saw Spread Hurdles and Extended Spread Hurdles as well as Tunnels. Kawdje's spirits lifted because he enjoyed jumping. Kissy's spirits sank because she did not. Kawdje was overjoyed to see that there weren't any Weave Poles. Kissy was distressed by the lack of them.

Kawdje preceded Essie into the ring with a jauntiness that was obvious. It wasn't an easy course. Two Extended Spread Hurdles had to be used consecutively with very little distance between them. In spite of the degree of difficulty, Kawdje had a swift and fault-free performance. He felt good.

"Dog Agility can be fun," he thought, "even if Michael and Topaz aren't with me!"

Kissy watched Kawdje's admirable performance as she sat high in her dad's arms. Her competitive spirit rose to the challenge. She resolved to do as well and, preferably, better.

It was difficult for Kissy to use her swiftness in this course to give her an advantage over Kawdje. So many jumps broke her stride.

She thought. "I'll pretend I'm flying when I jump over the Extended Spread Hurdle. I'll hold my front legs straight out and stretch my hind legs straight back. I won't waste energy jumping upward. I'll just jump forward. I won't try to run so fast between the jumps. I'll just take enough steps to prepare for the next hurdle." She began to find a rhythm. Whenever she encountered a Tunnel, she broke into a no-holds-barred run through it and was glad of the advantage the Tunnel afforded her.

As she cleared the last jump, she was profoundly relieved. She had learned how to pace herself and work more fluidly on a Jumpers course.

"I'll do better next time!" she vowed.

Essie and Evan were ecstatic because Kissy and Kawdje had not only qualified in their first Masters Level class but Kawdje had placed first in Jumpers, winning over two Tournament Masters, and Kissy had come third. Her parents recognized Kissy's effort and determination and that she had seemed to hit her stride about two-thirds of the way through the course.

Kawdje's mood remained buoyant throughout the tournament. He made qualifying scores in all his Masters classes. Kissy put the strategy she had learned in the dreaded Jumpers class to good advantage in the rest of her classes. She placed first in Snooker, thanks in part to Evan's shrewd choices, and first in the Master Standard Agility class. Kissy and Kawdje performed the Master Pairs Relay together and placed second against more experienced competition.

It was a great day for the Double K twosome!

CHAPTER TWENTY-FIVE

Fort Worth, Texas, where the South Central Regional Championships were being held, was unseasonably hot. On a whim, Sarah and Gordon had entered Michael in the Steeplechase and Grand Prix. Because of the heat, Sarah and Gordon were glad that Michael only had two classes today plus Round 1 of the Steeplechase.

Once Sarah was in the ring with Michael for the Masters Gamblers class, she forgot about the heat as the intensity and excitement of performing blotted out everything else. The Masters level of this class differed from the Starters and Advanced levels in that she would have to remain at least fifteen feet from Michael during the "Gamble" sequence instead of nine feet.

For this class, there were five obstacles designated as part of the "Gamble" and a time allotment of twenty seconds to perform them. Sarah was confident that Michael would remember the names of each obstacle as she called them out.

"He's smarter than I am," she thought. "He knows his right from left."

When the judge's whistle blew, signaling the end of the opening period and the beginning of the "Gamble," Sarah had barely managed to position herself in the designated handlers' area for this portion of the class. Michael had just emerged from the pipe tunnel and was facing the first obstacle to be used in the "Gamble."

As always, Sarah held her painted left hand in front of her, at chest level, so that she could easily see it and keep orienting herself to Michael's left. As she called out to him to turn left and climb the A-Frame, she made a half-turn to her left so that she kept her right and left aligned with Michael's right and left. This strategy made directing him so much easier.

They gave a stellar performance.

"Your strategy was impeccable," Gordon said as he pulled Sarah close and planted a kiss on the top of her head and then one on Michael's head.

Sarah and Michael took a well-earned break. After they had eaten their snacks, the three of them ambled over to the Point Accumulation Sheet.

They were ecstatic to see that Michael had placed second. It was a huge win, worth many points because of the large size of the class.

Jetson and his handler, Maureen Hanks, had won. Sarah had chatted briefly with Maureen while waiting to perform. Maureen had told her that Jetson was a four year old, Black Lab, mixed-breed dog that she had gotten from a relative when Jetson was a puppy and that he had earned several Gold and Silver Metallic Designations.

Sarah told this to Gordon and added, "Michael probably would have won if he had been teamed with a more experienced handler than me."

"Give yourself credit, golden girl. You and Michael have only been on the Dog Agility circuit for a few months and you're already placing near the top."

Later that day, in spite of being hot and tired and not at their best, Michael and Sarah placed fourth in Round 1 of the Steeplechase and were eligible to compete in Round 2, which would be held on Sunday. Placing fourth wasn't too shabby in a large, competitive class!

Saturday was a light day for Sarah and Michael because they only competed in the Grand Prix Qualifier. They were fresh and rested and placed first in Michael's jump height category. Sarah rejoiced at Michael's win over Jetson but confided to Gordon that she now felt pressured for them to do well in the Grand Prix Finals on Sunday.

On Sunday, the third and final day of the South Central Regional Championship, the darling duo, as Gordon had begun calling them, were entered in the Final Rounds of the Steeplechase and Grand Prix. The Grand Prix was similar to a Masters Standard Agility Class and was scored the same way; however, the Standard Course Time was even faster than at the Masters level.

Gordon found a bleacher seat just before Sarah and Michael's performance in Round 2 of the Steeplechase began. They appeared calm and assured as they walked briskly into the ring. Throughout their superlative performance, Gordon overheard favorable comments about the cool dog with the orange ear and the pretty woman with the matching orange hand.

A man said, "He's a homely-looking dog until he moves and then he metamorphoses into the most gorgeous creature I've ever seen."

He heard a young girl's voice ask, "What's metamorph, uh, what does that long word mean?"

The man replied, "Change. It means change or transform from one thing to another."

Gordon couldn't resist announcing, "That's my wife and our pet, Michael Archangelo."

"What breed of dog is he?" inquired a woman who was sitting beside the young girl and looked to be her mother.

"He's a Callé dog from San Miguel de Allende in Mexico," replied Gordon.

Spectators seated near enough to hear his reply smiled knowingly. Texas bordered Mexico and most people in the area had some knowledge of Spanish.

A man commented, "So that is how he came to be named Michael Archangelo!"

The young girl needed an explanation because she couldn't make the connection between San Miguel and Saint Michael.

An older woman in the crowd pronounced, "He is surely destined to achieve greatness with such an exalted name."

"Hear! Hear!" said Gordon.

The spectators whistled and applauded noisily after their performance.

Gordon left his seat to find Sarah and Michael. Michael spied him before Sarah did and galloped toward him pulling Sarah along as she determinedly held onto the leash with both hands.

Gordon pulled her close for a hug and then knelt to hug Michael. "The crowd around me loved your team performance."

They checked the Point Sheet and saw that, so far, Michael had posted the fastest time. Sarah and Michael sauntered back to their rest area and drank water and munched gingersnaps while Gordon purchased food from a vendor.

Gordon arrived with burritos and announced, "I checked the Point Sheet and Jetson has tied with Michael for first place. Unless another dog posts a faster time, they'll have a run-off. Hold off on eating. Neither of you should compete on a full stomach. We'll check the results again in ten minutes."

Twenty minutes later, Maureen Hanks and Jetson, Sarah and Michael waited patiently while the last competitor exited the Steeplechase ring. They remained tied for first place. Gordon hadn't waited with them near the entrance gate because he wanted to watch the spectacle from the bleacher seats.

Michael thought he was going to perform a Pairs Relay until he and Sarah paced into the ring without Jetson and his mom. He recognized that this was the same course setup he had run not so long ago and understood that something different was happening because he had never run the same course, back-to-back. He knew what the word "fast" meant and understood that Sarah wanted him to run and jump as quick as he could move his legs.

About three-quarters of the way through the course, Michael displaced the top pole of a jump and heard the clatter as it toppled to the ground. Sarah urged him toward the next jump, so he kept on running the course as fast as he could.

When Gordon saw Michael displace the top pole he thought, "That's it! Oh well, second place in a Steeplechase over so many competitors is an astounding feat for Sarah and Michael."

He heard some onlookers seated nearby groan, and someone commented, "There goes Michael Archangelo's chance of winning."

Someone else said, "What a great name! There must be an interesting story connected to a name like that!"

A gruff-voiced man said, "It ain't over till it's over. The other dog hasn't performed yet."

There was noisy, prolonged applause as Sarah and Michael exited the ring.

Jetson and Maureen Hanks began their performance and Gordon decided to delay congratulating and consoling his darling duo in favor of watching these two worthy competitors. "I'd like to see Maureen's handling technique," he thought. "Maybe she has a method I could advise Sarah about."

They were running the setup in a controlled, economical and practiced way. He saw Maureen check her watch and then command Jetson to move faster. Suddenly, Jetson was preparing to take a decoy jump. Maureen quickly signaled him to take the hurdle on the left. He swerved and used the correct jump, but didn't clear it cleanly and displaced the top pole.

"Aha!" thought Gordon. "We still have a chance. They have each accrued five faults."

Jetson and Maureen finished to a round of hearty applause after which the winning team was immediately announced. The crowd clapped and stomped and whistled as the homely dog with a neon-orange ear and the small, pretty woman with an equally bright orange hand strode to the center of the ring to receive their first place award for having had the fastest time. Gordon heard the onlookers around him yelling Michael's name over and over.

Michael understood that he had won the South Central Regional Championships Steeplechase over a much more experienced competitor. He was proud of his accomplishment and confidence filled him. He remembered having experienced that same feeling when performing with Patrick. He wanted that unshakeable faith in himself to always be inside him.

After the award ceremony, Gordon promised Sarah that he would buy a fantastic take-out dinner for the three of them, from a very expensive restaurant.

"We can eat it in our motel or in a park," he said.

"What if a top-notch chef refuses to cook a take-out meal?" Sarah asked.

"I'm betting the chef will when I explain your big tournament win."

Sarah said, "I've got to concentrate on getting through the Grand Prix Finals in another hour or so. I know I shouldn't feel pressured to win it just because we won the Round I Qualifier, but I do. I feel even more pressure now that Michael has won the Steeplechase. That reminds me, soon we will have participated in enough Tournaments that we should hit the number 10 mark and Michael will earn the title of Tournament Master. Hooray!"

The final round of the Grand Prix would be another huge class in Michael's jump height category. Gordon and Sarah were aware that Michael had been accruing a large number of points because he had either won, or placed well, over so many other competitors in his classes.

"Maybe he'll be on 'The Top Ten' list because of his high point accumulation," Gordon speculated. "If you both do as well next year, you could be offered a place on Team USA and represent our country at the International Federation of Cynological Sports the year after next. Whatever points Michael accrues this year won't count toward being selected, but whatever he accrues next year will. That's good for us because he just got started this year and didn't have a chance to collect a lot of points."

Sarah gulped and said, "Maybe you and Michael ought to practice together. You two could compete together next year. You would be a fabulous team."

Gordon laughed, "You and Michael are already a fabulous team. Are you nervous about the possibility of you and Michael representing our country at the International Dog Agility tournament?"

"You bet I am," Sarah said.

As they hugged, they automatically parted to allow Michael to nudge himself between them and get his share of the lovings.

They strolled around and stopped to watch the 12-inch jump height dogs compete in the Steeplechase. They applauded enthusiastically for a Papillon named Thumbelina who gave an outstanding performance. They watched until the last competitor left the ring and listened to the announcement that Thumbelina had won.

Gordon stayed with Michael near Ring 1 while Sarah sprinted to Ring 2 and took a pre-performance walk-through of the Grand Prix course setup. She noted the deceptive positioning of two hurdles side-by-side, one of which was a decoy. She knew she would have to be positioned near the decoy to point Michael toward the correct hurdle to use when he emerged from the Rigid Tunnel. She jogged backed to Ring 1 and found them.

Sarah watched Gordon find a bleacher seat at Ring 2 and then whispered in Michael's ear just before they entered the ring, "I love you no matter what our placement is, but please, perform FAST!"

Michael intuited what Sarah had said because the deep and abiding bond of love that opens a level of communication that transcends words connected them. Michael now understood what Topaz meant when she had described the thought and feeling transference that she and her mom had. He pressed his head against Sarah and looked directly into her eyes. Sarah knew that Michael was telling her he understood.

She thought, "We have that same mystical connection that Jeanette and Topaz have."

He entered the ring with assurance and Sarah saw the confidence that emanated from him.

"I believe he's telling me we'll win," she thought.

They did. They won the South Central Regional Grand Prix!

Gordon phoned the highly recommended French restaurant, "Tuilleries," and spoke with the chef. After explaining Sarah and Michael's huge wins at the Regional Championship Dog Agility Tournament, Chef Laurence Lafitte, cooperated fully. He suggested an appetizer of Shrimp New Orleans, followed by a Chateaubriand large enough for three rather than for two (as was the usual serving size), arugula and spinach salad with his special House Lafitte dressing, Lafitte mashed potatoes, a vegetable medley of green beans and shoestring zucchini flavored with his special herbs and warm French bread rolls that were baked on the premises.

"We 'ave many desserts, monsieur. Do you 'ave somet'ing particular in mind?" inquired the chef in a pronounced French accent.

"Crème Brûlée is a favorite of all three of us."

"Ah! A magnifique dessert that is always available at the Tuilleries. I desire all t'ree of you to dine elegantly, so I am prepared to supply our china and cutlery if you would kindly return those items before you depart town. A meal of such quality should not be eaten on plastique plates using disposable utensils. I will place hot food items in a special container designed to keep them warm and chilled food in another container that will keep them cool. When would you like to pick up your dinner, monsieur?"

Gordon thanked Chef Lafitte and said he would pick up the meal about 5:30 p.m. He promised to return containers and dishes several hours later.

"Monsieur, I request you to bring your wife and "magnifique chien" with the exalted, heavenly name to the back entrance of my restaurant when you return my goods. I would be honored to meet two grande champions."

They ate the world-class meal in a pretty park at a picnic table placed near a small lake. Folks enjoying an evening stroll were drawn to their little feast by the tantalizing fragrances of good food that wafted through the early evening air.

An elderly woman asked Sarah if she had prepared the meal herself. Gordon explained the circumstances and the origin of their feast. The woman and her husband congratulated Sarah and Michael. Michael was becoming used to receiving attention and rather enjoyed it.

As the couple walked away, they overheard the woman say to her husband, "Darlin', do that for my birthday, next month."

Gordon and Sarah decided to drive back to Pennsylvania early the next morning. They missed their home and were impatient to begin renovating the place, making it their own and starting their lives as a threesome.

CHAPTER TWENTY-SIX

September was a busy month. Essie managed to show Kawdje at some Conformation Dog Shows and was elated to receive acceptance to show him at the Westminster Dog Show that was always held in February. All four dogs and their parents competed in two locally held Dog Agility events.

The September 17th/18th event was held outdoors and weather conditions during the first day of competition were dismal. An oppressive, gray cloud cover looked as though, at any moment, it would fall down and envelope everyone and everything. There were intermittent showers of light rain and everyone expected a deluge of blinding rain to let loose.

Pavilions provided shelter and kept performance areas and equipment dry. Large, non-slip runners covered the grass adjacent to every entrance gate to each ring to absorb dampness from paws and shoes. In spite of these precautions, people and pets walking from wet, unprotected areas tracked in dampness. Fortunately, contact obstacles were always covered with a non-slip surface so that was not a safety issue.

Kissy was paired with Chrysee in the 12-inch category Masters Relay. Their pleasure in one another's company was obvious. They placed first by the narrowest of margins. Kawdje was paired with Marjie, a Manchester Terrier who was already well into earning a Bronze Metallic Designation. They placed second.

While Kissy and Kawdje performed in the Relay, Michael and Topaz competed in the Masters Standard Agility Class. Michael came first. A dog named Hubert the Best placed second. Topaz came third.

During lunch break, under cover of one of the large pavilions, Jeanette asked the others if they knew what breed of dog Hubert the Best was. Gordon said that he had been standing near the handler's wife and they had exchanged information about their pets.

"She told me that Hubert the Best is a Belgian Malinois and, in present company, I will refer to him as Hubert the Second Best because Michael has bested him in every class so far."

They all laughed and Cole said, "I don't blame you for being a proud dad. Michael has been spectacular."

When the pets were taken for a potty break before entering the first of the afternoon classes, it was raining steadily. Kissy hated being set down in wet grass. At home, piddle pads were placed on the garage floor for her use when it was raining and during winter blizzards when the snow was deep. Kissy didn't want to squat in wet grass and make it even wetter than it already was. She begged her dad to pick her up. Evan did so, assuming that Kissy had no need to relieve herself. He carried her into the shelter of the pavilion that covered Ring 1 where the Masters Gamblers Class was just about to start for her jump height category.

Kissy decided that the grass inside the ring was dry enough for her to relieve herself upon it and thought she had better do that quickly before performing the course. A tall, heavy-set, red-haired woman standing near the entrance gate loudly announced that Kissy had fouled the ring. The judge saw the deed, walked over to Evan and quietly informed him that Kissy was eliminated. Evan thought to himself, as he led her out of the ring, that at least she hadn't bitten the judge as she had done many months ago during a Conformation Dog Show.

The next competitor was a Lhasa Apso who made it obvious that he was male as he raised his leg and fouled the ring in the exact spot that Kissy had used. Once again, the red-haired woman, holding a small Terrier mixed breed dog who had not placed well in the morning classes, called out that another foul in the ring had been committed. The Lhasa and handler exited the ring. An assistant was called in and a solution was poured onto the fouled area.

The woman who had loudly announced the infractions of Kissy and the little male Lhasa entered the ring and put her dog down on the grass a few feet away from the fouled spot. As soon as she released her hold on him, he promptly ran over, sniffed the area, raised his leg and added to the mixture. This time, many voices announced that the ring had been fouled again!

Suddenly, a bone-rattling thunderclap boomed directly overhead and, in Ring 2 where the Masters Snooker class for the 22-inch height category was in progress, a Bearded Collie collapsed onto a hurdle while in mid-jump. She was so frightened she truly fouled the ring. Paper towels and a pooper-scooper were brought to the rescue.

Judges and officials conferred and, after several minutes, an official announced that competition was suspended for the day and would resume tomorrow pending better weather conditions. The decision to eliminate those dogs who had fouled the ring in the Masters Gamblers 12-inch jump height category class and the Masters Snooker 22-inch height category class was rescinded. The official said that those two classes would resume tomorrow and competitors who had completed the course were given the option to perform again under more favorable weather conditions or accept the course time achieved in today's class.

"Furthermore," the official stated, "competition will begin an hour earlier and end an hour later tomorrow pending the arrival of better weather conditions that are expected to move in overnight. The extra time will allow us to fit in today's cancelled classes."

Evan let out a huge sigh of relief and slogged through the downpour and wet grass carrying Kissy, accompanied by an equally relieved Essie carrying Kawdje. Everyone was glad to head home.

The next day was unseasonably cool with intermittent sunshine, but no one complained. Kissy won Gamblers and Kawdje placed third, just a fifth of a second behind Marjie, the Manchester Terrier. Chrysee was a close fourth. The Masters Snooker class was also won by Kissy. Kawdje was a half-second slower and took second place. Michael dominated his Masters classes, winning every class with the exception of Gamblers, which Topaz won. Topaz placed second in Snooker and Hubert the Best came third.

The following weekend, picture perfect early autumn weather smiled on the Opening Day of the Dexterous Dogs Agility Event. The morning classes began with the Masters Pairs Relay for the 12-inch jump height. Kawdje was paired with Olé, the Miniature Pinscher, and Kissy with Marjie, the Manchester Terrier. Kissy confided to Marjie that she wanted to win and that she definitely wanted to win over Olé.

Marjie said that she had been paired with Olé before. "We placed first. Olé told me how lucky I was to be paired with him and that we won because of his extraordinary performance. I'm sorry Kawdje is paired with him because he'll blame Kawdje if they don't earn first place, and they won't because you and I will win."

Kissy and Marjie marched into the ring with determination coursing through them and fueling their energy levels to an all-time high. Kissy performed first. She loved Relays because the course design was similar to a Standard Agility Class in which all the various obstacles were used with the exception of the table, which, to her delight, was never included in a Relay class.

Because she was performing outdoors and there was a breeze, she heard the rushing sound of the wind as it flapped her little ears. She was swift and superb and wished her performance would go on and on.

Tim Kreutzberg and Marjie were an exceptional team. After they exited the ring, Tim promptly checked the Point Sheet for their placement while Evan stood near the exit gate holding Kissy in his arms and watching Kawdje and Olé perform. He saw Tim walking toward him giving him the thumbs up signaling their first place lead.

Olé ran well, but in Evan's biased opinion, Kawdje gave a superior performance. After the last competitors exited the ring, to Evan's delight, Kissy and Marjie placed first. Kawdje and Olé came second. Chrysee and a Terrier mix called Bon Jon held third place.

Kissy and Marjie were standing close to one another while their dads checked the final placements. Both understood the phrase "We've won," and they were so happy they practically high-fived their paws together.

The whole day went well for the fabulous foursome. Michael Archangelo placed first in every one of his classes with the exception of Jumpers, which Topaz won. Topaz placed second in all other classes. Hubert the Best placed third in two classes and far down the list in others.

The second day of the event, the weather blessed everyone with a clear blue sky and a slight northwesterly breeze. Morning classes went well for everyone.

During lunch break, Gordon and Sarah invited everyone to a birthday bash for Michael on October 27th and said that they had decided on a Halloween theme because the party was being held just five days before All Hallow's Eve.

"Everyone come in costume," Sarah decreed.

Evan said, "That's your birthday, Gordon."

"I forgot you would know that's my birthday, Evan. Sarah and I didn't mention that it's my natal day because I don't want obligatory gifts."

Jenny asked, "How did you know what day Michael's birthday is? You found him when he was full grown, Aunt Sarah."

"I'd like to celebrate the birthdays of my two special guys on the same day. Both of them are big, intelligent, athletic, like fast cars and good food. They're so similar that I'm betting they have the same birth date."

Gordon stood up and took a mock bow and said, "We both have something else in common that you didn't mention. We both love you."

Jenny was enthralled with the idea of a costume party and begged to be allowed to invite a couple of her best friends from school. Her aunt began to scold her for being presumptuous, but Gordon interrupted Jeanette and said that kids and parties go together.

"Are the pets going to the party, too?" asked Jenny.

"You bet!" replied Sarah. "Pets and parties go together, too, and, it's Michael's birthday bash."

"Aunt Essie and Uncle Evan, could I borrow Kissy? I want us to go as Lilo and Stitch."

Essie laughed and asked, "How will you transform Kissy into Stitch, and how can you possibly make over yourself to look like Lilo?"

Jenny looked questioningly at her Aunt Jeanette who said, "We can look for a black wig for you at some costume stores. Maybe some pet shops have dog costumes. If Aunt Essie and Uncle Evan agree, I'll help you find a suitable costume for Kissy."

Essie and Evan assured Jenny that Kissy could be her sidekick for the party.

While party plans were discussed, the pets devoured their lunch of dry dog food and chicken breasts stuffed with seasoned rice that had been diced for their convenience. Kawdje couldn't finish his portion because he had eaten so many oatmeal cookie tidbits, a treat which Essie had hand fed him after he placed first in Jumpers that morning. Topaz and Michael hovered over him, waiting to clean up his bowl for him.

"Quit drooling on my head, Michael," grouched Kawdje as he backed away from his bowl. "I don't mind getting drenched by rain but not by drool."

Michael and Topaz's muzzles neatly divided the bowl and in less than three seconds, Kawdje's bowl was shiny clean.

"Does anyone have any exciting tales to tell about our morning activities?" asked Topaz.

Kawdje related his experience of being paired with Olé in yesterday's Masters Relay Class.

"You all know that Kissy and Marjie won. My mom and I are a good team and we did very well. In spite of our good showing, after we found out we hadn't placed first, Olé sneered and said it was his hard luck to be paired with a loser. At first I wasn't going to dignify his slur with a reply but then I looked him straight in the eyes and said, "Likewise." I walked away and left him sputtering.

They all laughed and agreed that his pithy comment was the perfect put-down.

Kissy said, "I had the bad luck to be paired with Olé this morning. We exchanged a nasty dialogue before the class began."

The other three begged, "Tell us."

"He had the nerve to say it was my lucky day because I was teamed with him. I reminded him that every class we've competed in, I've placed ahead of him. I told him that Marjie and I placed first in yesterday's Relay, thanks to his mediocre performance which held back Kawdje's placement."

"What did he say to that?" asked Kawdje, who was pleased that Kissy had defended him.

"He said that if my ears flapped as much as my mouth, I could be used in a cornfield to scare away crows."

The other three suppressed laughter, but they quivered from the effort. They could hardly wait to hear what quick-witted Kissy had retorted.

"I told Olé that I hadn't realized that he was a little farm dog whose only companionship was livestock and that his lack of exposure to society explained his absence of Dog Agility etiquette. Then it really got nasty. He said he hoped that I would fall into the Wishing Well Hurdle."

"What did you say to that?" asked Topaz.

"I said that such a calamity would prevent us from placing well and if he really wanted that to happen, he was not only slow but he was stupid. I followed that up by saying, 'furthermore, you little twit, if you don't run fast enough to suit me, I'll throw up all over you.' I told him I could throw up at will if I ate a little grass and that he wasn't worth cheering about, but perhaps he was worth throwing up on.

He had the gall to brag that he would perform the course faster than me. While he was competing I called, 'Olé, Olé, don't lose your way.' I almost regretted my comment because I could see that he nearly stumbled, but it proved that my taunt irked him. I refrained from calling out any other remarks because I decided I would rather do well than thwart Olé and lose my chance of winning."

By now, the others had given up trying to suppress their laughter.

Finally Topaz asked, "Who won your jump height Masters Relay?"

Kissy replied that she and Olé had.

"What did Olé say after he found out that you and he placed first?" Michael asked.

"I didn't give him a chance to twitch his whiskers. I said, 'Olé, Olé, I saved the day. No thanks to you, we won the Relay.' Then I turned away and walked fast ahead of my dad to hurry him along."

Kissy would have exulted in self-satisfaction had she known how much Olé had come to hate his name. He fumed with frustration because it rhymed with so many words. He bemoaned not having been called a name that was impossible to rhyme with anything else.

CHAPTER TWENTY-SEVEN

The weather was milder than normal for Gordon and Michael's Halloween/ Birthday bash. Sarah and Gordon turned off the heat and left the kitchen door and some windows open. The scent of mulled cider simmering in a pot on the stove filled the house and wafted through open windows.

Sarah, Gordon and Michael were dressed as Daphne, Fred and Scooby Doo. Essie and Kawdje were impersonating Dorothy and Toto. Evan was resplendent as Glinda, the beautiful and kindly Witch of the South from the movie, *The Wizard of Oz*.

He wore a blonde wig upon which a tiara glittered and sparkled with every movement of his head. He glided into the house in a long, pink gown made of layers of gossamer netting. He waved a sparkling wand and spoke in a falsetto voice. Long, pink satin gloves sheathed his hands and most of his arms. Essie had glued false eyelashes on him and had liberally applied mascara, eye shadow and rouge but no amount of makeup could hide the stubble on his chin and cheeks.

Jeanette, Cole, Jenny, Topaz and Kissy followed them into the house. They had caravanned over together because Jenny needed to stop by Essie and Evan's home in order to dress Kissy in her costume which consisted of spraying her with a non-toxic blue paint that could easily be washed off her fur. Kawdje had been sprayed with dark brown paint to make him look more like Toto. Essie was a credible version of Dorothy in a brown wig braided into two plaits. She wore a blue and white gingham dress and a pair of red sequined shoes.

Jeanette wore a 1940's style dress and hairdo. Topaz was dressed in a short, swingy skirt and a puffed sleeve, wraparound blouse in the same material as Jeanette's dress. They were impersonating the Pointer Sisters. Cole, posing as their manager, was garbed in a 1970's leisure suit.

No sooner had they begun to sip cider, when Jenny's friends were dropped off for the party by their parents. Alyssa Benton was dressed as Barbie Doll in Hawaii because she wanted to coordinate her costume with Jenny, who was wearing shorts and a blouse. Mark Wesley was a pirate. He told Jenny and Alyssa that he just wanted to wear a comfortable costume.

"You just want to wear a patch over one eye," retorted Alyssa.

"That too!" he admitted.

Pat and Ed arrived with apples for the apple-bobbing contest. They were dressed like contestants from the Dancing With The Stars television show. Joy came costumed as the Bride of Frankenstein and Sam was a large, tall Frankenstein.

Joy hugged her Uncle Gordon and wished him a happy birthday, then asked, "How old are you?"

"Younger than your daddy," replied Gordon.

Michael nudged in for his hug and Joy asked Michael as she wrapped her arms around his neck and laid her head on his, "Michael, how old are you?"

Sarah laughed and said, "We're celebrating his second birthday. I'm not sure what the equivalent is in dog years."

Kissy came into the living room and her hackles went up when she saw Sam. She barked at him. He took off his full-head Frankenstein mask and spent several minutes coaxing her to come before she would cautiously sidle up to him. Sam picked her up in his arms and told Joy that he thought he would like one of Kissy's puppies if and when she had a litter.

"I thought you liked big dogs," a surprised Joy said.

"I do, but I like Kissy. She's gutsy! As tiny as she is, she was ready to take me on until she finally recognized me."

The buffet table was draped in black cloth and laden with tempting dishes. There were stuffed cabbage rolls, Swedish meatballs, rice and burritos that Sarah thought might appeal to the kids' tastes, not to mention her own and Michael's. She had made a huge dish of seven-layer refried bean dip, and placed a large bowl of tortilla chips beside it. There was champagne for toasting, and bottles of sparkling, non-alcoholic carbonated juice for the kids to drink during the birthday toasts. A huge birthday cake decorated like a pumpkin with *Happy Birthday Gordon and Michael* written in black icing and a fake black spider perched on the top took center stage on the buffet table.

The house was draped with fake cobwebs and spiders. Several small

Jack O'Lanterns grinned on the buffet table plus a huge one scowled on the kitchen counter, and more of them dimly lit the front and kitchen door entrances. A witch, perched on her broomstick, was suspended from the kitchen ceiling and looked as if she were swooping toward the countertop.

When the festivities began, Mark won the apple-bobbing contest. Sarah awarded him with a movie theater certificate for $20. Mark quietly said to Jenny that he would like to take her to the movies next Saturday evening. Jenny simply smiled mysteriously: (at least she hoped it was a mysterious smile. She had been practicing in front of her mirror all week).

Next came a talent contest. Essie tap-danced and sang, *Somewhere Over the Rainbow,* while a barking Kawdje/Toto circled her and Evan waved his wand and intermittently joined her in song. When Essie finished, Evan brandished his wand and announced in his best falsetto voice, "I now change each of you into the most wonderful version that any of you could ever aspire to be and all your good wishes are granted for the next year."

Everyone clapped and cheered.

Pat and Ed put on a CD and did an elegant foxtrot to *Blue Skies.* They swayed, dipped and quickstepped. Everyone was dumbstruck by their expertise and several seconds of silence followed the end of their act before the enthusiastic and appreciative applause kicked in.

Jeanette played a CD of the Pointer Sisters hit song, *The Boogie Woogie Bugle Boy of Company B.* She had chosen that song because of the connection of Topaz being a Shorthaired Pointer. She and Topaz had practiced dancing to it. Jeanette lip-synced while she and Topaz paced and circled in intricate patterns. Occasionally, Topaz belted out a high note. Kawdje joined in at those times, as well as Michael and Kissy who refused to be left out of the chorus, so all four pets accompanied the Pointer Sisters. Jeanette and Topaz took a bow in the down dog yoga position at the end of their act. Everybody whistled and stomped and the applause was as thunderous as a small audience could make it.

Gordon took center stage and asked if there were any more contestants. No one spoke up, so Gordon declared that the winner would be chosen according to the loudness of the applause. It was a three-way tie.

Gordon announced, "Essie, Evan, Kawdje, Jeanette and Topaz plan to compete in the World Cynosport Games in Scottsdale, Arizona in three weeks, so the prize will be a ride in my helicopter plus a gourmet lunch prepared by a world class chef and dining will take place near my kiva site in the desert."

Everyone cheered.

He continued, "Pat and Ed, here is a gift card to Ralph's Italian Restaurant in downtown South Philly. I recommend the mussels in red sauce."

Mark whispered to Jenny, "Your family and friends are way cool. Are you going to the World Cynosport Games?"

"Yes," she replied. "I'm going to compete with Kissy in the Junior Handler class."

Jenny, Mark, Alyssa and the pets gravitated outdoors. It was dark, but outdoor lighting had recently been installed and a meandering path had been cleared all the way to the stream, which was situated downhill from the house. They all loped down the path with pets quick-stepping between, around and through legs.

Jenny was surprised to see how swollen and tumultuous the stream had become since she had last seen it three weeks ago.

"It's amazing how the week of continual rain that we had awhile ago changed this stream from a shallow, babbling brook into a fast-moving stream," she remarked.

Michael stood near the edge of the bank and bent his head to lap water. Topaz leaned her head close to Michael and drank, too. Kissy and Kawdje followed suit.

Kissy had to bend over so far to lap water that she accidentally nose-dived into the stream. The rush and tumble of fast-moving cold water somersaulted her and she lost all reference of up and down. She gulped very cold water and felt as though she was smothering. A thought flashed through her mind. "I don't want to leave my dad and mom and Kawdje and I'm not done running. I have lots more Agility Events to win." Suddenly, she felt air and coughed and struggled to breathe. She made a tremendous effort to swim and keep her head above water.

No one saw Kissy fall into the stream, but everyone saw her splashing close to the bank in a frantic effort to get out of the water. Jenny quickly knelt down and reached out to grab her, but the rushing water swept Kissy away from the bank and carried her downstream.

Jenny knew that Topaz was a strong and confident swimmer and swam, in her own personal pond almost everyday, for the joy of it. Jenny commanded her to "Get Kissy" but Topaz had already jumped into the stream. It was too shallow for her to swim, so she half jumped, half ran as fast as she could in a stumbling, clumsy fashion because the uneven, rocky bottom and the current kept her off balance. Michael jumped in, too, and because he was stronger, he made more headway with his attempt to reach Kissy, who was struggling and in obvious panic. Kawdje was well aware that Kissy couldn't swim, so he jumped in, too, and was immediately out of his depth. He swam with the current and reached Kissy first.

He positioned himself downstream from her. The current wedged her body alongside him. He tried to swim toward the water's edge, but the current was strong and they both were being swept downstream. When Michael reached them, he understood what Kawdje was trying to do. He positioned himself downstream of Kawdje and crouched so that Kawdje was pressed alongside his flank by the rush of water and Kissy was still pressed against Kawdje's flank by the current.

Kissy panicked as water splashed over her muzzle. She opened her jaws to bark, but water gushed in. Her front legs flailed in a vain attempt to swim.

Kawdje kept his cool and tried to dog paddle toward the bank, but with the current pressing a struggling Kissy against him, he couldn't budge. He was profoundly thankful that Michael was keeping him and Kissy from being swept downstream.

Alyssa ran back up the pathway to the house. Her legs felt as heavy as though she was wading through molasses. She burst through the open door into the kitchen.

"Kissy fell into the stream and the others are trying to help her," she gasped.

Everyone ran outside. Sarah and Gordon snatched a couple of flashlights from a kitchen drawer. They shone the light along the pathway as everyone hurried toward the river.

CHAPTER TWENTY-EIGHT

Kissy became aware that Topaz was beside her. She felt Topaz's jaws close around her neck. In several strides, Topaz reached the edge of the stream and dropped a frightened, exhausted Kissy onto dry ground; then Topaz immediately plunged back into the stream to help Michael maneuver Kawdje to the bank.

Topaz could only imagine how cold Kawdje must feel. The water just reached her underbelly and it chilled her to the bone. She knew Michael must also feel desperately cold, because he was partially submerged in a crouching position in order to keep Kawdje from being swept downstream. If he stood upright, Kawdje would be swept between his legs and the current would take him away.

She tried to encircle Kawdje's neck with her jaws, but his neck was thicker than Kissy's. Then she attempted to snag his collar between her teeth, but it wasn't loose enough for her to get a good grasp. She considered positioning herself behind Kawdje and nudging him toward the edge of the bank while Michael stayed beside him and prevented him from being swept downstream.

She saw, with profound relief, that Jenny and her friend, who had been stumbling along the stream's edge trying to catch up with them, had reached Kissy. Topaz knew they had seen her, Kawdje and Michael because Jenny called out to her. Jenny lifted Kissy into her arms.

Mark said, "Jenny, stay with Kissy. I hear everyone pounding down the pathway. Call to them so they can locate us. I'll help the other three pets." He waded into the water and splashed toward Topaz.

Mark was glad that the moon shed enough light for him to see the three dogs. Topaz was alternating between standing alongside Kawdje and trying to take hold of his collar between her teeth and standing behind him while trying to push him forward and toward the bank. Mark understood that Michael was preventing Kawdje from being swept downstream by staunchly standing his ground in the current, although crouching his ground would be more accurate. Mark could tell that Kawdje had not panicked and was trying to swim crosswise to the current toward the embankment, but couldn't make much progress. "The little guy must be frozen," he thought. "My feet already feel like ice cubes."

He lifted Kawdje into his arms and held him securely against his chest as he waded toward Kissy and Jenny.

Kissy had not been able to relax in Jenny's arms because she knew that Kawdje was still in that terrible and dangerous stream where she had almost drowned. She felt too weak to bark encouragement to him and had been too exhausted to thank Topaz for saving her. She didn't even have the strength to kiss Jenny.

By now, all the partygoers were surging toward them and Mark stumbled, almost falling backward as the beam of a flashlight momentarily blinded him. He felt Michael pressed against his right leg and he followed Topaz as she splashed in front of him toward the embankment. Arms reached out to pull him onto dry ground.

Kissy experienced a surge of strength when she saw Mark being helped out of the stream while holding Kawdje in his arms.

"Sweet, wonderful, loyal Kawdje who tried to save me without any thought for his own safety," she thought. Then she saw Topaz and Michael, who had helped to save them both. She knew she was unbelievably blessed and lucky to have such faithful and caring friends.

She managed to weakly yelp, "Thank you."

"I love them all!" she thought.

Just before Essie lifted Kawdje out of Mark's arms, he felt the little guy's cold tongue lick his cheek and Mark knew that he had been well and truly thanked. A longing swept through him to have a faithful, loyal friend who accepted him for what he was and who didn't argue.

"I bet Jenny would be faithful and loyal, but she would argue. A pet wouldn't," he thought.

After Mark and the pets were toweled dry, everyone slouched in chairs and lounged on couches while enjoying the buffet meal. Gordon and Michael blew out their birthday candles while everybody sang "Happy Birthday" to them. Jenny and her friends retired to the den and sprawled on the Oriental rug with the pets nestled between and around them. Jenny thanked Alyssa and Mark for their help in the rescue and then turned on a TV program that they wanted to watch.

Mark's parents arrived to take him home and Sarah and Gordon insisted that they sit down and enjoy cake and coffee while listening to the story about their wonderful son who had rescued one of the pets who had fallen into the stream on their property.

No sooner had they settled comfortably to hear the details of the story when Alyssa's parents were heard at the doorway, calling for permission to enter. When they, too, were seated and sipping coffee and nibbling on cake, the rescue tale unfolded with everybody contributing details and impressions.

Jenny, Mark and Alyssa were still cloistered in the den with the pets. During a lull in the party conversation, the adults heard Mark's voice saying, "If everybody tried to help everyone else the way these dogs helped one another, the world would be a peaceful and happy place."

"Amen," Pat said softly.

Jeanette smiled at both sets of parents and said, "Your children are wonderful. My husband and I are very happy that our niece has such good friends."

Mark's parents said, "We have to see these altruistic, agility wonder dogs who are such loyal friends to one another."

They and Alyssa's parents walked into the den and their hearts overflowed with tenderness as they looked at the group of kids and pets casually and comfortable interlaced while they watched TV.

As they were leaving, Alyssa hugged Jenny and said it was the best party she had ever been to and added, "I've never sung, 'Happy Birthday' to a dog before. That was so cool."

Mark seconded the sentiment, including the hug.

Essie, Evan, Jeanette and Cole remained after the party to discuss how to divide up the four pets into a Three-Dog Team for the upcoming World Cynosport Games.

Gordon said," Before you discuss the World Cynosport Games, I want to tell you that Sarah and I received our wedding video and the young man who filmed it has asked our permission to submit it to that TV show called 'World's Funniest Home Videos.' We want you all to watch it because you are in it and will be recognizable to anyone who sees the video on TV; therefore, you should have the option of deciding whether or not it should be aired. You can borrow and view it at your convenience."

Sarah said, "Now that we've settled the video issue, let's discuss the World Cynosport Games. We have the option of three of our pets comprising a team, and the remaining pet being paired with two other dogs that we've met on the Agility circuit or letting the Cynosport officials complete the team. Another option is to have two of our pets on one team and two on another team, let the Cynosport officials provide the third member of each team, or call up some of the folks we've exchanged contact information with to bring in the third member for each of the two teams. How do you want to play it?"

Jeanette said, "I vote that we have three of our pets comprise a team. Topaz and I should be left out because she will come into her fertile season very soon and will be barred from competing unless her cycle is over before the Cynosport Games begin."

Essie said, "I prefer to have three of the pets comprise a team and the only fair way to do that is to draw lots. Let the decision be made by the luck of the draw. If Topaz comes into season too late to compete in the Games, we'll deal with that circumstance if it arises."

Evan and Sarah agreed. Gordon said he would prepare three slips of paper with an "X" and the fourth with an "O". While Gordon was in the den, it was decided that Evan would have first pick because he was the only male handler.

Cole was sitting beside Jeanette with his arm around her shoulders.

"I can't be away from my practice for more than a few days and Jenny should miss as little school as possible so she and I will arrive the day before the Games begin and fly home immediately after the closing. I'm relieved that you're going to caravan across the country together and stay in the same motels and eat meals together. It's reassuring to know that Jeanette and Topaz will constantly be in the company of friends."

"Don't worry, Cole, we'll take good care of your ladies," Evan said.

Sarah said," You and Topaz can travel in our SUV to the Games."

"Not a good idea, Sarah. Topaz might still be fertile during the cross country trip and will need to be kept separate from Michael and Kawdje."

"Michael will be heartbroken not to see Topaz for a couple of weeks."

Gordon came back into the living room holding four pieces of folded paper.

"Who chooses first?"

Evan held up a finger.

"Okay, bro, pick!"

Evan made his selection and unfolded it. He smiled, but remained silent.

"I'll pick next since I'm closest to you," Essie said. Her face remained impassive as she looked at the mark on her paper.

"Who's next?" she asked, looking at Sarah and Jeanette.

"Let's close our eyes and pick whichever piece we each touch," Jeanette suggested to Sarah as they walked toward Gordon's outstretched hand.

"Okay," agreed Sarah.

They opened their folded papers simultaneously. Cole asked, "Which one of you four fabulous Dog Agility Teams has been left out?"

CHAPTER TWENTY-NINE

To everyone's great relief, Topaz came into her fertile season two days after the Halloween/Birthday bash. She finished her cycle just prior to starting the cross-country trip to Arizona. To be certain that no mishaps occurred, Jeanette kept her separated from Michael and Kawdje throughout the five-day drive to Arizona. The group arrived in Scottsdale, Arizona, in the afternoon of the day prior to the opening of the World Cynosport Games, and everyone checked into their rooms. Because he was familiar with the area, Gordon drove Jeanette and Topaz to the airport to pick up Cole and Jenny.

There were hugs all around when Cole and Jenny greeted the group. Jenny had to kiss each of the pets. That evening, the group strolled the beautifully landscaped grounds around the resort with the pets on leashes. For the first time in three weeks, Topaz mingled with Michael, Kissy and Kawdje. Tails wagged enthusiastically and they jumped around in excitement to be together again.

Cole remarked, "Michael and Kawdje aren't making advances toward Topaz, so she's definitely over her fertile season."

Everyone retired early. Jeanette lay on the bed to rest before taking a shower and promptly fell asleep while Cole watched TV. Jenny and Topaz were in an adjoining room. Cole heard Jenny knock on the door that separated their rooms and called her to come in.

"Topaz wants to go out, Uncle Cole. May I take her for a walk?"

"It's after dark. I know the grounds are well lighted, but I don't want you walking outside alone. I'll go with you. I could use the exercise."

They encountered Gordon, Sarah and Michael enjoying a late evening stroll and stopped to chat about tomorrow's activities.

"Gordon, tomorrow morning, let's meet for breakfast about 6:45. After we've eaten, we'll follow you to the Cynosport Games since you're the only one of us who knows this area. Will that give us enough time to get there when it opens?"

"Sure, Cole. It's less than a 15-minute drive from here."

Cole asked, "How hot will it be tomorrow? I forgot to check *The Weather Channel.*"

"The daytime high will be in the upper seventies and that is usually from 3-5 p.m. Even at that temperature, the sun is powerful, so everyone should wear sunscreen, plus a visor or hat."

Jenny pointed to clumps of tall, blue flowers highlighted by a tall streetlight.

"What are those pretty flowers? I've never seen them before."

They others looked toward the area that Jenny was pointing to.

Sarah said, "They're called agapanthus. Aren't they beautiful?"

Jenny tugged her Uncle Cole closer to the flowers to get a better look, and as he followed her, he abruptly halted when Topaz's lead played out to its full length and was pulled taut.

Sarah and Gordon walked toward the display of agapanthus flowers, too, and Gordon stopped suddenly as Michael's lead pulled taut. While they were admiring flowers, Topaz and Michael were learning about the birds and the bees.

Jenny was embarrassed, Gordon was amused, Sarah was dumbstruck, Cole was dismayed and Michael and Topaz were deliriously happy.

Gordon said hopefully, "Maybe it's too late in Topaz's cycle for her to get pregnant."

Cole smacked the palm of his hand against his forehead and dragged it over his head and down the back of his neck, which he began to massage. Instantaneously, he had a headache. "Yeah, sure, and bears fly," he muttered.

Jenny said, "It will be fun to have puppies in the house. I'll help look after them. They'll be very special puppies because Topaz and Michael are the best dogs anyone could ever have."

"That's the spirit, Jenny," said Sarah. "Gordon and I want one of the puppies. After all, it will be a puppy of Michael's as much as it is of Topaz's."

Gordon said, "I bet Pat and Ed will want one, too. Cole, we'll help with the expense of raising puppies. They're ours, too."

"The expense isn't what I'm worried about. I have to face Jeanette with the news of the mating and then eventually find great homes for them."

"Topaz and Michael love each other, Uncle Cole. I'm glad they're going to have puppies. My friend, Mark, keeps saying that if people were as nice as dogs, the world would be a better place."

"You tell that to your Aunt Jeanette as you break the news to her."

Sarah smothered a smile and said, "We should all tell her together. That way her anger will spatter over all of us and one person won't be flooded by the storm."

"Good idea," Cole said, feeling profoundly relieved.

"Are you scared of Aunt Jeanette?" asked Jenny as she looked up at her Uncle Cole with obvious concern and surprise.

"Of course not! Why would you ever think that?"

"Just a thought!"

A trembling Topaz pressed her wet nose to her mom's cheek to awaken her. She knew that her mom had kept her away from Michael during the past few weeks because her mom had not wanted her to mate with him.

Jeanette wondered why Topaz was shivering and, as sleep receded, she became aware of Cole, Jenny, Sarah, Gordon and Michael standing near the bed. She shot up into a sitting position and suddenly, she knew. Topaz continued to nuzzle her in a supplicating way. Because of their mystical connection, Jeanette understood that Topaz was pleading with her to forgive her act of mating with Michael and to welcome any puppies she might have.

She slid off the bed, knelt beside Topaz and wrapped her arms around her neck, whispering into her long, silky ear, "I love you no matter what."

Topaz felt dizzy with relief at her mom's acceptance of what she had done. She wagged her stump of a tail so vigorously that the rest of her body followed the rapid back-and-forth movement. She licked her mom's face and made soft woofing sounds.

Everyone watching understood the wordless exchange that had taken place. Cole felt his headache fade. Jenny smiled and felt an odd sensation in her chest and decided that her heart was smiling, too. Sarah was delighted at the prospect of having one, or maybe two, of Michael's puppies. Gordon felt deep-down happiness that these two extraordinary beings were making a gift of themselves to their families. Michael completely understood how

Topaz felt and also knew that her mom had accepted their puppies. He sensed a light, happy energy spread throughout the room and connect them all. He knew it was love.

Jeanette finally spoke. "We'll be grandparents and you'll be an aunt, Jenny."

Everyone laughed.

"Let's go tell Evan and Essie the good news," Gordon said, "and then let's head for bed. Tomorrow's contests will be challenging!"

CHAPTER THIRTY

World Cynosport Games was huge. Rows of bleacher seats surrounded each competition ring. Many RV's were parked and looked like houses on wheels, which was just what they were. Evan, Gordon and Cole set up their tent on the spacious grounds, well away from competition areas and rolled up the sides so that it just provided shade. Sarah, Jeanette and Essie set up the Pak 'n Fold kennels for the pets to use between classes if they wanted to nap. Jenny opened portable chairs and placed them under the shade of the tent cover.

Sarah asked Jeanette, "What is the name of your team? You promised to tell us who you and Topaz are teamed with after we arrived at the Cynosport Games. We've told you that USDAA named our team *The Quakers* because we're from Pennsylvania."

Jeanette answered, "I called Mark Lederman. He handles Harry Houdini, a large Border Collie mix. Harry has earned Gold, Silver and Bronze Metallic Designations. Although I contacted him so close to the Cynosport Games he, too, had not registered because he had expected to be out of the country and unable to compete; however, his plans fell through at the last minute. Mark thought Topaz was a great competitor when he saw her perform this past summer and expressed an interest in any future puppies she might have. We e-mailed our registration forms requesting to be teamed together and asking for a third team member. I received acceptance and notification that Topaz's team members are Harry Houdini and Patrick, an Irish Water Spaniel. Our team is called *Magic Gems.*"

Sarah exclaimed, "Patrick is a great competitor. He was teamed with Michael in a Pairs Relay and they won over a huge number of competitors. Are you going to meet with Mark and Patrick's handler to discuss baton-passing methods for the Relay class?"

"Yes. I'm sure I'll run into Mark sometime today. He told me that

Ryan Donohue handles Patrick and he's met Ryan and his wife during several Dog Agility Shows."

"What's up first?" asked Jenny.

Jeanette said that Topaz had been entered in Wave 2 of Dock Dogs at 1:00 p.m.

"What's a wave, Aunt Jeanette?"

"That's a term used which means group. There are so many competitors that they are divided into groups. Because water is involved, the groups are referred to as waves."

Essie said, "Jenny, I've entered Kawdje. Because there are no size divisions in Dock Dogs competition, small dogs are unfairly competing against large dogs. Kawdje loves the water so much that I've entered him for his own enjoyment and satisfaction and also to bring attention to the fact that there should be size divisions. He won't win, but that doesn't matter. He'll have fun."

Evan added, "Dock Dogs isn't an official USDAA sport, so any placements earned during any competition anywhere don't count toward titling."

"I think it should be an Olympic Sport for dogs. Are Dog Agility Championships an Olympic sport?" Jenny asked Evan.

"No."

"They should be," Jenny declared emphatically. She then asked when Michael and Kawdje were scheduled to perform because she wanted to watch them, too.

"They're part of Wave 2, so they'll be performing when Topaz is," Sarah said.

Gordon studied Sarah's schedule. "Michael and Topaz compete in Team Snooker at 11 a.m. They should be finished in plenty of time to recover for Dock Dogs competition at 1 p.m. and will be rested from that event when they compete in Ring 5 in Team Gamblers for their height category."

Essie said, "Kissy and Kawdje compete in Team Gamblers at 11 a.m. in Ring 5 and Team Snooker in Ring 2 at 3 p.m. We switch rings. That makes sense because Gamblers and Snooker setups will remain the same except for changing the jump heights."

Sarah finished spraying Michael's ear and her hand. "Now Michael and I are ready to perform."

Jeanette suggested to Cole, "Let's you and I, Jenny and Topaz wander the grounds. Maybe I can find Mark Lederman. He might know if Ryan Donohue has arrived. Perhaps he could introduce us or at least describe him to me. I know the Three-Dog Relay isn't until Sunday, but I'd feel more relaxed if I met Ryan and Patrick."

The foursome sauntered toward Ring 3, where the Time Gamble competition was taking place. After watching for several minutes, Cole asked Jeanette if she knew what the competitors were doing.

"Basically, yes. Each competitor is supposed to perform the class and finish at the exact time that it was estimated it would take."

She jumped as a male voice with an Irish accent asked her, "Would you be Jeanette Bancroft?"

She whirled and faced a couple with a chocolate brown, curly-coated Irish Water Spaniel standing between them. The man was slightly under six feet with very blue eyes and black, wavy hair. She would have guessed he was Irish even before she heard him speak. The woman was a blue-eyed blonde with abundant freckles.

"I am. Are you Ryan Donohue?"

"That I am, and this is my wife, Clodagh and our pet, Patrick."

Jeanette introduced Cole and Jenny and Topaz.

Patrick touched noses with Topaz and wagged his tail enthusiastically. He thought that he had never seen such a beautiful lady. Everything about her was perfect from the set of her sparkling brown eyes and long, silky ears to her shiny coat of short fur. He moved closer and Topaz immediately backed away.

"My boyo is smitten with your beautiful gem," Ryan said. "I'm guessin' we're named the Magic Gems because of Harry Houdini and Topaz's names.

Jeanette smiled and said, "Patrick is an obviously Irish name and the Irish, as you well know, are associated with fairies and leprechauns and their belief in magical beings and spells, so I think the magic part of our team is equally due to Patrick."

"Ah, you're a diplomat to the manor born, for sure," said Clodagh. "Mark Lederman described you as a beautiful, rather tall, Eurasian woman with an equally gorgeous female German Shorthaired Pointer. He wasn't generous enough in his description. You are both 'knockouts,' to use Yankee slang."

Jeanette felt flustered, but managed to thank Clodagh for the compliment and said with sincerity, "You are a fabulous-looking couple. Excuse me, I should say threesome and include Patrick."

Cole asked how long they had been in America and if this was now their home country.

Ryan explained that he and Clodagh were in the import/export business. "We have a home in the USA and in Ireland. Our business headquarters here is situated near New York City, and since we're both from Dublin, that's where our business is located in Ireland."

"How often do you have to travel?" inquired Cole.

"More often that we'd like," answered Ryan. "Because of Patrick, we seldom travel together. One of us stays home with him. We don't take kindly to the thought of our boyo being stashed in cargo with the luggage. Oh, we know full well that he'd be kept separate from the suitcases, but if the accommodations aren't fit for Clodagh and me, they're not fit for Patrick as far as we're concerned."

"Cole and I and some of our friends looked into starting an airline that specifically catered to people traveling with pets. We want to have a portion of the passenger cabin dedicated to housing pets. We researched the idea and decided it would be too costly for us to fund the project. We keep hoping to get a backer with deep pockets."

"What a grand idea!" exclaimed Clodagh.

Ryan said thoughtfully, "What we would be able to contribute financially wouldn't help much, but I'll keep the idea in mind. Keep a positive frame of mind regarding the venture. You never know what might come of it. Miracles do happen."

The conversation then turned to the technicalities of passing the baton during the Relay.

Jenny asked, "Did you enter Patrick in Dock Dogs?"

Clodagh said, "We most certainly have. Why, water's his element! He's an Irish Water Spaniel."

At the sound of his name, Patrick turned his attention from Topaz to his mom. Topaz was relieved to have someone else be the focus of Patrick's interest. She had let him know that she was going to be a mother and that the father of her puppies was Michael Archangelo. Patrick had not been warned off. He merely suggested that maybe he could help her have a few more puppies.

"What Wave is he in?" Jenny inquired.

Ryan said, "He's scheduled at 1:00 p.m. with Wave 2."

"That's when Topaz, Michael and Kawdje perform,'" Jenny said.

"And who might Michael and Kawdje be?" asked Clodagh.

Jeanette said, "They're great friends of Topaz's and we're close friends of their families. We all began Dog Agility training together and it was because of the pets and our desire to have them become Agility Dogs that our friendship began. Ryan, I think you know Sarah Kilmer and Michael. She told me that Patrick and Michael ran a Pairs Relay at the South Central Regional Championships and that they won the class. Cole and I would like to introduce you to Sarah's husband, Gordon, and his brother, Evan and sister-in-law, Essie. Sarah met Gordon through her friendship with Essie and Evan, who handle Kawdje and Kissy, two Tibetan Spaniels. Do you have time to come to our tent for introductions?"

"We'd love to," replied Clodagh.

Michael was sitting with his head on Gordon's lap; his mind was at rest as he enjoyed the rhythmic stroking of his dad's hand on his head. He was content to stay in the moment forever. He was jarred out of his repose by a familiar bark. It was Patrick! He stood and wagged his tail in greeting. He stopped wagging his tail as jealousy coursed through him. Patrick was standing close to Topaz!

Topaz immediately sensed Michael's swift change of mood. She rather enjoyed his adoration even if it was occasionally accompanied by jealousy. She paced toward him and touched her nose to his.

Kissy was resting on Evan's lap and when Kawdje, who had been sitting on the grass, sensed the tension between Michael and Patrick, he immediately jumped onto Essie's lap.

"So, Michael boyo, are these wee ones with you?" asked Patrick.

"Topaz, Kissy and Kawdje are my team partners. We've trained together and our parents are all good friends of one another."

Patrick felt an emotion that was foreign to him. He couldn't put a name to it because the word "envy" was not part of his vocabulary. He felt uncomfortable and excluded. He hadn't felt that anything was missing from his life but, as he looked at the four friends, he longed for the companionship of another dog in his life. He had a close bond with his parents, but now he wanted another pet to chase around his yard and share a bone with.

He said, "You're lucky to have such fine friends, Michael."

There was something in his voice and manner that transmitted his underlying feelings to the four of them. Kissy and Kawdje jumped off the safety positions of their parents' laps and, as if it had been rehearsed, all four pets walked toward Patrick wagging their tails. Kissy barked hello, Kawdje did a down dog yoga position while wagging his tail, then raised his head as high as he could. Patrick lowered his head and touched Kawdje's nose and then Kissy's. Michael laid his muzzle next to Patrick's and they both woofed. Topaz briefly touched Patrick's nose, then immediately retreated to stand slightly behind Michael. Patrick knew he had been accepted. He felt great!

CHAPTER THIRTY-ONE

Evan and Kissy, Essie and Kawdje ambled to Ring 5 for Team Gamblers. Kawdje was so relaxed that he felt drowsy. Kissy nudged him and ordered him to wake up.

"Get on alert! We may have to compete soon."

"Is it going to be a Pairs Relay?" he murmured. He kept his eyes closed.

"No. I see a dog about our size with the biggest ears I've ever seen compared to the rest of her. Her ears are held upright and higher than the top of her head. Her mom is taking her into the ring alone."

Kawdje stood upright on his hind legs, planted his front paws on his mom's knees, signaling for her to pick him up. Kissy, too, had signaled her dad to pick her up. They both craned their necks to see the big-eared dog.

Essie and Evan watched the Papillon perform.

"She's a fantastic Agility Dog," said Evan. "If she has equally good teammates, we've got serious competition."

Kissy and Kawdje picked up on the admiration and concern in their dad's voice. They knew from sensing their parents' attitudes that the big-eared dog was a top-notch performer. That was the impetus Kawdje needed to produce the juices of competition in him. Kissy was always competitive and didn't need any stimulus to push her to her best performance.

Kawdje and Essie were scheduled to perform just before Kissy and Evan. Kawdje felt brisk and energized as he jauntily paced into the ring. When he reached the "Gamble Sequence" setup, his mom stood in one spot while she called out commands and signaled with her arms and hands what direction he was to take and which obstacle to use. He thought he performed faster than he ever had before. He finished well before the Standard Course Time. His mom carried him through the exit gate and then spun round and round in a victory gesture until he felt dizzy.

Essie situated herself so that she and Kawdje could watch Kissy and Evan perform the Gamblers class.

She overhead someone refer to Kissy as a whirlwind. She half-turned and saw another handler holding a Welsh Corgi. She smiled and introduced herself and Kawdje.

"That's my husband and our female Tibetan Spaniel. We refer to her as 'Kissy the Comet.'"

The young man laughed and said that was the perfect nickname for her. Owen Gylliam introduced himself and his pet Merlin and said he was from Great Britain. After finishing their performance, Evan and Kissy joined them. Essie introduced Owen to Evan.

"Merlin's an Agility Champion at home. I had no idea that competition would be so stiff here. Your pets are incredible performers."

"Thank you, Owen. I'm sorry that Evan and I missed seeing you and Merlin perform, but I expect that sometime during these World Games, we'll watch you in the ring together."

As an afterthought she added, "Are you here alone?"

"Not exactly. One of my teammates is a man from Japan that I met at the International Cynological Games earlier this year. They're other Brits here, too. Actually, I'm Welsh, but I live in England. Also, there are Spanish, German and Ukrainian competitors here as well."

Owen explained that, even though no competition points would be accrued, he and other international competitors competed in the World Cynosport Games because they enjoyed the November weather in Arizona and the desert topography. The Games gave them a chance to look over the competition they might encounter at the next International Dog Agility event sponsored by the IFCS.

"Aha! You're here to spy on the American and Canadian teams," Essie said playfully. "I'll be sure to watch you and your friends perform so that I can gauge the overseas competition."

Evan said, "I've read that the sport of Dog Agility was founded in Great Britain."

"That's so," Owen replied. "But America and other countries have taken it up with a vengeance."

"Let's check the Point Sheet," suggested Essie.

Thumbelina, the Papillon, who was part of *The Storybook Tailers* team, so named because the other two dogs were called Chrysee and

Hansel, had posted the fastest time. Kawdje was in second place, with Kissy placing third. However, the Gamblers class was still open and other competitors could change those placements.

Owen smiled ruefully and stroked Merlin. "We'll have to try harder, buddy. We're not even in the top six teams."

Essie said, "This is the first day, and a lot can happen before the Games end."

A lot was happening in Ring 2. Sarah saw the great Jetson that she and Michael had competed against before, and knew that he was teamed with Zelda, the Weimaraner and Hubert the Best. Sarah thought, "I'm betting that Hubert the Second Best," as she privately referred to him, "is probably the weak link in that team.

She spoke softly to Michael, "Let's try to do our best. Win, lose or draw, I love you, my special gift from the universe."

Michael didn't know all the words, but his heart, which was joined with Sarah's, translated the general meaning.

Snooker was a class that called for strategy on the part of the handler. Sarah felt lucky that Michael didn't have any weaknesses and he had improved tremendously in strength and agility during the past few months. She thought with pride, "He commands attention with his attitude of determination, concentration and joy."

Michael paced confidently into the ring with Sarah. The shaggy dog with the orange ear and the small, pretty woman with the bright orange hand performed flawlessly. It was a jolt back to reality for both of them when they heard the loud applause.

Gordon greeted them as they exited the ring, "Well done, my darling duo. The crowd loved you."

They watched Harry Houdini and Mark Lederman perform expertly and exhibit wonderful rapport with each other. Jetson and Maureen Hanks were next. Sarah marveled that just two months ago she and Michael had competed against them. It seemed so long ago. She looked down at Michael, sitting between Gordon and her and thought, "Michael, you're my good luck charm. My life is a treasure chest of riches since I met you."

Michael nudged her thigh and Sarah though in wonderment, "He knows I'm thinking of him."

Jetson and Maureen had a fault-free performance, but to Sarah's surprise, they just barely finished the course before the Standard Course Time was up.

"He's off stride today," she thought.

Sarah watched Topaz pace confidently into the ring.

Topaz was feeling happy because she was certain she would have puppies. Her mom would look after her and the puppies and find wonderful homes for them. She hoped she could keep one of them, but the thought of sharing her mom with one of her puppies troubled her. "I won't think about that. It may never happen. I'm going to perform with my mom. It's just the two of us in the ring together and I love it."

Jeanette was delighted that they finished several seconds before the SCT with no faults accrued.

Oshi Yakamuri watched with admiration as the beautiful and elegant Eurasian woman and her equally beautiful and elegant German Shorthaired Pointer performed the Snooker class. It was obvious to him that the two had a bond that transcended the ordinary.

"She looks as though she has Japanese heritage," he thought. "I'll wait near the exit gate and introduce myself after she leaves the ring."

Jeanette and Topaz exited the ring to enthusiastic applause and were hugged and kissed by Cole and Jenny. A middle-aged, oriental gentleman approached them. A dog of the Akita breed walked beside him. The man smiled, bowed slightly, then introduced himself and his pet. Jeanette then introduced Cole, Topaz and herself.

Oshi Yakamuri complimented Jeanette on her excellent performance. "Topaz is a superb athlete. Is there any possibility of puppies in her future? If so, I would be honored if you would entrust me with the care of raising one of her offspring. My beautiful Aiya is now five years old. She may have another year or two at the championship level before I retire her."

Cole cleared his throat to speak, but Jeanette, afraid that her husband might put a negative spin on the mating between Topaz and Michael, quickly said, "Mr. Yakamuri, Topaz had an unplanned mating yesterday with a dog who is also competing here. His name is Michael Archangelo and he is a superb athlete as well as being very intelligent, affectionate, loyal, and intuitive but he has a mixed breed background."

"Perhaps I have seen him, Mrs. Bancroft. Would you describe him to me?"

Jenny broke into the conversation. "He's a big, gray, shaggy dog with a bright orange ear."

Oshi Yakamuri smiled, "A very succinct explanation. I do, indeed, remember him. One could not forget such a commanding presence and superlative performance. The orange ear gives him a certain 'Je ne sai quoi'."

"What's that mean?" asked Jenny.

"It means, literally, I don't know what!" answered Jeanette. Figuratively, it means unique, or unexplainable quality."

"How do you spell that 'je ne whatever'?" I want to spring that phrase on my friends. I'll throw it in a conversation real casual like to impress them."

Jeanette put an arm around her niece's shoulders and pulled her close. "I'll write it down for you later."

She continued, "We thought that Topaz was well over her fertile cycle when the unplanned mating occurred so nothing may come of it but if she does birth puppies you may not be interested in acquiring one whose breed background is mixed."

"Mrs. Bancroft, I mean no offense when I say that you are of mixed heritage and I see nothing but a blending of the best qualities of your Caucasian and Asian backgrounds. The same is true for Michael Archangelo and will also be so for Topaz's puppies. I would be honored if you would consider me as a suitable and potential candidate for one of the puppies. I am willing to pay whatever you decide to charge."

Cole asked, "How would you transport a puppy to Japan, or do you live here in this country? My reason for inquiring is that my wife and I and some of our close friends and family are very concerned about air travel conditions for pets. They are housed in the cargo section. We want to start an airline that caters to comfortable air travel for pets, but our plans are on hold because we don't have the financial resources."

"I share your concern and distaste for the air travel conditions that pets are subjected to. I believe Aiya's performance has been adversely affected by the long flight she had to endure to take part in these Cynosport Games. I am very interested in your idea to start up an airline company that provides the type of accommodations for pets that would satisfy us. I am not a poor man but I do not have unlimited wealth. I wish I could help you accomplish your goal."

Jeanette said, "Mr. Yakamuri, please give me whatever information I need to contact you if Topaz births puppies."

He wrote his home contact information on a business card and passed it to Cole who gave one of his business cards in return.

Jeanette said, "I've forgotten to check my team's results."

They all walked over to the Point Sheet. So far, the Magic Gems held first place in Team Snooker.

"Which team is Aiya with?" Jeanette asked Oshi.

"We're called *The Internationals* because my teammates are from Britain and Germany and I am from Japan. We don't have our results because one team member is a Welsh Corgi competing in the 12-inch jump height category. His class isn't scheduled to compete in Snooker until this afternoon; however, your team has probably won Team Snooker."

"Maybe not. Two of Michael Archangelo's teammates are also in the 12-inch category and will compete when Merlin does."

Oshi Yakamuri raised eyebrows questioningly. "I had presumed that Michael Archangelo, sire of Topaz's future puppies, would be teamed with his canine lady love."

Jeanette, Cole and Jenny took turns explaining the situation. Oshi bowed and said, "A very democratic method of selection."

Michael, Topaz and Kawdje stood in line for Wave 2 of Dock Dogs competition. Kawdje looked around uncertainly from the security of his mom's arms. He was definitely the only small dog in the lineup.

"What have I gotten myself into?" he thought.

Kawdje watched the dog at the front of the line climb the stairs. He heard splashing, followed by applause after which, the big, black Lab descended the stairs. The same routine was followed with each dog in front of him. He watched a very wet Michael descending the stairs and saw that his ear that was always sprayed a different color from the rest of him before every practice was dripping colored drops of water.

Michael said as he walked by, "There's a dock that's long enough to get a running start before you make your jump. No one else will be there except for you, your mom and the judge."

Kawdje relaxed, knowing that he wouldn't be sharing the pool with any large, four-legged strangers. He was carried up the stairs by his mom and was grateful for the lift because he didn't want to tire his legs before he even got to compete.

He ran as fast as he could down the long dock toward the pool. He didn't even brake his speed as he neared the pool. He jumped upward and outward with the mightiest effort he had ever made. He heard applause and looked up to see people sitting on bleacher seats above the walls that surrounded the big pool of water.

An electronic device measured each jump from the edge of the pool to the base of each dog's tail, where it joined the backbone, as it hit the water. Kawdje jumped an astounding 11 feet, 11 inches—a monumental jump for a small dog.

The judge congratulated Kawdje and Essie. "Unfortunately, we don't have size categories in Dock Dogs. If Kawdje was competing against his own size, his jump could have been the winning one."

"I'm doing this for Kawdje's enjoyment and not for placement. If you don't mind me asking, what is the length of the world record jump?"

The judge replied that it was about 27 feet. Essie was amazed.

Essie went directly to their tent to towel dry Kawdje. She found Sarah re-spraying Michael's left ear, but his fur was too damp for the non-toxic, water-based paint to stick. Jeanette, Cole, Jenny and a very wet Topaz arrived on the scene. All three went to work toweling her dry.

"I've got to hustle over to Ring 5 in fifteen minutes," Sarah fumed. "I don't think I can function in the ring without Michael's orange ear for a reference to his left side. What will I do?'

Jenny tore the bright red bow from her hair. "Aunt Sarah, use this on his left ear in place of the paint."

"What a great idea, Jenny! You have a quick, creative, problem-solving mind. Help me tie it on his ear."

Michael's ear felt odd to him. He never noticed the paint but the ends of the ribbon flapped and fluttered annoyingly.

Gordon arrived with lemonade and tortilla chips. "You could all use some liquids and a salty snack," he announced. He did a double-take when he saw Michael. "What have you done to Michael?" he asked Sarah.

"His ear-paint came off during his Dock Dogs jump and his fur isn't dry enough to take the orange paint before we have to perform Team Gamblers. I think he looks cute."

"He looks like a dork and I bet he thinks so, too," Gordon retorted.

"I need to have a reference point for his left side when we're competing," Sarah practically wailed.

"Okay, okay, honey. I'm sure Michael can stand it for one class. I bet the spectators will get a charge seeing an obviously male dog sporting a big, red bow tied to one of his ears."

As Michael waited near the entrance gate for his turn to perform, Jetson said with a lisp, "You look tho thweet."

Patrick was close enough to hear the remark and added, "Isn't he a darling boyo?"

Michael lifted one side of his muzzle to show a big, white fang and said to Jetson, "My ear-tie matches your neck bandana."

Jetson said, "Lots of us wear neck bandanas. It's a fad."

Michael briefly replied, "This is the latest fad and I'm starting it."

Jetson wondered how he could let his mom know that he wanted an ear-tie.

While Gordon, Cole and Jenny sat together on a bleacher watching Michael perform, they overheard comments murmured around them concerning Michael's bow.

"Hey, that's an intact male dog with a bow tied on his ear. What's his handler thinking of?"

Jenny explained Sarah's right/left difficulty and that she usually sprayed Michael's ear, but that the paint had soaked off during Dock Dogs competition. Other spectators sitting close enough to hear her said they remembered watching the orange-eared dog compete that morning.

Sarah and Michael gave an outstanding performance. Jenny understood that they were a great team and had a special bond like her Aunt Jeanette and Topaz.

Topaz and her Aunt Jeanette were equally dazzling to watch.

"I don't know who I want to win," Jenny thought. "Too bad Topaz isn't on the same team as Michael, Kissy and Kawdje."

That evening, in a nearby park, the friends discussed the day's activities while sitting at a picnic table and eating food they had purchased from an Italian restaurant.

"Move over Jetson and Harry Houdini," said Gordon with obvious pride. "Michael Archangelo has arrived. He and Sarah won Snooker in his height category and placed second in Gamblers."

Cole quickly responded, "Topaz and Jeanette won Gamblers and came second in Snooker."

Essie said, "Kawdje and I placed second in Snooker and in Gamblers. We're a consistent team."

Evan picked up Kissy and nuzzled her. "Did you all notice how proud and happy Kissy was when she was presented with a first-place ribbon and certificate for winning Snooker in her height class?"

Jenny, smiling in amusement at the display of ego by the adults, said, "I sure did, Uncle Evan. I also noticed that she wasn't happy about placing third in Gamblers. I'm sure she understood that Thumbelina, the Papillon, won and that Kawdje placed second."

Gordon said, "Team-wise, *The Quakers* won Snooker, *The Hoosiers* came second and *The Magic Gems* placed third."

Cole responded, "And team-wise, *The Magic Gems* won Gamblers, *The Hoosiers* placed second and *The Quakers* came third."

Sarah said, "We have serious competition from *The Hoosiers*. Those three peppy Border Collies in the 22-inch category are nipping at our heels."

CHAPTER THIRTY-TWO

The next morning everyone arose at dawn, hustled through breakfast and set up their tent by 8:15 a.m.

The first events on the schedule were Team Jumpers, the Grand Prix Quarterfinals and the Steeplechase Semifinals. All the pets had earned a bye for the Grand Prix Quarterfinals because each had performed so well in Regional Grand Prix Tournaments that they only had to compete in the Semifinals tomorrow to try to qualify for the right to compete in the Finals. Only Michael, who had won the South Central Regional Grand Prix and Steeplechase, had earned the right to bypass both of those Semifinals.

Team Jumpers began with the 26-inch jump height category and, while Topaz, Michael and Patrick waited to compete, Topaz asked Patrick what his favorite Dog Agility Class was. Michael hovered near Topaz with a possessive attitude as Patrick answered that he liked Pairs Relay best.

"It gives me a chance to meet others. I wish I had the companionship you two have with each other and those two small dogs."

Patrick watched Zelda performing. He thought she was almost as attractive as Topaz—almost, but not quite.

Meanwhile, Kissy and Kawdje were competing in the 12-inch category of the Steeplechase Semifinals. They were held high in their parents' arms as they watched the little dog with the oversized ears perform. She ran unerringly from one obstacle to another in perfect rhythm with her mom. They now knew her name was Thumbelina. Kissy's resolve to compete faster than Thumbelina rose up inside her and she felt the top of her head grow warm.

Evan knew that Kissy was excited when they entered the ring. She gave a couple of short, sharp barks.

"Settle down," Evan warned her.

Kissy felt energized and invincible and tackled the course as though it were a mountain to be climbed. She conquered it! She heard loud applause as she exited the ring with her dad.

At lunch, under the shade of their tent, while the dogs snoozed, the group discussed the morning's events. Kissy and Kawdje made the top 15% of their jump height category in the Steeplechase Semifinals and were eligible to compete in tomorrow's Finals. Topaz narrowly won Jumpers in the 26-inch height category over Michael who placed second. Patrick placed third. Jetson came fourth and Harry Houdini placed fifth.

Gordon said, "It looks as if *The Magic Gems* will pull ahead of *The Quakers* unless Kissy and Kawdje do well in Jumpers. By the way, I checked the Dock Dogs list and, so far, Topaz and Michael are clustered near the top. They may end up being two of the twelve dogs that comprise the 'jump off' tomorrow afternoon."

"Well, let us gird our loins for the afternoon competition," Evan said.

"It's too warm for girdles," said Essie.

Jenny snickered, "What exactly does gird mean, Uncle Evan?"

"It means to prepare or clothe oneself for action. One girds oneself for battle," he replied.

"Uncle Evan, it's called World Cynosport Games, not World Cynosport Battle."

"For Kissy, it's a battle. She's out to conquer," he replied.

Jenny said, "I hope she has that attitude when we compete in the Junior Handler Class. She can carry us to victory."

They all gathered beneath their tent cover after Kissy and Kawdje had competed in Team Jumpers and Topaz had performed the Steeplechase Semifinals. Kissy and Kawdje snoozed in their kennels. Michael and Topaz drowsily lay side by side on the grass between Gordon and Cole.

Jeanette said, "Topaz qualified for Steeplechase Finals tomorrow as did Patrick and Harry Houdini. Also Jetson, Zelda and Hubert the Best qualified, too."

Cole said, "My understanding is that the Steeplechase and Grand Prix don't count toward Team accomplishments."

"Correct," Jeanette said. "They're separate events."

Evan returned to the tent after checking the final placements of the 12-inch category in Jumpers. "Kawdje narrowly won Jumpers over Thumbelina and Kissy placed third so *The Quakers* and *The Magic Gems* are still jockeying to be the Number One Team overall."

"What about *The Hoosiers?*" Jenny asked.

"They're cleaning up in the 22-inch jump height category but their times, adjusting for jump height differences, may not be any faster, or even as fast as our teams. That's for the officials to work out," Gordon replied.

Jeanette suggested, "Let's check the Dock Dogs roster. By now, the officials will have posted the top twelve dogs eligible to compete in tomorrow's 'jump off.'"

They ambled over to the swimming pool setup. Gordon scanned the list and saw that Michael and Topaz were included in the top twelve as were Patrick, Harry Houdini, Jetson and Zelda. Kawdje's name was not on the list, but they knew he had made a heroic jump for such a small fellow.

Jenny silently wished for Topaz to win.

"I do love Michael Archangelo but Topaz is a girl like me and she saved my life. I want a girl to win," she thought.

Saturday, to everyone's relief, was cooler. The dry climate made everyone feel thirsty. Gordon made sure that bottled water and Gatorade was always available. The pets were offered water hourly.

The Team Standard Agility Class for the 12 and 16-inch jump heights was to be held in the morning and the 22 and 26-inch categories in the afternoon. Grand Prix Semifinals for the 22 and 26-inch height was scheduled in the morning and in the afternoon for the 12 and 16-inch categories. Steeplechase Finals for all jump height categories was scheduled for late afternoon.

The group checked the line-up lists to help them judge the approximate times each would be competing. Topaz and Jeanette would be competing early in the 26-inch category of the Grand Prix Semifinals. Kissy and Kawdje would be almost the last to compete in their height category of the Team Standard Agility class. In the afternoon, Topaz and Michael would compete second and third to last in the 26-inch category of the Standard Agility class. Kissy and Kawdje were scheduled to compete early in their height category of the Grand Prix Semifinals, so once again, the friends could watch each other perform.

As Topaz entered the ring to compete in the Grand Prix Semifinals, she was thinking of puppies and felt so happy at the prospect of motherhood that she wondered if she could hold any more of that joyful light feeling without floating like a balloon. She heard her mom say "Topaz, run fast" and suddenly she was in the present moment and completely aware of her mom.

Jenny, Cole, Gordon, Sarah, Michael, Evan and Essie with Kissy and Kawdje in their arms all applauded noisily at the flawless and elegant performance. The pets didn't beat their paws together, but they barked. Gordon judged that Topaz's performance was faster than her teammates, although Harry Houdini and Patrick gave great performances.

There was enough time to watch several other competitors in the 26-inch category so that was how they happened to see Hubert the Best accrue 10 faults and Jetson lose time and accrue faults because he jumped the wrong obstacle.

The friends trekked over to the ring where the Standard Agility course was set up and settled on bleacher seats to watch Kissy and Kawdje perform. Kissy followed Evan's directions but it was a toss-up as to who was spurring on whom during their performance. It was obvious that Kawdje waited for Essie's direction.

They watched Merlin's performance and, in their estimation, he wasn't as fast as Kissy and Kawdje.

The group convened at their tent and enjoyed a leisurely snack and fluid break. Everybody was elated that Topaz had qualified for Grand Prix Finals. Sadly, Hubert the Best and Jetson had not. Evan walked to the Point Sheet and checked the final placements in the 12-inch category of the Team Standard Agility class. He whistled as he walked back to the tent to announce the good news that Kissy had won, Kawdje had placed second and Thumbelina had come third. The others congratulated Evan and Essie. Evan broke a gingersnap into bite-size pieces and hand-fed them to Kissy while Essie hand-fed pieces of her homemade oatmeal cookies to Kawdje. Topaz and Michael devoured gingersnaps, barely bothering to crunch them before gulping them. The group hustled to the ring where the Grand Prix Semifinals for the 12-inch category, was about to begin.

Kissy felt great as she performed the Grand Prix Semifinals. She loved a course that had a variety of obstacles. "I'm the best! I'm the fastest," she repeated over and over in her mind. "I'm faster than that little dog with the big ears! I know I am!"

She was unaware of everything except her dad and the next obstacle. After she paced through the exit gate, her dad picked her up in his arms and she was shocked back into reality by loud applause.

"You're my fabulous Kissy the Comet," Evan whispered into her ear.

Kawdje had a fast, fault-free performance, but the group thought that Kissy's performance had been faster. The group stayed as long as they could to see if another competitor bested Kissy's performance. A little Rat Terrier had a great performance, as did Thumbelina. It would be close.

They all stopped at their tent to get bottled water and give Kissy and Kawdje a drink, then went to the ring where the Team Standard Agility class for Michael and Topaz's 26-inch jump height category was being held. They found a bleacher empty enough to seat all of them then held spaces for Jeanette, Topaz, Sarah and Michael who walked toward the entrance gate of the Ring. Jenny crossed her fingers as she silently wished for Topaz to win.

Topaz and Jeanette had a fast time and a fault-free performance. Michael and Sarah entered the ring as Topaz and Jeanette exited so Jenny and Cole remained seated to watch their performance.

Michael was extraordinary. He made everything look so effortless that his performance didn't appear to be as fast as it actually was. From not having had to compete in the Grand Prix Semifinals that morning, he had the advantage of being fresh.

When they checked the results of the Grand Prix Semifinals in the12-inch category, Kissy and Kawdje were listed as eligible to compete in the Finals. In the 26-inch category of the Team Standard Agility Class, Michael won. Harry Houdini came second, Topaz was third, Patrick placed fourth and Zelda was fifth.

"The Magic Gems and The Quakers are still jockeying for first place," commented Gordon.

Essie said, "Don't forget that there are great teams in the 16 and 22-inch categories, too."

They had time to rest and chat before the Steeplechase Finals.

Gordon said, "Keep in mind that you're performing for money in the Steeplechase. Having said that, stay calm and don't be nervous."

Sarah said privately to Gordon, "I feel nervous and pressured because Michael won the South Central Regional Steeplechase plus the Grand Prix at that Tournament. Any advice on how to be calm?"

Gordon asked, "Will you be disappointed in Michael or love him less if he doesn't win?"

"Of course not."

"I feel the same way about you and Michael. Win, lose or draw, we all love one another. That's the important part of our lives. A Steeplechase win is just one of life's nice desserts," he said as he hugged her. As always they had to part to let Michael in for his share of the lovings.

In the Steeplechase Finals, the 12-inch jump height class was scheduled to compete first, followed by the other categories in order of ascending height. Kissy and Kawdje gave great performances, as did Thumbelina. The last competitor in the class was a Rat Terrier who was fabulous. No one recalled seeing him in the Team classes. To their collective amazement, the Rat Terrier whose name was Dustin won the Steeplechase. Kawdje was second. Kissy placed third. Who was this new guy?

The 22-inch class consisted primarily of Border Collies. Two of *The Hoosiers* team placed first and second. A beautiful Samoyed placed third.

Michael, Harry Houdini, Patrick, Topaz, Zelda, Jetson and Hubert the Best were among those who competed in the 26-inch category of the Steeplechase Finals. Despite his poor showing in the Grand Prix Semifinals, Jetson gave a great performance. Hubert the Best accrued faults because he dislodged a top pole during a jump. He would definitely not win! Patrick had a fast and fault-free performance. Zelda, the Weimaraner, had a terrific run until she displaced the top pole of the second to last jump. Harry Houdini exhibited assurance, competence and style during his performance. He had a fault-free performance and Gordon said he thought it was a toss-up between Harry and Patrick for the fastest time so far. Topaz had a fault-free run and her time appeared to be as fast as Patrick and Harry Houdini's.

When Michael, with his bright orange ear, and Sarah, with her equally bright orange hand, entered the ring, everyone became silent. So far, most people had judged there was a three-way tie. Michael was superlative. He performed with the same easy, effortless manner he had exhibited in the Team Standard Agility Class, which he had won.

"He's won," declared Gordon.

The others voiced the same opinion.

Indeed, Michael won by a two-second lead. Topaz placed second with an extremely narrow lead over Harry Houdini, who had beaten Patrick by a quarter of a second.

Gordon suggested they use some of their winnings to treat themselves and the pets to a meal to be eaten in the same park where they had dined the previous evening. The others agreed that was a great idea.

"I know of a good restaurant," Gordon said. "I'll call and order a fabulous take-out meal. By the time we photograph and videotape the Award Ceremonies, pack up our gear and drive to the restaurant, it should be ready for pick-up."

Kissy was obviously delighted to be front and center as she and Evan were presented with a huge blue ribbon and a first place certificate for her individual performance in the Team Standard Agility Class. Kawdje always appeared imperturbable whether he won or not. He didn't play to an audience and didn't seem to require any feedback regarding his performance: he took his second place without any show of emotion other than wagging his tail. Thumbelina appeared to be as happy with her third place as Kissy was with her first place.

Michael looked as regal as a shaggy dog could look as he sat between Topaz and Harry Houdini and received his blue ribbon and first place certificate for his individual win in the Team Standard Agility Class for the 26-inch jump height category. Michael was glad that his center position separated Topaz, who won the second placement from Harry Houdini, who placed third.

Cameras flashed and camcorders rolled during the presentation of the Steeplechase Awards in each jump height category. Michael, Topaz and Harry Houdini remained where they were because the 26-inch category awards were presented first. Sarah, Jeanette, and Mark Lederman accepted checks for Michael's first place, Topaz's second place, and Harry's third place.

Gordon and Cole videotaped all of the Steeplechase Awards. They knew *The Hoosiers* team consisted of the three Border Collies whose names were John, Jake and Jordan, but they weren't sure which of the two were on the platform for their first and second placements. The handsome white Samoyed who placed third was called Rush.

Bogey, a Shetland Sheepdog, or Sheltie as the breed was referred to, took first place in the 16-inch category. He didn't seem to care at all about receiving a blue ribbon and gold-tone trophy, but his handler was ecstatic about receiving a hefty check. Gracie, an "All American" who appeared to be a Beagle mix and reminded Gordon, Cole and Jenny of Kissy in attitude, but not in appearance, was obviously happy to be on the platform for her second place win. Julie, a black Cocker Spaniel mix, took third place.

Gordon and Cole grinned as they filmed the 12-inch category and Jenny giggled. It was obvious that Kissy knew she hadn't won the Steeplechase and wasn't happy about placing third. She barked at Dustin, who was sitting between her and Kawdje. Dustin's handler snatched the huge check he received and grinned broadly.

Later that evening, the friends shared a sumptuous seafood medley plus a chicken dish for the pets in case they didn't want fish, shrimp or scallops. Persnickety Kawdje ate chicken and some of the rice. The other three pets ate everything offered except for Kissy, who wouldn't eat broccoli, whereas Kawdje loved it. Everyone dined on cheesecake dessert. It was the perfect end to another perfect day. They all looked forward to tomorrow's finals.

CHAPTER THIRTY-THREE

Sunday morning, as the friends ate the buffet breakfast provided by the resort in the dining room area, they discussed the final day's agenda. The Three-Dog Relay was to be held in the morning, as was the Junior Handler Preliminary Class. The Grand Prix Finals, Dock Dogs Finals and Junior Handlers Finals were scheduled for the afternoon. Jeanette, Essie and Evan had checked with event officials, on the first day of the World Cynosport Games, to be sure there wouldn't be any scheduling conflicts.

Jenny and Kissy competed at the Intermediate Level and had an excellent, fault-free performance that guaranteed their advancement to the Finals that afternoon.

After Jenny and Kissy's performance, the group jogged to the Three-Dog Relay ring and found bleacher seats to watch the performances. The pets hadn't realized that they were not all on the same team because each had performed individually, until now. As they watched, they saw that there were always three dogs and three handlers in the ring and one dog and one handler performed while the other two teams waited their turns. They had never before been part of a Three-Dog Relay. They had only competed in Pairs Relay classes; however, they could tell that this was a Relay class in spite of there being three teams.

Jeanette and Topaz left the others and made their way toward the entrance gate in preparation for their upcoming performance.

Michael was shocked and dismayed when Topaz and her mom entered the ring with Patrick and Harry Houdini and their dads. He couldn't understand why he wasn't in the ring with his ladylove. He barked to her and saw Topaz looking around for him.

Sarah offered to take Michael for a walk so that he wouldn't disturb Topaz's performance or annoy other spectators but Gordon insisted that Sarah watch *The Magic Gems* perform. He passed the digital camera to her because Cole was videotaping the performance. Michael reluctantly walked with Gordon. He dragged his paws. Knowing that Topaz was in a Relay with Patrick and Harry Houdini puzzled him and he felt despondent. Several minutes later, he and Gordon greeted Topaz and Jeanette at the exit gate.

"How did it go, Jeanette? I took Michael for a walk because he began barking when he saw Topaz in the ring, and Sarah and I could see that it distracted her."

"Topaz had a fault-free round. Harry had an excellent run, but Patrick slipped and almost fell. He lost some time. In spite of Patrick's stumble, I think we did well."

They rejoined their group and watched other teams in the 26-inch category perform. Cole estimated that, so far, none had been as fast as *The Magic Gems.*

They watched the 22-inch category performances, and *The Hoosiers* appeared to be the leaders in that jump height class; however, one of the Border Collies didn't completely clear a spread hurdle. Gordon was timing the performances with his stopwatch and, although it wasn't as accurate as the electronic timer that the event officials used, he thought another team in that height category, with a slightly slower performance, might win because they hadn't accrued faults.

The 16-inch jump height category proved a surprise for the friends. There were several very strong teams. *The Film Stars* were a black Cocker Spaniel mix named Julie and two Shetland Sheepdogs called Bogey and Pitt. They had a great Relay run. Another team comprised of Gracie, a mixed breed referred to as an "All American," plus Robin, an English Cocker Spaniel and Chris, a black Poodle, were called *The Comedians.* They looked to be having a really good performance, but the group couldn't watch all of it because they had to hustle over to Ring 1 where the 12-inch height Relay was in progress.

Kissy and Kawdje were the first team scheduled in the 12-inch jump height class and because Michael would be performing with them, one part of the course was set up for Michael's height category while the other part of the course was set up for the 12-inch category. The Internationals would follow them on the same setup because Merlin was in the 12-inch category and his two teammates were in the 26-inch category.

Kissy, Kawdje and Michael were surprised to find themselves walking into the ring together. They realized, from having watched Topaz, Patrick and Harry Houdini perform together earlier that this was a Relay and they were a team.

Kissy declared, "I want to win."

"Me, too," Michael said.

They looked at Kawdje, who said, "Of course, I want to win." Then he asked Kissy, "Are you going to eat grass and throw up on me if I don't run quickly enough to please you?"

Michael looked confused and asked, "What?"

Kawdje explained that he hadn't wanted to perform in a Pairs Relay with Kissy when they were at an Agility practice by themselves because he missed him and Topaz.

"Kissy can vomit at will if she eats grass. She threatened to throw up all over me if I wouldn't compete with her or didn't perform fast enough to please her. I believe I gave one of my best performances in that Relay."

Michael asked, "Would you run even faster if I threatened to throw up on you? I would probably drown you if I did."

Kawdje asked with alarm, "You're kidding, aren't you?"

Michael teasingly said, "Maybe."

Gordon, Jeanette, Cole and Jenny heard compliments all around them as they watched the team's fantastic performance. Several spectators commented on Michael's bright orange ear and others said they had seen the orange-eared dog perform before and that he was always fast and fabulous.

When Kissy was performing, they overheard someone in a bleacher behind and above them say, "I didn't think it was possible for such a little dog to be so fast."

Jenny turned around and proudly announced that she would be performing that afternoon in the Junior Handler Finals with Kissy and that the dog's nickname was Kissy the Comet.

"That's an apt nickname for her," the woman replied.

Kawdje surprised them all with his aggressive performance. The spectators applauded enthusiastically as *The Quakers* exited the ring.

Several minutes later, Essie and Evan, Kissy and Kawdje, Sarah and Michael joined the group in the bleacher seats. While they were getting seated, they missed seeing Oshi and Aiya perform. He was passing the baton to Hans Leibkin, who had a fast and smooth start with Rudolph, the Giant Schnauzer. Rudolph was a handsome and impressive dog who gave a strong performance. Owen Gylliam and Merlin ran the same portion of the course as Kissy and Kawdje had because it was set up for the 12-inch jump height category. Although *The Internationals* gave a really good performance, Gordon said he didn't think they were nearly as fast as *The Quakers*. Cole and Jeanette agreed.

"*The Quakers*," Jenny said as though asking a question, "Oh, yes, I almost forgot. That's Kissy's team."

Essie immediately thought, "No, that's Kawdje's team."

Sarah and Gordon were thinking, "You mean Michael's team."

After snacks and fluids and a potty break for the pets, the group ambled over to the Junior Finals area.

Jeanette and Cole hugged their niece, telling her that she gave such an excellent and self-assured performance that morning that she shouldn't be at all nervous now.

Jenny hugged them back and declared, "I'm not a bit nervous. Kissy is the best and we work well together."

They did, indeed, work well together. Jenny had absorbed so many of the subtleties of handling from watching her Aunt Jeanette and her honorary aunts and uncles that it offset her limited experience and she was helped by Kissy's unflagging enthusiasm. They had the fastest time in the 12-inch height division with no other contestant even close.

Evan said, "I hope Jenny will continue with Dog Agility handling. She's a natural."

Essie remarked, "I wonder if she should be coached in Conformation Dog Show handling. I bet she could be a renowned dog handler by the time she's in her twenties."

They watched the entire Junior Handlers Spotlight Finals and applauded until their hands hurt during the award ceremony. Jenny was the youngest handler on the podium. She was given a plaque and a tee shirt with World Cynosport Games Junior Handler emblazoned on it, plus a ribbon that she attached to Kissy's collar. Jenny beamed as her picture was taken holding Kissy. Kissy looked equally proud of their accomplishment.

Everyone in their group recorded the event on their cell phones, digital cameras, and camcorders. When Jenny and Kissy rejoined the adults and the congratulatory hugs and kisses were over with, the entire group walked briskly to the Point Accumulation Sheet to check the Three-Dog Relay results.

Sarah said, "I can't look. Someone else please check the results."

Jeanette, Essie and Evan bravely walked to the Point Sheet while Sarah, Gordon, Cole and Jenny held the pets. Sarah knew *The Quakers* must have done well because Essie and Evan were jumping up and down and hugging one another like a pair of kids. Evan turned to Sarah and gave a "thumbs up" gesture. Then he and Essie turned toward Jeanette and hugged her. Cole thought *The Magic Gems* must have done well because his wife was smiling.

Jenny yelled impatiently, "Come on, tell us who won. I can't stand the suspense any longer."

Evan exclaimed, "*The Quakers* won!"

Essie added, "Remember that cute team called *The Film Stars* in the 16-inch category? Well, they placed second."

Jeanette said, "*The Magic Gems* came third. *The Comedians* placed fourth."

"How did *The Hoosiers* do?" asked Cole.

"They came in sixth, placing behind *The Storybook Tailers* who were fifth. That's the team Thumbelina is on," Jeanette replied.

"Three cheers for our teams," said Jenny. "Can we all have a snack before the Grand Prix Finals? I'm hungry."

Essie said, "I'm all for taking a sit-down break at our tent and sipping some water or Gatorade."

As they sat relaxing and sipping fluids, Jeanette suddenly smacked her palm on her forehead. "Sarah, we have Dock Dogs Finals right now," she yelped.

Sarah's mouth gaped open, and she checked her watch. "We've got enough time to make it if we leave pronto."

Evan said, "Essie and I can't watch you perform because we have to compete in the Grand Prix Finals in ten minutes. The 26-inch category performs the Grand Prix last so you'll have enough time to compete in both events."

The group split as Sarah, Gordon, Michael, Jeanette, Cole, Jenny and Topaz paced briskly toward the Dock Dogs setup.

"Aunt Sarah, I'm still wearing my lucky red ribbon. I'll loan it to Michael for the Grand Prix Finals."

Sarah groaned, "I'd forgotten that his ear paint will wash off. Thank heaven you're here, Jenny. What would we do without you?"

There were twelve competitors for the final jump, and the Awards Ceremony was scheduled to take place immediately afterward. Michael performed before Topaz and as he and Sarah descended the stairs, Sarah said she knew Michael wouldn't win but that didn't matter because he enjoyed the sport.

"Michael jumped 24 feet, 10 inches, which was fantastic for him. Good luck to you and Topaz."

There was just one competitor to perform after Topaz. Jeanette looked for Sarah, Cole and Michael among the group of handlers holding onto their wet dogs while waiting expectantly for the results to be announced.

When the last competitor joined the waiting group, the judge announced that Topaz placed first with a jump of 26 feet, 4 inches. Sarah gave Jeanette a quick hug just before she and Topaz ascended the awards platform. A medal was hung around Topaz's neck. Everyone whistled and cheered and applauded loudly. Topaz knew she had won and felt glad because she knew her mom was happy.

The judge then announced that Patrick placed second with a jump of 25 feet, 11 inches. As Patrick and Ryan Donohue stood next to Jeanette and Topaz, the two pets touched noses. Michael watched with jealous eyes. Harry Houdini came third with a jump of 25 feet, 8 inches. Jeanette had just finished shaking hands with Ryan when Mark and Harry positioned themselves on her other side and she shook Mark's hand. Harry Houdini leaned toward Topaz and as they touched noses, Michael lurched forward. He desperately wanted to be alongside Topaz. Sarah grasped him firmly. She understood that Michael didn't want Topaz to be in close proximity to Patrick and Harry.

The judge announced that she wanted to make special mention of a Border Collie named Brew, who made an astounding leap of 22 feet, which was remarkable because he only measured 19 inches at the withers. She went on to say that during this competition, they had the smallest competitor ever to participate and that he measured just 10 inches at the withers.

"Considering his size, a Tibetan Spaniel named Kawdje made an equally prodigious jump that measured 11 feet, 11 inches. Because there are no size divisions in Dock Dogs, smaller dogs are at a disadvantage competing in this sport. Perhaps, in the future, as this sport gains in popularity, that disparity will be addressed and size divisions will be instituted. Thank you all for your participation and cooperation. I hope to see you here next year."

Jenny called out, "Three cheers for the winners and Kawdje and Brew."

CHAPTER THIRTY-FOUR

Jeanette, Cole, Jenny, Topaz, Sarah and Michael jogged over to Ring 1 to watch the Grand Prix Finals. Kawdje and Essie were exiting the ring when they arrived. The applause was noisy so the new arrivals assumed Kawdje's performance had earned the admiration of the spectators. Gordon stood and waved them toward his bleacher where he had saved them aisle seats so they could exit unobtrusively with the pets when their performance turns came up. Michael and Topaz were sopping wet, but Sarah and Jeanette reasoned that they probably felt comfortable in the mild weather and decided to watch Kissy's performance and towel-dry the pets later. Jenny wordlessly removed her red ribbon from her waist pack and passed it over to Sarah, who smiled her thanks.

Kissy knew she had not been the best in the Steeplechase. That little dog she had never met before had won and Kawdje had placed before her, too.

"This practice class is mine!" she vowed.

After using the first few obstacles, Kissy realized it was a course setup that didn't have lots of jumps. Her mood lifted from grim determination to pleasure. She bounded through the setup effortlessly and saw her dad point to the table. She quivered in resting pose, watching her dad's hand in the stay position. When he said "off," she exploded off the table. She jumped through the tire and the exit gate was in front of her.

Cole said, "Even I can see that Kissy wants to win and gives her performance everything she's got."

Everyone, except Gordon, who remained to continue videotaping and save their seats, left and walked toward the exit gate area to congratulate Essie, Evan, Kissy and Kawdje.

Sarah said, "Sorry we missed Kawdje's performance. We'll have to watch Gordon's videotape of it when we get home. We did see Kissy and she was fabulous."

Evan said, "There are only two more competitors, so Essie and I will hang around until all results are tabulated. We'll see you at our tent in ten minutes."

After Sarah and Jeanette towel-dried Michael and Topaz, Sarah tied Jenny's red ribbon onto Michael's left ear. Everyone smothered grins. Michael was so very obviously male that the red bow looked ridiculous on him.

Evan and Essie walked into the tent with huge grins on their faces. Even Kissy and Kawdje appeared to be grinning.

Essie announced, "Kissy won and Kawdje placed second. Thumbelina came third and Owen Gylliam is very proud that Merlin, his Welsh Corgi, placed fourth."

Jenny grabbed Kissy and danced around with her. Everyone else stroked Kawdje.

Evan said, "Too bad the Grand Prix doesn't award money. We would have cleaned up."

Two hours later, they gathered for the Three-Dog Relay Awards Ceremony. Michael, Kissy and Kawdje were photographed on the awards platform with Sarah, Evan and Essie standing directly behind them. Kissy knew they were the best because they were positioned in the center and higher than the teams of dogs on either side of her. She didn't recognize *The Comedians*, who came second in the Three-Dog Relay, but she knew Topaz and Patrick and recognized having seen the big dog called Harry Houdini when he was performing in the ring with Topaz and Patrick. *The Magic Gems* placed third.

An event official announced that the Grand Prix Awards were next. No sooner had they left the platform when Kissy's dad carried her back to the same place. This time she was alone on the high, center platform, except for her dad, who stood behind her. Her dad was given a gold trophy and a big, blue ribbon, which he attached to the collar that she always wore between performances. The ribbon was almost as big as she was. Her dad placed the trophy beside her and it was almost as tall as she was. She turned to Kawdje, who was now sitting to one side of her. He had a silver trophy and a big red ribbon. Thumbelina was on the other side of her and she had a yellow ribbon and a brown trophy.

Kissy knew she was the best! She couldn't ever remember being this happy except for that day long ago when she had first met her mom and dad and had run round and round the huge tree.

"They chose me because I can run fast and now everyone knows that I'm the best and the fastest. Hooray for me!" she thought.

She was disappointed when they had to leave the awards platform, but so many people spoke her name and touched her paws and stroked her head that she was mollified. She looked over to Kawdje, who was being held in their mom's arms and saw that he was receiving lots of attention, too, and didn't begrudge him.

She watched other dogs that she didn't recognize pace onto the platform and receive trophies and ribbons. Her dad clapped for those dogs and she jiggled and rocked in his arms when he did that. Then she saw Michael and his mom walk to the center platform. Sarah had taken that bow off his ear. Kissy wished her dad had tied a bow onto one of her ears. She knew that Michael had been the best just like her because he was standing in the center and his mom was given a gold trophy and blue ribbon. Harry Houdini paced onto the platform and stood to one side of Michael. After his dad was given a red ribbon and silver trophy, Topaz and her mom walked onto the platform and stood on the other side of Michael. Topaz had the same brown trophy that Thumbelina had been given.

Kissy rested drowsily on her dad's shoulder. She felt too sleepy to be interested in anything that didn't directly involve her. Suddenly, a cheer erupted all around her and she snapped awake on full alert. Her dad carried her back to the platform. Her mom and Kawdje and Michael and his mom were standing beside them.

"Yippee! I've won something else," she thought.

Gordon was very proud of Sarah and Michael and clapped until his hands were sore. He heard comments about *The Quakers* team who had won first place because they had accrued the most points overall.

"Look at those two cute little dogs teamed with that big, shaggy dog who won the Grand Prix and the Steeplechase," a woman said.

Someone else said, "That little blonde dog won the Grand Prix in the smallest height category and the little amber colored one came second in the Grand Prix and the Steeplechase."

A woman asked, "Anybody know the name of that big, shaggy dog with the orange ear?"

Several voices said, "Michael Archangelo."

The same woman said, "With a name like that, he must have special blessings from above. No wonder he's dominated these Games. I wonder how he came to be called such a fantastic name."

Gordon snapped pictures as he spoke in the direction of the woman's voice, "My wife rescued him from the streets of San Miguel de Allende in Mexico and brought him home with her to Pennsylvania. She named him Michael because he was from San Miguel and added Archangel because she thought he was an angel in disguise. She gave him an illustrious name to make up for his lack of pedigree."

The crowd around Gordon laughed appreciatively. The woman who had inquired about Michael's name said, "How wonderful that an unwanted, abandoned street dog is now a member of the Number One Team at these World Cynosport Games! It's a 'rags to riches' story. Is there an interesting background story about the two little dogs who are also part of the winning team?"

Gordon replied, "They're part of my brother and sister-in-law's family and are Tibetan Spaniels with illustrious pedigrees. They live an idyllic life and have always been pampered."

A man standing nearby said, "A mixed breed dog from humble beginnings paired with purebred dogs who have never known hunger—only in America."

The three Border Collies called John, Jake and Jordan of *The Hoosiers* team that had placed second overall paced onto the platform with their Handlers. Someone in the crowd commented that they looked like triplets. Someone else said maybe they were.

The Magic Gems placed third overall. Topaz, Harry Houdini and Patrick took their turn on the platform and received the applause of an adoring crowd. Cole was gratified to hear compliments about Topaz.

"She's so sleek and beautiful."

"She's gorgeous."

He suddenly wondered if they were referring to Topaz or Jeanette.

The next morning, they all drove to the airport. After a quick round of goodbye hugs and kisses, Cole and Jenny walked inside the airport terminal and the cars caravanned to Arno's Belle Époque Restaurant.

Gordon had spoken to the chef the previous evening, explaining that his friends, family members and pets had won prizes at a Halloween party talent contest that he and his wife had given. The prize was a helicopter ride into the desert and a fantastic gourmet lunch to be eaten and enjoyed at their chosen landing site. The chef had been most cooperative and had suggested various foods that would travel well and not become flavorless and soggy.

After they were settled into Gordon's Bell Jet Ranger 427 and the propellers began to rotate, Michael explained to his three friends that flying was noisier than driving and they wouldn't be allowed to hang their heads out the windows but that everything would be okay. He was pleased to be the experienced passenger. The pets were securely strapped into their individual seats, so moving around wasn't an option. Kissy and Kawdje were bored because they weren't big enough to see out the windows.

Topaz was shocked to be so high above the ground and avoided looking out the window that she was seated next to. The pets were glad when the rride was over and they were walking on solid ground once again.

Gordon proudly showed the others his find. They all appreciated the painstaking effort required by the ancient tribes of people who cut stones and fit them together so securely that their work remained standing many centuries later as a monument to their craftsmanship and ingenuity.

Topaz was drawn to an area that held the scent of bones. The odor was not at all like that of the bones that her mom sometimes allowed her to gnaw on. Suddenly she was nose-to-nose with Kawdje. He, too, had picked up the strange yet oddly familiar scent. She asked his opinion about the peculiar scent. He said he thought it was bones even though they didn't smell like any he had ever known. They both dug a little at the earth, but the ground was so dry and hard-packed that they gave up.

Michael and Kissy followed Topaz and Kawdje, who slowly walked while thoroughly sniffing the area like detectives examining a crime scene.

Gordon and the others stopped walking the ruins and watched the pets with interest.

Gordon said, "I believe the pets are archeological sleuths. I'm going to mark that whole area they are sniffing so thoroughly. I have stakes, rope and spray paint in the helicopter. Anyone up for some pre-lunch exercise?"

As they cordoned off the area that the pets had been interested in, they all had an immediate reaction of goose bumps as Topaz began a long, mournful howl. Kawdje immediately joined in. Michael and Kissy added their voices to the dirge.

Topaz, whose extraordinary perception of her mom's thoughts and feelings and those of the animals and birds who lived on her property, divined that people and pets had lived and died in this place. She wasn't singing for the loss of their lives, she was acknowledging their ancient existence.

Gordon, Sarah, Essie, Evan and Jeanette stood transfixed.

At last Gordon said, "This was an ancient community and I believe that the bones of those beings are in the earth directly below our pets. If any of you would ever like to help me excavate this site, I'd appreciate the help and that most definitely includes the pets. They have special powers for finding old bones, especially Topaz and Kawdje. Who knows what lies waiting for us?"

CHAPTER THIRTY-FIVE

Several days after arriving home, Jeanette knew for certain that Topaz was in the "family way" because she refused to eat anything except dry crackers for a day and a half. After that, her appetite returned with gusto and she didn't exhibit any symptoms of impending motherhood other than an expanding waistline.

Pat confirmed the pregnancy and estimated that the puppies would arrive sometime during the second or third week of January. Pat also said that she and Ed wanted one. She promised to take excellent care of Topaz throughout her gestation and be with her during the delivery.

A week after their arrival home, Sarah and Gordon pet-sat Kissy while Essie, Evan and Kawdje attended the Philadelphia Dog Show. Kawdje won Best of Breed and the Non-Sporting Group but lost Best in Show to a handsome Gordon Setter.

As November drew to a close, Jeanette and Cole hosted Thanksgiving Day dinner for everyone. They watched videotapes of the World Cynosport Games taken by Gordon and Cole and expressed relief that the Dog Agility circuit had wound down for the winter season.

Sarah and Gordon wanted to show off improvements they had made to their home since the Halloween Party and asked if everyone was agreeable to gather at their place on Christmas Day. Essie and Evan said that was fine with them because they planned to host a Christmas Eve Open House and invited the group to attend. Joy, Sam, and Ed worked full-time, and Pat was busy studying, attending classes and working in a clinical situation: their generation was happy not to bear the burden of a Christmas get-together. Jeanette was relieved to not cook Christmas dinner because she and Jenny planned to fly to Chicago and spend an early Christmas celebration with Jenny's parents. They would arrive home in Pennsylvania just two days before Christmas. Sarah and Gordon offered to keep Topaz while Cole was away during the day or whenever he was on call.

Christmas Eve day was crisp, clear and cold. A light dusting of snow decorated lawns, but roads were clear. Essie's buffet table was laden with tempting food.

Essie had bundled together clippings from the pine, spruce, fir and holly trees that grew on the property with big, red velvet bows. They hung on the mailbox, the outer doors and the doors inside the home. The entire house was redolent with the scent of fresh greens.

Everyone arrived laden with gifts that they placed under the tree. As Essie and Evan knelt to sort gifts, Evan commented that he thought Kissy and Kawdje were going to receive more gifts than they were.

He lifted several brightly-wrapped packages. "Here are gifts from Jenny to Kissy and Kawdje and more for them from Jeanette and Cole." He passed a box to Essie saying that it was for Kawdje from Michael.

Essie laughed. "Evan, I bought gifts for Michael and Topaz from us and more gifts for them from Kissy and Kawdje. I also bought a gift for Jenny from us, plus one for her from Kissy and another from Kawdje. I expect Jenny and the pets will be kept busy for at least an hour opening their gifts."

Evan sighed with longing, "I wish I were a kid again."

Essie kissed him on the forehead. "You still are."

The pets strolled from room to room amidst the visitors, seeking out dishes laden with food that were within the reach of their tongues. Jenny sneaked them Christmas cookies that Kawdje the Particular refused, and some ham that they all devoured.

Kissy told Topaz and Michael that she and Kawdje were going to have puppies.

Michael said to Kawdje that he was lucky to be living in the same home as Kissy. "You'll be with your puppies every day. I'm not sure how often I'll get to see Topaz and our puppies."

After the last of their neighborhood friends departed the Open House, Essie said, "I have an announcement to make."

She looked so serious that the group unconsciously held their collective breath waiting for the sky to fall. "Kissy is expecting puppies sometime during the second or third week of February. Evan and I think Kissy and Kawdje are too young to be parents, but they didn't consult us."

Everyone let out a collective breath with a whooshing sound. They all began laughing and talking at once.

Sam loudly said over the hubbub, "I want one of their boy puppies."

Jenny jumped up from her chair, "I want a girl puppy."

After the conversation quieted, Essie said, "Tibetan Spaniels usually have two or three puppies per litter. If Kissy has two, one goes to Sam if there is a male, and one to Jenny if there is a female."

Sarah asked Jeanette if she had takers for Topaz and Michael's puppies. "Gordon and I want a puppy. You and Cole want to keep one. Do you have anyone else on your list?"

"The Irish couple, Ryan and Clodagh Donohue want a female and Oshi Yakamuri, the Japanese gentleman will take either gender. Mark Lederman wants a puppy because Harry Houdini is just tipping over to the down side of the performance hill. I phoned John and Marie Colbert, owners of the B and B where we stayed when Topaz competed in an Agility event in Ohio, and explained about her mating with Michael. They said they trusted Topaz's selection of a daddy for her puppies and assured me that they definitely want a puppy. Then there's your daughter, Pat, who wants one."

Sarah ticked off her fingers and said, "That makes a total of seven puppies that Topaz needs to birth."

Jeanette added, "I have names of people who saw her perform at Dog Agility events and requested future puppies. I'm sure they thought she would be having purebred German Shorthaired Pointer puppies, but I'll call them if she has a dozen."

As the evening drew to a close, Essie and Evan distributed Christmas gifts to their friends.

"You can open them now or take them home to open Christmas morning," Essie announced.

Everyone elected to open their gifts in the morning with the exception of Jenny, who immediately began tearing wrapping paper off her gifts. Kawdje gave her a nail polish kit. Kissy's gift was a pink belt glittering with rhinestones. Michael gave her a tee shirt with a red heart made of sequins sewn onto the front. Sarah and Gordon's gift was a pair of jeans with a matching red sequin heart on a back pocket. There was a video game from Joy and Sam and movie tickets and several books from Pat and Ed. She received a gift card to spend money at her favorite department store from Essie and Evan. Jenny was delighted and went around kissing and hugging her thanks to everyone!

Jeanette said that Topaz's gift to Jenny was at home under their tree, as were the gifts from herself and Uncle Cole. Jenny implored that Kissy, Kawdje and Michael be allowed to open their gifts from her. Kawdje loved his small, soft, stuffed wolf toy that howled whenever he bit it firmly. Kissy wasn't sure if she liked the small, glittering thing called a tiara that Jenny placed on top of her head and secured it by tying ribbons under her chin. Kissy did, however, love the attention she received when she was wearing it. Michael tore open his gift and was almost intimidated by a gigantic rawhide bone, but after a few seconds of contemplation, he decided he was big and strong enough to conquer it. Jenny brought Topaz's gift with her because she didn't want her to feel left out if the other pets were allowed to open their gifts at Aunt Essie and Uncle Evan's home. Topaz was happy to feel the softest blanket she had ever rubbed her muzzle against.

"It's for your doggy bed, Topaz," Jenny told her. "Let's go home and try it out."

Christmas Day was overcast. A sharp wind scattered intermittent flurries across roads and onto lawns. The gloomy weather couldn't diminish the happiness in everyone's heart. After everyone had opened their gifts, they sat at Sarah and Gordon's dinner table, chatting, laughing and toasting the accomplishments of the pets, their friendship, the passing year, the closely approaching New Year, the soon-to-be-born puppies and everything else they could think of to be grateful for.

Sarah and Gordon's Christmas tree was a sight to behold. It was decorated with gold lights and angel ornaments. There were not only angel ornaments of the traditional sort, but dog and cat angels, chipmunk and squirrel angels, fox angels, pig angels, horse and cow angels and many other animal angels. The area under the tree was piled high with gifts that had been opened and wrapping paper that hadn't yet been collected and disposed of.

Kawdje started a game by grabbing a balled-up piece of Christmas wrapping paper in his teeth and running around the house daring the others to try and take it from him. Topaz did not feel agile enough to take up the challenge and enter the chase. Kawdje easily eluded Michael by running under Kevin's bed, but Kissy ran under the bed in hot pursuit and everyone heard their mock battle. After a minute or so, Kissy charged out from under the bed with the wrapping paper in her mouth and Kawdje chasing her. She ran behind the Christmas tree. When the ornaments and lights shimmied, Essie got up from the table and ordered the two of them to come out from behind the tree.

As she sat back down at the table Essie said, "They're too young to be parents. They haven't really grown up yet."

Gordon his raised his wine glass for yet another toast, "Lots of us haven't. Here's to being young at heart forever!"

Jenny said, "For sure—and puppies are even better than the desktop computer my parents gave me. Let's all have another toast to the future puppies."

They all raised their wine glasses except for Jenny, who raised her glass of sparkling fruit juice and everyone said in unison, "To puppies."

CHAPTER THIRTY-SIX

In the early dawn of January 10th, a strange squeezing pain in her lower abdomen awakened Topaz. Just as she was about to bark to tell her mom that she needed her, Jeanette awakened with the absolute certainty that Topaz was in labor. She got out of bed and walked over to Topaz, who was lying quietly on her dog bed. Jeanette rested her hand on Topaz's abdomen for several minutes, feeling it harden during a contraction and then soften. She decided not to say anything to Jenny, who would want to stay home from school for the event.

Cole awakened and Jeanette said that Topaz was in the early stages of labor.

"You and Topaz have a mystical connection with one another. If you say she's in labor, I believe you."

"I'll phone Pat in a half hour. No need to awaken her yet." Jeanette said. "I'll also phone Sarah and Gordon, then Essie and Evan. They'll want to know."

As she listened to the sounds that her dad and Jenny made as they dressed and ate breakfast and then left the house, Topaz lay on her dog bed quietly enduring the intermittent pain that escalated in intensity with every reoccurrence. Her mom offered her breakfast but the pain reoccurred and she had to focus all her attention to it and strangely, food didn't interest her right now.

"That clinches it," Jeanette thought. "Topaz never refuses food, so she definitely is in labor."

Pat arrived about 9:00 a.m. She checked Topaz and estimated it would be another hour or two before the first puppy arrived. Topaz understood that Pat was there to help her. Sarah, Gordon and Michael arrived an hour later. Jeanette served coffee, tea and sweet breakfast rolls. Essie and Evan had wisely said that they ought to remain at home and out of the way. They requested progress reports and promised to notify Joy and Sam.

Michael nuzzled Topaz, who lay panting on her bed. He wanted to know what he could do for her. She asked him to stay near and keep her company. Indeed, Topaz had lots of company. Jeanette, Pat, Sarah, Gordon and Michael were all present to lend her moral support. Soon a puppy was born.

Pat announced, "It's a male."

She passed the puppy to Jeanette, who wiped it with a towel and then held it close to Topaz, who sniffed it and licked it all over. During the next couple of hours, Topaz birthed seven more puppies.

Jeanette said, "We're lucky that she's had four males and four females. We have homes for seven of them and I believe that the eighth puppy has a wonderful family awaiting him, too."

After fresh padding was placed on Topaz's bed, the puppies all nursed vigorously. Michael, who had been sitting quietly near the bedroom door, got up, paced over to Topaz and then bent his head to sniff his puppies. He felt so happy and proud to be a daddy!

Topaz snarled, "Get out of here, Michael. I don't want you near our puppies until they can walk."

Michael hastily backed away. He felt shocked and hurt. Topaz had never, ever snarled at him before. He asked her, as he slowly walked toward the bedroom door, "Why won't you let me stay near you and our puppies?"

"Because they only need me right now. The fewer people around them, the less chance that harm will come to them."

Topaz suddenly understood with absolute clarity why the momma deer had charged her when she approached her fawns.

Pat explained to the puzzled spectators, that this was normal behavior and that she was surprised Topaz had let Michael remain with her throughout the birthing process. Sarah and Gordon asked if Topaz would allow them to visit her and the puppies. Pat admitted she didn't know and suggested that if Topaz objected to anyone coming close to her puppies, her objection would have to be honored.

Jeanette stroked Topaz's head and when she picked up a puppy, Topaz made no protest.

Pat said to Jeanette, "She completely trusts you and won't mind you handling her puppies."

Sarah, Gordon and Michael sat in Jeanette's kitchen. Sarah phoned

Essie and Evan to report that eight puppies had been born and the genders had been evenly divided. She also described Topaz's behavior toward Michael after the birthing.

Essie asked if she and Evan could visit the next day to see the puppies. Sarah replied that they were welcome to try, but if Topaz objected to anyone being close to her puppies, Pat had said her objection had to be honored.

Sarah, Gordon and Michael left because it was clear that Topaz didn't want Michael around. Pat remained another hour and said before departing, "If you have any concerns about Topaz or any of the puppies, call me immediately."

Jenny arrived home before Cole. She was ecstatic that Topaz had birthed eight puppies and she wanted to see them right away. Jeanette discussed Topaz's behavior toward Michael and cautioned Jenny not to go near the puppies unless she was with her. Topaz proudly showed off her puppies, but seemed anxious whenever Jenny handled one of them.

Now that the puppies were dry, Jeanette noticed that the fur over their shoulders was longer than anywhere else on their bodies. They seemed to have more of Topaz's coloring than Michael's, but their ears were not as long as hers.

The next day, Jeanette notified everyone on the waiting list for a puppy about the birthing and that she didn't want them to leave Topaz until they were three months old because she felt that eight weeks of age was too young for a puppy to be parted from the mother. Oshi Yakamuri said that somehow he would make arrangements for his puppy to be flown to Japan in the cabin of an aircraft and not in cargo.

Pat started Topaz on daily calcium supplements soon after the birth of the puppies. She described symptoms Topaz would exhibit if her blood calcium level dropped below normal.

"If her head or any part of her appears to wobble or tremble, or if you feel tremors in her muscles, or her heart rate increases, call me immediately and I'll come over and give her calcium intravenously. Topaz is a big healthy girl but her body is providing nourishment for eight rapidly growing puppies."

Ten days later, the puppies had their eyes open and they squirmed and propelled themselves on their bellies for short distances. Their legs were not yet strong enough to carry them upright, but Jeanette knew that in another week, they would be able to wobble around. She had prepared for that eventuality by purchasing linoleum floor covering and placing it over the greenhouse brick flooring and setting up a portable, folding fence around the perimeter of the linoleum. It transformed the area into a very large playpen. Topaz's Pak 'n Fold kennel was set up inside the playpen area and padded with lots of towels. Piddle pads were in one corner of the playpen to begin toilet training early. She wanted Topaz's puppies to be housebroken before they went to their new homes so as to add to a wonderful first impression.

"First impressions are lasting," she thought.

She surveyed the arrangement and was satisfied with the setup. She hustled into the kitchen to make the trifle dessert that she planned to serve this evening when Pat and Ed, Sarah and Gordon, Essie and Evan paid a visit to see the puppies. It would be the first time that Sarah and Gordon had seen the puppies since their birth. Essie, Evan and Ed would be seeing them for the first time.

When the group arrived that evening, Topaz caught their scent as soon as they walked into her home. She knew that Michael, Kissy and Kawdje weren't with them, so she relaxed.

Sarah, Gordon, Ed, Essie and Evan walked slowly into the room. Topaz wagged her stump of a tail. Everyone could tell that she was very proud of her puppies.

Pat picked up the little female she had chosen.

"This one is ours," she said as she showed the puppy to Ed.

"How can you tell the difference between her and the others?" Ed asked.

"Her tail is entirely white."

Sarah said, "They all have longer fur on the upper back."

Jenny said, "I bet it will grow like angel wings."

Gordon commented that all the puppies had fur that was more like Topaz's than Michael's. "It's longer than Topaz's very short, close-lying fur, but the texture is not as wiry as Michael's. Maybe that's because they still have soft puppy fur."

Jeanette said, "If they have a growth pattern of longer fur that is localized to the upper back area, it might look as though they have angel wings, as Jenny suggested. They could be called Angel Pointers."

Evan said, "Pointers are a hunting breed, although Topaz is the exception. Angel Pointers implies that anything one of these dogs pointed to would be an angel. No hunter could shoot an angel. Of course, if these puppies turn after Topaz, none of them will want to hunt anyway. Why not just call them Angel Dogs?"

The others thought that was a great idea and Jenny said, "All dogs are angels. It's just that most people don't know that."

The following week, Jeanette and Pat transferred the puppies to the big playpen that had been set up in the greenhouse room.

Topaz approved of the new arrangement because it confined her puppies and kept them out of harm now that they had reached that stage where they wanted to explore. Topaz was able to easily jump over the portable fence and gain access to her puppies whenever she wanted to.

She felt well and strong in spite of nursing eight big, healthy and fast-growing puppies, but she was relieved when her mom began giving them a daily supplement of cooked rice cereal. She tasted it before allowing her puppies to lap it.

Jeanette, Cole, Pat and Jenny laughed uproariously at the puppies' attempt to lap the cereal. The dipped their noses into it and then snorted, sneezed and shook their heads. Some of them walked into it and accidentally ate it as they licked their paws clean. That gave Jeanette and Pat the idea of dipping their fingers into the cereal and offering them to the puppies to lick. They continued to feed them this way while slowly lowering their fingers toward the bowl until the puppies lapped it directly from the bowl.

Pat said, "Next week, we'll pulverize dry puppy food in the blender and mix it with milk and white syrup and add some of that mixture, which I call 'puppy mash', to the rice cereal. We'll decrease the cereal until they're only eating 'puppy mash.'"

At three and a half weeks, the puppies were scrambling all over their huge playpen. Miraculously, they caught on to the idea of piddle pads. Jeanette always lavished praise and affection on whichever puppy she caught in the act of using the piddle pad. This encouraged the others to flock to her for their share of the lovings and, after a few episodes, some puppies would immediately squat on the pad and use it when they saw her.

Finally, Pat pronounced that she thought it was time for Michael to be introduced to his offspring. Sarah and Michael arrived within the hour. Sarah bustled through the door and apologized for not waiting until evening when Gordon could accompany her.

"He's having an interview with the University of Delaware's Department of Anthropology. He has already been interviewed by the University of Pennsylvania's Museum of Archeology and Anthropology and Kutztown University's Archeology and Anthropology Departments. He's negotiating a deal to be on their staffs as guest lecturer and to be connected to the U of P Museum. So far, there is great interest in having him provide fieldwork for their students at his sites in Arizona. Gordon's excited about extending his work and being on the staff at universities in Arizona and Pennsylvania. He'll tell you more about it this evening when he comes over to see the puppies. I hope you won't mind seeing me twice in one day. I know how busy you are. Also, if Topaz accepts Michael being in proximity to their puppies this morning, I'd like him to accompany Gordon and me this evening."

Jeanette hugged her and said how happy she was for Gordon and that she had missed them terribly the past few weeks.

Then she confided, "I think Topaz is beginning to feel cloistered and I am, too. I'm betting she'll be real happy to see Michael."

CHAPTER THIRTY-SEVEN

Michael walked cautiously into the greenhouse-turned-puppy playroom. Jeanette folded back a portion of the portable playpen. The puppies surged toward the opening and all tried to squeeze through at the same time. They bumped and crawled over each other, tumbling and then righting themselves. Several stopped suddenly and sniffed the air and those behind them fell onto the front line of puppies. The puppies waddled toward Michael and sniffed him curiously. He carefully lowered his head and sniffed them, too.

Topaz walked toward Michael until she stood about three feet from him. She was very happy to see him again. He was afraid to move his paws because puppies were milling around his legs in disorderly abandon. They were intrigued by Michael's unfamiliar scent. He licked their faces. Topaz was used to carefully picking her way among the puppies, so she moved toward Michael. They touched noses and rubbed muzzles. Michael thought Topaz was even more beautiful than he had remembered.

Sarah asked Jeanette if she had chosen a puppy for herself and Cole yet.

Jeanette said she loved them all and couldn't select one over another. "I'm watching to see if Topaz has a favorite, but so far I don't detect any preference she may have."

Sarah asked "Is it okay if I make a selection for Gordon, Michael and me?"

"Sure, Sarah, although they're all so adorable I don't know how you can choose one over the others."

"The little female sitting between Michael's legs and licking his muzzle has chosen him."

Pat said, "Mom, you had better put a collar on her so that you will be able to recognize her from now on."

"I'll recognize her," Sarah replied. "She has a liver-colored patch across her shoulders so she'll have dark brown wings and her legs are solid liver.

Topaz intuited that Michael and Sarah would have the little female who was licking her daddy's muzzle and that Michael was besotted with her. She was satisfied that two of her puppies would eventually leave her—one to live with Pat and Ed and the other to live with her daddy, Sarah and Gordon. She felt a little sad, but at the same time, she was comforted knowing that she would see them often after they left to live in their new homes.

Topaz had never seen her own mother again after she had come to live here, but she hadn't ever missed her mom nor even thought of her until this moment. She sent a fervent wish to the moon that she so often sang to, that each of her puppies would live in a happy home with a mom and dad as wonderful as her own.

That evening, Sarah and Michael returned with Gordon. Pat brought Ed over to visit and bond with their chosen puppy. Essie, Evan, Kissy, Kawdje, Joy and Sam all paid a visit to admire the eight Angel Puppies. The little puppy who had chosen Michael earlier that day once again claimed him by snuggling between his paws and licking them.

The puppies chased Kawdje and Kissy, who easily out-maneuvered them and managed to stay out of their reach. Kissy quickly tired and became peevish, so Essie rescued the dog by lifting her onto her lap. Kissy had become too rotund to make the jump herself. The group began making bets about the number of puppies Kissy would deliver and when.

Essie turned to Evan, "I have to show Kawdje in the Westminster Dog Show, which takes place close to Valentine's Day. Kissy will probably have birthed her puppies before then. Can you handle Kissy and newborn puppies without me?"

"Pat and Joy promised to help. We'll manage without you if we have to."

Topaz walked over to Kissy, who was still sitting on Essie's lap and asked how she was feeling.

Kissy whined, "I can barely waddle, much less run. I'm so huge and ungainly that I can't jump onto the couch. My mom had to lift me onto her lap. Your puppies are cute, Topaz, but honestly, I hope that I don't birth eight. One would be enough for me, two would be plenty and three would be a crowd."

Topaz said soothingly, "You'll feel better after your puppies are born. You can't believe how much you'll love them. Why, they'll mean so much to you that you would die to protect them."

Kissy looked alarmed and said, "What a dreadful thought! I don't want to die for any reason other than old age."

"I mean that you'll love them so much more than you ever thought you could love anyone or anything. Don't worry. Your mom and dad will look after you and the puppies and keep you safe and comfortable. Maybe Pat will look after you, too."

"I wonder if I will love them as much as I love my mom and dad and Kawdje, or as much as I love winning at Agility practices. Do you love your puppies as much as you love your mom? You've always said that you and your mom have a special connection."

"I love my puppies in a different way. I want to nurture and protect them. They're going to leave me after they grow a little bigger and stronger. I'm happy that one of my puppies is going to live with Pat and another to live with Michael. I'll be able to see them often. I'll always love them, but after they leave me I don't think I'll feel as close to them as I do to my mom. If we keep one of my puppies, I hope my mom won't have that special connection with anyone else besides me."

Topaz kept alternating her attention from her puppies to Kissy. Two puppies were pulling and untying Sam's shoelaces. As Michael sheltered the puppy sleeping between his paws, another was trying to crawl onto his back. Kawdje rested near Michael and managed to keep moving his tail just out of reach of the puppy who was attacking it. Pat held her chosen puppy on her lap. Joy had another on her lap. Gordon was seated on the floor with legs outstretched and back propped against the couch. Two puppies kept trying, unsuccessfully, to jump over his legs.

He said, "Here are two future Dog Agility Steeplechase Champions. They'll give Michael serious competition in a couple of years."

Kawdje asked Michael if he liked being a father.

"This is the first time I've been allowed to see my puppies since they were born. Immediately after their birth, Topaz ordered me stay away until they could walk well enough to get out of my way. I felt very hurt that she didn't trust me to be gentle and careful with them."

Kawdje was surprised and asked Michael if he thought Kissy would keep him away from his puppies after their birth.

"I don't know, Kawdje. You should ask her. I don't understand Topaz's behavior."

During the ride home, Kawdje asked Kissy if she was going to keep him away from their puppies during the first few weeks after their birth the way Topaz had made Michael stay away.

Kissy was amazed by the question. "Why would I ever do that? I expect you to help me keep them clean and warm. It's too bad you can't nurse them but I guess I'll have to do that myself."

Kawdje told Kissy that Michael's feelings had been hurt because Topaz wouldn't let him near the puppies until this evening. Kissy confided that she thought it was because Michael didn't share the same home and parents as Topaz. Kawdje relaxed. He knew Kissy could be difficult at times and he didn't want to think about a situation with their puppies that could keep him away from them.

CHAPTER THIRTY-EIGHT

Kissy began labor in the wee hours of the morning on February 8th and awakened Essie and Evan with her barking. Essie immediately phoned Pat, who arrived at 5:00 a.m. Evan gave Pat a hot, freshly-made mug of coffee. Pat asked if they had contacted Joy yet. Evan said they hadn't and were waiting to be sure that Kissy was in true labor. They walked into the bedroom where Essie was sitting beside Kissy's whelping box. Whenever Essie attempted to leave the bedroom, Kissy struggled follow her. Although Evan was Kissy's partner for Dog Agility events, for this event she wanted her mom with her

Pat checked Kissy. "She's in hard labor, but it will be a while before she births puppies because this is her first pregnancy."

Joy arrived at 6:30 a.m. Essie asked Evan and Joy to make breakfast for everyone while she and Pat remained with Kissy. When no puppies had entered the world by 7 a.m., Pat discussed the possibility that Kissy might need a caesarian section or, at the very least, an ultrasound to be sure there wasn't a problem.

Kawdje kept running back and forth between the bedroom to check on Kissy and the kitchen to be hand fed bacon and pieces of fried egg. Kissy refused all offers of food, but she drank some milk. Kissy had a very healthy appetite and her refusal of food terrified Essie, who couldn't eat any breakfast herself because of her anxiety. Pat reassured Essie, saying that Kissy was concentrating solely on giving birth to her puppies and that she would eat heartily afterward.

At 7:30 a.m., Kissy assumed a crouching position, gave a mighty push, yelped and a big male puppy with light fur and dark paws, was born.

"Wow!" Pat exclaimed. "No wonder she took so long to birth the first puppy. He's huge for a little lady like Kissy."

Kissy licked her puppy and Essie helped dry him off. Ten minutes later, a big female with white fur was born. At 8:00 a.m., another female puppy, with dark fur and light paws, entered the world.

As each puppy was born, Kawdje would check it and then touch Kissy's nose.

He asked with concern, "How are you, Kissy?"

She looked at him wearily and snapped, "Can't you tell? I'm suffering!"

"What can I do to help you?" he asked.

"Just get out of here. I can smell fried egg on your breath and I wish I could have some, but I don't think I could keep it down. I wish you could birth some of our puppies so that we could split the chore."

"Good grief! What a thought!" Kawdje said to himself as he beat a hasty retreat back to the kitchen and resumed resting comfortably on his dad's lap while Joy hand fed him bacon. At 9:00 a.m., just as Pat was beginning to worry that Kissy might have encountered a problem because she had palpated her abdomen and felt another puppy yet to be born, Kissy delivered another male puppy who had dark fur and four white paws.

"That's the last puppy," Pat said, "and he's the biggest. What a time of it Kissy's had! She's delivered four top-size puppies and she normally weighs fourteen pounds."

Essie cleaned and dried the last puppy as Pat directed her attention to Kissy.

After the puppies were clean, warm and dry, Kissy lapped a bowl of milk.

Pat walked into the kitchen and saw that Sam had arrived and was sipping coffee.

"You're just in time for the first viewing of the puppies," she said to him as she took liverwurst from the refrigerator and cut it into bite-size pieces. Everyone followed Pat into the bedroom. They clustered around Kissy, praising her and admiring her puppies. Kissy beamed with appreciation at the attention lavished on her and her puppies. She gratefully gobbled the liverwurst that Pat handfed her.

When Sam saw the biggest puppy with dark fur and four white paws, he claimed it for himself.

"That big boy is mine. I'm naming him Sneakers because those four white paws make him look as though he's wearing sneakers."

Essie said, "That puppy will be your birthday gift from Evan and me. By the time Sneakers is old enough to leave here in three months time, it will be your birthday."

"Sneakers will be the best birthday gift I've ever received."

Kawdje poked his head into the whelping box to check on his puppies. Kissy trusted anyone who walked on two legs because she had been conditioned by her mom and dad to expect that all humans were kind and trustworthy, but she did not feel the same way about her own kind. She trusted Kawdje, but she remembered that Topaz had driven Michael away during the time when her puppies were dependent and helpless and needed only her. She knew Topaz hadn't wanted Michael around until they could walk well enough to scoot out of harm's way or at least be able to bark loud enough to be heard if they were in trouble. Kissy now understood Topaz's concern because she felt the same about her own puppies.

She snarled at Kawdje, telling him to get out of the room and to stay away from the puppies until she told him otherwise. Once again, Kawdje beat a hasty retreat to the kitchen. Essie was sitting at the kitchen counter sipping coffee and chatting on the phone. She had just hung up from telling Sarah about the puppies and was now inviting Jeanette, Cole and Jenny to come visit whenever they liked, but to leave Topaz at home for the next few weeks. She had also asked Sarah to keep Michael away for a while.

"Jeanette, Kissy has two female puppies and one of them is Jenny's."

After Essie and Pat rejuvenated themselves by eating breakfast, Essie showed everyone what she planned to wear at the Westminster Dog Show. It was a blue two-piece outfit with wide-leg palazzo pants and a three-button jacket adorned by a subtle sequined pattern. She explained that the wide palazzo pants would conceal the motion of her legs and provide a solid blue background while she was walking with Kawdje so that the judge would be able to see his movement and top line better.

Everyone admired her outfit and agreed that her reasoning was sound.

"Kawdje and I have to leave in three days. I hate to leave Kissy and the puppies, but Kawdje should have his chance at Westminster."

"Don't worry, Essie, I'll be over every day to check on Kissy and the puppies," Pat assured her.

"Mom, Sam and I will be here, too. I'll cook dinner for dad."

Essie handed an envelope to Pat. "This is a gift for being with Kissy throughout her delivery and for all the checkups, puppy shots and vet care that you will be supplying."

"Essie, you know that I won't take money from you and Evan. You're like family. I'm happy to help you."

"It isn't money. Open the envelope."

Pat did as she was told and a grin lit up her face. "Tickets for two to the two biggest Broadway hit plays that are coming to Philadelphia in March and April," she exclaimed. "Looking at the seat numbers, I'm guessing these are about the best seats in the theater. What a fabulous gift! You've overpaid me for my services," she said as hugged them.

Kawdje felt lonely all by himself in the kitchen so he walked toward the bedroom and stood at the door peering in. Kissy spied him and snarled warningly. Everyone laughed as Kawdje ran back to the kitchen.

"I expect he'll be happy to be away from home for a few days," Evan said.

CHAPTER THIRTY-NINE

Kawdje's mood lifted as he watched his mom and dad put suitcases, his Pak 'n Fold kennel and his water bowl into the van. That meant he would be traveling and staying overnight somewhere and he was delighted to leave Kissy at home.

He was sick of scuttling past the bedroom where Kissy and the puppies stayed, to reach the other bedroom where he was now sleeping. Whenever Kissy left the puppies to go outdoors to relieve herself or to hastily eat a meal in the kitchen, she barely acknowledged his existence. He couldn't think of anything he had done to deserve such treatment. They were his puppies, too!

After a drive of several hours his mom parked, lifted him out of the vehicle and into his kennel. She wheeled him into a hotel lobby and he saw other dogs who were also confined inside kennels.

He spent a relaxing evening in a hotel room with his mom. She shared her chicken dinner with him. She stroked his back and rubbed his ears as he lay beside her on the bed while she watched TV. It was a relief to be away from Kissy.

The next morning he and his mom entered a huge building and Kawdje knew this was another Conformation Dog Show because he didn't see any agility obstacles set up anywhere.

He thought. "This won't be as exciting as an Agility practice, but it's better by far than being home with that tyrant, Kissy."

As soon as Essie began showing Kawdje, she knew that he was "on." To anyone who saw him, he appeared to be focused and enjoying himself and, indeed, he was. The relief of not having to try to be invisible, so as not to incur Kissy's wrath, was liberating. He won Best of Breed over thirty-five other competitors.

Essie flipped open her cell phone and called Evan with the good news.

Evan congratulated her and said he would alert their friends to watch the show and that Joy and Sam would be with him to watch it.

"How are Kissy and the puppies?"

"Kissy misses you but she and the puppies are fine. Pat is putting her on a calcium supplement and plans to start the puppies on cooked rice cereal when they're two weeks old just like she did with Topaz's puppies. I wonder if Kissy will recognize you and Kawdje on TV."

"Let me know how she reacts. I'll talk to you tonight and again tomorrow. I'm going to put my cell phone to Kawdje's ear. Say something to him."

The next day, the weather was cold but not so cold that Essie couldn't take Kawdje for a long walk. Kawdje soaked up his mom's undivided attention. She had almost ignored him since the birth of the puppies. He had been so happy to have puppies and had expected that it would be fun and games but so far, it had been a dismal experience. He hoped that he and his mom would stay away from home another day. He would rest easier away from Kissy the Tyrant. He knew from past experience that winning meant hanging around a dog show longer.

"I'll do my best to win," he vowed.

They returned to the hotel room and Essie ordered room service, making selections she could share with Kawdje. After lunch, they both napped. At mid-afternoon, Essie dressed, brushed her hair, then brushed Kawdje, packed his grooming gear, her makeup kit, his Pak 'n Fold kennel, her portable fold-up chair and called a hotel porter to help her transport the paraphernalia to the lobby and load it into a cab. The cab driver was aware that the Westminster Dog Show was being held at Madison Square Garden and Kawdje wasn't his first canine passenger. The driver warmly wished them luck as she alighted from the cab.

It was not as crowded as it had been the previous day. Essie noticed that Kawdje was still exuberant and surmised that he was still happy to be away from Kissy.

Essie phoned Evan and he picked up on the first ring. She reported that she and Kawdje were ready to perform.

"Joy and Sam are arriving in an hour and they're bringing dinner. Pat and Ed will join us for dinner, too. We'll all watch you and Kawdje in our bedroom right beside Kissy and the puppies."

Kawdje wanted to win, not only to stay away from home another day to avoid Kissy but also to have his mom all to himself a while longer. When it was his turn to pace around the ring and be examined by the judge, he lit up like a thousand-watt spotlight. He looked up at the judge with as beguiling and endearing an expression as he could manage. He wagged his tail while he paced around the ring. The applause of the crowd inspired him to wag his tail even faster. His turn was over all too soon and then he and his mom waited in the lineup as the judge evaluated other dogs.

Meanwhile, Evan, Joy, Sam, Pat, Ed and Kissy watched Kawdje perform like a talented and seasoned actor. They listened to the announcer talk about the Tibetan Spaniel breed and give a history about Kawdje.

"Kawdje is a Master Agility Dog. He participated in the World Cynosport Games held annually in Arizona and was a member of the team that won first place overall at those games. He became a first-time daddy of four puppies born February 8th and the mother of those puppies is a Tibetan Spaniel named Kissy and she resides in the same household as Kawdje. Kissy also is a Master Agility Dog and was a member of that winning team at the World Cynosport Games. Kawdje is being shown by owner/handler, Essie Kilmer. Her husband handles Kissy at Dog Agility events.

Something else of interest is that the third dog of that winning team at the World Cynosport Games, whose name is Michael Archangelo, is a large dog who was rescued from the streets in Mexico and brought to this country by the mother of Kissy's veterinarian. Apparently it's permitted to have dogs from two different jump height categories on the same team. Michael became a first-time daddy of eight puppies last month. He mated with a German Shorthaired Pointer called, Topaz, who is also a Master Agility Dog and owned and handled by another close friend. What a heart-warming story!

Essie Kilmer says that her husband Evan, and daughter, Joy, and son-in-law, Sam Albright, as well as Kissy's veterinarian, Pat Palliser, and her husband, Ed are all watching this show from her home."

The second announcer asked if the son-in-law, Sam Albright, was the famous basketball player by that name. The first announcer replied that he was, indeed.

Joy, Sam, Ed, and Pat high-fived one another after the mention of their names.

Evan asked, "Kissy, did you hear that man on TV talk about you?"

Kissy checked on her puppies and because they were all sleeping, she carefully stepped out of the box and jumped onto her daddy's lap.

"Hey, girl! This is the first time you've left your puppies since you birthed them except to eat or take a potty break."

During a commercial break, Ed and Sam raided the kitchen for more snacks to bring back to the bedroom. Evan took Kissy outside for a potty break while Joy cut up some of the leftover roast they had eaten for dinner into bite-sized pieces for her. As they all hurried back to the bedroom to resume watching the dog show, the judge was just beginning to select her choices from the Non-Sporting Group.

She pointed to an adorable French Bulldog, a silver-colored Standard French Poodle, a Tibetan Terrier, a Bichon Frisé, a Sheba Inu and Kawdje. Pat, Ed, Sam and Joy bounced up and down on their chairs and clapped and cheered. Evan dropped his head forward, his heart pounding. His boy had made the first pick! Wow!

They watched, silent and intent, as each competitor followed the judge's instructions. The crowd applauded enthusiastically as the judge pulled out the Standard Poodle, then the Tibetan Terrier, the Bichon Frisé, the Sheba Inu, Kawdje and lastly, the French Bulldog. She instructed the handlers to take them around the ring at the same time.

The first announcer said, "The judge has placed them according to size and the speed at which each can pace around the ring with the swiftest dog in the front and the slowest bringing up the rear. This placement may not be her final choice."

Evan was so tense that he didn't want to watch, but he couldn't seem to look away. The judge pointed toward the French Bulldog and Kawdje. Who had won? It was Essie who joyfully ran to the first place spot. Kawdje won the Non-Sporting Group! The crowd applauded wildly.

The announcer commented that history had just been made as this was the first time a Tibetan Spaniel had won the Non-Sporting Group and that the American Kennel Club had only recognized the breed since 1986.

Evan sat speechless as Kawdje jauntily paced to the head of the line, then the French Bulldog stood behind him, third place went to the Tibetan Terrier and fourth to the Standard Poodle.

Pat, Ed, Sam and Joy laughed and applauded and hugged one another.

The commotion awakened Kissy. She felt confused because she had been more deeply asleep and more completely relaxed than she had since the birth of her puppies. She was physically exhausted from providing the sole nourishment for her four big puppies.

Her dad whispered quietly to her as he caressed her ears and smoothed the fur on her back, "You're a winner, too, my girl. You're such a devoted and diligent mommy. I'm just as proud of you as I am of Kawdje. We're lucky that you are both part of our family."

Kissy licked her dad's hand. She felt such love for him. She loved him as much as she loved her puppies, but she jumped off his lap and returned to her box because her puppies needed her more than her dad did.

The phone rang. Evan took the call in the kitchen because the others were still noisy and excited by Kawdje's big win.

It was Sarah and Gordon. They congratulated him and said they appreciated Essie mentioning Michael and the sport of Dog Agility in the write-up that she had given the Westminster Dog Show officials. Evan heard the click that signaled an incoming call and said he thought Jeanette and Cole were probably trying to phone him. They rang off and Evan pressed the button to take the next call. Sure enough, it was Jeanette and Cole, who were very happy and excited by Kawdje's win and the mention of Topaz. Jeanette passed the phone over to Jenny and she, too, offered her congratulations.

Fifteen minutes later, Essie phoned and took turns chatting with everyone. She said she was glowing from all the congratulations and good wishes bestowed upon her and Kawdje and that she had been given business cards by breeders requesting Kawdje's services as a stud dog, plus many requests for puppies. She said she was too exhausted to watch the rest of the show and hoped that Evan was taping it because she and Kawdje were going back to their hotel room to get a good night's rest. She said that she should have bought another outfit to wear. Joy suggested that she buy a scarf to wear with the jacket because it would make her outfit look different. The home team said their goodbyes to Essie and watched the Herding dogs being televised. The win was given to the Old English Sheepdog. It was late when Joy and Sam, Pat and Ed departed, promising to gather at Evan's house tomorrow evening to watch the second half of the show.

CHAPTER FORTY

Before ordering a room service for herself and Kawdje, Essie phoned Evan.

Later that day, when Essie and Kawdje were once again at Madison Square Garden, she was surprised to see Ryan and Clodagh Donohue and hurried over to speak to them.

"I didn't know that Patrick was a Conformation Show Dog."

"Essie, we didn't know that your Kawdje was Champion Starlite Kawdje of Darling Acres until yesterday evening. We were seated during the show and had no chance to talk to you. Congratulations on your impressive Group Win!" Clodagh replied.

Ryan introduced her to Patrick's handler and they both congratulated her. Then Ryan said, "I'm going to request to change the information that we wrote for the announcers. I want them to know about our Dog Agility connection to Topaz, Michael, Kawdje and Kissy and their families."

He said over his shoulder as he turned to leave, "By the way, Essie, my congratulations on becoming a grandmum to four puppies."

"I'll bet you have bidders for them now that Kawdje is famous," Clodagh said.

"The supply can't meet the demand. My son-in-law has chosen one as his upcoming birthday present. Jeanette and Cole Bancroft's niece, Jenny, whom you met at the World Cynosport Games, wants a female puppy. One of Sam's teammates wants a male puppy. Evan and I are debating whether or not we should keep one. I have a list of folks who want a puppy and another list of those who want stud service from Kawdje."

Meanwhile, Patrick and Kawdje were carrying on their own conversation. Patrick asked where Topaz, Michael and Kissy were. Kawdje explained that Topaz and Michael had puppies and that he and Kissy just had puppies. He related that Kissy was being very nasty and wouldn't let him near his own puppies.

"Michael warned me this would happen because Topaz behaved the same way toward him. He told me that he was present during the birth of his puppies and when the birthing was over she snarled at him and more or less told him to get lost. He wasn't allowed to see his puppies until about a week ago. He was wonderful with them —so gentle. I don't know why Topaz kept Michael away and I can't think why Kissy is keeping me from my puppies. Frankly, Patrick, I'm glad to be away from her. She makes me feel uncomfortable and unwelcome in my own home."

"Well, boyo, sounds like you've had a time of it," Patrick said sympathetically.

Ryan rejoined the group just as Essie asked if Patrick had won Best of Breed.

Ryan laughed, "Holy Trinity! Clodagh and I forgot that you just arrived and didn't know he had won his Best of Breed. Isn't it wonderful?"

Essie congratulated them, then said, "Jeanette told me that you want one of Topaz and Michael's female puppies. Will that eventually be a problem because of the possibility of Patrick and the little lady mating?"

"Ryan and I are excited about the possibility of becoming involved in helping to make Angel Dogs a distinct breed. Jeanette and Sarah will need to bring in some unrelated dogs and we're hoping that Patrick will be included in the breeding program."

That evening, as Evan, Joy, Sam, Pat and Ed gathered near Kissy, in the bedroom, to watch the last half of the Westminster Dog Show the announcer said that tonight the Working, Sporting and Terrier Groups would be shown, followed by Best in Show.

As they watched the Working Group, Evan exclaimed, "I've seen that dog at a Dog Agility event."

The announcer said, "This is Komondor Number 13. He is Champion Swish 'n Mop of Keystone Corners and is called Mop. He is also an Agility Dog."

Mop made the judge's cut along with a Great Pyrenees, a Mastiff, a Standard Schnauzer, a Great Dane and a Newfoundland. They watched each dog pace around the ring and then stand stationary as the judge walked slowly by each one looking at head and facial expressions. At last, the judge motioned the Great Pyrenees to first place, then the Newfoundland, followed by the Great Dane and then Mop.

Next up was the Terrier Group, which always had a lot of competitors.

It was narrowed down to a handsome Airedale, a jaunty Sealyham, a smooth Fox Terrier, a Border Terrier and an Irish Terrier. As the dogs stood in "stacked" pose while the judge took her final look, she pointed to the Irish Terrier whose red coat made him obvious.

During a commercial, Evan took Kissy outdoors for her break while the others refilled bowls of snacks and refreshed drinks. The last group before Best in Show was the Sporting Group. Evan told the others to watch for Patrick, an Irish Water Spaniel, who had been one of Topaz's teammates at the World Cynosport Games. They watched one fabulous dog after another present themselves to the judge and the crowd. At last, it was Patrick's turn.

The announcer said, "Irish Water Spaniel Number 9 is Champion Boru's Patrick of Kildare's Keep. Patrick is a Master Agility Dog and was on the team that was third best overall at the World Cynosport Games held last November."

The announcer then went on to relate Patrick's connection to Kawdje, Kissy, and Michael.

The second announcer said, "It's wonderful that people and pets in the dog world become friendly with one another and their circles of friendship widen and encompass new situations and more friends."

As Sam watched the judge choose Patrick and six other dogs, he commented, "That's a big final cut."

"I'm rooting for Patrick," said Evan. "Wouldn't it be something if he and Kawdje are rivals for Best in Show?"

They watched intently as the judge gave a final look at each dog and then instructed the handlers to go once around the ring together. As they were pacing back to their starting point, the judge pointed to Patrick.

The announcer said, "Once again, history is being made at this Westminster Dog Show with the Sporting Group win by an Irish Water Spaniel. Champion Boru's Patrick of Kildare's Keep was born and bred in Ireland."

The other announcer added, "Ireland is well-represented at this Westminster Dog Show. The Irish Terrier, Champion Erin's Heart of Kilkenny, and known as Kenny, won the Terrier Group. He was not born in Ireland, but his sire and dam were."

During the commercial break, Evan gave Kissy her bedtime snack.

As everyone reseated themselves for Best in Show, Kissy saw that all her puppies were asleep and decided to sit on her dad's lap. She padded over to Evan and sat looking up at him, willing him to pick her up. He automatically reached down, and without taking his eyes off the screen, scooped her up and positioned her comfortably on his lap.

One of the announcers introduced the finalists. "We have the Old English Sheep Dog called Busy Betty from the Herding Group; the Great Pyrenees called Awesome from the Working Group; Lacey, the Saluki from the Hound Group; Kawdje, the Tibetan Spaniel from the Non-Sporting Group; Kenny, the Irish Terrier from the Terrier Group; Patrick, the Irish Water Spaniel from the Sporting Group, and Peewee, the Chihuahua from the Toy Group."

As the dogs and their handlers made their appearance into the ring, Kawdje was feeling great. The brilliant spotlight that engulfed him and his mom did not intimidate him one bit. It was so bright that he couldn't see the spectators, but he heard the roar of applause and was gratified that lots of people appreciated him even if Kissy didn't.

Joy said, "Mom did buy a scarf to make her outfit look different. I think it's sharp looking."

Pat agreed and added, "Kawdje looks happy and interested. He's still 'on.'"

They mostly watched in silence as each of the seven Group winners paced the ring and then stood "stacked" for the judge. The spectators loudly applauded approval for each competitor. They watched the judge walk over to a table, pick up the huge winner's ribbon and point to Lacey, the Saluki. The crowd went wild.

Evan let out a long breath that he had unconsciously been holding. "Lacey is a good choice. She's elegant and beautiful."

Pat said, "Any one of them would have been a good choice."

Joy said, "I was afraid Mom would faint if Kawdje won. I'm proud of them both. They were terrific."

Sam stoutly maintained that he thought Kawdje should have won and Ed agreed.

Patrick admitted to Kawdje that he was disappointed that he lost out to Lacey and asked Kawdje if he minded not winning.

Kawdje replied, "Not really. Winning wouldn't have kept me away from home for a longer time. I'm still going to have to face Kissy the Tyrant tomorrow."

CHAPTER FORTY-ONE

Several days after the Westminster Dog Show, Essie and Evan received a phone call from a man who identified himself as Aaron Breslin of ABCD Realty. He informed them that he and his partner, Cecil Diamond, were part owners of Sam Albright's basketball team and that he and his wife, Mimi, had watched the Westminster Dog Show and had been enchanted with Kawdje. The couple loved the human-interest story about Kawdje and Kissy being teamed with a big, Mexican street dog and the three dogs becoming the number one team at the World Cynosport Games. He asked if he and his wife could see the puppies because they very much wanted to have one.

Evan replied that he and Essie would be delighted to have them visit but added, "Kissy is still very protective of her little ones and won't even let Kawdje near them; however, the puppies have opened their eyes and are beginning to crawl around, so I judge that she'll be ready to introduce them to the world in another week."

Aaron suggested the 25th of February about 2 p.m., pending weather conditions. Evan agreed that would be fine.

Essie and Evan immediately phoned Jeanette with the good news. Jeanette said she had received a call from Cecil Diamond of ABCD Realty ten minutes prior and was just about to call them. Cecil and his wife had also watched the Westminster Dog Show and were interested in having one of Topaz's puppies.

"Cecil's beloved Irish Wolfhound succumbed to old age six months ago. He and his wife decided not to have another Irish Wolfhound because of that breed's rather short life expectancy. He said his wife, Arielle, was fascinated by Michael Archangelo's name and thought he must have divine protection. That, combined with the fact that Cecil and his family had a German Shorthaired Pointer when he was growing up, convinced them that they were meant to have one of Topaz and Michael's puppies.

He and Arielle prefer a female puppy but are open to having a male if no female is available. I always had a strong hunch that the eighth puppy who didn't already have a family waiting to claim it with open arms was going to have a wonderful home, too."

Essie, who was listening to the conversation from the bedroom cordless phone while she stroked Kissy and checked the puppies said, "Aaron Breslin and Cecil Diamond must have deep pockets if they're part owners of Sam's basketball team. I wonder if there's any chance of getting them to back our People Pet Airline."

Evan spoke from the kitchen phone, as Kawdje rested on his lap. "Let's wait until we know for sure that they want our puppies before broaching the subject. I'll alert Sarah to tell Ed to dust off the documents he drew up for the proposed PPAL Company. Gordon has a set of blueprints of Kevin's design that modifies an aircraft cabin to accommodate a designated space for pets. No harm in having the information ready in case they're interested."

Jeanette agreed and said, "Cecil and Arielle are coming over Sunday to see Topaz and the puppies. I promised Cecil that Michael Archangelo would be here with Sarah and Gordon. I described Michael looking as though he has Irish Wolfhound somewhere in his background and being about the size of a German Shorthaired Pointer."

As they said their goodbyes, each had a heart full of hope that maybe their goal of providing safe, comfortable air travel for pets would fly.

During the drive to Jeanette and Cole's home on Sunday afternoon, Sarah said, "I hope they're worthy of having one of Michael and Topaz's puppies. They may be filthy rich, but that doesn't guarantee they will provide a loving home."

Gordon replied, "Let's watch how Michael and Topaz react toward them. That's the crucial test."

They saw a Lexus SUV parked in the driveway.

"I guess they're already here," Gordon observed.

Jenny was surrounded by puppies, prepared to bolt outside, when she opened the door. Gordon and Sarah pushed Michael inside before quickstepping into the midst of the puppies and closing the door. The puppies pulled on the towel that Sarah used to wipe Michael's paws. As Sarah and Gordon slowly and carefully wiped their shoes on the back hall floor mat, puppies attacked their shoelaces. The couple hung their jackets out of reach of mischievous puppies. They walked into the living room carefully picking their way through the wave of puppies who jumped, skidded and frolicked around, in front of, behind and between them. Gordon scooped up their puppy, telling Sarah that he intended to hold her in his arms throughout the visit to make sure the Diamonds didn't try to select her for themselves.

Michael and Topaz greeted one another affectionately and settled side-by-side in resting pose while their puppies crawled around them and jumped on them. Topaz confided to Michael that she welcomed his daily visits and was getting an overdose of puppies who were now exuberant and rambunctious to the degree of being pesky.

"Until this past week, I never thought I could ever let them go to other homes."

Arielle pointed to Topaz and Michael. "They're like a happily married couple nuzzling each other affectionately."

She walked toward them and knelt down. She stroked their heads and said, "Michael, you're like a smaller, shaggier version of my beloved Muldoon who died about six months ago."

Cecil joined his wife and stroked Topaz's long, silky ears, telling her she reminded him of Max, the wonderful German Shorthaired Pointer that he had grown up with.

Arielle said, "Honey, we've got to have one of these puppies!"

Michael and Topaz sensed that this man and woman were going to be mom and dad to one of their puppies and they approved. Topaz licked the man's hand and she wuffled deep in her throat as he laid his head on hers. Jeanette saw that Arielle and Cecil had met with Michael and Topaz's approval. She asked if they would like to choose a puppy and said she would put a collar on their puppy to identify it. She picked up Pat's puppy saying that she was named Pearl Angel Mary of Heaven Sent and belonged to Sarah's daughter, Pat, who was the puppies and Topaz's veterinarian.

Arielle exclaimed, "What an enchanting name!"

Jeanette decided this was a good opportunity to tell Arielle and Cecil about her aspiration to introduce a new breed known as Angel Dogs and to explain the official name requirements and agreement obligations that each family must legally adhere to.

Jeanette suggested they sit down while she and Sarah explained the agreement that must be signed by each person who takes a puppy to become part of their family. She told them that she and Sarah planned to start a new breed known as Angel Dogs and that a strict breeding program, approved of and directed by herself, Sarah and Pat must be adhered to. Precise records of matings and progeny would have to be kept. Each puppy's official name must begin with the name of a gem, followed by the word Angel or Archangel or a deity, then the name that identifies the Angel/Archangel/Deity and the suffix, Heaven Sent.

"Do you still want a puppy in spite of these requirements and restrictions?"

Arielle said, "I'm even more eager to have one of these precious puppies."

She turned to her husband and asked, "How about you?"

Cecil said, "I loved Topaz and Michael the moment I saw them. I'd be proud to take part in establishing this new Angel Dog breed. When can we take our puppy home with us?"

Jeanette replied that the puppies must be three months old before they left for their new homes.

Sarah said, "Whenever you decide on a name, let Jeanette know and we'll begin using that name for your puppy."

Arielle said that she loved the little puppy who was chewing the laces on her sneakers. Cecil reached down and lifted up the puppy who looked at him and barked hello.

He said to his wife, "She's a girl."

"That's perfect. We can look forward to having puppies in the future." Arielle added, "Let's name her Diamond Archangel Gabrielle of Heaven Sent. For obvious reasons, diamond is my favorite gem and Gabrielle is because she's talkative. Besides, Gabrielle sounds good with Arielle. We can nickname her Gabby."

"I like it, Sweetheart." Cecil kissed the puppy who reciprocated by licking him all over his face.

Jeanette excused herself to prepare some refreshments. While she was in the kitchen, Jenny said she thought that the puppy's new name was just about the prettiest she had ever heard. Arielle asked Jenny if she was going to have one of the puppies and Jenny told her about Kissy and Kawdje's puppies and that she had picked one of those puppies for herself.

She mentioned that she was working toward her Junior Handler's Senior Agility Certificate.

Just as she said that, Jeanette brought a tray of hot beverages and cookies into the living room and she proudly said that her niece had won first place in the Junior Handler's Intermediate Level at the World Cynosport Games and that Jenny was the youngest handler at her Level.

Arielle and Cecil were impressed and said so. Jenny beamed with pleasure and told of her airplane ride with Uncle Cole because her Aunt Jeanette and Topaz had to drive to Arizona for the Games.

"Why didn't you all fly together?" asked Arielle.

"Because Topaz would have had to ride in cargo with the luggage," Jenny replied.

Sarah spoke up. "Air travel conditions for pets are abysmal. My husband, Michael and I drove to Arizona, too, as did the Kilmers, who made the cross country trip with their pets, Kissy and Kawdje."

Sarah described the experience of bringing Michael from San Miguel de Allende to Pennsylvania via air travel. Cecil asked questions about air travel conditions for pets and Gordon filled him in on all that he knew, mentioning that he, Cole, Evan, their wives and children had tried to start up a pet-friendly airline.

"We have a charter for our new airline company and blueprints for modifications that could be made to aircraft to accommodate pets in the main passenger cabin and then have kenneled pets boarded via a lift. We couldn't swing it financially and we couldn't get backers with deep pockets."

"Interesting," Cecil said. "I want to discuss air travel conditions for pets with my partner. I have some ideas that I'm going to propose to Aaron before I get back to you about your pet-friendly airline company."

When the Diamonds were leaving, they asked how often they would be permitted to visit Gabrielle. Jeanette suggested they phone ahead whenever they wanted to come over and she would try to accommodate them.

Before Cecil and Arielle's car had reached the end of her driveway, Jeanette was on the phone telling Essie and Evan all about their visit.

"Be sure to casually bring up the subject about our pet-friendly airline to Aaron Breslin and his wife when you see them. Jenny introduced the topic when she told Arielle and Cecil about flying to Arizona with her

Uncle Cole while I had to drive with Topaz to avoid having her put in cargo with the luggage. I could see the two of them look at their little puppy and imagine her shut up in cargo and being all alone and afraid. They practically shuddered!"

Before Sarah, Gordon and Michael departed, Sarah announced she had chosen the official name for their girl puppy. "It is Joaquinite Archangel Michelle of Heaven Sent. She has patches of brown, or liver, colored fur and Joaquinite is a mineral that ranges in color from honey yellow to brown. It is known as the "Sweetheart Stone" because it stimulates love in relationships. We'll call her Michelle because that is the feminine form of Michael."

Jeanette exclaimed, "What a wonderful name! I wish I could decide upon a name, but since Cole and I don't know which puppy we'll be keeping, I can't."

CHAPTER FORTY-TWO

The next afternoon, Aaron and Mimi Breslin were stroking Kissy and cooing over the puppies. Kawdje was hanging around outside the bedroom door, unsure of his welcome. Kissy hadn't seemed as hostile toward him lately and she had been spending more time away from the puppies. He crept into the room and looked longingly at his puppies crawling outside their box. He wondered why Kissy allowed these strangers to play with them but would not let him near them. He decided he'd had enough of her mean treatment.

Evan spied Kawdje sidling into the room. He walked toward him, picked him up, carried him to the puppy box and placed him on the carpet beside two of the little ones. Kawdje looked fearfully toward Kissy, who was soaking up the attention she was receiving from the lady stranger. Kawdje sniffed the two puppies close to him. They crawled all around him, licking his muzzle and peering into his mouth. Kawdje was enchanted with them. He felt such love well up inside him that it flowed outward to include everyone in the room. Another puppy waddled toward him and then another so that all four of his puppies were around him.

Essie said, "This is the first time since the day they were born that the puppies have encountered their daddy."

At Aaron and Mimi's questioning expressions, she described Kissy's behavior toward Kawdje immediately after birthing the puppies.

Aaron stroked Kawdje. "You're a handsome fellow. My wife and I enjoyed watching you on TV."

He said to Mimi, "I'm partial to the puppy who looks like Kawdje," as he picked it up and announced, "She's a girl."

His heart melted when the little puppy began to lick and suck his fingers.

"She's the one for us. What shall we name her?"

Mimi thought a few moments before saying, "Darling Acres Kissy's Caressa, and we'll just call her Caressa."

"I like it," said Aaron as he nuzzled Caressa.

"Aaron, I want to take Caressa with us when we travel to Belize. I don't want to be parted from her. I can hardly bear to walk away from her today, even knowing she's too young to leave Kissy and Kawdje."

Evan quickly said, "Whenever you fly to Belize, Caressa will be housed in cargo with luggage. She'll grow too large to fit comfortably into a carrier that can slide under a seat in the cabin area. Any pet who can't fit into a carrier that can slide under a seat has to travel in cargo."

Aaron said, "My partner and I are preparing to open a resort in Belize. We envision it as being a family resort, and family includes pets. I'm going to discuss putting in pet facilities with him."

Evan said, "Most people I know drive to vacation destinations because they are loath to subject their pets to current air travel conditions. Is there any chance you and your partner would consider starting up a pet-friendly airline? My son-in-law, Sam Albright, whom you know, is willing to put up some money to back the venture, as I am and some of my friends are. We have a lawyer in the family who has drawn up a charter for PPAL, which stands for People Pet Air Lines. His wife is Pat Palliser and she is our vet and the daughter of my brother's wife. Pat has drafted a document detailing the rules and regulations of PPAL's air travel conditions for pets. My nephew, Kevin, will soon graduate from Purdue University as an aeronautical engineer and he has designed an aircraft passenger cabin that has space to house pets."

Aaron said, "Sounds like the whole family is involved with PPAL. My first thought is that we could start flight paths between some northeast cities to our Belize family resort. If it takes off, no pun intended, we could open up more routes. I'm meeting with Cecil this evening. I'm definitely interested and I promise to get back to you about this."

Kissy watched Mimi's interaction with her puppy and knew she would come back to take her away sometime soon. She felt sad and glad at the same time. She remembered how much she had wanted to leave the home where she had been born and to have her own people and be the queen of her own home. She had left her mother that day long ago and hadn't even said goodbye. She had always been happy living here with her mom and dad and Kawdje. She had known from the moment her puppies were born that they, too, would leave to live with other families and bring love and joy into their new homes. She hoped she would be able to see all of her puppies occasionally, just to be sure they were happy and to hear about their adventures.

After Aaron and Mimi Breslin departed, Kawdje remained in the bedroom with his puppies. He was delirious with joy because Kissy was back to being, well, Kissy. She walked toward him, carefully stepping between puppies and snuggled beside him. His heart overflowed with love and contentment. What more could he want? His world was perfect!

Several days later, Aaron phoned Evan to arrange a meeting at his and Cecil's downtown office, regarding PPAL. They wanted everyone who had contributed in any way to the idea, to be present.

Evan explained that his nephew, Kevin, was at university and probably wouldn't be able to attend the meeting, but could meet with them at a later date. Aaron said that would be fine. He said that Cecil would inform Cole and Jeanette about the meeting because he had met the couple when selecting one of their puppies. Evan promised to get back to Aaron, after conferring with everyone, with several possible dates.

Evan hung up and ran excitedly through the house calling for Essie. He found her in the laundry room folding freshly washed and dried puppy towels, a task which she did every day. He related his conversation with Aaron.

Essie said, "I've got a hunch that our pet-friendly airline company will be an immediate success, and I think that encouraging clients to bring their pets along on a vacation to the resort in Belize will increase business a thousand fold. Best of all, you and I will help their business flourish by taking a relaxing vacation at their Belize resort with Kissy and Kawdje."

Evan wrapped his arms around his wife's still slender waist, pulled her close and said, "You bet we will."

It was a chilly day in February when everyone gathered in a posh meeting room in downtown Philly to discuss PPAL. Ed distributed copies to everyone of the charter he had drawn up the previous year. Pat had copies of her proposed Rules and Regulations for pet air travel, which she, too, passed around. Gordon brought copies of the blueprints of Kevin's design for an aircraft cabin that housed pets and people as well as the changes that could be made to existing aircraft to install a hydraulic lift that could be used to transport pets contained in kennels directly from ground level into the cabin area.

Aaron and Cecil perused the documents.

At last Cecil said, "I'm impressed. We'll have our attorneys look over this charter. We work with a large engineering firm because of the hotels and resorts that we buy and renovate, or have built from the ground up, so we'll have engineers study Kevin's blueprints. We don't have any veterinarians at our disposal, but we want to have our legal consultants look over the Pet Rules and Regulations. We have great confidence in the work that all of you have done; however, we firmly believe in second opinions."

Aaron added, "I think PPAL is a great idea and if Cecil and I commit ourselves to it, we want it to be successful. We know that you are prepared to make a financial commitment and although your percentage of ownership would be small, we want you to take an active part in managing and/or promoting the airline, because we believe that your involvement will be crucial to its success."

The meeting lasted several hours. Aaron and Cecil were impressed by Ed's knowledge of the international legalities of pet travel and Pat's comprehension of how to keep pets safe during travel and after reaching a destination, as well as knowing vaccine requirements for pets entering other countries. They listened to Sarah, Gordon and Pat discuss the logistics of a pet entering an airport, being placed into a PPAL kennel and the boarding path from the check-in point to the cabin destination.

Pat explained, "The goal is to have pets be as comfortable temperature-wise as people are, independent of outside weather conditions. We want them to be safely housed inside the airport terminal until they are put inside the aircraft cabin. Flight attendants would not be expected to attend to pets, but they would be expected to assist a family member who required help while attending to their pet. For example, if a pet became airsick, a flight attendant would be expected to provide cleanup wipes for the family member to clean the kennel. We don't want them to travel under conditions where there is the potential to become lost like our luggage sometimes is."

Pat took a deep breath and continued. "I think PPAL should have a Veterinary Consulting Department of which I wish to be head honcho."

Aaron grinned. "I agree. There should be a Vet Consulting Department, and you get my vote to be in charge of that department."

Cecil said, "You've got my vote, too. Since ABCD Realty doesn't have a Vet Consulting Firm, I suggest you take the Pet Rules and Regulations and have them checked by other vets such as some of your professors at the Veterinary School of Medicine where you attended. Second opinions are helpful even if only to have your own opinion validated."

After more discussion, Jeanette said, "It's because of my niece, Jenny, that we have the catchy name of PPAL for the airline. Could she be recognized or rewarded in some way."

Sarah suggested, "Feature her in a commercial with some of our pets."

Everyone was enthusiastic about the idea, each envisioning their pet in a PPAL commercial.

As the meeting came to an end, Aaron and Cecil promised to keep everybody updated on progress and arrange for Ed and Pat to meet with the ABCD Realty Legal Department soon.

CHAPTER FORTY-THREE

Several days after the meeting with Aaron and Cecil, Gordon logged onto the USDAA website and checked the Agility Top Ten lists. The highest ranked competitors, at the Masters Level, in each jump height division of each class were listed for the previous year. Michael placed fifth in the Tournament Top Ten because he had won the South Central Regional Championship's Grand Prix and Steeplechase. He earned seventh place on The Top Ten list for the Masters Relay, tenth place on the Masters Jumpers and Masters Standard Agility Top Ten Lists, and held ninth on the Masters Snooker list. It was a remarkable achievement considering the brief time he had been on the Dog Agility circuit.

While Michael had competed at the Masters Level in the Southwestern and South Central Regional Championships, Topaz had done so in Ohio and Kissy and Kawdje in Massachusetts where their excellent placements hadn't been over nearly as many other competitors as Michael's had been so they hadn't accrued as many points.

Gordon called for Sarah to come look and see how famous she and Michael were. Sarah's name had been listed beside Michael's because the handler was just as important, it not more so, than the dog.

The phone rang and it was Evan calling to congratulate Sarah. As they talked, Evan mentioned that he doubted that Kissy could recuperate from the physical demands of birthing and nursing four big puppies in time to compete at the start of the Dog Agility competition season, then wondered aloud whether Topaz would be ready to compete when the season began.

"The Dog Agility season begins in April," Evan said. "I think I'll give Jeanette a call."

After Evan had said goodbye to Jeanette, who was sure that Topaz would be ready to compete in late April or early May, he noticed Kissy sitting at his feet. Her head was wobbling. He called to Essie who came running because she heard the alarm in his voice.

"Kissy's head is wobbling. I touched her neck and I can feel tremors underneath my fingers. I think she has a serious calcium deficiency."

Essie ran out of the room, found the calcium supplement and quickly gave some to Kissy.

"I've been giving her this every day and increasing the dose according to Pat's instructions. I'm going to phone Pat right away."

She dialed Pat with trembling fingers. After five rings, the message machine kicked in and she described Kissy's symptoms, adding that if she didn't hear from her within fifteen minutes and Kissy's condition hadn't improved by that time, she would take her to the closest animal emergency hospital.

Fifteen minutes later, Essie gave Kissy another dose of calcium supplement and bundled her in a warm blanket while Evan shrugged into his winter jacket. He insisted that Essie stay home with the puppies and Kawdje while he took Kissy to the hospital.

An hour later, Ed phoned and said that he had just arrived home and listened to their message.

"I can't reach Pat either. She's attending a seminar and must have turned off her cell phone. I'll have her get in touch with you as soon as I can relay the message."

"Don't worry, Ed. Kissy is being looked after at the Animal Emergency Clinic. I expect to hear from Evan at any moment. I'll keep you updated on the situation."

Essie had just hung up the phone when it rang. She snatched up the receiver and was relieved to hear Evan's voice. He told her that the vet had taken a blood sample and then given Kissy intravenous calcium in a bag of I.V. fluids.

"Kissy's blood sample showed that her calcium level was only slightly below normal. The vet thought the calcium doses you gave her before I brought her in had been absorbing into her system, which was why her serum calcium hadn't registered as being dangerously low. He said the puppies have to be completely weaned within the next few days. They'll be almost six weeks old by then. During the weaning period, we are to give Kissy her calcium supplement three times daily and if she shows any signs of deficiency, she is not to nurse the puppies again, ever."

Kissy was feeling much better the next morning. Her heart was once again beating at a normal rate and her muscles no longer felt painfully knotted and stiff. She padded up the stairs and followed Kawdje into the bedroom where her puppies were. They ran to Kawdje and crawled all over him when he lay down. They sniffed his ears, licked his muzzle and peered down his throat when he opened his jaws in a big yawn. He talked to them and they made happy sounds, telling him, in puppy babble, that they loved him.

Kissy clenched her jaw. It was so unfair that the puppies made such a fuss over their father. She felt like pounding her paws on his head. She was the one who nursed them. She was the one who licked them clean and watched over them to make sure they didn't do anything to hurt themselves. She was diligently teaching them to use the piddle pads that her mom put between their sleeping box and the playpen area. She taught them how to lap the thickened formula and cereal that her mom supplied and she licked their muzzles clean afterward. She always stood guard over them while Kawdje came and went as he pleased.

"I'll bet they love him more than me," she thought. "I do all the work and he gets all the reward." She charged across the bedroom carpet and snarled in frustration at Kawdje. She accused him of never helping to clean their puppies or keeping them safe or teaching them the good habits and manners each would need to become a loved and respected family member of a household.

The puppies raised their innocent eyes and gaped at their mother in stupefaction.

Essie had been hanging freshly washed clothes in the bedroom closet and paused to watch this altercation. Kawdje hastily got up and fled into the hallway. Essie knew the puppies were stunned by their mother's angry outburst. All their playful activity had abruptly stopped. Essie continued to watch as Kissy licked their muzzles and attempted to get them to resume their playful activities with her, but they wouldn't move. Essie walked over to the puppies and sat down among them. They clustered to the shelter of her lap.

Essie empathized with Kissy. She recalled the times that Joy had seemed to have a closer bond with her father than with her. Essie remembered Joy running to her father's arms after having been bussed home from her first day at school and how unappreciated, jealous and left out she had felt. As Essie placed the puppies in the playpen that she and Evan had taken from its storage place in the attic a couple of weeks ago, she fondly reminisced about placing Joy in that playpen so many years ago. She walked downstairs in search of Kissy.

She found her sulking under the dining room table. Essie coaxed her out, lifted her into her arms and spent the next fifteen minutes cuddling Kissy, telling her how much she loved her and that she was the best mommy any puppies could ever have. Kissy calmed down and listened drowsily to the endearments her mom whispered in her ear. She felt somewhat appreciated and was mollified. She decided to make up with Kawdje tomorrow.

"Let him sweat it for the rest of today," she thought.

CHAPTER FORTY-FOUR

On a beautiful and unseasonably warm spring day, Topaz, Michael and their puppies were outdoors. The portable fence from the greenhouse had been transported outside and set up to confine the puppies inside its perimeters.

Topaz and Michael paced about thirty yards away and when Topaz judged they were out of earshot she said, "I'm certain that our puppies are going to leave here soon to go to their new homes. We need to tell them how to behave so that their families will be pleased with them."

"Why? No one ever told me how to behave in a new home, and I didn't do anything that displeased Sarah after she rescued me."

"Michael, you were older and wiser than our puppies when Sarah took you into her home. Also, remember, you didn't fare well in your first home. I want our little ones to make a great first impression. My mom and I have been teaching them to use piddle pads if they are unable to get outdoors. However, there are other rules that they need to be told so that they can impress their new families."

"Um-m, okay, but you go first, Topaz."

Topaz paced to the portable fence and jumped inside its perimeters. She instructed the puppies to listen up because she had some important things to tell them. She explained that soon each of them would be going to a new home.

"That's the way of life. I left my own mother when I was younger than you, so I don't remember her. I've always been happy here and I have a special connection with my mom."

She had the full attention of her puppies, who looked at her with serious and trusting expressions.

"Here are my rules to live by:
- Always greet your family members with joy when they come home.

- Use a piddle pad or newspaper if you can't wait until you get outdoors to relieve yourself.
- Bark at a door to let someone know whenever you want to go outside or come in.
- Bark to alert your family if a stranger comes to the door or tries to get inside your home.
- Always protect your family and your home.
- Listen for your name and come when you're called.
- Don't pull on your lead when you're being walked.
- Dig holes in the part of the lawn that is farthest from your home and preferably behind a bush that will conceal the hole.
- Never bite anyone unless you absolutely must in order to protect your family.
- Always love your family no matter what. That's what we're here to do —to love people. They need it. If you are loved in return—that's crème brûlée."

Mary asked, "Mommy, what's crème brûlée?"

"It's the most delicious dessert anyone could ever eat!" Topaz saw that her puppies looked puzzled so she elaborated and explained, "If your families love you in return, then life is giving you something extra special that is as sweet and enjoyable as a dessert like crème brûlée."

She jumped over the portable fence and paced toward Michael. He knew it was his turn to tell his puppies what they needed to know to live well and enjoy life. He wasn't sure what to say, but as he walked toward the puppies and jumped over the portable fence, thoughts flowed into his mind and he shared them.

- "Hang your head out a car window every chance you get and let the wind whistle through your teeth, flap your ears and vibrate your muzzle and whiskers.
- Don't throw up inside your home or car. Try to get outside before you do.
- If you have an upset gut, eat grass and that will help clear things out of one end or the other.
- Don't howl if you are ever up in an airplane.
- Always ask to go along on every car ride. Enjoy the ride.
- Learn to swim if you have the opportunity.

- Protect your home and property from varmints, and never run from deer.
- Always eat dessert.
- Remember this—you can always come home to daddy if you're not loved and treated well by your family."

The puppies looked worried by their daddy's last remark. Topaz jumped back inside the circle and said, "I'm sure your new families will love you."

One of the male puppies asked, "How will I be able to get back to daddy if my family doesn't love me?"

"Just send thoughts to me that you want to come home and then I'll send those thoughts into my mom's mind. Don't worry! Your daddy and I will get your message."

On a Saturday afternoon about a week later, all the families for Topaz and Michael's puppies descended upon Jeanette and Cole's home to claim each new family member. Sarah, Gordon and Michael arrived before the others. Sarah helped staple together the Breeding Program Agreement and the instruction sheet about the feeding, training, vet care and timely advice for raising a healthy puppy that Pat and Jeanette had composed. Each family would have to sign the papers.

When John and Marie Colbert arrived, they were so happy to see Topaz that they kissed and hugged her before greeting Jeanette. Jeanette introduced them to Sarah and Gordon and Michael. Michael liked them and immediately showed it with tail wags and friendly licks. This greatly relieved Jeanette and Sarah, who felt that his seal of approval meant a lot.

Jeanette had told John and Marie the previous week that all the female puppies had takers. The couple plopped down amidst the male puppies who swarmed over them. A darker colored male who was slightly larger than the other three stood on John's lap and licked him on the lips.

John cradled the puppy to his chest. "I've been chosen. This is our boy."

Marie said, "We've been thinking about a name ever since your phone call when you explained the protocol of how each Angel Dog is to be named. We've decided to call our boy Malachite Archangel Raphael of Heaven Sent. John's great-grandfather's name was Raphael. John's first gift to me was a pair of green malachite earrings. A friend of mine, who is into New Age teachings, told me that Raphael is associated with the color green and that malachite assists in clearing and activating all chakras and is a stone of transformation. I'm not sure I understand exactly what that means, but it sounds good."

John pulled a collar from his jacket pocket. "We've brought a green collar with Raphael's name and our telephone number stitched onto it."

Jeanette and Sarah were delighted with the name and also that John and Marie had brought a collar. As Sarah and Pat were explaining the agreement to John and Marie, Jeanette went to the door to greet Mark Lederman.

After introductions, Mark also sat down among the male puppies. Michael and Topaz remembered him. They picked up the scent of Harry Houdini on him and relaxed. They felt certain that Harry would be a good mentor and pal to one of their puppies.

Mark stroked them both. "Don't worry. I'll provide a good home for one of your puppies. He will be well taken care of and greatly loved."

He said to Jeanette, "I don't anticipate any rivalry between the puppy and Harry. Harry was neutered at eight months. It will be two to three years before my puppy is ready to be the alpha dog and by then, Harry will be eight to nine years old and ready to pass over the alpha mantle."

Jeanette asked if he had chosen a name yet, and Mark replied, "My wife researched minerals, crystals and stones and came up with Kyanite. The mineral is blue and never needs cleaning or clearing because it will not accumulate or retain negative energy or vibrations. She chose Archangel Jeremiel because her father's name is Jeremy. So, our puppy's name is Kyanite Archangel Jeremiel of Heaven Sent. On a mundane note, we'll call him Jerry. It goes well with Harry."

Everyone loved the name and said so. Marie told Mark the name of her puppy while he was looking over the remaining male puppies to select his. One of them had liver colored ears and a liver patch on his hindquarters and another on the chest. The rest of his coat was a mixture of grey and white. He reminded Mark of Harry Houdini. Mark picked up and cuddled the puppy who looked directly into his eyes.

"Hey there, Archangel Jeremiel, you and Harry and I are going to spend many a happy hour practicing dog agility. With those wings of yours, I expect you to fly over the jumps."

The doorbell rang and Jeanette, Cole and Jenny left the group to answer it.

Oshi Yakamuri said, as Cole took his overcoat and hung it up, "I am honored to be your guest, Dr. and Mrs. Bancroft. You have a most beautiful home."

"Please call me Cole, Mr. Yakamuri."

"And please call me Jeanette."

"Thank you, Cole and Jeanette, and you must please call me Oshi."

"You have met our niece, Jenny, at the World Cynosport Games," Jeanette said.

"I remember her well. It's nice to see you again, Jenny."

Cole said, "Oshi, come into the greenhouse where everyone is gathering and I'll introduce you to people and puppies."

Sarah and Gordon shook hands with Oshi and introduced him to Pat and Ed, John and Marie. As he was introduced to Mark, both men said they remembered having seen one another at the World Cynosport Games. Oshi then greeted Michael and Topaz. John, Marie and Mark proudly showed their puppies to him and gave an explanation of the names they each had chosen.

Oshi sat on the floor and crossed his legs underneath him. "Please show me which puppies are available for my selection," he said.

Gordon picked up the two remaining puppies and placed them in front of Oshi.

Jeanette said, "Please don't feel you're getting leftovers. All the puppies are wonderful and Topaz, Cole and I will keep and love whichever one you don't select."

Oshi said, "They are all superb puppies. I can see the resemblance to wings that the growth pattern of their fur gives them. It is most unusual and very striking."

The puppy near his left knee crawled onto his lap and flopped on his back, exposing his belly for a tummy rub. The puppy had gray, liver and white ticking all over.

As Oshi stroked the puppy's belly he said, "I have been chosen by Jade Angel God Ida-Ten of Heaven Sent."

Jeanette exclaimed, "I remember my grandmother invoking that Japanese God whenever she wanted victory or success in some venture or issue."

"Ah," said Oshi. "You do remember something of your oriental heritage. My wife and I chose that name, not only for its meaning, but because saying 'That's a ten,' is the ultimate compliment or best rating in this western culture. We shall shorten this little one's name to 'Ten' for daily usage."

Everyone broke into spontaneous applause. This noise startled the puppies and one of them ran toward the piddle pads on the floor near the greenhouse door to squat. Two more ran over to the pad and followed suit.

Marie exclaimed, "How wonderful that they're housebroken!"

Jeanette said, "They're still too young to sleep through the night and stay dry. I suggest withholding fluids for an hour before bedtime, and taking them outside, weather permitting, for a last stroll, and then getting up very early in the morning for an outdoor potty break. Place piddle pads in front of the door that you will use most often to let them in and out of. They'll use them if no one is available to let them outside. In a few months, it won't be necessary to go through that ritual because they will have matured enough physically to sleep throughout the night without needing a potty break. They will also have learned to bark to let you know when they want to go out and come in."

The doorbell rang. Jeanette and Cole excused themselves and went to greet the Donohues. They had brought Patrick but had left him in their vehicle with the windows open so that he would be comfortable.

After they had been introduced to the other families, Jeanette brought the female puppies into the greenhouse. They had been sequestered in the study so as not to confuse the selection process of the male puppies.

"This is your little lady," Jeanette said.

"O-o-oh, she's beautiful. She really does have wings," exclaimed Clodagh as she pointed to the puppy's upper back area.

Their puppy barked and wagged her tail.

"She wants to play with us," Ryan said. "She has spirit. She suits the name we chose for her."

Clodagh announced, "She's Emerald Goddess Brigit of Heaven Sent. Emerald is, of course, because we're from the Emerald Isle. Brigit is an Irish and Welsh warrior goddess who is the perfect balance of femininity and power. The name means bright and/or powerful one. Brigit is the female equivalent of Archangel Michael and there is a shrine erected in her honor in the town of Kildare. Patrick's official name is Boru's Patrick of Kildare's Keep. We liked the connection. We'll call her Brigit."

The group applauded and then broke into conversion all at once, sharing the special meanings of the names of their puppy.

Jeanette slipped away unnoticed to answer the doorbell but suggested to Sarah before she did so, that she prepare everyone for the explanation of the rules of their breeding program and distribute the agreements that everyone had to sign.

Cecil and Arielle greeted their puppy by name as they entered the greenhouse and Gabrielle ran toward them.

Arielle picked up Gabrielle and held her close. She turned to Jeanette and asked, "What have you and Cole named your puppy?"

"We chose the name Sunstone sun god Hugh of Heaven Sent. The sunstone color range includes grey, green, yellow, brown, orange, peach, pink and red. Since the coloration of the puppies includes grays and browns, we thought it would be an appropriate choice. We chose the name sun god Hugh, which is Celtic, because both Cole and I have Celt in our heritage. Hugh is a youthful sun god who is supposed to be multi-talented and a jack-of-all-trades. We thought sunstone and a Celtic sun god went together well. Cole said that whichever male puppy remains with us will be called Sonny. And since he is Topaz's son, that nickname will be very apropos."

Jeanette concluded by asking if everyone had brought a collar and leash for their puppy. Everyone had.

"Let's put on their collars and walk them before we have lunch. Remember, they are very young and need potty-break walks frequently."

Clodagh and Ryan separated Brigit from the rest of the puppies and walked toward their car. They let Patrick out on his leash and introduced him to Brigit. He sniffed her and recognized that she was Topaz and Michael's puppy. He instantly loved her.

During lunch, Jeanette and Sarah answered questions and clarified points about the breeding program and explained the obligations of the participants to keep accurate records of all matings that first had to be approved by Sarah and Jeanette, and of all matings of the present puppies' progeny that must also be approved by Sarah and Jeanette. They added the stipulation that any future families of the progeny must sign the breeding agreement.

Topaz, Michael and the puppies ate in the greenhouse. Linoleum still covered the brick floor, which was fortunate because the puppies always dropped food when they were eating.

Michael said quietly to Topaz, "I hope the puppies are as well fed in their new homes as they have been here."

Topaz couldn't eat. She had a lump in her throat and zero appetite. Michael understood that while he would be gaining one of his puppies on a full-time basis, Topaz would be losing all of them except one.

"Don't be sad. You'll see Michelle almost every day. I liked every person that I met today. I could tell that each of them loved the puppy they had chosen. You'll see them again and so will Michelle and I."

Topaz just stared at her food.

Michael continued his attempt to cheer up Topaz. "Just think how noisy and messy and hectic it would be around here in six months if you still had them all with you. You'd never get any sleep."

Topaz still looked down at her bowl.

"Don't let our puppies see that you are sad. We want them to think that leaving here is a positive experience for them."

Topaz remained silent and Michael asked, "If you're not going to eat your crème brûlée, may I have it?"

Topaz raised her head and looked at Michael. "I'm sad but I'm not THAT sad!" And she bent her head and ate her dessert in two big licks. She then briefly wondered how Kissy would react when her puppies left to live in other homes.

CHAPTER FORTY-FIVE

On a sunny day, early in the month of May, Joy and Sam arrived at Essie and Evan's home. They had been invited to dinner to celebrate Sam's birthday and to take home his birthday-present puppy. Evan opened the door and hugged his daughter as Sneakers ran out and stood as tall as he could on hind legs while bracing himself with his front paws on Sam's shins. Sam picked him up in his arms.

Sneakers loved being up so high. He looked around and it seemed as though he could see everything in the world. He had inherited his father's love of heights and the desire to be taller. Sam followed Joy and Evan into the house holding Sneakers nuzzled next to his cheek.

Flashbulbs popped and voices shouted, "Happy birthday!"

Jenny stood beside Jeanette and Cole, holding her white puppy that she had named Candy. Sam's teammate Beau Benadar and Beau's wife, Selma, were also there. Selma was cuddling their male puppy. Sam saw Aaron and Mimi Breslin.

Mimi said, as she cuddled Caressa, "My birthday is the end of this month and Caressa is Aaron's birthday gift to me. This is the best birthday gift he has ever given me!"

Kissy and Kawdje were comfortable with Joy and Sam taking Sneakers to live with them and Jenny taking Candy to live with her. They loved them and knew they would see the puppies often. They were familiar enough with Aaron and Mimi to trust them to provide a happy home for Caressa.

They turned their attention to Beau and Selma Benadar, who held their big male puppy with the light fur and dark paws. They kept repeating the name Hershey. Beau was a really tall man, almost as tall as Sam. Kissy and Kawdje both sensed that he was a friend of Sam's.

"Any friend of Sam's must be okay," pronounced Kawdje.

Kissy was not so easily convinced. She walked purposefully toward

Beau and Selma. She stood on her hind legs and braced herself for support by placing her front paws on Selma's legs. She looked up at her inquiringly. She wanted to familiarize herself with this person who was to become her puppy's mom.

Selma passed Hershey into Beau's arms, then reached down and lifted Kissy into her arms. She sensed what Kissy was thinking. She laid her cheek against Kissy's muzzle and whispered, "Don't worry, Kissy. My husband and I will take very good care of your boy. I hope that Hershey will be a great Agility Dog competitor like you and Kawdje because he and I are going to become an Agility team."

Kissy showed her approval by kissing Selma.

It was a fun-filled evening. Kissy and Evan, Essie and Kawdje gave an agility demonstration using the obstacles they had on their lawn. The puppies waddled over the stretch hurdle and under the jumps. Essie and Evan gave pointers on training the puppies to agility, and also on housebreaking. Jenny demonstrated her agility handler's prowess by running the little setup with Kissy.

As twilight set in, everyone went indoors and helped themselves to a bountiful buffet dinner. Essie had included foods that Kissy and Kawdje liked and some that the puppies enjoyed, too.

Essie served crème brûlée for dessert, plus rice pudding because she thought crème brûlée was too rich for the puppies. She had a bowl of oatmeal cookies tidbits for Kawdje, which Evan hand fed to him, one by one. Sam grabbed some and offered one to Sneakers, who readily ate it and then another and another until Sam's hand was empty. Jenny offered one to Candy, who declined it. Mimi fed an oatmeal cookie morsel to Caressa who gobbled it. Essie advised Mimi to use them as treats when training Caressa for Conformation Dog Shows if Caressa disliked dried liver treats, as did Kawdje. Selma Benadar tried to tempt Hershey with a piece of oatmeal cookie, but he wasn't interested. Essie promised to give Mimi her recipe for oatmeal cookies.

While desserts and beverages were served, Aaron told everyone that he and Cecil planned to open their resort in Belize within six months and that PPAL would be making its maiden flight to Belize in time for Christmas.

"I hope you will all be open to the idea of spending Christmas in Belize with your pets. It will be a trial run for the airline and the resort.

We want to remedy any glitches in our service that show up. No one will be charged for accommodations, but tips will be expected by the employees of the resort."

What an awesome Christmas present! The group clapped and cheered. The puppies vocalized their approval by barking.

CHAPTER FORTY-SIX

When the Dog Agility season resumed, Jeanette and Sarah noticed an increase of smaller dogs competing in the 26-inch jump height category and wondered why they weren't in the 22-inch division. They checked out the 22-inch category and found that there were competitors in that division that they would have expected to be in the 16-inch category.

Essie saw pets in the 16-inch jump height category that were of a size to fit in the 12-inch division.

The friends checked the USDAA website and learned that the International Federation of Cynological Sports had size divisions that differed from USDAA and that points earned in one height division could not be reallocated to another jump height division. Height breakdowns were posted in centimeters and the equivalent in inches.

They studied them and were relieved that nothing changed for them. Kissy and Kawdje were well within the IFCS height breakdown for the Toy Division as were Topaz and Michael for the Maxi Division. The greatest variance occurred in the IFCS Maxi Division, which was the equivalent of the USDAA 22-inch jump height category. The Maxi Division included all dogs who measured 50 cm at the withers or greater (19.69 inches)—a difference of almost two and on half inches!

Although motherhood delayed Topaz and Kissy's entry back into the agility circuit, they and Michael and Kawdje achieved Agility Champion titling and Tournament Master status and were working toward attaining Bronze Metallic Designations.

Essie entered Kawdje in some Conformation Dog Shows so that he would remain familiar and comfortable with that routine in case she decided to enter him in the Westminster Dog Show the following year.

Jenny's parents were discharged from the extended care facility in time to attend Jenny's school graduation ceremony and celebrate her twelfth birthday. Prior to their discharge, Jeanette and Cole spoke to Aaron and

Cecil about the possibility of a job for Don in the insurance department of their fledgling airline company. After looking into Don's background and experience, Aaron and Cecil offered him a "second in command" job in the insurance division of PPAL with the possibility of eventually becoming Department Head. Don and Iris sold their home in Chicago and bought one near Jeanette and Cole.

PPAL commercials were made and scheduled for release during the summer and fall. One was of Cecil, Arielle and Gabby and Aaron, Mimi and Caressa. Another featured Sam with Sneakers and Beau with Hershey using the caption, "Big Guys and Their Little Pets—All sizes can travel in comfort by flying PPAL". Jenny and Candy were featured in a commercial that was due for release just before Christmas.

In order to accrue as many points as they could, plus achieving titling, the friends drove all over the country competing in Regional Championships, plus many local Dog Agility events.

In October, Jeanette entered Topaz in the Singing Dog Contest held in New York City. They performed their rendition of *The Boogie Woogie Bugle Boy of Company B* and did their dance routine while singing. Topaz held a note for so long that she amazed everyone, including herself. She won!

All the families of Topaz's puppies called to congratulate Jeanette, including Oshi Yakamuri, who happened to be in New York City at the time of the contest and saw it featured on the news. He told Jeanette that Ten had inherited Topaz's strong and melodious voice and that they had flown inside the passenger cabin of the company corporate jet for the flight home to Japan. The other passengers must have kept quiet about the incident or had assumed that Oshi had been given permission.

Because of the hectic Dog Agility schedule they had adhered to since the spring season, Essie and Evan, Jeanette and Sarah decided to forego competing in the World Cynosport Games held in November. Any honors achieved at the World Cynosport Games would not accrue points to add to their total, plus attending the World Cynosport Games would require spending almost two weeks driving to and from Arizona because, as yet, there was no pet-friendly airline they could use to shorten travel time.

Ed resigned from his law firm in June to become head of PPAL's Legal Department. Immediately after graduating from the University of Pennsylvania's School of Veterinary Medicine in May, Pat was hired as both the Veterinary Department Head of PPAL and the airline's full-time veterinarian. Because Pat and Ed were away from home all day fulfilling the duties of their exciting and demanding jobs, they requested permission to bring Mary to work with them. Permission was readily granted.

Aaron and Cecil decided that ABCD Realty would be a vanguard company in allowing pets to accompany employees to their workplace. This decision was due, in no small part, to the fact that each thought his wife hogged the time and attention of their pet while they were at work. Each negotiated with his wife that their pet accompany him to work at least twice a week to set an example for their employees. Morale had always been good at ABCD Realty, but it soared to an unprecedented high after pets showed up at the workplace. Pat established Rules and Regulations for pets in the workplace.

By Thanksgiving, PPAL commercials advertising pet-friendly travel to ABCD Realty's pet-friendly resort in Belize aired on television. The slogan was, "Welcome in the New Year with all your family members." Some ads included Kissy and Kawdje, their puppies and families. Others featured Michael and Topaz, their puppies and families. One commercial just featured Jenny and Candy.

PPAL began booking flights to Belize and ABCD Realty's pet-friendly *Familias* resort in Belize quickly booked up for New Year's. Soon afterward, January, February and March months were booked solid.

CHAPTER FORTY-SEVEN

The maiden flight of PPAL was scheduled to take place from Philadelphia to Belize City. The families of puppies who were out-of-towners arrived a day early and stayed in pet-friendly motels. ABCD Realty's pet-friendly hotel in downtown Philly was under construction and not ready for occupancy.

December 22nd, the morning of departure, dawned bright and crisply cold. Everyone was thankful that the previous week's snowstorm was now reduced to patchy covering on lawns and that the roads were clear and dry.

Pat arrived at the airport terminal early to supervise and make sure that the pet pathway from the kenneling of pets prior to arrival at the ticket counter, the weighing of the kenneled pet at the ticket counter area and subsequent delivery to the hydraulic lift, followed by the positioning and securing of each kennel at its destination in the allotted cabin area went smoothly. Ed and Mary accompanied her, as did Kevin, who wanted to be there to remedy any mechanical glitches.

Pat's first problem occurred when Mary began barking and refused to quiet her noisy objection to being kenneled. Pat quickly discovered the reason for Mary's uproar. Because of the deviation from her daily routine, her gastrointestinal system was upset and she soiled her kennel. There weren't any piddle pads or moist disposable towels hand, so Ed located a dolly and loaded it with boxes of the pads and towels and rolled it to the ticket counter check-in area.

That proved to be a wise decision because Jerry and Hershey each fouled their kennel. Jerry was upset and frightened because he was kenneled separately from Harry Houdini. Hershey had eaten bacon, egg and grits for breakfast, plus dried dog food. He upchucked while his kennel was being rolled from the ticket counter area to the hydraulic lift. Pat accompanied the attendant who transported him and Pat quickly cleaned him and his kennel after it had been positioned and secured.

"Our flight attendants need to be trained to service a pet requiring a cleanup or have them alert the pet's family member to do so before take-off," she thought. "I also need to add to PPAL's Rules and Regulations for pet travel, the suggestion that pets be given a light, bland meal, preferably a few hours before check-in time, and a potty break just prior to leaving for the airport. It won't be a rule, just a suggestion."

After all kennels were secured in the pet cabin area, Michael saw that Michelle was situated directly across from him and he was glad that she had the security of knowing that her daddy was traveling the journey with her. Sonny and Brigit flanked either side of her. He knew that Patrick was kenneled on one side of him and Topaz on the other.

He heard Harry Houdini's voice reassuring Jerry, who had asked what was happening. He detected a familiar, yet elusive scent and suddenly recollected that it belonged to Aiya. He asked how she liked sharing her home with Ten and if she had ever traveled like this before.

Aiya replied that she had traveled the way birds do, but in a much smaller flying house than this and was kept in a kennel much like the one she was in now. She also related that on several journeys she had been kept alone in a dark room for a very long time. She told Michael that during her first trip, she had been very frightened, but the next trip she had known that her dad would rejoin her once again after she had been taken out of the house that flew like a bird.

Michael told Aiya of his first terrifying experience of being flown from Mexico to his new home. Aiya asked if he had been in Mexico to compete in Dog Agility games and Michael explained that he had been born there. She wanted to know more, so he told the story of his life in Mexico. His puppies listened with rapt attention, as did Patrick, Harry Houdini and Kissy and Kawdje's puppies. As his tale unfolded, they were entranced and barely noticed the aircraft taking off.

Mary said, "That's why you told us that we could always come home to you if our families didn't love us and treat us well."

They all recognized pain in Michael's voice as he simply said, "Yes."

Harry Houdini spoke next and said that he, too, had sometimes traveled in the building that flies like a bird and it had always been an unpleasant experience until now, because he had been left outside in cold weather with lots of suitcases around him before being put inside a small dark room and left alone. "This is the first time I've ever traveled in a lighted place with others for company."

Jerry asked with obvious nervousness if he would ever be put into a dark, lonely room inside a house that flew like a bird.

Harry replied that he didn't know, but if Jerry ever were he shouldn't be nervous because their dad would always come and get him at the end of the journey.

Kawdje was nervous and decided not to say anything that might upset or worry any of his puppies. He kept his thoughts on them to avoid thinking ahead about how this flying building was going to manage to land on solid ground somewhere.

The puppies had been absorbed by the tale of Michael's childhood and in the general conversation for more than halfway into the flight when Pat and Arielle walked into the pet area and disturbed their concentration. Pat thought she ought to accompany the other passengers during their first experience of their pet's in-flight potty break and hug time. Gabby was happy to see her mom, but secretly wished she had arrived a little later because Kissy was in the midst of her tale about Olé. Their families all took turns visiting them. Harry Houdini was last and as soon as he was securely back in his kennel, Kissy resumed telling about her altercations with Olé and how she had outperformed and outwitted him on every occasion. The puppies enjoyed her tale of victory, as did their parents.

The others were spellbound as Michael described his big win over Jetson at a huge Dog Agility practice. Topaz, Michael, Kissy, Kawdje, Patrick, Harry and Aiya told the puppies about their adventures in last year's World Cynosport Games. The puppies were fascinated when they learned that their parents were top winning teams. Michael described the Dock Dogs competition and proudly said that Topaz had won. Topaz told them about Kawdje's great Dock Dogs performance.

Topaz described her experience about winning a dog-singing contest with her mom. At everyone's urging she demonstrated her best long and loud note. Kawdje joined in and so did the others.

While the pets were having this conversation, Aaron Breslin was thanking everyone for their cooperation and enthusiasm that had helped to make PPAL's first flight an uplifting experience. Everyone smiled at his pun. They applauded as he sat down. To their collective amazement and amusement, they heard Topaz belt out a high note and assumed their applause had inspired her to sing. They heard Kawdje exercise his vocal cords in accompaniment. Then all the dogs added to the canine chorus but none could hold a note as long and strong as Topaz.

While everyone was laughing, Pat jotted notes to tell Kevin that the pet cabin required insulation to muffle sounds from that area.

After Aaron sat down, Cecil Diamond spoke about the Pet Rules and Regulations at their Belize resort called *Familias*.

He explained, "Pets are not permitted in the indoor dining areas, but are allowed to be with their families at outdoor dining areas. Pets must be leashed at all times except within the confines of the pet pool and exercise area or in their hotel room. Pet pool and exercise areas are available, according to pet size, at those times posted. Time slots are available to accommodate for different-size-but-same-family-pets, to play and exercise together. This must be scheduled in advance with management. There are at least two pet pool guards on duty at all times from 6 a.m. to 10 p.m. in the pet pool and exercise areas.

Biodegradable pet cleanup bags and disposal waste bins are available throughout the resort.

Pet amenities include the following:

- A pet-friendly shuttle to and from the airport and the resort is provided by *Familias*.
- A pet-grooming salon is on the premises. This facility is not included in the resort fee.
- Dog walkers are available for a reasonable fee.
- Kennel and pet sitting services are available for a reasonable fee.

You are our first clients and your input will be invaluable. We want to correct any problems that you encounter. *Familias* is committed to providing a fabulous and memorable vacation experience for people and pets."

After a smooth landing, everybody deplaned from the aircraft in sunny, warm Belize. None of the pets had been airsick and the in-flight breaks had been uneventful. Shuttles transported everyone to *Familias* and their Christmas vacation.

CHAPTER FORTY-EIGHT

Familias was an enchanting place. The new arrivals immediately thought of the Garden of Eden. An abundance of trees and shrubs flowered in vivid colors. Low-growing shrubs fringed walkways and concealed solar powered lights. Jasmine and plumeria sweetly scented the air.

A spectacular freshwater pool consisted of three pools connected by two caves whose entrances were concealed by waterfalls. A saltwater pool had a partially submerged bar where clients could sit on a barstool and imbibe, plus another bar situated beside the pool.

There were three separate fenced-in pool and exercise areas specifically for dogs. One area had a deep pool to accommodate large dogs. Another had a wading pool that catered to small dogs. The third exercise area had a pool with a deep diving end and a shallow end with a gradual descent to accommodate all size breeds. All were landscaped with bushes and trees tall enough to provide shade, and each had a portion dedicated to an agility set-up consisting of a dozen obstacles. Drinking water dispensers had been set up in each of the exercise/play areas for pets to quench their thirst. Doggy-duty bags were available at each enclosure.

The aviary exercise area was topped with a fine mesh to prevent escape. Several fountains bubbled and dripped water in the enclosure. Trees shaded some areas and other parts were open and sunny.

The cat enclosure was equally picturesque. There were trees for climbing and stumps of varying heights to leap upon plus small platforms attached to some tree limbs so that a cat could sleep or survey the kingdom from a high perch. A winding staircase had been provided for cats who didn't care to expend the energy required to claw their way up a tree trunk. They could walk up the stairs and step onto any one of several large tree limbs. As in the dog enclosures, drinking water dispensers were placed in each corner. Litter boxes were discreetly placed.

Familias was situated on oceanfront property and owned a spectacular private, sandy beach. Leashed pets, accompanied by family, were permitted on the beach.

White lights sparkled around the trunks of palm trees and festooned the branches of other varieties of trees. Indoor potted trees were decorated with Christmas ornaments and lights were woven intricately through their limbs. The décor was a subtle mix of south-seas casual and vintage European. A large gathering room beyond the lobby check-in area had soaring ceilings, large windows and sliding glass doors that washed the room in sunlight.

Birds trilled and flitted among the indoor trees. They, obviously, had taken up residence of their own volition because none were tethered to perches or confined in cages.

Cole and Jeanette, Sonny and Topaz walked down a long hallway, open on each side to the lush gardens that surrounded *Familias*. The roof overhang was adequate to keep rain from wetting the hallway during a storm. Jeanette and Cole gasped in awe at the beauty of their room. It was almost hexagonal in shape. The large casement windows had indoor screens that could be removed or replaced as desired and indoor shutters that could be closed over them for privacy.

Everyone had rented dog beds from *Familias* rather than bringing along their own pet beds. Jeanette had packed a large bed sheet, which she now arranged over the hotel's bedspread to protect it, since Topaz and Sonny were accustomed to lounging on their parents' bed at home.

Cole opened the large armoire and sighed in relief at the sight of a television. Vacations to get away from everything were all well and good, as long as he could keep up-to-date with the world situations that he had traveled to get away from.

Topaz plopped down on one of the dog beds. She felt that her status as mommy gave her the unquestionable right to decide which of the two beds would be hers. It didn't occur to Sonny to argue the point.

It was late afternoon when everybody gathered outdoors near the pet enclosures. They divided the pets into three groups. Kissy, Kawdje and their puppies went into the pet enclosure for small breed dogs. Michael, Topaz, Michelle, Sonny, Mary, Gabby and Raphael went into another exercise enclosure. Harry, Jerry, Aiya, Ten, Patrick and Brigit took the remaining one.

Kissy walked into the enclosure and immediately began using the agility setup. She was in her element showing off her agility skills to the puppies, who were as big as or bigger than she was.

Kawdje watched her showing off before their puppies and was inspired to display his agility prowess.

Candy was as competitive as her mother. She slithered in and out between the weave poles. She wasn't as fast as her mom—at least not yet. Sneakers followed his daddy's routine. He was a good jumper and easily cleared the spread hurdle. He was not quite as fast as Candy because his legs weren't as long, but, because of that, he had the potential to be a winner in Conformation Dog Shows just like his dad, Kawdje.

Hershey was well-proportioned, but large for the Tibetan Spaniel breed and that eliminated him from being shown for Conformation. He was strong and a good jumper and he and Selma, had been practicing at a local Dog Agility Club for the past few months. He blundered clumsily through the Weave Poles, but he easily cleared jumps and hurdles and climbed the A-Frame with ease.

Caressa was the smallest and very beautiful. She was being shown in Conformation Dog shows and already had a collection of blue ribbons. Mimi hadn't introduced her to Dog Agility, so Caressa watched the others. One of the pet guards coaxed her to try a jump. Caressa managed to clear the jump and was thrilled when everyone applauded her accomplishment. "Wow! I'm great!" she thought. She had inherited Kissy's love of attention, which helped her to show well in Conformation Dog Shows.

All of Topaz and Michael's puppies were familiar with Dog Agility. They alternated demonstrating their skills with watching their parents perform.

Everyone had brought a Christmas stocking for their pet. After some discussion, everybody decided that the pets should open the stockings in the privacy of their individual rooms to prevent any possibility of scuffles. No one was sure how possessive the pets might be over the contents in their stockings.

Everybody had paid for their own airfare, and husbands and wives had agreed that would be a sufficient Christmas gift to one another. Sarah and Gordon gifted Kevin with his airline ticket, as did Iris and Don Prescott for Jenny, but they also brought a Christmas stocking stuffed with gifts that a twelve-year-old would treasure. Jeanette and Cole gifted Jenny with a sweater that she had seen and pronounced to be cool when she and her aunt had been shopping early in December.

When Christmas morning arrived, everyone discovered to their delight and surprise that a Christmas stocking, beckoning to be opened, awaited each of them.

It was a joyous Christmas Day. Everybody opted to eat Christmas dinner outdoors so the pets could remain with them. It was a grand buffet and, although it wasn't the traditional turkey dinner with cranberry sauce that they were used to, it was still a very special meal made even more so because of the privilege of sharing it with friends and family members in such a special paradise.

CHAPTER FORTY-NINE

Early in February, Gordon browsed the USDAA website and saw that the Tournament Top Ten rankings had been posted for each height category. He scanned the 26-inch jump height category, and when he saw that Michael Archangelo held the number one spot, he felt almost as proud a daddy as the day he first held Kevin in his arms.

He ran to fetch Sarah in the kitchen where she was preparing dinner. "Michael is numero uno in his height category in the Tournament Top Ten. Hallelujah!"

They hugged and immediately felt two pets nudging them to be included in the lovings. They all walked into the den and he and Sarah checked the rest of the results. John, a Border Collie, held the number two spot. They heaved a sigh of relief when they saw that Topaz had placed third. They saw the name Jake in seventh place and Jordan in eighth. Both were listed as being Border Collies.

Sarah said, "John, Jake and Jordan are *The Hoosiers* who competed in the 22-inch category at the World Cynosport Games. They measured too tall at the withers to qualify for the Midi Division in the World Dog Agility Championships, so they competed all last year in the 26-inch category to qualify for the Maxi Division. I remember that John performed well in the tournaments but I didn't think he did as well as Topaz. I'm surprised he edged her out for the number two placement."

Gordon thought a moment before replying. "Due to motherhood, Topaz probably began the season later than John. She didn't begin Dog Agility until late May."

Sarah scanned the list and said, "Hubert the Best was bested once again by at least ten dogs. I can't find his name."

Gordon said, "Jetson came fourth, Harry Houdini placed fifth and Patrick came sixth. Ryan and Clodagh didn't enter him in as many Dog Agility events as we attended."

Gordon scrolled to the 16-inch division. He and Sarah recognized some of the names from having competed at the World Cynosport Games. Bogey, who had been on *The Film Stars* team at those Games, headed the list. Gracie, of *The Comedians* team placed third

"Get to the 12-inch division," Sarah commanded. "The suspense is killing me."

Dustin, the Rat Terrier who won the Steeplechase at the World Cynosport Games they had participated in, headed the list. Kawdje was in the number two slot.

"Oh no!" wailed Sarah. "Thumbelina, the Papillon who was part of *The Storybook Tailers* at the World Cynosport Games that we attended is third. Kissy placed fourth which eliminates her from competing with Team USA at the International Dog Agility Games. Evan and Essie must be feeling grim, especially Evan. Kissy didn't enter a Dog Agility event until near the end of June. The others had probably accrued a hundred points by then."

"I bet you're right," said Gordon. "In spite of her late start, only seventeen points separate her total and Dustin's."

They were both silent and then Gordon said, "I have to call Evan. Maybe he has already seen the results."

Evan hung up after talking with Gordon. He had neither the will nor energy to log onto the USDAA website and look for himself at the results. He dragged himself upstairs and dropped onto the bed.

"I have to pull myself together for Essie's sake," he thought. "I don't know if I should accompany her and Kawdje to the World Games or stay home with Kissy. I was so sure that Kissy could make up for lost time. She performed even better after her venture into motherhood."

Dismal thoughts circled around in his mind until he slept. He awakened to the sounds of Essie lugging in bags of groceries. He felt two warm bodies pressed against him, one on either side, and glanced down to see Kissy and Kawdje gazing at him with concerned expressions.

"They're psychic," he thought. "I can't hide my feelings from them. They know I'm upset and depressed." He sat up and stroked them.

"Come on. Let's help mom put away groceries."

As soon as Evan walked into the kitchen, Essie knew something was wrong. She could see that he was trying to put on a smiley face, but he had the posture of a man who bore the weight of Mount Everest on his shoulders.

"Are you ill?" she asked anxiously.

"Kissy is number four on The Top Ten list. Kawdje and you will represent Team USA at the IFCS World Agility Games. He's in the number two spot."

Evan felt shaky; so he sat on a kitchen stool, planted both elbows on the counter and propped his chin on his fists. It was the only way he could hold his head up. Essie stood behind him, pressed herself against his back and wrapped her arms around him.

"Thank heavens you're okay! I thought you were going to tell me you had just been diagnosed with an incurable disease. I'm sorry that you and Kissy won't be competing at the IFCS Agility Games, but they are, after all, games. We're well and healthy. Our pets and families and friends are well and healthy. We have safe drinking water and many amenities that make our lives pleasant. Most of all, we have lots of love in our lives."

Evan swiveled the stool around so that he faced his wife. He hugged her tightly.

"The best decision I every made in my life was to marry you. You're right—we've got love. Not competing in the IFCS World Agility Games is a disappointment but it's not a disaster. I'll accompany you to the games. Maybe we'll take Kissy or maybe we'll leave her with Joy and Sam while we're away. We have plenty of time to decide."

The evening crawled by. Neither of them had any appetite. Kissy and Kawdje, who sensed their dad's depression were anxious and puzzled and left much of their dinner untouched. Essie suggested that they not tell Joy and Sam until they had decided whether or not to take Kissy to the World Agility Championships.

"I don't think she'll be allowed on the premises of the IFCS World Agility Games," Evan said. "I think I can be there as a spectator, but I would have to leave Kissy kenneled somewhere else."

"We need to ask someone at USDAA Headquarters what we can and can't do," Essie said.

The phone rang and Essie answered. It was Jeanette, who sounded just about as despondent as Essie herself. After Essie hung up, she let Kissy and Kawdje outside for a potty break before bedtime.

Kissy and Kawdje discussed the dark mood that had pervaded their home.

"I wonder why dad is so gloomy," Kissy said.

"He walks as though he's exhausted," Kawdje observed and was about to add that he thought maybe his dad was tired but yelped instead when he stepped on something sharp.

One of his front paws hurt terribly and he gingerly avoided walking on it. Kissy asked what was wrong when she saw him hobbling. After Kawdje explained that he thought something sharp had cut his paw, she suggested that they go back inside and let their mom look at it.

"I'm going to call it a day," said Evan.

"I'll join you as soon as the mutts come back inside," Essie said.

Evan felt exhausted as he climbed the stairs to the bedroom. He had just kicked his shoes off when he heard Essie let Kissy and Kawdje back inside and then call him frantically. He ran back downstairs.

Kawdje pulled away whenever his mom tried to examine his paw because she made it hurt worse but he allowed her to wrap a towel around it.

"He's bleeding from his right front paw. I think the pad is cut. He won't let me examine it."

Evan wasn't able to get a good look at the paw either. Kawdje seemed to be in pain and the bleeding continued.

"I'll take him to the animal emergency clinic, Evan. Hold him while I put on my coat."

Kawdje knew that his mom was going to take him to the vet. He allowed her to wrap a blanket around him, carry him into the garage and put him in his car booster seat. Boy, did his paw hurt!

"I'll call you," she shouted as she backed out of the garage.

Thirty minutes later, Essie phoned telling him that Kawdje was going to be sedated in order to have splinters of glass removed from his paw and that the wound required suturing. A couple of hours after that, Evan was alerted, by Kissy's barking, to their arrival.

"How is he?" Evan asked as Essie placed a sleepy Kawdje into his arms.

"He'll be okay. The vet said to keep him confined as much as possible for the next four or five days to give the paw a chance to heal. There goes Westminster! He can't possibly perform in a week's time. He won't be up to pacing properly and his lower leg and paw have been shaved."

Evan asked, "Do you mind very much?"

"Not really. He had no place to go but down as far as the Westminster

Dog Show is concerned. He almost won last year but perhaps this year he might not get the Group win."

As they climbed the stairs to their bedroom carrying Kissy and Kawdje, Evan said, "I'll be glad to crawl into bed and turn the light out on this dreadful day."

The next morning, neither of them wanted to get up, but Kissy and Kawdje needed to be put outside. By the time they were ready to come back inside, Essie and Evan were too awake to get back into bed and pull the covers over their heads and keep out the world. Essie gave the pets their breakfast. Evan turned on the computer and, while sipping coffee, spent an hour checking his portfolio and making trades. Essie showered and washed her hair. By the time she reappeared in the kitchen, she felt as though she could manage to eat some breakfast.

She made pancakes, slathered with butter and maple syrup—great comfort food. While talking about whether or not to take Kissy to the IFCS World Agility Championships, they were startled by the loud ring of the kitchen phone. Essie choked on a sip of coffee. Evan grumbled as he walked over to pick up the handset.

"I've got to turn down the ringer volume. It's loud enough to wake a dormant volcano."

While Evan talked on the phone, Essie cleared away breakfast dishes. She had just finished loading the dishwasher when Evan grabbed her and hugged her so tightly she could barely breathe.

"Kissy and I are going to the World Agility Games! We're all going to England!"

Kissy and Kawdje immediately sensed the happy, buoyant mood that filled their home.

After they were cuddled on the couch in the den with Kissy and Kawdje snuggled on their laps, Evan explained, "Thumbelina's handler will be six months into her pregnancy when the games take place in May so she declined the invitation to participate in the World Agility Games. Bottom line is that she's happy and I'm happy. It's a win/win situation."

Evan phoned Gordon with the good news. After Gordon finished congratulating Evan, he called to Sarah to pick up the phone in the kitchen. Essie got on her kitchen phone and they had a four-way conversation.

Sarah said, "The IFCS World Agility Games are going to be held from May 6th through the 8th in Birmingham, England. That's where the huge, famous Conformation Dog Show called Crufts is held. I guess the Agility Games will be held in the same building as Crufts. There must be plenty of hotels, motels and B & B's in the area that accommodate pets as well as people."

Evan asked Gordon if he planned to attend. Sarah answered saying that she couldn't do without him.

Gordon said, "Before you make any decision about participating in the IFCS World Agility Games, we have to arrange comfortable air transportation for the pets. None of us want them relegated to cargo. I'll find out if a PPAL aircraft can be spared to fly Team USA to England. If that isn't possible, we can look into the expense of chartering personal jet service, provided we are permitted to have the dogs travel in the cabin area."

Gordon knew that Aaron and Cecil were planning to lure business travelers to use PPAL and indulge themselves in the luxury of enjoying the companionship of their pets in a PPAL aircraft and in one of ABCD's pet-friendly hotels to and from their business destinations. They had recently purchased a fleet of aircraft with plans to have connecting flights from New York City to Los Angeles and a future goal of having routes connecting all the major cities.

Gordon's phone call to Cecil proved productive. Cecil said that some of the aircraft they had purchased had been reconfigured to accommodate pets traveling in the cabin area and that one of the smaller aircraft could be used to fly Team USA to the World Agility Games. Gordon and Cecil discussed an airfare that would cover flight costs without profit to PPAL.

"Gordon, if there are any empty seats, I may send a couple of my international realtors to look for hotels that would be good for ABCD Realty to purchase. Our eldest son is enthusiastic about having a worldwide chain of pet-friendly hotels, motels and resorts called *Families* and *Familias*. Catering to the needs of pet family members has changed my life and the change has been great. I have a feeling that it's only going to get better."

CHAPTER FIFTY

When Michael alighted from the aircraft, he knew he was far from home. The quality of light was different and a breeze carried the scent of some unfamiliar plants and trees.

"Do you think this will be a wonderful and relaxing time like we had at Christmas?" he asked Topaz.

"I doubt it. Our puppies aren't with us but others that we've competed with in Agility practices are."

"You're right, Topaz. We're here to compete even though we've always traveled by car to agility practices."

"Michael, I love competing in Agility practices because I'm with my mom, but I'm already missing Sonny. When we traveled so much and competed in all those agility practices, I missed our get-togethers with some of our puppies and Kissy and Kawdje and their puppies and all the parents."

"I know what you mean, Topaz. I didn't get to spend time in the desert with Gordon when he went looking for old bones. Michelle kept him company, but she told me that she knew he missed Mom and me and that she did, too. I'm glad that I'm with Sarah and Gordon on this trip, but I wish Michelle were here."

They had been walking toward a bus during their conversation and now climbed into it and, after Sarah spread a towel over the seat, they sat side-by-side on it.

Kissy and Kawdje were held in Essie and Evan's arms. Kissy knew they had traveled a long way to compete in another Agility practice and decided that it must be a very important one. Dustin had come on this trip, too. He had been faster than she had in some of the agility practices last summer. Sometimes, she had won. Occasionally, Kawdje had been the best. Her resolve to be the winner in this important practice caused her to stiffen her body. Kawdje noticed.

"What's up, Kissy? Plotting your course to win before the practice begins?"

"I like being the best and getting the biggest ribbons and hearing the applause," Kissy said honestly.

"I miss our puppies," Kawdje replied. "We see them often when we're not traveling from one agility practice to another. I'd rather compete less and just enjoy everyday life."

Michael and Topaz said they felt the same way. Kissy became worried that the others might not try their best to win.

She said, "Remember, when we all competed at that big agility practice and afterward we flew in a helicopter into the desert place where we sang over the old bones of people and dogs that were buried deep in the earth and then ate a great-tasting lunch. Maybe we'll do something exciting like that after this agility practice."

The others brightened visibly. Michael and Kawdje's stomachs rumbled at the mention of lunch. Kissy knew that she had captured their interest and seized the opportunity to dangle the idea of a rewarding, fun trip if they won.

She slyly asked, "Who knows what kind of wonderful adventure and food we'll be treated to if we all win?"

"Sounds like Kissy's giving a pep talk," commented Evan. He had no idea how close to the truth he was.

The bus drove up to a moderately sized inn that was large enough to accommodate Team USA and their family members. Belva Tufts, their team manager, advised everyone to meet in the lobby after getting settled in their rooms.

"You must get registered at the IFCS World Agility Championships, and that includes an official health and height check of each dog. After that has been done, the rest of the day is yours to do as you wish. Tomorrow begins with the Grand Opening Ceremony."

Sarah told Belva that she always sprayed Michael's left ear and her left hand an orange color for competitions. At Belva's questioning expression, she explained her right/left dilemma.

"Will the officials object to Michael and me competing in such a colorful fashion?"

Belva said she didn't think so, but that they should clear it with the officials during registration.

By the time Team USA completed registration, the dogs and their families were ready for a meal and a good night's sleep. Sarah was greatly relieved that the officials had not objected to her spray paint solution for her right-from-left difficulties.

The next day at the Grand Opening Ceremony, they saw Oshi with Aiya. The twosome had competed in Japan the previous year in order to be eligible to represent Japan at the World Dog Agility Games. Oshi told them that, his wife, Susu, was trying to institute a Singing Dog Contest in Tokyo as a way to showcase Ten's melodious voice and that he was training Ten in the sport of Dog Agility.

"Ten is a very talented agility athlete. Maybe two years from now, he and I will compete at the next World Agility Games if my legs hold out."

Gordon smiled and said, "Perhaps Michelle and I will be at those championships, too."

The group watched as the flags of each participating country were carried into the room and raised on flagpoles that were placed against the wall behind the platform upon which the president of the IFCS stood. He gave a short speech praising the special bond between humans and dogs and the efforts of everyone present and all the countries comprising IFCS to promote events that call for teamwork between man and dog.

The day's agenda began with Power and Speed for the Maxi Division, working down the height divisions and finishing with the Toy Division. That class consisted of two parts, the first being the Power section, which was of a setup of Weave Poles and contact obstacles. Any competitor who accrued faults in the Power section was eliminated from performing in the Speed section, which was a course that consisted of Jumps and Tunnels. Michael and Topaz would begin their day performing that event.

While the Maxi Division was competing in the Power and Speed class, the Toy Division would perform in the Agility All 'Round class, which was comparable to a Standard Agility class. It, like all the classes in the World Agility Championships, was performed under Masters Rules. Kissy and Kawdje would start with the Agility All 'Round class.

The Biathlon was a two-part event that consisted of a Jumping class, which would take place on Day One in the afternoon, and an Agility class that would be held on Day Two. The winner in each height division would be the competitor who accrued the most combined points in the Jumping and the Agility classes.

Michael, Sarah, Topaz and Jeanette watched the three teams in the Russian Maxi Division perform the Power and Speed Class. One of them was a mixed breed beauty who had a deep red-toned coat and bore resemblance to a Golden Retriever.

"I thought I heard her name announced as Mikhaila. That's the Russian female equivalent of Michael," Sarah said.

The third dog in the Russian team accrued a fault in the Power section, which eliminated him from performing the Speed section. He and his handler immediately exited the ring.

Next up were the three teams from Hungary. Darda, a gorgeous Vizsla, and a Kuvosz named Oszkar each had outstanding performances.

"I know that Oszkar means leaping warrior. He's a natural jumper so he suits his name. He is smaller than the standard for that breed," commented Jeanette.

Sarah said, "His smaller stature sure hasn't hurt his performance. He's fabulous."

The Italian contingent performed next. Of those three dogs, Antonio, who appeared to be a mix of Standard Poodle and some other breed, had the best performance.

Of the British Maxi Division group, Annabella, an elegant black and white Pointer, who moved with speed and grace gave a performance that was far superior to the other two dogs on her team.

"Now it's our turn," Sarah said to Jeanette.

As Michael entered the ring, he heard his name spoken very loudly—"Michael Archangelo." His mind cleared of all thought except Sarah and the next obstacle to be used. His body performed with split-second reactions without his thinking about it. He never had to consciously gauge the height of a jump and the effort needed to clear it: his body automatically did all the fine-tune adjustments. Everything just flowed.

When they exited the ring, the Russian handler who was teamed with Mikhaila, approached her and spoke in heavily accented English, "I watch very carefully your performance when I hear wonderful name of Michael Archangelo. We have something in common. My girl called Mikhaila. Your Michael Archangelo not so looking good until he perform. But orange ear helps him look good. Why orange ear?"

Then he noticed Sarah's left hand and pointed toward it. Sarah explained her left/right dilemma.

The man introduced himself as Gregori Lomonisov. He congratulated Sarah on "super good performance." Sarah thanked him and extended her own congratulations and praise for his and Mikhaila's excellent performance.

Gregori said that he wished his Mikhaila and Sarah's Michael to mate. "They would have most terrific puppies ever."

Sarah explained Michael and Topaz's mating and their very special puppies that she and Topaz's family were planning to become a distinct breed known as Angel Dogs.

Sarah then suggested to Gregori that they watch Topaz and Jeanette perform so that he could see the mother of Michael's puppies.

Topaz and Jeanette performed as one and their almost supernatural connection was obvious to all who watched.

Gregori said, "Topaz is most beautiful bitch I ever have been looking at. She move like graceful swan. If you have second mating of Michael with Topaz, please to let me have a puppy. My dog is treated as good as my wife and two children. Mikhaila is my third child. I would love a puppy of Michael and Topaz like my children."

Sarah said to Gregori as Jeanette and Topaz exited the ring, "The decision of another mating between Topaz and Michael is up to Jeanette. I'll introduce you to her and you and she can discuss the matter."

CHAPTER FIFTY-ONE

Evan watched Essie and Kawdje perform in Agility All 'Round and was relieved to see that Essie was relaxed and Kawdje was focused and enthusiastic. He had watched Dustin, the Rat Terrier, perform superbly just prior to Kawdje's performance and thought that Kawdje just might be the superior jumper and Kissy the fastest on a course that didn't consist mostly of jumps.

"Well, we'll see," he said to himself as he and Kissy entered the ring.

He had been feeling queasy shortly after having eaten breakfast and he now felt ominous rumblings in his gut. The start whistle blew. He knew Kissy would recognize a Standard Agility course after she performed the first few obstacles, which were the A-Frame, Spread Hurdle and See-Saw that, here in England, was called a Teeter Totter. He sensed Kissy's enthusiasm bubbling up as she cleared the Spread Hurdle. He was almost to the See-Saw and calling her to use it when he experienced a spasm in his gut. He suppressed a yelp of pain and fervently hoped that he could hold it together and finish the course. He unconsciously speeded up the tempo of their performance, which was normally executed at an incredibly fast speed.

Essie gasped and said to Breen Cronin, "Lordy, they're traveling at warp speed."

Breen's jaw went slack as he stared in disbelief at Kissy's fantastic performance. He admitted to himself that Kissy the Comet was faster than his beloved Dustin and that she would probably have earned the number one ranking on The Top Ten list in the 12-inch jump height category if she had not been prevented from starting the Agility circuit at the beginning of the season because she was physically recovering from having birthed puppies in February of last year. He now coveted one of those puppies.

"I'll ask Evan and Essie if Kissy and Kawdje are going to mate again. If so, one of their puppies has to be mine," he thought.

The Spanish team members, who were waiting to perform next, watched in appreciation and dismay at the phenomenal performance.

"We haven't got a chance of winning the Agility All 'Round," one of them said to his team members.

Kissy's heart was pounding and she was panting as her dad urged her on. She couldn't seem to perform fast enough to please him. She sensed that he was agitated. She kept pushing herself to go faster until, suddenly it seemed effortless and she experienced greater pleasure and ease of performance than she had ever felt before. She was disappointed to see the table obstacle and to assume resting pose on it because that signaled the finish. As soon as they exited the ring, her dad picked her up, raced toward her mom and practically threw her at her mom before running away. Kissy was bewildered but mollified when her mom and that man who was Dustin's dad stroked her.

Essie chuckled and whispered in her ear, "Kissy, your daddy urged you on to the performance of a lifetime and you'll probably never know why but, due to unusual circumstances, I'll bet you've won Agility All 'Round."

Later when Evan, who was now feeling better, and Essie and Breen checked the Point Accumulation Sheet, Kissy had won handily. Second place went to Seeka, an Affenpinscher from Belgium. Dustin placed third and Kawdje was fourth.

"Do you think that anyone else watching Kissy and me knew that I had an intestinal upset?" Evan asked.

"I didn't know until after you dumped Kissy into your wife's arms and said that you hoped you could make it to the men's room in time. I doubt that anyone else knows, other than Essie and me. Maybe I should eat something that disagrees with me and see if that brings out a phenomenal performance response from Dustin."

The Jumping part of the Biathlon was being held today for all height divisions. The friends decided to watch as many performances in all the height divisions as their agendas permitted. Tomorrow, they would also try to watch all the height divisions perform the second part of the Biathlon, which would be the Standard Agility course.

The Mini Division was scheduled to perform first, followed by the Toy, Midi and Maxi Divisions, in that order.

Before they positioned themselves to observe the Jumping part of the Biathlon, Sarah and Jeanette checked the Point Sheet for the final results of the Maxi Division in Power and Speed. Michael was first. Jeanette gave Sarah a congratulatory hug. Darda, the Vizsla from Hungary, had narrowly beaten Annabella, the Pointer from England, for second place. Topaz held fourth place.

The Maxi Division results for Agility All 'Round were also available. This time, Annabella of Britain placed first, Michael second, and Topaz third.

Evan and Essie checked the Power and Speed results for the Toy Division. Kissy hadn't left her competition in the dust in this event because she wasn't at her best when she had to perform one jump after another, which is what the Speed part of the course consisted of. Being the focused and determined competitor that she was, she managed to take fourth place. Dustin won and Kawdje placed a close second. Zsa Zsa, a Bichon Frisé from Hungary, was third.

Essie, Evan and Breen were in high spirits when they joined Sarah, Gordon, Jeanette and Cole to watch the Mini Division performances in the Jumping Biathlon. They all agreed that Emi, a pretty female from the Japanese Team, who looked to be part Beagle and who knew how many other breeds, was fabulous. From Britain, a male dog called Arrow gave a very good performance. Austria's best performer was Zack, a Petite Basset Griffon Vendeen who, in appearance, reminded them of a small Michael Archangelo. Zack was a natural jumper and gave a fabulous performance.

Bogey of the USA, who had the number one Tournament Top Ten ranking in the 16-inch jump height division, had a terrific performance. Bogey's attitude reminded them of Kissy's.

They gave the pets a quick break before the Toy Division began the Jumping Biathlon. By the time they returned, all the teams in the Mini Division had performed. They listened to an announcement that there was to be a runoff because of a first place tie between Zack, the Petite Basset Griffon Vendeen from Austria, and Bogey, the Sheltie from the USA. Many other competitors who had not been watching the event converged around the performance ring as the runoff began. Because Zack had performed before Bogey and had the advantage of being more rested, he was scheduled to go first. He had another fast and flawless performance and finished to appreciative applause. Bogey and his handler, a young woman named Shelley Hansen, also gave another fabulous performance and applause for them was equally enthusiastic. Zack of Austria edged out Bogey for first place. Emi, the mixed breed from Japan was third.

Kawdje had been held high in his mom's arms during the Mini Division performances. He watched as the jump heights were adjusted. He knew that he would perform soon and understood that the course to be performed upon was his favorite—a setup of jumps and tunnels.

He and his mom competed before Kissy and his dad. There was a winged jump that had to be performed upon after using an Ascending Spread Hurdle, with very little distance between the two obstacles to give a competitor time to adjust stride or gather focus and intent for the liftoff to clear it. He aced it! He knew from the noisy applause that lots of people besides his mom and dad thought that he was terrific.

Dustin's performance was as topnotch and reliable as ever. Kissy's performance was excellent but Evan knew that she just wasn't as good a jumper as Kawdje or Dustin.

It was a very competitive class. Gordon had been timing all the teams with his stopwatch, but there were so many great performances that it required electronic timing to separate the placements.

The handlers clustered around the Point Sheet.

Essie reminded Evan, "This is only Part One of the Biathlon. A first placement here isn't a win. We have to perform the Agility portion tomorrow before placements are final."

Kawdje edged out Tilly of the Netherlands for first place. Stubby of Britain was third. Dustin placed fourth. Kissy came sixth.

Evan whistled and said, "There is less than three seconds separating fourth place from tenth place. It's still anyone's win. Let's hope that Kawdje, Kissy and Dustin are in top form tomorrow. Us, too," he added as he remembered his intestinal upset from early that morning.

By the time Essie and Evan made their way through the crowds, the Midi Division of the Jumping Biathlon was well underway. Jeanette, Cole, Sarah and Gordon were anxious to hear the results of the Toy Division and grinned when they heard that Kawdje was in the lead. They, too, agreed that it was still anybody's win when they heard how close all the results were. Gordon told Essie and Evan they hadn't missed much because so far, none of the performances had been electrifying.

The first two British teams gave good performances. The third member of the team was a young male dog who appeared to have barely qualified for the minimum competition entry age of eighteen months. He still moved like an ungainly puppy. He looked like a Smooth-Coated Fox Terrier but his bone structure was a little heavy for that breed. By now, Breen and Dustin had joined their group, along with Belva Tufts, the Team USA manager and advisor.

Belva said, "Maybe he's the result of a mating between a Harrier and a Fox Terrier."

His name was The Artful Handful. They heard his handler, a man who looked to be close to fifty years of age, call him Artie.

Artie galvanized the onlookers. In spite of his youthful ungainliness, it was obvious that he had tremendous potential.

The group heard someone with a British accent say, "I'll bet the middle-aged codger handling him will have a tough time keeping up with Artie when the next World Agility Championships are held."

The applause was enthusiastic as Artie pranced out the exit gate.

The first team from Spain entered the ring and Sarah went on alert as the name of a mixed breed dog who looked like a cross between a Field Spaniel and an Italian Greyhound was announced. He was called Miguel. He was an odd-looking dog, to say the least but, just like Michael Archangelo, he transformed into a thing of beauty as he conquered the course.

All three USA teams in the Midi Division of the Jumping part of the Biathlon did very well. Jeanette and Sarah did not have time to check the results because the Maxi Division was scheduled to begin as soon as adjustments had been made to accommodate the taller dogs on the jumps and hurdles. Belva checked her agenda and informed them that Team USA would be the third country to perform in the Maxi Division. Jeanette and Sarah decided to position themselves near the entrance gate in readiness for their turn.

While waiting to perform, Jeanette and Sarah watched the teams from Georgia perform, and the best of the three was a male dog who had the appearance of an Otterhound. His name was announced as being Dzaglika, but his lady handler called him Zag.

Four Dogs and Their Tales

The Canadian team performed next. Matelot looked to be a large Briard and, although he was a good jumper, he was prevented from gaining any real speed by the placement of the obstacles. His handler was a woman who spoke her commands in French. Luke Earthwalker, a Border Collie, was the second Canadian competitor and he gave a great performance. The last Canadian team consisted of a young woman and a female red Doberman Pinscher named Vixen. Vixen and her young handler were a terrific team and their performance earned prolonged applause.

Topaz and Jeanette entered the ring. Cole felt such love and pride for them that tears welled up in his eyes.

Topaz looked inquiringly at her mom, who quietly said two words—"fast" and "jumps." Topaz knew that this course would be mostly jumps.

The spectators became quiet as they watched the beautiful woman and the beautiful German Shorthaired Pointer move in a fast but unhurried way. The woman's commands were spoken quietly and her gestures almost unseen, but all who watched recognized a special communication between the two that transcended gestures and commands. When they exited the ring, there was a moment of silence before the thunderous applause began.

John, the Border Collie, and Breen had a terrific performance, but it was anticlimactic after Topaz and Jeanette's almost ethereal display of perfect teamwork.

Michael Archangelo's name was announced and then his country. Essie, Evan, Gordon and Cole heard some folks speak his name in various languages. The homely dog with the orange ear who was named after an Archangel intrigued them. Gordon looked around at some of the faces in the crowd and saw that they were smiling and speaking to one another in a jocular manner and pointing to their ears.

As soon as the small woman with the golden brown hair, golden eyes and golden tanned skin began to move as though she had just been given a shot of adrenaline and the shaggy, gray dog began to perform with the grace of a gazelle and the strength of a mountain lion, silence prevailed as everyone became absorbed in the extraordinary performance taking place. Once again, there was a moment of silence before the huge applause began for Sarah and Michael.

The two exited the ring and joined Jeanette and Topaz, John and

Josh, who were waiting for them near the exit gate. They all made their way through the spectators to find the rest of their group. After taking a break, they clustered around the Point Accumulation Sheet to check the results of the Jumping portion of the Biathlon. Michael won. Topaz placed second. Vixen, the Doberman from Canada, came third.

CHAPTER FIFTY-TWO

Saturday, day three of the World Agility Championships, was sunny and cool. Although the event was being held indoors and rainy weather wouldn't matter, everyone liked the option of being able to take a break outdoors and stroll in the sunshine.

Essie, Evan, Jeanette and Sarah checked the schedule. Because so many events were taking place simultaneously throughout the day, in the three agility rings, it was perplexing to make order of it.

After they studied the schedule for several minutes, Jeanette said, "Bottom line is that Topaz and Michael perform Gamblers in Ring One followed by Jumpers in Ring Three, then Snooker in Ring Two."

Evan said, "Right. It's best to ignore schedules for jump height divisions that you won't be competing in."

The Agility part of the Biathlon would be the last event of the day. The Jumping part, held on Day Two, had been a very close competition especially in the Toy and Maxi Divisions. Many of the leading contenders were great jumpers. Today's Agility Biathlon was comparable to a Standard Agility class and some dogs who were not good, natural jumpers excelled on the Standard Agility course setup. Anticipation for the second part of the Biathlon was high.

Sarah and Jeanette, Essie and Evan were kept so busy performing the classes in their different height divisions that their paths rarely crossed. None of them had time to check the Point Accumulation Sheets for results, other than their own.

Gordon and Cole found out results from Belva Tufts, and told Essie and Evan, while they were taking a break, that Topaz won Gamblers, Darda, the Vizsla from Hungary came second and Michael placed third.

Gordon said, "Too bad you couldn't watch Jeanette and Topaz perform in Gamblers! I swear they communicate by ESP."

Cole smiled and said, "Michael and Sarah won Jumping All 'Round and I'm proud to say that Topaz and my wife came second. Vixen of Canada came third.

"How did Topaz and Michael do in the Snooker Maxi Division?" asked Evan.

Gordon replied, "John, the Border Collie, won for the USA. Oszkar claimed the number two spot for Hungary. Topaz placed third and Michael fourth. Anyway, it was almost a sweep for our country. We placed first, third and fourth."

Essie couldn't contain herself any longer and almost jumped up and down when she said, "Kawdje won Jumpers."

They all high-fived one another.

Essie continued, "Dustin placed second in Jumpers so that was a one-two win for the USA. Tilly, that lively little Schipperke from The Netherlands, placed third and Stubby, the adorable Norwich Terrier from Britain was fourth. Kissy came fifth.

Evan demanded, "Ask me how Kissy the Comet did in Snooker."

Cole said, "Okay. How did Kissy the Comet do in Snooker?"

"She won!"

Essie chimed in, "Kawdje came second."

Cordon and Cole congratulated them and then Cole asked, "Who won Gamblers?"

"It was a surprise win by Kenji, the Papillon from Japan," Evan said. "Kissy placed second and Seeka, the Affenpinscher from Belgium, was third. Dustin came fourth and Kawdje was fifth."

Evan asked Cole and Gordon if they'd had time to watch the USA competitors in the Mini and Midi Divisions.

"Essie and I have been kept busy with our own competitions. We didn't have time to watch our three USA teams in the Midi Division perform but I know that they were clustered in the fourth, fifth and sixth slots."

Essie said she thought that the odd-looking dog from Spain called Miguel had won the Jumping portion of the Biathlon in the Midi Division and that The Artful Handful from Britain had been second.

Sarah and Michael, Jeanette and Topaz, Josh and John waited near the entrance gate for their turn to perform in the Agility biathlon. Knowing that their performances were scheduled third from last, they had chosen to take a leisurely stroll outdoors with the pets rather than watch the other teams in the Maxi Division perform.

They saw Belva walking toward them. As she drew near, Sarah asked, "Who has had the best performance so far?"

"I haven't checked the Point Accumulation Sheet, however, in my opinion, Annabella, the Pointer from Britain, and Vixen, the Doberman from Canada, had great performances."

The Russian Team of Mikhaila and Gregori Lomonisov were entering the ring so they stopped their conversation to turn their full attention to that performance. Mikhaila had an excellent performance on the Agility Biathlon setup. Jeanette said that she thought Mikhaila had placed sixth in the Jumping Biathlon.

Sarah said, "If she wins the Agility part of the Biathlon, that will bring up her combined score, but not so much that she'll win unless Michael, Topaz and others in the top five placements of the Jumping part of the Biathlon fall down on the Agility setup and don't get up."

John, the Border Collie, and Josh Barnes were the first of the American teams to perform the Agility Biathlon. They had a fabulous performance. Belva remarked that it was too bad they hadn't done well in the Jumping Biathlon because, in spite of the great performance they'd just had, it wouldn't put them in any of the top three spots.

Just before Jeanette and Topaz entered the ring, Jeanette bent down and whispered, "It's almost over my beautiful gem. Let's give it all we've got. Fast. Go very fast."

Topaz intuited what her mom had said to her. She felt secure in the strong, steady love that always spread outward from her mom and enfolded her like a soft, warm blanket. Even when her mom sometimes sprinted away from her and toward the obstacle that she wanted to be used next, Topaz felt as though there wasn't any distance between them. She was acutely aware of every signal, no matter how subtle, that her mom made, so she almost always knew which obstacle was to be taken next. She was sorry to see her mom indicate that she was to use the table next because that meant the end of this special time together. She gazed into her mom's eyes as she assumed resting pose on the table. They each gave a slow blink of the eyes to one another, which was their way of silently saying, "I love you."

As Topaz paced out the exit gate with her head pressed against her mom's leg, she was shocked back into reality by thunderous applause. Cole pressed his way though the onlookers and hugged his wife, then bent over and hugged Topaz.

Michael and Sarah also had an outstanding performance and, as always, he became a thing of beauty when he competed.

The three competitors from Hungary also had great performances, especially Darda, the Viszla. However, none surpassed the elegant and ethereal quality of Topaz, whose swiftness was camouflaged by the ease and sheer beauty of each movement that made her performance look like a beautiful dance.

The Point Accumulation Sheet showed that Topaz won the Agility part of the Biathlon. Michael was second. Vixen of Canada placed third, and because she had been third in the Jumping part of the Biathlon, she would definitely hold the number three placement in the Biathlon. Topaz and Michael had each achieved the same number of points in the two-part event by each placing first in one part and second in the other. The winner was chosen by combined times. Topaz won by .015 seconds. Michael was second and Vixen of Canada came third.

Sarah, Gordon, Jeanette and Cole didn't watch the Midi Division perform the Agility part of the Biathlon in favor of taking a well-earned break.

Jeanette fed Topaz gingersnaps as a treat for her sublime performance. She added a shortbread cookie for good measure. Michael greedily ate a gingersnap and drooled for another. Sarah gave him another, and then ate one herself. Gordon and Cole each munched on shortbread cookies.

Later, after a stroll outdoors with dogs, Sarah and Gordon, Jeanette and Cole kenneled Michael and Topaz and then walked over to Ring Two to watch the Toy Division Agility Biathlon. They arrived too late to watch Essie and Kawdje. Dustin and Breen were performing and gave a tremendous, fault-free performance. Gordon, Cole, Jeanette and Sarah looked around and saw that handlers from other height divisions had gathered to watch the Toy Division Agility part of the Biathlon because they had heard of the close results in the Jumping Biathlon. It was going to be a neck-and-neck race for the top three spots.

When Kissy and Evan walked into the ring, they heard several people say Kissy, prefixed by "ah" or "aha."

Kissy quivered while she waited to hear the whistle and, because she was so revved up, she gave a short, sharp bark, which was her way of saying, "Come on! Hurry up!"

The whistle blew. The action began. Her dad pointed and sprinted

Four Dogs and Their Tales

toward the first jump. She cleared it easily and after using several more obstacles, she recognized this was one of the course setups that she loved, and she felt even more energized.

Her dad was running toward a winged jump and she caught up with him at that obstacle. She gave another short, sharp bark commanding him to move faster.

Evan got the message. Kissy was not only telling him to ratchet up speed, but that she thought she could go faster.

Essie smiled when she heard Kissy telling her dad to "get the lead out of your shoes." She said a silent prayer of gratitude that she wasn't teamed with Kissy, and all because of that embarrassing incident more than two years ago when Kissy bit the judge and she had told Evan she was too mortified to handle her in the ring anymore.

"That breach of etiquette was a blessing in disguise. If it hadn't been for that incident, I'd be out there right now trying to keep up with her. I'll bet she keeps Evan competing until they're both old and gray and barely able to hobble around," she thought.

Breen and Dustin had been waiting near the exit gate, too, and he said as Evan walked through it, "Kissy told you to speed up your act, didn't she?"

Evan gasped, "She needs a younger man."

Everyone was still applauding as Evan slowly walked away from the exit area carrying Kissy in his arms.

He said to Essie, "Kissy wants her gingersnap cookie reward, and I'm sure Kawdje wants oatmeal cookies and I need a drink. Water will have to do for now. Tomorrow, after the games are finished, I'll treat myself to some British stout at the nearest pub."

By the time Evan had recovered enough to accompany Essie to check the Point Sheet, they found Sarah, Jeanette and Belva in the crowd, clustered around the roster. Cole and Gordon were standing off to one side.

Gordon smiled at his brother and said, "You almost won with that Agility Biathlon performance which was the fastest, but Kawdje and Tilly, the Schipperke from The Netherlands, are ahead of her in points. Kawdje was awarded first place because his combined performance was about a quarter of a second faster than Tilly's, plus he had placed first in the Jumper Biathlon. Kissy pulled up to third place and Dustin came fourth, so Team USA placed first, third and fourth in the Toy Division of the Biathlon."

Belva Tufts joined them. She congratulated Essie and Evan and laughingly said, "Evan, I heard Kissy scolding you for being such a slug in the ring."

Belva went on to inform them that she wanted to meet with all the team members that evening because she had selected the three teams who would represent the USA in the Country Team Competition tomorrow.

CHAPTER FIFTY-THREE

Kissy, Topaz and Michael waited at the entrance gate to perform the Three-Dog Relay that was the last of the Team Country events.

After totaling the number of points each competitor had accrued, Kissy placed first overall in the Toy Division with a close second by Kawdje. Topaz was first overall in the Maxi Division with a close second by Michael. The Mini and Midi Divisions of Team USA had not done as well.

The three competitors chosen by each country to comprise its Country Team could come from no more than two height divisions. The choice for the third competitor of Team USA was between Michael and Kawdje. Michael had accrued more points.

During the Country Team Standard Agility event, smart, little Kissy figured out early on that this was some kind of runoff because so few other dogs were competing. Most important of all, she was still in the running. She knew that Kawdje and Dustin were not. She ran her heart out on the Agility course setup, and so did Evan.

During the Jumping event, Kissy had not yet performed with Michael and Topaz, so she didn't realize that she was part of a team. She attacked the Jumpers setup with determination, but did not attempt to hustle her dad to move faster. She didn't accrue faults, and although her performance was not as stellar as her Agility performance had been, it was outstanding, nevertheless. She wasn't quite sure what was going on, but she knew that she and a few others were stars. "Everyone knows that I am the best and I am! I am!" she thought.

When she saw Topaz and Michael and their moms walking into the same ring with her dad, who had been carrying her in his arms and now set her down beside them, she caught on that this event was a Relay. She asked them if they had competed in the Agility and Jumping practices.

They said they had and Kissy commented, "We're a team just like Michael, Kawdje and I were at that big agility practice."

"Yes," said Michael. "I'm not sure why Kawdje is not part of the team and Topaz is. I'm glad we're on the same team, Topaz," he added hastily.

"I wonder if Kawdje is on another team with two other dogs," said Topaz.

"No, he isn't performing today. My mom and Kawdje have been meeting my dad and me every time we leave the ring. Also, once I saw Dustin and his dad, too."

"I'm very happy to be on the same team with both of you," said Topaz.

They looked over the obstacles. Michael and Kissy immediately recognized two separate setups—one half of the ring had jumps set for Kissy's size and the other half for Michael and Topaz's height category. Topaz had never been exposed to this kind of course arrangement because she had been part of a team at the World Cynosport Games with Harry Houdini and Patrick, both of whom were her size. Michael and Kissy explained to her that Kissy would perform in the half of the ring that had some of the obstacles adjusted for her size and she and Michael would compete in the other half.

Sarah snapped off Michael's lead and whispered into his ear, "Do your best my special friend and companion. Let's go for the gold."

Michael knew he had earned awards for being faster and better at the Agility practices than most other dogs. He remembered that he, Kissy and Kawdje had been the best team over Topaz, Harry Houdini and Patrick. He vowed to try to do better than he had ever done so that Topaz could be on the very best team today.

Michael performed with incredible speed and dexterity. Sarah understood just how Evan felt as she pushed herself to the limit to stay ahead of Michael in order to direct his path through the setup. He never verbally urged her on, but she knew he was giving everything he had to this Relay.

As Topaz watched Michael competing, she resolved to make her best effort ever because Michael was trying his best, so this must be important to him. She knew for sure that Kissy would want to win. Topaz slithered through the Weave Poles with a fast rhythm. She used to dislike them, but now they seemed effortless. She wasn't even panting when her mom passed the stick to Kissy's dad. She sat beside Michael and they both watched Kissy the Comet blaze through the setup so fast that her tail looked as though it had difficulty keeping up with the rest of her.

Michael said, "I bet she likes performing Agility more than eating gingersnaps or crème brûlée. Well, almost!"

Kissy performed with joy in her heart. She quickly switched her mind from gauging the spring and push needed for the various jumps to the ebb and flow of running fast between obstacles and the quick, yet precise placement of paws on the contact obstacles while keeping her dad in her sight and following the path that he directed her to take through the course setup. She was a comet—on course, swift, blasting through the setup without hesitation. She was still running so fast when she came to the finish area, that she almost somersaulted when she tried to stop quickly. If her paws had been tires, they would have screeched.

Essie held Kawdje in her arms so that he could watch Kissy, Michael and Topaz perform. She reminded him that when he had been in the Westminster Dog Show enjoying his moment of fame, Kissy had been at home tending to their puppies.

"Now it's Kissy's turn to bask in the spotlight."

Kawdje intuited what his mom said and he involuntarily shuddered as he recalled how nasty Kissy had been to him after their puppies had been born. He thought that she would probably be just as mean to him if he had been chosen to compete with Topaz and Michael and she had not. He decided that peace and contentment was a fair trade-off for relinquishing the spotlight of fame.

The Awards Ceremony took place in Ring One.

Individual Standard Agility

<u>Toy Division</u>
  Kissy of the USA—Gold
  Dustin of the USA—Silver
  Seeka of Belgium—Bronze

<u>Mini Division</u>
  Emi of Japan—Gold
  Bogey of the USA—Silver
  Arrow of Britain—Bronze

Midi Division
The Artful Handful of Britain—Gold
Miguel of Spain—Silver
Van Zeeman of The Netherlands—Bronze

Maxi Division
Annabella of Britain—Gold
Michael Archangelo of the USA—Silver
Topaz of the USA—Bronze

Individual Jumping All 'Round
Toy Division
Kawdje of the USA—Gold
Dustin of the USA—Silver
Tilly of The Netherlands—Bronze

Mini Division
Zack of Austria—Gold
Bogey of the USA—Silver
Emi of Japan—Bronze

Midi Division
Fodor of Hungary—Gold
Miguel of Spain—Silver
The Artful Handful of Britain—Bronze

Maxi Division
Michael Archangelo of the USA—Gold
Topaz of the USA—Silver
Oszkar of Hungary—Bronze

Individual Snooker
Toy Division
Kissy of the USA—Gold
Kawdje of the USA—Silver
Zsa Zsa of Hungary—Bronze

Mini Division
    Emi of Japan—Gold
    Bladerunner of Australia—Silver
    Zack of Austria—Bronze

Midi Division
    Miguel of Spain—Gold
    Sheena of the USA—Silver
    Van Zeeman of The Netherlands—Bronze

Maxi Division
    John of the USA—Gold
    Oszkar of Hungary—Silver
    Topaz of the USA—Bronze

Individual Gamblers
Toy Division
    Kenji of Japan—Gold
    Kissy of the USA—Silver
    Seeka of Belgium—Bronze

Mini Division
    Miguel of Spain—Gold
    The Artful Handful of Britain—Silver
    Gamesman of The Netherlands—Bronze

Maxi Division
    Topaz of the USA—Gold
    Darda of Hungary—Silver
    Michael Archangelo of the USA—Bronze

Individual All Around
Toy Division
    Kissy of the USA—Gold
    Kawdje of the USA—Silver
    Dustin of the USA—Bronze

Mini Division
Emi of Japan—Gold
Bogey of the USA—Silver
Arrow of Britain—Bronze

Midi Division
Miguel of Spain—Gold
The Artful Handful of Britain—Silver
Van Zeeman of The Netherlands—Bronze

Maxi Division
Topaz of the USA—Gold
Michael Archangelo of the USA—Silver
Annabella of Britain—Bronze

The Biathlon

Toy Division
Kawdje of the USA—Gold
Tilly of The Netherlands—Silver
Kissy of the USA—Bronze

Mini Division
Emi of Japan—Gold
Bogey of the USA—Silver
Zack of Austria—Bronze

Midi Division
The Artful Handful of Britain—Gold
Miguel of Spain—Silver
Fodor of Hungary—Bronze

Maxi Division
Topaz of the USA—Gold
Michael Archangelo of the USA—Silver
Vixen of Canada—Bronze

Power and Speed

<u>Toy Division</u>
>Dustin of the USA—Gold
>**Kawdje of the USA—Silver**
>Zsa Zsa of Hungary—Bronze

<u>Mini Division</u>
>Bogey of the USA—Gold
>Zack of Austria—Silver
>Emi of Japan—Bronze

<u>Midi Division</u>
>Miguel of Spain—Gold
>Fodor of Hungary—Silver
>The Artful Handful of Britain—Bronze

<u>Maxi Division</u>
>**Michael Archangelo of the USA—Gold**
>Darda of Hungary—Silver
>Annabella of Britain—Bronze

Country Team Competition featuring Standard Agility, Jumping
All 'Round and Three-Dog Relay.

<u>Team USA—Gold, represented by</u>
>**Kissy (Toy Division)**
>**Topaz (Maxi Division)**
>**Michael Archangelo (Maxi Division)**

<u>Team Britain—Silver, represented by</u>
>Bonny (Midi Division)
>The Artful Handful (Midi Division)
>Annabella (Maxi Division)

<u>Team Austria—Bronze, represented by</u>
>Schatzi (Toy Division)
>Otto (Mini Division)
>Zack (Mini Division)

Kissy quivered with excitement and pleasure every time she walked up onto the award platform with her dad. Some of that pleasure drained away if she wasn't positioned in the very center and on the highest part of the platform because she knew that meant she hadn't won the award for being the very best. She was, nevertheless, delighted with all the cups and ribbons that her dad kept collecting for her.

Kissy reveled in the applause and the flash of cameras. When she, Michael and Topaz sat together on the award platform between two other teams, she knew they were the very best team because they were in the center. Michael was sitting between her and Topaz. She wanted to be in the center position, so she walked in front of Michael and squeezed herself between him and Topaz. She sat as tall as she could, which wasn't tall enough to suit her, so she balanced herself in a semi-standing position by sitting on her hocks and using her tail to steady herself. She held her front legs in front of her chest, and the overall effect was one of a dog begging for a treat. She heard her dad and Michael and Topaz's moms laughing and lots of clapping and cheering. Kissy was relieved when the large award cup was placed in front of her. She rested her front paws on it for support.

Michael said to Kissy, "You really love Agility, don't you?"

"Of course. Don't you?"

"I enjoy it because it's a challenge and because I'm doing it with Sarah and we're a team," and then he added, "I miss Michelle."

Topaz said, "I love being part of a team with my mom, too, but I love being at home with her and my dad and Sonny even more. I wish Michelle and Sonny were here with us."

Kissy suddenly realized that she hadn't given a thought to her puppies during the whole time she had been at this big Agility practice. She felt a little guilty about that, but then she remembered that none of her puppies were living with her and Kawdje.

She said, "All my puppies were taken from me. They live in other homes."

Topaz said sympathetically, "I'm so sorry, Kissy."

Michael echoed "Me, too."

Kissy admitted only to herself that she didn't mind not having any of her puppies hanging around her every day, all day, all the time.

"Kawdje and I get to see them frequently. It's okay."

The World Agility Championships closed with the Grande Finale Ceremony. The flag of each participating country was carried out of the building.

It was 6:00 p.m. After a quick walk in a nearby park, the group of friends returned to the Inn, kenneled the pets in their motel rooms and drove to a pub. Evan treated himself to the mug of stout that he had promised himself. The others joined him. They ate hearty sandwiches made of roast beef and compared them to Nick's in Philadelphia.

Jeanette said, "This is a complete change of subject, but do you all recall me telling you prior to this trip that I wanted to see some crop circles? We have two and a half days before we fly home. Is everyone up for getting on the road early tomorrow morning and searching for crop circles? Areas around Avebury and Stonehenge are good places to look for them. Both are situated near Swindon, a town large enough to have some pet-friendly hotels, inns, or B & B's. We could stay overnight in or near Swindon and explore the surrounding countryside tomorrow and most of the following day."

Cole said that he knew of a rental car agency nearby.

"We couldn't fit all eight of us and the four pets plus the Pak 'n Fold kennels and our luggage into one vehicle so I suggest renting two vehicles."

Gordon said, "I have my satellite phone and you all brought your cell phones, so we can talk back and forth even though we'll be in two cars."

They ordered steak and kidney pie so that they could bring a hot meal back to the pets. While they waited for the take-out meal, they discussed driving on the wrong side of the road, directions to Swindon and how they would pair up in the vehicles.

CHAPTER FIFTY-FOUR

Cole, Evan and Gordon took a cab drive to the car rental place and chose a Land Rover and a Mitsubishi Colt. They drove back to the inn and decided over breakfast how they would divide themselves. They settled on Essie and Evan, Kissy and Kawdje riding in the small Mitsubishi and the others in the Land Rover.

They drove for about an hour, then stopped at Stratford Upon Avon to do the tourist thing at Shakespeare's birthplace. Because of that detour, they didn't arrive at Swindon until noon. It was cloudy and cool enough to leave the pets in the vehicles while they ate lunch at a pub. They asked their waitress, Lucy, a cheerful woman with an engaging smile, if she knew of any pet-friendly accommodations nearby. The waitress inquired about their pets. They told her they had four dogs and that they had competed in the World Agility Championship Games that had just been held in Birmingham.

Lucy said, in her very British accent, "I know about that. T'was Annabella, that beautiful Pointer, and Artie who both done so well for us. Our team won the Silver medal. I know the Yanks won the Gold in the Country Team competition. How did your dogs do?"

When they explained that they were the Yanks who had won the Gold medal and that their pets had won many individual medals, Lucy asked where the pets were now. Jeanette replied that they had left them in their rental cars parked outside the pub.

"I've got to see them," Lucy said. "We had telly coverage of the Agility games, and mum and me had a good laugh when that wee blonde cutie squeezed herself between those two big dogs and stood on her hind legs to make herself taller. As for pet-friendly inns, my brother and sister-in-law have a small farm just outside town. They fixed up one of the outbuildings into a house that they're planning to rent. I'll ring up Nigel and see if he'll rent it to you. How long would you want it for?"

They decided on two nights. After Lucy left to make the call, they discussed what their rental fee limit would be.

Lucy bustled back. "Nigel said he'd be honored to rent the place to the winning team at the World Agility Games. He says it's sparsely furnished right now as he and Prissy haven't quite finished decorating the place, but there are enough beds for all of you, plus comfortable chairs to sit on and a dinette set."

Cole asked, "How much will your brother charge us?"

Lucy looked stunned. "Lord love a duck! I forgot to ask. I can tell you this; he'll be as reasonable as anything else you might get around here. Want me to ring him back and ask?"

Gordon said, "Why don't we drive out to the place and take a look?"

The others nodded in agreement.

They told Lucy they wanted to order take-out lunch for the pets and asked what she would recommend.

"Hang on a minute," she said as she bustled away in the direction of the kitchen. Several minutes later she reappeared carrying two bags. "Here are scraps from last night's roast beef special with some leftover Yorkshire pudding. This isn't leftovers from customers' plates. It's from the trimmings and ends of the beef roast. I've put in leftover cooked turnips, mashed spuds and gravy. You can heat it up at my brother's place."

They thanked her profusely. When Essie inquired how much they should pay for the dog meals, Lucy made a dismissive gesture.

"Their meal is on the house. I usually save the scraps for my mum's dog." Seeing the look of consternation on their faces, she quickly added, "Don't be worrying. There's enough left for Wiggins. I'll follow you out so that I can have a look at your pets."

They had no difficulty finding Nigel and Prissy Marden's farm and thought the rental fee was very reasonable. They loved the outbuilding that had been transformed into a charming cottage. Fortunately, it had three bedrooms so each couple could enjoy privacy.

Sarah searched through kitchen cupboards and found a saucepan that she heated gravy in and then drizzled it over the meat and vegetables that Essie had diced into bite-sized pieces and mixed with dry dog food. The pets gulped the food while Gordon, Cole and Evan carried in luggage and kennels.

They had just seated themselves at the kitchen table when they heard a knock at the door. Cole let in Nigel and Prissy who were carrying an electric kettle plus coffee and teabags, sugar and cream. Jeanette invited them to sit down and have a cup of tea.

After the tea had steeped and their cups filled with the fragrant brew, Jeanette told Nigel and Prissy about their quest to find crop circles.

Nigel said, "You've come to a good area for that. I've seen some myself. The animals won't go into a crop circle. They'll stand at the edge or walk around it. Come to think of it, I don't believe I've ever seen a bird fly over one."

Jeanette asked, "Have either of you ever walked into one?"

Prissy answered, "I have twice but that was some years back. The first time that I walked into one, I don't remember anything out of the ordinary happening. Six months later, I walked into my second crop circle and I felt a strange sensation in my body—sort of a wave-like vibration that went through my body. It happened three times. Each wave occurred about five to ten seconds apart from the ending of one to the beginning of another. I remember thinking at the time that I'd had all of me scanned by something or someone."

Prissy added, "By all of me, I mean my physical body and all my thoughts and everything that is me had been looked at or into."

They noticed Prissy shuddering as she recalled the experience.

Jeanette asked, "Did you have any impression that whoever, or whatever, had scanned you meant any harm?"

Prissy thought a moment before replying, "No. Whatever it was it just seemed to be curious."

She immediately corrected herself. "Curious is the wrong word because that has emotion attached to it. I had the impression that whatever it was, it wanted information and was collecting data. There wasn't any emotion attached."

Nigel added that he had walked into one several years ago, but hadn't experienced anything unusual. "Prissy and I have been busy fixing up this place, so we haven't gone roaming for crop circles. I'll mark areas on your local map that would be good places to look. You'll have enough light until about 8:00 p.m."

Prissy asked if they planned to take the dogs along. Essie explained that Kawdje and Topaz seemed particularly sensitive to the vibrations of ancient bones and briefly spoke about Gordon's kiva excavations. Nigel and Prissy were very interested and requested that Gordon tell them about his work when they returned.

Prissy offered to make enough stew for all of them to eat and that she would keep it warm so that they could have a hot meal whenever they returned in the evening.

Sarah said, "We always cook something that we can share with the pets. We certainly don't expect you to share your stew with them; however, we'll need to add something to their dry dog food. Where do you suggest that we purchase something during our drive back here?"

Prissy replied as she looked at the four dogs snuggled together and snoozing on a rag rug, "I don't mind sharing my stew with the pets. Nigel and I feed his mum's dog whenever they come over for a meal. We're charging you extra rent for the dogs so they deserve to be fed, too. I must say they really are exceptional pets. Nigel and I have promised ourselves a dog and a cat when we're done with renovations."

Nigel said, "We saw you and your dogs on the telly yesterday. I can hardly wait to tell the folks around here that you stayed at our place." Then he added, "If you drive near to a crop circle, maybe your dogs will alert you to it."

CHAPTER FIFTY-FIVE

Topaz was dozing beside Michael in the back of the Land Rover when faint, strange vibrations penetrated her consciousness.

She roused and said to Michael, "There's a hole ahead."

Michael asked, "So what? We've dug lots of them."

"It's not like a hole in the ground. I don't know how to describe it. It's more like an opening than a hole. I've never experienced anything like it before so I can't compare it to anything. I just know that it frightens me."

"Topaz, deer used to frighten you."

The parents knew when Topaz began to tremble and "talk" that they must be nearing a crop circle. Gordon was driving so Cole immediately phoned Evan and Essie, who were following them. Essie answered and Cole described Topaz's behavior. Essie said she had just been about to contact them about Kawdje's display of whining and uneasiness. She suggested they park near a hill that was a little ways ahead.

"We can climb the hill and get a view of the countryside. If there is a crop circle in this area, we should be able to see it."

"Good idea," Cole replied. "If we can't see one, the pets can lead us to it."

They drove about five hundred yards before spotting a perfect pull-off place. They parked, climbed out of the vehicles, snapped leashes on the pets and began to ascend the hill. When they reached the crest of the hill, they had a 360-degree view.

They saw the crop circle near the bottom of the hill and opposite to the side that they had climbed. They immediately began their descent toward the circle although it was obvious that the pets were disturbed and reluctant to follow.

Evan said, "We can return to the vehicles by walking around the base of the hill toward the road."

They had not been able to get a completely unobstructed view of the crop circle from the top of the hill because of a grove of trees situated close to it. In spite of that, they had been able to get a good enough view to appreciate the intricate pattern. It was a series of curves of varying lengths, arranged in such a way as to give the impression of a rose in full bloom. A long, narrow, straight line extended from the rose and connected to a miniature replica of the large rose. "Rose" was the word they all used when referring to the crop circle.

When they arrived at "the rose," they discovered that it had been formed in a field of barley. They examined the plants and found that each stem had been bent so carefully and cleverly that none was broken, just bent and twisted, folded and interwoven in such a way so as to give subtle shadowing and depth to the overall pattern.

The pets were reluctant to enter the circle but Sarah, Gordon, Cole, Jeanette, Essie and Evan did not want to leave them unattended outside the circle or tie them to a tree in the nearby grove. Evan carried Kissy in his arms and walked into the circle. Essie followed with Kawdje held in her arms. Michael walked between Gordon and Sarah with Gordon holding onto his leash. Sarah kept her hand on Michael's head to reassure him. Topaz walked on trembling legs between Jeanette and Cole and she pressed herself against her mom.

They walked carefully through the circle, following the curved areas that they judged to be about four to five feet in width and which varied from about twelve to fifteen feet in length, with the longer areas on the perimeter of the circle and the shorter ones near the center. When they reached the center, they saw a circle shaped by barley stalks that had been flattened in a clockwise direction. It was an area large enough for all of them to stand in together. They exited the center circle and made their way to the side of the crop circle opposite from their entrance point until they reached the point where the long, narrow connecting path to the miniature replica began. It was wide enough to accommodate two persons walking side by side.

Evan led with Kissy walking beside him rather than being carried. Essie and Kawdje followed in similar style. Sarah walked in front of Gordon, who walked with Michael close beside him. Jeanette and Topaz followed Gordon and Michael. Cole brought up the rear. When they reached the miniature "rose," they found that it was not large enough for all of them to stand inside it, so they stood in a circle just outside its perimeter.

Suddenly, the sky darkened and they wondered if a rainstorm was imminent. Michael sniffed the air and thought that it didn't smell like rain. Topaz thought that everything smelled different and Kawdje agreed. Kissy decided that she wanted to go someplace where they could have a picnic, because she felt hungry. Evan felt tuckered out from all the sprinting that he'd had to do at the World Agility Games to stay a step ahead of Kissy and he agreed with her that a picnic would be great.

"You had to sprint but I had to run faster than the wind because I'm so much smaller than you. If anyone has a right to be tired, it's me," she thought.

Topaz thought, "We're all tired and hungry. We'll find a place somewhere soon where we can just relax and have something to eat."

"I enjoy eating the food in this land," Michael thought. "It's very flavorful."

Gordon checked his satellite phone to get the latitude and longitude bearings of the crop circle. He was perplexed when he realized that his phone wasn't working. When Essie saw that Gordon's phone wasn't working, she immediately pulled her cell phone out of her waist pack.

"Well, neither is mine," she thought.

Cole reached his for cell phone but it wasn't attached to his belt. He had left it in the vehicle.

"Oh well, it isn't as though we're in the wilderness," Jeanette thought.

"I have a really good sense of smell and can easily scent the location of the car and maybe even where we slept last night except that for some reason, I can't smell anything remotely familiar," Topaz thought and Kawdje immediately agreed.

Kissy stood on her hind legs and touched her dad's knee. She wanted to be up high so that she could see everything better. Her dad reached down and lifted her up in his arms.

"I don't recognize anything," she thought with dismay.

Evan picked up her mood and thought that he, too, didn't recognize the terrain.

Everyone looked at the ground. They couldn't see any trace of the miniature replica of the crop circle, nor even the barley. There were patches of stubble and reddish soil and small rocks.

"Where's the crop circle?" Evan thought.

"Beats me," Cole said.

At the sound of Cole's voice, they all looked at one another in astonishment. They had been communicating by thought, all eight of them.

"This could open up Pandora's box," said Sarah.

"What's Pandora's box?" asked Kawdje wordlessly.

Jaws dropped and Essie, Evan, Sarah, Gordon, Jeanette and Cole stared at one another in disbelief.

"We're all communicating telepathically," Cole said.

"You don't have to say it, just think it," Jeanette thought.

"Sometimes I don't even want to admit to my own thoughts, much less have them known by anyone else," Gordon thought.

"I echo the sentiment," thought Evan.

Michael thought, "Sarah and Gordon, I'm always sending thoughts to you. That's how I communicate. Eventually you let those thoughts into yourselves."

"I wonder if we've slipped through a portal into an alternate universe or something," thought Gordon.

"Or something, for sure," replied Jeanette wordlessly.

Cole was thinking hard and his formed-thought-suggestion that they should just step forward toward one another and into the now invisible miniature crop circle replica to see if they could return to their own reality was greeted with relief.

"Try to retrace your exact steps," he thought, "and that includes Michael, Topaz, Kissy and Kawdje."

Everyone thought back on every step taken.

Kawdje closed his eyes in thought and then communicated, "It's easier to retrace your steps with your eyes closed. Remember which way your body was turned, even if it was slightly sideways and go back that exact way."

"Good thinking," Evan thought. "You're well named. Kawdje is a name your mom and I made up. It's short for cogitate, which means to think or reflect on things.

Gordon thought, "I'll give you fifteen seconds to think about how you will retrace your steps and then, on my count of three, we all start together. Okay?"

About twenty seconds later, the group found themselves in the long, connecting strip close to the miniature rose. They were all facing the replica. They jogged toward their vehicles as fast as they could. When they reached them and were putting the pets inside, Evan said, "Remember, Kissy and I are hungry. We want lunch."

They drove for about fifteen minutes before sighting a restaurant. They elected not to dine inside because they didn't want any discussion about their crop circle experience to be overheard, plus, they were reluctant to leave the pets in the vehicles. They all felt shaky and unnerved and thought that the pets probably felt the same way. They bought sandwiches and hot coffee and tea to go, then drove on until they found a clearing and stopped to have their picnic lunch. There were some stones large enough to use as sitting perches and flat enough to put some food upon. After filling pet bowls with food and water, they settled themselves onto stones and talked while munching on sandwiches.

Cole said, "Maybe we should have remained in the alternate world a little longer and explored."

"Maybe we wouldn't have found our way back to the exact spot where the portal was," said Jeanette.

"We could have had half of us stay at the point where we left our reality while the rest of us explored a little," he replied.

Gordon said, "Maybe we were able to return to our world only by exactly retracing our steps and movements. Those of us who left to explore might not have been able to place ourselves exactly where we were standing when we entered the alternate world, or whatever it was. Maybe it wouldn't have mattered, but maybe it would have. I'm glad we didn't take that chance. It would be unthinkable for some of us to have been left in the alternative world."

Michael walked over to Gordon, rested his head on his knee and looked up at him inquiringly.

Gordon stroked Michael's head. "Hey, buddy, I've lost the ability to communicate with you telepathically."

Kissy, Kawdje and Topaz were resting near one another. Although they physically talked with one another by barking and making other audible sounds, it was natural for them to communicate by mental and emotional telepathy. They were now telling each other that they regretted the loss of that special way of sending and receiving thoughts with their families. Topaz reminded them that she had that special connection with her mom.

"It's not as clear as when we were in that strange place awhile ago. I'm going to send my mom the thought that we're all chilly. This ground is cold and slightly damp. I sense that you both feel the same way."

Kawdje said, "Good idea. Kissy, let's you and I send that same thought to our parents."

All three concentrated.

Jeanette said, "I'm ready to get back on the road. It's chilly and I'm thinking the pets find the ground cold to rest upon."

Essie said, "I was just thinking the same thing."

"Me, too," agreed Evan.

They gathered their belongings while debating what to do next. They decided that another crop circle, if they could find one, would be anticlimactic after their experience.

"Let's drive back to our cottage. Tomorrow we can visit Stonehenge," suggested Sarah.

Later that evening, in the comfort of their cottage, they once again discussed their experience.

Sarah said, "I have a better understanding of the limitations imposed upon all of us by the bodies we inhabit. I think that the life force, the beingness, or whatever you want to call it, that is our true self is the same in all of us and in everything. When we were in that other dimension, or wherever, I felt that there wasn't any difference between humans and dogs, except for the way in which we must express that life force because of our physical differences. For example, dogs will never be able to master calculus. Well, forget that. It's not a good example because I, for one, will never be able to master calculus either."

The others laughed. She continued, "Dogs can't write; their paws aren't designed for that. Humans don't have the incredible sense of smell that dogs have. We have gifts unique to our species that we use and rely on that other species don't have and vice versa. Apart from the differences in how we must live and function that are imposed upon us by our bodies, our true beingness is very similar. Dogs and humans have the ability to think and reason; we feel the same emotions; we are both a sociable species and enjoy companionship; we can give and receive love, demonstrate loyalty and so on."

Jeanette said, "Lots of people develop special relationships with barnyard animals, wild animals and even plants. That life force is, indeed, in everything."

Cole said, "I don't want to go there. I'm going to feel guilty every time I eat meat, fish and vegetables. Maybe water is alive, too."

Gordon said, "According to recent studies, water has consciousness and responds to thoughts directed to it."

"I've got to eat and drink," Evan said. "Let's stop this conversation."

Essie asked how they felt about discussing their crop circle experience with anyone else. After a brief debate, they unanimously agreed to only tell their children and their children's spouses.

Jeanette said, "I've never heard of anyone else having had the strange experience that we had."

Sarah replied, "Maybe lots of folks have and like us, they decided to keep quiet about it."

Gordon said, "I'd want to be better prepared if I ventured into a crop circle again. Instead of a satellite phone that won't work unless there are satellites orbiting, I'd take an old-fashioned compass, which also may not work. I'd have instruments that measure magnetic fields and atmosphere. Plus, I'd bring sterile tubes to collect soil, air, plant and water samples. I'd also take stakes and spray paint to mark our exact entry spot. I'd also place markers at intervals to make the path retraceable."

Cole interrupted with enthusiasm. "We should take food and water supplies, plus lightweight camping gear and, I hate to say this, but I think we should have small firearms with us. You never know what we might encounter that we would need to protect ourselves from."

Jeanette said, "This is scaring me. I would only want to explore a little and remain close to our entry point."

Evan said thoughtfully, "If much time passed, perhaps we couldn't exit from the point at which we entered."

"That's a possibility," Gordon said.

Cole rubbed his forehead. "I've been feeling edgy ever since my experience in the crop circle." Then he surprised himself, his wife and the others by announcing that he thought he would retire from the practice of medicine. "PPAL is doing so well that my share in the company will bring in enough money to enable me to retire if I choose to. I'd like to learn everything I can about crop circles. I'd also like to have time to train Sonny and myself in the sport of Dog Agility."

Jeanette gaped at him. After a few moments she said, "That crop circle experience must have had a profound effect upon you."

Cole shrugged, "I guess it did."

Gordon said, "Maybe because of our strange experience, we now understand just how tenuous our existence is and we feel pushed to decide what we really want."

Meanwhile the pets were having their own discussion. They all admitted to missing the instantaneous communication that they had with their families while in "that strange place" and wondered how they could recreate it.

Kawdje said thoughtfully, "Maybe it can only happen in that particular place and if so, I wonder why."

Topaz admitted that she didn't want to go back to that place. "It was so different as to be alien. Let's remember that our parents weren't sure that we could find our way out of that place. I sensed their underlying fear. I don't want to go anywhere that would prevent me from ever seeing any of my puppies again. On the plus side, I was with my mom and dad and all of you."

Michael agreed that he would miss his puppies and then suggested that they send the thought to their parents that if they ever go to "that strange place" again, they should also bring all their puppies.

Kissy announced, "I don't want to get stuck someplace where I wouldn't ever be able to compete in Dog Agility practices. What would I do for recreation?"

Kawdje said, "I'm still wondering what Pandora's Box is. I sure wish I could ask Sarah to explain that to me."

CHAPTER FIFTY-SIX

The day after arriving home, Gordon phoned Cecil and reported that everything had gone well during the flights to and from the World Agility Games. He related in detail the great showing that Team USA had made at the competition.

Cecil asked Gordon to pass on his congratulations to Sarah and then asked, "When is that son of yours planning to work full-time for PPAL?"

"Real soon. Sarah and I will be attending his graduation late this month."

"Have him call me at home any evening. By the way, Aaron and I want to have a PPAL commercial made using all the Team USA competitors who performed at the World Agility Games—people and pets. It will say something to the effect that pets who fly in comfort perform better."

Gordon and Sarah spent the remainder of the morning playing catch-up on all the details that require attention after having been away for a week. They were in the den when the phone rang. Sarah answered. Gordon heard her talking enthusiastically to whoever was on the other end of the line and giving out Essie and Evan's, Jeanette and Cole's telephone numbers. After she hung up, Sarah dance-stepped over to him and kissed his cheek.

"That was the program director of my favorite national morning television show. You know that the Best-in-Show winner of the Westminster Dog Show always makes the morning TV show circuit. Well, Jean Miles wants Michael, Topaz and Kissy on TV because they won the Country Team Triathlon for the USA at the World Agility Games. She also wants Kawdje on the program because he won Gold in Jumping All 'Round, plus the Biathlon, and Dustin because he won Power and Speed. I told her that Bogey won the Silver medal in the Individual All Around, so she may want him, too."

"That's wonderful news, golden girl."

Sarah said, "Obviously we can thank Cecil and Aaron for the upcoming publicity. It will help promote PPAL and their chain of hotels and resorts. It's good for us, too. We have founding stock in PPAL. Aside from the five minutes of fame and the financial benefit to us and our families and friends, we're the instigators and promoters of an enhanced lifestyle for pets. That has been our goal and still is. This publicity will help."

Being on the morning television show circuit meant a trip to New York City. Everyone lodged at ABCD Realty's *Families Hotel*. It wasn't as gloriously beautiful as the *Familias Resort* in Belize, but there was an outdoor pet exercise area and a pet-grooming salon on the premises. The dogs were treated to a bath and fur trim and had their nails clipped and buffed and their teeth brushed. For their television appearances, Michael, Kawdje, Dustin and Bogey each sported a bowtie and Topaz and Kissy wore a silk flower attached to a ribbon that encircled their necks.

They appeared on three national morning television shows. The pets adjusted easily to the rushed morning schedules and to sitting sedately under bright, hot lights. Michael was puzzled because Sarah sprayed paint on his left ear and her left hand before the shows. He waited expectantly to perform, as did Topaz, Kissy and Kawdje who also associated Michael's colored ear with an Agility practice, but none of them saw an Agility setup. They had no way of knowing that Sarah had been requested by the television program personnel to paint Michael's ear and her hand because it added to the human interest appeal of someone who struggled to quickly differentiate left from right.

PPAL had free national advertising as everyone praised the comfortable accommodations provided for themselves and the pets representing Team USA on the flights to and from the World Agility Games held in England.

The idiosyncrasies and preferences of the pets were discussed during the national morning television shows. The week following their television appearances, a national cereal company offered Essie a contract to endorse their brand of oatmeal because it had been aired that Essie's homemade oatmeal cookies were used as performance bait and competition rewards for Kawdje. A cookie company requested Evan and Sarah to feature Kissy and Michael in their gingersnaps advertisements. A national, well-known supplier of hunting and fishing gear approached Jeanette about using

Topaz in their company's advertising campaign to lure people who didn't like to hunt or fish to try camping and other outdoor activities.

Several weeks after their appearances on the national TV morning shows, the friends were interviewed on Barry Baldwin's live, nightly primetime television show. This time, Gordon, Cole, Kevin, Aaron, Cecil, Pat and Ed, Jenny, Joy and Sam were included, but Breen and Shelly and none of the pets were.

The thrust of the interview was PPAL, its inception, immediate success and the profound effect it was having on the way people vacationed and did business now that comfortable and safe air travel conditions for pets was available. Aaron and Cecil gave credit for the inception of PPAL to the others present.

Barry began with Sarah who described Michael being housed in cargo during the flight from Mexico to the USA and her desire for better air travel accommodations for all pets. Gordon spoke about Sarah and himself researching the aircraft accommodations afforded pets and his idea to start their own pet-friendly airline and subsequently, asking his son to redesign aircraft cabins to accommodate pet quarters. The group took turns telling about their initial meeting where guidelines for safe, comfortable pet travel were discussed.

Barry congratulated Kevin on his recent graduation from Purdue University with a degree in aeronautical engineering. "You are young to have taken on the project of reconfiguring the body of an aircraft to accommodate an elevator that lifts kenneled pets into their cabin area."

Kevin thanked Barry and gave a brief explanation about the elevator lift, saying that it could be operated mechanically in an emergency situation if there were enough able-bodied persons to operate the lift by using its mechanics. He mentioned that wheelchair-bound persons could enter the aircraft via the lift if needed or desired.

Next, Barry turned his attention to Pat and she discussed PPAL's air travel requirements for pets. Barry congratulated her on being head of PPAL's Veterinary Consulting Department and then focused on Ed, asking him about the responsibilities involved in being second in command of PPAL's Legal Department and Legal Division Head of PPAL's International Travel, which had not yet gotten off the ground. Barry chuckled at his own pun. Wisely, Ed did not go into the boring details of PPAL's charter and avoided talking in legal jargon. He spoke concisely about the legal aspects of international pet travel and said that he and his wife worked closely on all aspects of safe and comfortable pet travel.

Barry turned to Sarah. "My understanding is that you all connected, one way or another, because of the dogs. You met Essie and Evan Kilmer at a Conformation Dog Show where the sport of Dog Agility was being demonstrated and they subsequently introduced you to Gordon. Your pet, Michael Archangelo, is a Mexican street dog that you rescued and brought to this country. Michael can't be entered into Conformation Dog Shows because he isn't a purebred dog but you wanted him to have some training and worthwhile activity, so you decided that Dog Agility was the way to go. Had you planned from the start that he would eventually be on the team that represented our country in the World Agility Games?"

"No, but I quickly realized what a talented Agility Dog he is."

Barry shifted focus to Jeanette and Cole and asked why they decided to have their purebred German Shorthaired Pointer become a Champion Agility Dog rather than a Champion Conformation Show Dog or even a Field Champion. Jeanette explained that Topaz showed complete disinterest in Conformation Dog Shows and her professional handler had advised that Topaz would never win because of her obviously bored attitude. Cole told Barry that deer chased Topaz instead of the other way around, so she would never make it as a Field Champion. Everyone chuckled.

Jeanette described seeing Essie carrying Kawdje and the huge blue ribbon he had just won at a Conformation Dog Show and striking up a conversation with her and Evan who subsequently spoke about a woman who had a partial Dog Agility setup on her property because she was interested in having her dog become an Agility Champion.

Evan entered the conversation saying that Kissy also had been bored by Conformation Dog Shows and her attitude, combined with the fact that her legs were slightly too long to become a top show dog, clinched their decision to introduce her to Dog Agility because she had shown great interest when watching a demonstration of the sport.

Essie said that Kawdje was a star in Conformation Dog Shows, but was entered into Dog Agility training because they wanted to make it a family activity.

"I understand that your daughter, Joy, and son-in-law, Sam, have one of Kissy and Kawdje's puppies," Barry said.

Joy entered into the conversation, saying that she and Sam were training Sneakers in the sport of Dog Agility and were also having him shown in Conformation Dog Shows.

Sam told Barry that he and Joy wanted to have the option of having Sneakers travel in comfort with him when he was flying around the country during the basketball season, but had invested in PPAL before Sneakers had joined their household. He mentioned that his teammate, Beau Benadar, also had one of Kissy and Kawdje's puppies.

Barry commented that he remembered their being featured in one of PPAL's commercials and that he also recollected seeing Sarah and Gordon's wedding ceremony, which included Michael, Topaz, Kissy and Kawdje, being aired on the *Funniest Home Video* television program.

"I thought it was hilarious when they sang during the ceremony, but it was heartwarming, too."

After everyone stopped laughing, Aaron said that he and his wife had one of Kissy and Kawdje's puppies and that Mimi was big time into the Conformation Dog Show circuit with Caressa. Cecil told Barry that he and his wife had one of Topaz and Michael's Angel puppies.

Barry asked Jeanette to tell him about the puppies. She described their fur growth pattern resembling wings that inspired her and Sarah to develop a new breed called Angel Dogs, and the protocol to be followed when developing a new breed. She mentioned that Pat was also involved in the Angel Dog breeding program and was their advisor.

At last, Barry spoke to Jenny, "I understand that you have one of Kissy and Kawdje's puppies and that you are active in the sport of Dog Agility. Tell me about that."

Jenny described achieving her Senior Level in the Junior Handler Program and competing with Kissy and Topaz to do that. She said that she and Candy were into Dog Agility big time and wanted to eventually be on Team USA at a World Agility Championship. When Barry asked why she had a puppy of Kissy's rather than one of Topaz's, Jenny explained that she had only been eleven years old when she had lived with her Aunt Jeanette, Uncle Cole, and Topaz, and at that time, a smaller dog suited her smaller size. She said that she loved Kissy's outgoing personality and her obvious "desire-to-win" attitude. She also described the special bond that she had developed with Topaz, who ran from deer and wouldn't chase the local wildlife, but had attacked and saved her from a burglar.

At Barry's prompting, she described the incident. After she finished, Barry said, "I've been told that it was your idea to name the pet-friendly airline PPAL. Why did you choose that acronym?"

Jenny looked puzzled for a few seconds and then her expression cleared and she said, "Because pets are our pals."

Barry replied, "They are, indeed."

Barry said, "Aaron and Cecil, you are the "deep pockets" that was needed to get PPAL off the ground, and from your involvement in a new pet-friendly airline company, you made sweeping changes to your real estate holdings. Tell me about that."

Aaron said that he and Cecil realized that hotels needed to accommodate pets traveling with their families and that the *Families/ Familias* hotels arose from that need.

"All our facilities have pet salons plus dog walkers and pet sitters. Outdoor exercise areas exist at some facilities with plans to have them installed in all our places."

Cecil summed up the situation saying, "Traveling pets need a comfortable place to stay at their destination just as much as people do."

Cecil continued explaining that PPAL was expanding as fast it could while still remaining fiscally sound. He emphasized that PPAL flights were appropriate for people traveling without pets, even though the premise upon which the airline company was founded was to provide safe, comfortable accommodations for pets and people.

Barry looked directly into the camera and said, "Kissy and Kawdje, purebred Tibetan Spaniels, with illustrious pedigrees, who have always lived in privilege; Michael Archangelo, a mixed breed street dog from Mexico, who, in spite of being fearful of people, decided to take a leap of faith and trust a woman who befriended him; and Topaz, a gentle German Shorthaired Pointer who has always lived in love and harmony with the animals that she is supposed to hunt and chase according to her breed, formed an incredibly gifted and successful Championship Dog Agility Team that reached its pinnacle when they represented Team USA at the World Agility Championships this year. These four dogs and their families came together for the common purpose of becoming Champion Dog Agility Teams and all their lives became intertwined as happy and unforeseen trails were blazed.

From that alliance has come a pet-friendly airline, a chain of luxurious pet-friendly hotels, dog walker and pet sitter hotel jobs, business travelers who are now able to have their pets accompany them and a new breed of dog called Angel Dogs.

The families of Kissy, Kawdje, Topaz and Michael Archangelo, inspired by their love for these four dogs, are making the world a safer and happier place for pets everywhere as they break traditions that don't support the close companionship with people that dogs desire."

Jenny's parents watched Barry Baldwin's television show while pet-sitting Michael, Topaz, Kissy, Kawdje, Mary, Sonny, Michelle, Candy, Sneakers, Gabby and Caressa at Jeanette and Cole's home. An après TV Show party had been planned.

The pets chased one another upstairs, downstairs, around furniture and in and out of rooms except for the dining room whose French doors were closed to prevent them from sampling the food buffet before the appointed time.

The doorbell rang. Don and Iris Prescott ushered Beau and Selma Benadar inside. Pets immediately surrounded them. Beau set Hershey down on the foyer floor and he disappeared into a sea of wagging tails as all the pets ambled into the family room and settled themselves onto throw-covered couches and chairs or lounged on the plush Oriental rug.

Kissy said, "This is a party."

"That means a lot of tasty food," said Kawdje.

"You bet," Topaz said. "That's why the dining room doors are closed. It's to keep us from eating anything until our parents are here."

Sonny said, "I hope we'll have crème brûlée for dessert. It's one of the best perks of life."

"What's the very best perk of life, Dad?" Michelle asked Michael.

"It's loving your family and being loved in return. Love is the best perk of all. But crème brûlée is a close second!"